The Golden Touch

The instant Trace's lips came in contact with Cassie's mouth, he knew he was a lost soul. He could no more have turned away than he could have refused water after being on the desert for days without a drink. All thought of right and wrong abandoned him; and blind instinct assumed control of his actions with a need so basic that it would have frightened him if he'd been rational enough to recognize it for what it was.

And if anyone had tried to tell Cassie it wasn't the clanging of bells she heard, but simply the frenzied pounding of her own pulse, she'd have insisted that they were dead wrong. For surely the flame of Trace's kiss blazed through her, weakening her muscles like so much melting wax, and she heard bells. Loud, magical, glorious bells . . .

DEFIANT SPLENDOR

MICHALANN PERRY

ZEBRA BOOKS
KENSINGTON PUBLISHING CORP.

The fiery brilliance of the Zebra Hologram Heart which you see on the cover is created by "laser holography." This is the revolutionary process in which a powerful laser beam records light waves in diamond-like facets so tiny that 9,000,000 fit in a square inch. No print or photograph can match the vibrant colors and radiant glow of a hologram.

So look for the Zebra Hologram Heart whenever you buy a historical romance. It is a shimmering reflection of our guarantee that you'll find consistent quality between the covers!

ZEBRA BOOKS

are published by

Kensington Publishing Corp.
475 Park Avenue South
New York, NY 10016

First printing: June, 1988

Printed in the United States of America

To my dear friends, Francis Ray, Patti Barricklow, and Nancy Gramm, who never fail to make me feel good about myself;

To my agent, Ruth Cohen, who's always there for me;

And to the members of the North Texas chapter of Romance Writers of America, who invariably "recharge" me time after time.

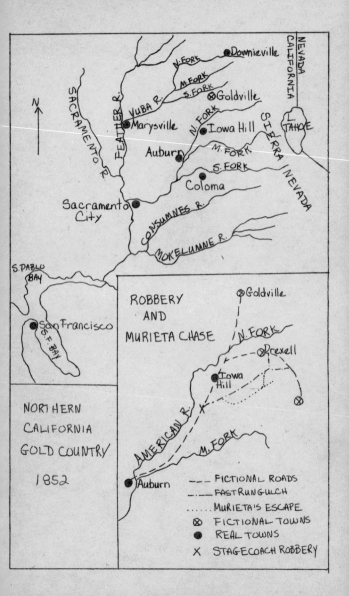

N

SACRAMENTO R.

FEATHER R.

NEVADA
CALIFORNIA

•Downieville

N. FORK

M. FORK

S. FORK

⊗Goldville

VUBA R.

YUBA R.

•Marysville

N. FORK

•Iowa Hill

SIERRA NEVADA

L. TAHOE

Auburn

M. FORK

S. FORK

•Coloma

Sacramento
City

CONSUMNES R.

MOKELUMNE R.

S. PABLO
BAY

San Francisco

S.F. BAY

ROBBERY
AND
MURIETA CHASE

⊗Goldville

N. FORK

⊗Rexell

•Iowa
Hill

⊗

AMERICAN R.

X

M. FORK

•Auburn

NORTHERN
CALIFORNIA
GOLD COUNTRY
1852

– – – FICTIONAL ROADS
–·–·– FAST RUN GULCH
······ MURIETA'S ESCAPE
⊗ FICTIONAL TOWNS
• REAL TOWNS
X STAGECOACH ROBBERY

Foreword

In 1852, the great American adventure, the California Gold Rush, was in full force. Thousands of "forty-niners" had already come from all over the world in frenzied response to the electrifying news that in California there were "golden nuggets lying around loose on the ground." They had abandoned farms, businesses, families, and sweethearts to swarm west with blind faith in the stories they'd heard: "In California a man could take a fortune out of the hills and streams with no more equipment than a tin pan and a shovel!"

So they came — in covered wagons, on ships, by foot, on horseback, and any way they could to reach the fabulous "El Dorado" of the West. But not all were fortunate enough to find gold in the hills and streams of California. Some did, but most did not. Instead, many of the great fortunes the Gold Rush produced were made by merchants, entertainers, and laborers, as well as gamblers, prostitutes, and thieves, who had all found the secret of striking it rich without ever panning an ounce of gold.

One such "success" story is that of Joaquin Murieta, the Mexican *bandido* who, with his gang of desperadoes, was pursued and feared from one end of the gold country to the other. There are several differing stories about Murieta—in fact, he may not have existed at all, or there may have been as many as five Murietas at one time. But whichever "truth" we choose to believe, the fact remains that in 1852 every crime committed in California by Spanish Americans was blamed on Joaquin Murieta—and no one with any amount of gold was safe.

Chapter One

Goldville, northern California — late spring, 1852

Trace McAllister sat slumped in a corner of the stagecoach, his long legs stretched out in front of him and crossed at the ankles. The tanned fingers of his hands were interlaced on his flat, lean middle, his black Stetson pulled down low over his forehead, hiding his face. To any but the most astute observer, the man was totally relaxed and already had a head start on a plan to sleep all the way to Sacramento.

However, Trace McAllister was not asleep and had no intention of relaxing. He knew he couldn't afford to miss anything that happened that day, however slight and seemingly inconsequental. Not if this trip was going to be successful. No, there would be no sleep for him during the next few hours.

Peering out the window from under the brim of his hat, he idly studied the newly-founded town of tents and hastily erected shacks scattered along what was said to have been an old pack-mule trail.

Through slitted eyes, Trace noticed two miners approaching the stagecoach. At first glance, they looked like any of the thousands of men who had flooded the hills of northern California since the discovery of gold at Sutter's Mill in early 1848, but there was something about the younger miner that held Trace's attention. Both men were dressed in knee-length black coats, durable canvas jeans tucked into heavy leather boots, faded red flannel shirts, and wide-brimmed gray felt hats; and neither of them was particularly clean looking.

Deciding there was probably nothing to be learned by watching the two prospectors, Trace resumed his covert perusal of the wagon- and people-congested Main Street of the gold camp. But when the older man snatched the sweat-stained slouch hat from his head and waved it in the air, Trace couldn't resist veering his attention back in their direction.

"Hold that there stage," the miner shouted to the driver, who was just ready to close the door on the half-full stagecoach.

Obviously anxious to collect another fare or two, the driver turned to greet the last-minute passengers. "Sure thing, mister," he said, holding out his hand in a sweeping gesture of welcome. "Tom Newman's the name, an' we still got plenty o' room."

There was no doubt in Trace's mind that the two new arrivals had been lucky and that their bags were full of gold dust and nuggets. The fortunate ones who'd "seen the elephant"—found gold—had a look about them that could be spotted every time. Besides, less fortunate "Argonauts" didn't flag down a stage. They walked.

It was clear the approaching men's worth was just as evident to the stagecoach operator as it was to Trace. For, undaunted by the miners' appearances, his face split in a welcoming grin as his gaze homed in on the bulging saddlebags slung over the miners' shoulders.

12

"Got 'nother passenger for you," the older man announced in a gruff snort as he heaved one heavy bag on top of the waiting coach, revealing a strength his tall wiry frame disguised. "How much is it gonna cost me?"

"The usual nine ounces," the driver answered the gray-bearded man. As he spoke, he whipped out his own trusty pennyweight scale to weigh the $144 worth of gold dust. It was easy for Trace to see this was one businessman who had found a less back-breaking way to strike it rich than panning and digging for his gold.

No doubt accustomed to the inflated prices in the gold camps, the older miner didn't balk at the exorbitant fare being charged for the short trip. He dropped a pouch of dust into the callused, outstretched hand. "That oughta cover it," he said, turning his attention to his younger, beardless companion. "You all set, Cass? You ain't forgot nothin', have you?"

"No, I ain't forgot nothin'," Cass answered with a smile, then added, "You know I don't have to go, Pa. I'd just as soon stay here 'n keep workin' with you."

"You'll do nothin' o' the sort. I'm dependin' on you to go show that old woman a thing 'r two, an' I ain't gonna let you wangle your way outta goin'.'"

"Then quit your fussin' 'n worryin'. I'll get on jus' fine. I ain't a kid no more, you know. I'm full-growed an' can take care o' myself. 'Sides, I got everythin' I need in here," the younger miner said, giving the second set of saddlebags a pat and tossing them on top of the stagecoach with almost the same ease as the father had pitched his up there.

At the sound of "Cass's" voice, Trace's eyes had widened in surprise, and the driver's head had jerked up, his mouth hanging open foolishly. "I'll be galdurned!" he finally managed to say. "You ain't no miner. You're a female!"

"If I ain't no miner, then that there dust you're a weighin' must be sand," the girl returned with a hearty laugh at the man's stunned expression. "An' any minute now, them horses of yours're gonna sprout wings 'n fly all the way to Sacramento."

The driver glanced over his shoulder at the four horses hitched to his stagecoach, then back to the girl, the expression on his face sheepish. He shrugged his shoulders and chuckled. "I don't guess that's gonna happen anytime soon," he conceded, returning his attention to the gold dust he was weighing—but giving it extra-close scrutiny, Trace was amused to notice.

I can't blame him. It wouldn't be the first time a miner sanded his dust to cheat an innocent and unsuspecting businessman! he reminded himself, his talent for observing the most minute details of his surroundings honed to the maximum.

I bet there's quite a story behind that girl, Trace chuckled to himself as he peeked out from under the brim of his Stetson and studied her.

She wasn't pretty. Of course, who could tell with all of her hair tucked up under that beat-up hat, which was pulled down so far on her head that the tips of her ears were folded over slightly by the misshapen brim. Still, there was something about her that fascinated him.

Perhaps it was the way she carried her tall, slender frame—he assumed she was slender under the baggy miner's clothes. At least eight inches over five feet, he decided; and there was a certain pride and majesty to her carriage that could not be disguised by her rough exterior.

Maybe it was the luminous excitement and humor that glimmered uncontrolled in her large tawny-colored eyes as she teased the stage driver and tried to ease her father's mind. Or maybe it was her smile that intrigued him. Open and honest, it displayed nicely shaped teeth that were surprisingly white and even. And Trace found himself sitting up a bit straighter for a better view.

"An' if what's in them bags there don't do the trick, I always got Mr. Colt's 'equalizer' here," she told her father with a mischievous grin as she wrapped her fingers around the butt of the revolver on her hip and whipped it from the holster in one smooth motion.

Not bad for a female, Trace thought. As a matter of fact, he hadn't seen a lot of men who had a draw much faster, he admitted reluctantly. *Of course, she probably can't hit the broad side of a barn.*

Just as the derogatory thought crossed his mind, the girl's gun fired; an instant later, the weather vane on the livery stable was sent spinning. *So much for that theory!* Trace goaded himself with a silent smile.

He released a weary sigh and shifted in his seat, uncrossing and recrossing his ankles restlessly before settling back into his pretended nap. This trip had the definite potential of being a profitable one if everything went according to plan. *With Cass's fat saddlebags added to the ante, Joaquin will be glad to see us coming,* Trace told himself, happy to realize that before the day was over he would probably be on his way to San Francisco for a well-earned rest and to celebrate his success.

Taking a quick glance out the window at Cass and her father, Trace's conscience was suddenly pricked by a twinge of guilt when he considered what it would mean to the girl and her father if they lost the gold in their saddlebags.

Again he rearranged his lean hips in his seat and shook his head. *Don't think about them. Nothing's going to go wrong,* he assured himself emphatically.

The girl gave her father a last hug and, ignoring the

15

stage driver's offer to help, stepped up into the coach with an unladylike bound.

"Howdy, folks. Name's Cassie Wyman," she announced with a wide grin as she plopped herself down between a bespectacled young man in a rumpled suit and a large black man dressed in miner's clothing.

"Ma'am," the black man acknowledged with a soft, mannerly voice, his gaze remaining on the street outside the window.

The blonde woman across from the black miner wrinkled her pretty upturned nose distastefully and raked her gaze over Cassie from head to muddy-booted foot. "I've never heard of a woman miner before," she said with a disdainful sneer.

"Well, I guess you have now, ain't you?"

Shooting Cassie a look that made her disapproval of a female who dressed and acted like a man obvious, the young woman directed a sick smile at the brown-haired man beside Cassie and said, "How nice."

"Horace Gilbert — boots and work clothes," the man introduced himself with an effeminate sniff that made no secret of his sense of self-importance.

Seemingly untouched by the blonde's sarcasm and the cringe of disgust behind Horace's stiff smile, Cassie grinned and grabbed his hand and began to pump it eagerly. "Right pleased to know you, Horace."

Definitely the smile, Trace said to himself, unable to remember having ever seen one as captivating and sincere. She reminded him of an affectionate — and particularly obnoxious — Irish setter he'd had when he was a kid. Like that fool lovable dog, it didn't seem to occur to Cassie Wyman that everyone wouldn't immediately warm to her friendliness.

"How 'bout you, mister? You got a face under that there hat?" Cassie asked, bending forward and tilting

16

her head to peek under the dark brim of Trace's Stetson.

Taken off guard by Cassie's bluntness, his face broke into a grin. He'd been caught. The little vixen had seen right through his pretense. He sat up straight and shoved the Stetson back on his head. "Trace McAllister" he said, offering his extended hand.

Surprised by the genuine friendliness in Trace McAllister's expression, Cassie took his strong hand and gripped it eagerly, searching his expression for an indication that his manner was insincere. Obviously tall, if the long legs that seemed to go on forever were any indication, he wore his almost-black hair full and combed back without any hair pomade. Brushed back over the tops of his ears, it was longer than was stylish, waving over his coat collar in back. His eyes were the most unusual shade of green Cassie had ever seen, tucked beneath a shelf of straight dark eyebrows; and the grin he directed at her was slightly crooked. "Howdy, Trace McAllister," she finally said. "It's right nice to meet you."

"Well, it's 'right nice' to meet you too, Cassie Wyman," Trace returned, surprised by the impact her small-boned hand in his made on his senses. She seemed so innocent and vulnerable. *You'd better get yourself to San Francisco fast, old boy. You're in bad shape. Only a desperate man would give this one a second glance—much less consider her "vulnerable" with that gun on her hip!* He dropped Cassie's hand as if it were hot.

"Stage'll be under way in a coupla minutes, folks," the driver announced in the doorway. "Just had a messenger tell me to hold up for one more passenger."

The other female passenger took a deep breath and sighed, turning to study Trace with a seductive smile. Trace sliced a sidelong glance at the petite blonde

17

who sat at the opposite end of the seat where he was sitting. *Now, that's what a woman's supposed to look like!* he told himself, still slightly shaken by his reaction to Cassie Wyman. *She may not be a miner, but from the looks it, she's sitting on a gold mine that's going to make her rich real quick!* Trace thought dryly, appreciating the way the young woman's full bosom pillowed above the edge of the low-cut neckline of her alpaca traveling suit. He returned the woman's inviting smile with a nod of his head. *Wonder if she's going all the way to Sacramento, or if she's going to stop over in Auburn,* he mused, determined not to give Cassie any more of his thoughts. Directing a last appreciative glance at the appealing display of bosom, he dragged his hat over his eyes with a sigh and slumped down in his seat again.

Horace took out his pocket watch and gave it an irritated glance; the black man continued to stare out the window; and Cassie relaxed back in the seat, her disappointment impossible to disguise.

Well, let them all ignore her. If they wanted to spend the entire trip in silence, it was no skin off her nose. *Not a bit!* There would be plenty of folks to talk to in Sacramento. *Plenty of folks!* she told herself with a less-than-genteel sniff of her nose — which she proceeded to wipe with her sleeve.

"I beg your pardon," a deep voice interjected into the strained silence. "Do you suppose it would be possible for me to sit beside the window?"

Cassie looked up into the face of the best looking — actually, *beautiful* was the word that came to her mind — man she had ever seen in her life. Standing in the doorway of the stagecoach, the handsome stranger was asking Horace Gilbert to exchange seats with him so he could sit beside the window — and beside her.

Horace shot the newcomer a look of indignant outrage.

It was all Cassie could do not to lift the hesitant salesman out of his seat by his collar and hurl him to the opposite bench so the place next to her would be available.

The nattily dressed newcomer's grin widened, showing perfect white teeth and a dimple in his left cheek.

Cassie's heart tripped clumsily, then raced in her chest. Her breathing grew shallow and she could feel her palms begin to sweat.

"I hate to admit it but I'm quite prone to motion sickness and always have to sit beside the window."

Seeing an opportunity to snuggle between two handsome men, the young woman wearing the low-cut bodice scooted up close to Trace. "Here, sir, you may have my seat by the window," she offered with a pat on the bench that was still warm from her own stylishly round bottom.

Cassie's heart crashed to the pit of her stomach and a stunned gasp formed in her throat. The witch was going to try to steal that man right out from under her nose! Her golden-brown eyes raining shards of fire, Cassie opened her mouth to protest. But before she could think of a way to keep him next to her, the object of her enthrallment spoke.

"That's kind of you, Miss—uh . . ." His fair eyebrows arched quizzically, his blue eyes glittering more charm than Cassie had ever imagined a mere human being could possess.

And she was sure this had to be what love felt like!

"LaRue. Lovey LaRue," the woman purred with a suggestive lick of her lips and a coy flutter of her eyelashes.

"Miss LaRue," the man repeated with an appreciative grin, "there's nothing that would give me more pleasure than to share my journey with you."

Lovey's face lit up. Cassie's fell.

"But, alas, I'm afraid that riding backward does not agree with me either."

Cassie let out a relieved sigh that was louder than she realized. Everyone in the coach turned a questioning glance in her direction. She feigned a cough to cover her embarrassment. As she leaned forward, she could have sworn that out of the corner of her eye she saw Trace McAllister's mouth twitch upward in an amused grin under the brim of his hat. But when she turned her gaze directly on the dozing man, the smile was gone. Slightly open, his mouth was relaxed, and he was breathing softly as though he were sound asleep.

The smile must have been her imagination, Cassie decided, turning her attention back to her objective: getting the handsome stranger the seat beside her.

Unwilling to take a chance that Lovey LaRue would yet find a way to *steal* her man from her, Cassie grabbed Horace's arm with one hand and hit him on the back with the other. Ignoring the sound of the shocked *whoosh* of air expelled from Horace's lungs, she prodded him toward the opposite bench. "You sit over there by Lovey, Horace, an' let this here gentleman sit by me . . . I mean the window. You wouldn't want him to get sick, would you?"

The inviting smile melted off the face of Cassie's buxomy competition as Horace allowed himself to be shuffled across the coach by the meddling female prospector.

"Here you go, mister," Cassie announced, smiling broadly as she whisked a bandana from her pocket and dusted the space beside her. "Here's your seat next to the window — an' facin' front, jus' like you wanted."

20

The man blessed Cassie with a special smile that sent goose bumps skittering over her flesh from head to toe. "Thank you, my dear," he said, accepting the offered seat and settling in before Horace could change his mind and reclaim it.

My dear! Cassie repeated silently. Never in her entire twenty years had anyone called her "my dear." Dearie, yes. And honey. Even sugar. But never "my dear." As though she was a lady. A real lady.

"Name's Cass—*Cassandra* Wyman," the besotted girl introduced herself, caring for the first time in her life what a man besides her father thought of her. She wiped her damp right hand on her pants leg and held it out to the man.

"A gold miner named Cassandra!" Lovey interjected with a spiteful smile in Cassie's direction that said, *You may have won the first battle, honey!* "Have you ever heard anything so outlandishly entertaining?" she asked the man beside Cassie.

To Trace, Cassie looked as though she'd been kicked in the stomach and didn't know why. *Just like that dumb Irish setter when someone got fed up with her and told her to get,* he remembered sympathetically.

"One name's pretty much as good as another," the man said, giving Cassie a half smile and turning his attention to the street, seeming not to have noticed her outstretched hand. His disinterest was obvious to everyone in the coach. That is, to everyone but Cassie, who looked at her ignored hand and gave a shrug before returning her adoring gaze to the man beside her.

The dandy's dismissing smile had been all it had taken to bring that radiant grin back to her face. *Just like that poor old pup. Give her a pat on the head or a kind word and she forgets you just kicked her,* Trace

21

reminisced with a sad smile of his own.

"You folks all set in here?" Tom Newman asked, peeking his head in the door to visually answer his own question before slamming it shut.

"All set, driver," the newcomer answered, ignoring the angry glares he was receiving from the displaced Horace Gilbert, the pouting disappointment on Lovey's face, and most of all the adoring worship evident in Cassie's honey-colored eyes.

In the next minute, they heard the crack of Newman's whip, accompanied by a shout at the horses as the stagecoach lurched forward.

"You didn't tell us yours," Cassie said to the last-minute passenger.

"I beg your pardon?" he returned, not bothering to hide the fact that he was enjoying the view of Lovey LaRue's cleavage, which was being deliberately displayed for his pleasure.

Cassie's eyes shifted irritably to Lovey's bosom, then back to the man—the man she was already sure she was going to make love her as much as she loved him! If she could just get him to notice her. "Your name. You didn't give us your name."

"Barton Talbot," he responded, his gaze never wavering from the attractive show in the opposite seat.

"What is your business, Mr. Talbot?" Lovey asked in a husky sort of whisper that suggested an intimacy the others in the coach were not privy to. Slowly moistening her lips with the point of her tongue, she ran the tips of her graceful fingers down the column of her neck to within inches of the shadowy cleft between her breasts, then back up to her chin.

Making no secret of the fact that he'd received Lovey's obvious message, Barton smiled suggestively. "I deal monte, Miss LaRue. And you? What brings a sweet lady like you to the rough mining towns of the

Sierra Nevada?"

"I'm an entertainer," Lovey offered with a saucy bounce of her golden ringlets.

"I'll bet you're a good one, too!" Barton said with a wink.

"I'm billed as 'The Lovely Lovey LaRue.' I'm surprised you haven't heard of me. Perhaps you'll come hear me sing at the Imperial Theatre in Auburn tonight."

"I might do that."

Cassie sagged back in her seat and crossed her arms over her chest sullenly. This was not going well at all. Lovey wasn't letting the distance between her and Barton slow her down in the least.

During the next hour, Cassie's worried gaze sawed from Lovey to Barton and back to Lovey again as she followed their conversation with mounting frustration. It was as if he'd forgotten all about her, and it was quite apparent she'd better think of something fast if she didn't want "Lovely Lovey LaRue" to take Barton away from her.

Glancing down at her own, unattractively disguised curves, Cassie made a face. Up until that very moment, she'd never had much use for female clothes with all their frills and ruffles; but now she suddenly wished with all her heart that she owned a dress that would make Barton Talbot look at her the way he was looking at Lovey.

Soon's I get to Sacramento and get Pa's gold in the bank, I'm gonna buy me one, she swore silently. *Maybe two or three.* But Sacramento might be too late. *Hell, Auburn might be too late!* By the time they got that far, Lovey could have wangled a proposal of marriage out of the handsome monte dealer. Women weren't exactly plentiful in California, and pretty ones like Lovey LaRue were almost nonexistent.

23

"I do swear, you're 'bout the prettiest smellin' thing I ever did get a whiff of," Cassie suddenly said to Barton, leaning closer to him and taking loud, exaggerated sniffs of his neck beneath his ear.

"It would give me great pleasure to be able to return the compliment," Barton said, shrinking away from Cassie, his lip curled in obvious displeasure. He and Lovey exchanged understanding smiles. "If you don't mind." He gave Cassie a gentle shove away from him and raised the leather window shade beside him.

"Don't open the shade!" Cassie warned, having missed his insulting innuendo. "You'll let the dust in an' get your fancy duds all dirty."

"Sometimes fresh air is worth a little dust," Horace said with a relieved sigh as he raised his shade too. His eyes focusing intently on the hilly terrain whizzing by the window, he pulled out a white linen handkerchief and mopped delicately at his forehead and upper lip.

After several more miles of uncomfortable silence, something shiny caught Trace's attention outside the window of the stagecoach. His face still deliberately hidden from his fellow passengers, he shifted in his seat and rested his head in the corner to attain a better view outside the coach.

There it was again. Two shiny flashes. Someone was using mirrors to signal ahead.

Suddenly Trace knew what the signals were saying. As if confirming his knowledge, the sound of the driver shouting orders to the horses and the cracking of his whip over their heads cut into the lulling silence. The six passengers were jounced unmercifully as the stagecoach picked up speed.

This is it, Trace congratulated himself. All the frustrating hours of waiting were about to pay off. He sat up straight, adjusted the hat on the back of his dark head, and raised the window shade beside him.

"What is it, Mr. McAllister?" Lovey squealed, grabbing his arm and cradling the muscular biceps between her generous breasts.

Trace glanced down at the frightened woman and said quite seriously, "I'm not sure." Showing none of the guilt he was feeling, his green eyes veered uneasily to Cassie, flitted over the black miner, then went back to Lovey. "But if I'm not mistaken, this stage is about to be robbed."

As if to support his theory, the first gunshots sounded, and an armed bandit rode alongside the coach, shouting in Spanish for the driver to halt.

"Ain't you gonna do somethin'?" Cassie yelled, staring at the men aghast.

"What can we do?" Horace asked, his eyes wide with terror. "If we resist they'll kill us all!"

"They probably outnumber us four to one," Barton suggested. "All we can do is hope they'll be satisfied to only take our gold and not our lives."

"Well, they ain't takin' *my* gold!" Cassie spat angrily, jerking her revolver from the holster and aiming toward the Mexican outside the window.

With the speed of one of her bullets, a tanned hand shot out and grabbed her wrist before she could fire. "What the hell do you think you're doing? Trying to get yourself killed? Don't you realize that's probably Joaquin Murieta out there? He'd just as soon kill you as look at you!"

Cassie looked from the hand on her wrist into deadly green eyes. "Let go o' me, McAllister, or you won't be around to see who makes it out alive 'n who don't!" She twisted her hand against his grip, determined to fire on the attackers.

Trace's hold tightened on her slim wrist, squeezing until the feeling was gone from her fingers and they opened of their own accord. The gun clattered to the floor.

Already the stagecoach was slowing down, and the thunder of the approaching bandits' horses roared in Cassie's ears — along with the sound of her father's life savings and her dreams of the future evaporating into the cool mountain air.

Chapter Two

"I must ask you to throw out the weapons, *senōrs*. Then you will please to step out of the stagecoach one at a time," the lone bandit announced in a thick Spanish accent.

"Give me my gun," Cassie hissed at Trace. "He's alone! I can take him down easy with one shot!"

"Look again," Trace ordered, jerking his head toward the other window.

Cassie and the rest of the passengers turned to see two more Mexicans riding along the other side of the stagecoach.

"And there are probably more in those rocks over there," Horace added shakily as he quailed away from the window.

"They're no doubt hidden all around us, just waiting for us to do something stupid like fire at them," Barton said.

Trace nodded his head in agreement. "Out in the open and surrounded like we are, we don't have much choice. If we resist, none of us will live through this. If we don't, we might have a chance."

Detecting the slight moment of hesitation from his victims, the robber added, "You will do as I say—that is, unless you wish to meet with the same unfortunate fate as the driver and guard."

Against Cassie's continued protests, Trace and Barton tossed their pistols, along with her revolver and the other passengers' weapons, out the door ahead of them, then stepped out of the stagecoach into the glaring sunlight.

Too angry and frustrated by what was happening to be afraid, Cassie bounded out of the stagecoach and stood between Barton and Trace. She had no intention of cowering down to these yellow-livered desperadoes.

An irate sneer on her face, her feet planted wide apart, Cassie balled her fists on her hips, jutted her chin in defiance, and narrowed her eyes to glare threateningly up at the umber-skinned Mexican who sat atop his snorting black stallion waiting for the waylaid travelers to assemble before him.

It was then she recognized the man who had all of northern California quaking with fear. *Joaquin Murieta!* McAllister had been right.

Though she'd never seen the famous Mexican *bandido* before, she had no doubt this was him. His description was on wanted posters in towns and gold camps from one end of the gold country to the other; and there was not a person in all California who hadn't heard the frightening stories about Murieta.

Just as she'd heard him described, he wore a large black sombrero pulled low on his face, a black velvet jacket, and tight black trousers with silver ornaments decorating the side seams. Around his waist was the famous red sash that had become one of his trademarks; and starting deep in the bushy black mustache that covered his upper lip, a jagged scar, puckered and red, slashed its way upward to the corner of his left eye, giving his thick-jowled face a permanent, recogizable sneer that was enough to cause the stoutest of hearts to race with fear.

"I must ask you to please lift up the hands," Murieta said, his unspoken threat chilling in the very politeness of the request — and in the way he motioned his instructions to them with two large silver-mounted revolvers.

Her original bravado suddenly wavering, Cassie raised her hands as she glanced uneasily over her shoulder to see what was happening behind her.

Her lungs constricted in a reflexive gasp when she saw the other two sombrero-wearing *bandidos* on top of the stagecoach, already tossing a trunk and saddlebags — her saddlebags — over the side. The driver, Tom Newman, had been wounded and was slumped over in his seat, precariously close to falling, his eyes glazed with pain. She looked around frantically for the guard, but quickly realized the man who'd ridden shotgun would be no help. He was nowhere to be seen and must be back on the road somewhere, dead or wounded.

A shiver of realization and fright tentacled its way over Cassie's skin, and her belligerent stance slumped perceptibly. If she'd had any doubts as to the bandit's identity before, they were all resolved now. This man was a heartless killer, and he was going to kill them all if they didn't do as he said.

Still, a stubborn inner voice nagged at her, there must to be something they could do to stop this gang of killers and thieves from stealing her gold.

Taking a cursory inventory of the other passengers to determine who would be the most likely to help, her eyes passed quickly over Lovey LaRue, who was doing her best to make herself invisible behind Trace as tears streaked down her rouged cheeks. Certainly no help there.

29

Cassie's gaze cut to Horace Gilbert, who was standing immediately behind Lovey. His watery eyes were bulging with fear, his face glistening with sweat. She could swear she saw tears in his eyes. By comparison, Lovey looked the braver of the two, she realized, discounting both of them for possible assistance.

She glanced from left to right, first at Trace, then at Barton Talbot, thinking that if each of them took one of the men on top of the stagecoach, she could take down Murieta. But neither of the men seemed as though he had any intention of pitting himself against the confident robbers.

Suddenly she remembered the miner who'd been beside her! He was the size of a small mountain, at least five inches over six feet. Surely he wouldn't be afraid to help! She shot a hurried glance over her shoulder in the black man's direction. But her hopes were immediately dashed. His upper lip beaded with sweat, as though he had a grave decision to make, his brown eyes shifted nervously from Murieta on the horse to the men on top of the stage. She couldn't even get his attention.

Grunting her disgust, yet refusing to let her fear show, Cassie directed her most intimidating stare toward Murieta and waited for her chance. They weren't going to steal her pa's gold. Not if she could help it, anyway. If she had to, she'd take them alone.

"Are you going to take our money?" Lovey suddenly ventured in a trembling voice.

Cassie's irritated gaze jerked toward Lovey, who peeked out from behind the protective shield of Trace McAllister's broad back. "No, they don't want our money," she blasted the other woman sarcastically, frustration burning in her throat at the thought of how long it had taken her and her father to pan that much gold. "They jus' dropped by to talk 'bout the weather!"

Murieta's eyebrows arched inquisitively and he turned his attention to Cassie. "What is this?" he asked, his accent silky with amusement.

Keeping one gun trained on Trace McAllister—who was a good five inches over his own five-foot-nine-inch height, and obviously the man most likely to give him any trouble—he holstered one gun and dismounted. His dark eyes darting threateningly over the rest of the passengers, he ambled up to Cassie. "Is it possible there is a treasure I have overlooked beneath this miner's clothing?" he laughed, wrinkling his nose at the mention of her clothes. Cupping her chin in a gloved hand, he pushed his own face up to Cassie's for a close examination and grinned.

"Are you a *senōr* or *senōrita?*" he asked with an amused laugh, making no secret of the fact that he knew the answer to his question.

"Get your slimy hands off me, you murderin' varmint!" she snarled, narrowing her eyes into an intimidating stare at the man who stood no taller than she.

"So, the *senōrita* spits fire. I like that!"

"That's not all I *speet,* you thievin' lowlife skunk!" Without taking time to consider the consequences, she spit in the Mexican's face.

The grip on her face tightened. His black eyes slitted dangerously. He brought the gun toward her, its barrel pointed directly at her gut. "You have made the mistake to insult *Joaquin Murieta.*"

Watching the drop of spittle slide off Murieta's cheek, Cassie didn't need to be told she had made a serious blunder. And though this wasn't the first time her tendency to act before thinking had gotten her into a mess, it showed definite signs of being the last. She hazarded a helpless look from left to right in a panicked search for help.

31

She thought she saw Trace McAllister's brows flinch together in a worried frown when his eyes met her questioning gaze. But the look of concern was gone as quickly as it had appeared, and she wasn't sure if she had imagined it or not. His total attention was focused on the large gun pointed at her middle. The only evidence that he was aware of what was happening to her was in the knotted muscle that flexed and relaxed in his strong jaw.

Murieta's grip on her face loosened and his free hand slid down her throat to the top button of her flannel shirt. "You must learn some respect, señorita." His fingers slid slowly and deliberately inside her shirt at the vee between her shirt and longjohn-covered breasts. "Perhaps Murieta will teach you that respect," he said with a taunting smile. He popped the first button off her shirt.

"There's no need to rough up the girl, Murieta," Barton Talbot said. "Just take the gold and leave us alone."

"You dare to give Joaquin Murieta orders, señor?" the bandit said, releasing his grip on Cassie's shirt-front and backhanding the taller man.

Taken off guard by Murieta's speed and strength, Barton flew backward and landed in a heap on the dusty road.

"Leave him alone!" Cassie growled, bringing her booted foot upward with a hard kick at Murieta's groin.

Though the aim of her foot missed its mark, she managed to send the silver-mounted pistol flying through the air.

The expression on Murieta's hard, brown face was one of total astonishment. Before he could react, Cassie dove across the space that separated her from the dropped pistol. Her fingers wrapped around the ivory handle, she rolled over and sat up, cocking the hammer as she did, all in one efficient motion.

"Very clever, *señorita,* but not quite fast enough!" Murieta said, his dark face as frightening as the idenical revolver he held pointed at Barton Talbot's temple. "You will put down the weapon or I will kill this pretty *señor* you seem to prize so highly."

"Do as he says, Cassie," Trace said in a low voice.

Cassie had heard too many stories about Joaquin Murieta to think the man was bluffing. She had no choice. She was beaten. All the gold in the world wasn't worth Barton's life. She lowered the pistol to the ground.

"That is better," Murieta said with an ugly smile, moving away from Barton and aiming his gun at Cassie now. "You make the foolish mistake when you spit in the face of Joaquin Murieta. For that I can perhaps forgive you, because Joaquin Murieta is a generous man. But no one who draws the gun on Murieta has ever lived to tell the story." The gleam in his black eyes left no doubt as to his plans as he put his thumb on the hammer of the revolver and smiled. With exaggerated emphasis, he aimed the barrel at Cassie's head and eased back on it.

Refusing to give her murderer the satisfaction of seeing her die afraid, Cassie fought the desire to squeeze her eyes closed as she waited for the sound of the gunshot that would end her life.

Hesitating under the courageous glare of the girl, Murieta shifted his gaze, an expression of uncertainty tripping across his face. He cast a side glance at Barton, then at Trace and Horace, then brought his full attention back to the girl.

Damn! Where in the hell are they? Trace cursed silently. It was up to him to do something. But what? Murieta was several feet away from him—too far to jump him. Besides, one wrong move, and the girl would be dead.

Trace sliced an annoyed glance up the road. Nothing! He was on his own. There was no other choice.

Lowering his hands slowly, he hoped the girl would keep the Mexican distracted long enough for him to draw out the spare gun he had hidden under his coat in the back waistband of his trousers. His only chance was to get the drop on Murieta. Of course, if he was too slow, it would mean the girl's death — and his. A thought occurred to him.

"I was told Joaquin Murieta is a man of honor!" Trace said, his voice displaying none of the uselessness and anger he was feeling. "I guess folks lied about that!"

Joaquin looked away from Cassie in surprise, his expression strangely tense.

Trace could have sworn Murieta let a relieved sigh.

"What do you mean?" Murieta asked, directing the barrel of his weapon toward Trace.

At least the danger to the girl wasn't quite so immediate. "No man of honor would shoot an unarmed girl in cold blood."

Before Murieta could respond to Trace's taunt, he was interrupted by a loud shout. "Rangers!"

Everyone looked up to see a fourth sombrero-clad rider coming toward them at frantic speed. "Not a mile behind me!" he yelled, pointing over his shoulder in the direction from which the stagecoach had come. "Let's get out of here."

"It's about time," Trace mumbled on a relieved sigh.

"You are fortunate this time, *mi amigos*," Murieta snarled, snatching his second pistol off the ground and leaping onto the black stallion. "But we will meet again. Of that you can be certain." His silver spurs dug into the horse's sides and he rode away, disappearing into the hills with his gang as though they'd never been there.

Cassie dashed for her revolver, managing to get off one shot, but it was too late. Murieta and his gang were gone — her gold with them. "Dammit!" she ground out, giving Trace a dirty look.

"What was that for?" he asked, stooping to retrieve his own weapons.

"For all the help!" she growled. "If you hadn't 'a took my gun in the first place, that varmint'd be dead by now! 'Stead, you let him get away!"

"And we'd all be dead right along with him, you hot-tempered little fool!" Trace returned. Here he'd been ready to shoot it out with Murieta to save her and she was accusing him of doing nothing.

Resisting the guilt he felt for his part in the botched plan to catch Murieta, he yelled, "You may be in a hurry to die, but me, I've got a peculiar hankering to keep on living! And there's no way in hell I'm going to let a skinny little kid who doesn't even know how to act like the female she's supposed to be get me killed!"

" 'Skinny little kid' " Cassie shrilled. "Who you callin' a skinny little kid, you overgrown ox?"

A group of twenty mounted Rangers rode up before Trace could respond, to be greeted by excited shouts and instructions from the robbery victims, all speaking at once, frantically detailing what had happened and pointing toward the route Murieta and his men had taken to escape.

"Don't worry, folks! He's not goin' to get away this time!" the leader shouted with confidence as he signaled his men to follow him toward the hills Murieta had disappeared into moments before.

"I'll believe that when I see it," Trace gritted through his teeth.

"What'd you say?" the wounded stagecoach driver

asked, righting himself with effort.

"Nothing! I just got something stuck in my craw. Are you going to be all right?" he asked, eyeing the blood-soaked sleeve of Tom's shirt.

"I think so. It's just a flesh wound."

"Miss LaRue, can you come over here and help me?"

Still visibly shaken, her rouge garishly bright on her color-drained cheeks, Lovey hurried to Trace's side.

"Will you bandage up this shoulder for Tom while I go check on the guard?"

Lovey paled even more, her blue eyes widening with fright. She looked hesitantly at Tom's bloody shirt, her face screwed into an expression of aversion. Still, she didn't want the handsome Trace McAllister to be angry with her—and she really did want to do her part. Swallowing the bile that rose in her throat with a determined gulp, she gave both men a weak smile. "I've never done any nursing, but if you'll tell me what to do, I'll try."

"First thing is to take off one of your petticoats."

Lovey's eyebrows raised suspiciously. "My petticoat? I fail to see how my—" she began, her voice quivering with indignation.

Trace heaved an exasperated sigh. "For bandages, Miss LaRue. You up to telling her what to do, Newman?"

"Sure," Tom answered without looking at Trace, his senses already reeling intoxicatedly with the feminine smell of lilacs and Lovey LaRue. "Guess I ought to get this shirt off first," he said to her, his voice hoarse. He made a feeble try at unbuttoning it with one hand.

"Here, I can at least do that without special instructions," Lovey offered, reaching for Tom's blood-stained shirtfront and pushing his hand aside, her own hands shaking visibly because it was necessary to

36

ouch the bloody shirt.

"This is real nice o' you, Miss LaRue," Tom choked, he Adam's apple in his throat jumping spasmodically as he swallowed his nervousness. And a new pain, far greater and more demanding than the one in his injured shoulder, began to burn in Tom's groin.

"Call me Lovey . . . Tom," she offered with a smile. "And it's the least I can do for a man who was wounded defending us all." Steeling herself not to show her revulsion at seeing all the blood and the ugly tear in Tom Newman's arm, she gingerly slipped she shirt off his muscular shoulder when it was unbuttoned.

Trace rolled his eyes heavenward and spoke to the other four passengers. "I need one of you to come with me to see what happened to that guard."

"I'll go," Cassie offered, relieved that the Rangers were on Murieta's trail, but anxious to keep busy until word came they had retrieved the stolen gold.

"I meant one of the others," Trace pointed out disapprovingly. "This is man's work."

She stomped over to Trace and poked an index finger in the middle of his chest. "So's minin' an' defendin' stagecoaches from desperadoes, mister! An' it ain't never stopped me before!"

He brought his face down to the same level as hers. "Well, something sure as hell should have. Your stupidity could have gotten us all killed!"

"Stupidity, huh? At least I didn't jus' stand there like some yellow-livered, panty-waisted—"

"Why don't you see if you can help Miss Lovey, Miss Cassie?" the black man interrupted, his soft voice surprisingly cultured. "I'll go with Mr. McAllister. Seems like I remember that guard being a mite heavier than a lady could probably heft."

Cassie turned her glare on the big man, ready to

37

lambaste him too. Who did these men think she was, anyway? Some weak female who couldn't lift anything heavier than a prissy fan or her batting eyelashes?

But the expression in the sad brown eyes wasn't the least bit condemning or judgmental. Instead, it was a look of kindness and concern. He simply wanted to help. Her eyes roved up the mammoth length of him, and even through the red haze of her anger she could see the sense in his words.

"I'll go help Miss LaRue with the driver," she said to him, leaving Trace to stare after her with a dumbfounded look on his face.

"You may not talk much, mister, but when you do, folks sure listen, don't they? How'd you do that?" Trace asked with a jerk of his head toward Cassie as he started walking back up the road to look for the fallen guard. "I told her the same thing you did and she was ready to pull a gun on me!"

The miner laughed. "*What* you were saying isn't as important as *how* you were saying it, Mr. McAllister."

"None of that *Mr. McAllister* stuff. Just Trace is good enough. Men are all equals as far as I'm concerned."

The light in the man's kind eyes seemed to dim. "That would be real nice. But you don't extend that thinking to women, do you, Mr. Mc— I mean Trace?"

"Sure I do," Trace answered too quickly, thought a moment, and then added, "I mean as long as they—"

"As long as they stay in their place and bow down to the menfolk?" the man finished for him.

Trace stopped in midstep and stared at the smiling man for a full minute before speaking. Then, when he did speak, it was with an astonished laugh. "I'll be damned. I'll be goddamned! How'd you get so smart—uh—What's your name?"

"Noah Simmons." The man chuckled sadly. "And I'm not smart. I just know there's nobody, black or white, male or female, who likes to be talked down to and treated like they're dumb. Everyone needs to be treated with a little respect."

The conversation was brought to an abrupt halt as the two men spotted the stagecoach guard on the ground ahead. Just as they got to where the guard lay sprawled and unconscious in the road, they heard the sound of horses and a stagecoach coming toward them.

"What the hell?" Trace grabbed the wounded man and dragged him to the side of the road before they could all be run over.

The vehicle came to a creaking, harness-jangling halt to the sound of "Whoa there, horses!" only inches from where the guard had been lying.

Their pulses racing wildly, Trace and Noah looked up to find Cassie Wyman sitting in the driver's seat, her expression guileless. "Thought it would save time if you fellers didn't have to carry that guard back down the road."

"*You* thought?" Trace started—at the top of his lungs—only to be brought up short by the light pressure of a massive chocolate-brown hand on his arm.

"Remember. Respect," Noah said out of the corner of his mouth.

Trace shifted his gaze to Noah, then back to Cassie, his eyes narrowed with indecision. But all of his intentions to make up to the girl for the way he'd yelled at her dissolved into uncontrollable anger. "You want respect? I'll give her respect—with the palm of my hand on her backside!" He grabbed the edge of the seat to hoist himself up to the driver's seat of the coach. "I'll teach her to scare the hell out of us!"

"That's real nice of you, Miss Cassie," Noah interceded, his voice loud and cheerful. "Real smart think-ing. Don't know why one of us didn't think of it! Isn't that right, Trace?"

One foot on the wheel hub, the other in midair, the expression on Trace's face was a curious mingle of determination and doubt. He stopped his ascent and stared at the expectant man. "Yeah, that's right," he finally said with a disgruntled sigh. He lowered his boot down to the road and stepped back. "Real smart. As long as the brakes were working!" he couldn't help adding to himself.

Within minutes, Cassie had turned the stagecoach around and the men had settled the wounded guard inside the stagecoach. Trace climbed up beside Cassie and reached to take the reins from her hands. "I'll drive."

Cassie's fingers tightened on the leather straps. "Says who?"

"Give them to me, kid!" he ordered through gritted teeth. "I'm not in the mood to argue with you about it."

"Tom Newman told me to drive this rig, McAllister. Not you. An' that's what I aim to do!"

"Over my dead body!"

Cassie's mouth thinned into a confident grin and she placed her hand on the butt of her gun. "That can be arranged real easy."

Trace took a deep breath and prayed for patience. *Respect,* he reminded himself over and over. "Look, kid, I shouldn't have gotten so riled at you before," he began.

"That's the first smart thing I've heard come out of your big mouth." She took her hand off her gun and looked straight ahead.

With a side glance at Noah that said, *I told you it wouldn't work,* Trace ignored her sarcasm. "And bringing the stage so we wouldn't have to carry the guard was real smart thinking. But driving this rig is man's wor—"

"I'm drivin'!"

"That's it!" He'd given Noah's way his best effort. "Give me those reins!" he commanded, jerking at the leather straps she held tightly wound around her hands.

Noah stepped in quickly—before the two on the driver's seat could come to blows. "Why don't you let Miss Cassie drive and you ride shotgun?" he suggested, offering the guard's weapon up to Trace.

Though he wouldn't admit it, Noah's idea made sense. "I guess that would work."

"I don't want him ridin' shotgun for me," Cassie said to Noah, wondering even as she spoke why she was being so contrary.

"Then get in the goddamned coach where you *females*—and I use the term in its loosest sense—belong!" Trace grabbed for the reins again.

"I'll get *in* it, when you get *under* it—where all you *snakes* belong!"

Trace opened his mouth to speak, sputtered a few unintelligible sounds, then clamped it shut. Without another word to her, he bounded down from the driver's seat. "You ride shotgun!" he shouted at Noah, thrusting the gun into his middle.

She'd won! Cassie smiled her satisfaction. Trace McAllister had backed down. That would show him to try to boss her around.

Then a strange thought blared through her mind. *What did you win, Cassie?* And the grin slid off her face, to be replaced by an expression of puzzled disappointment as she heard Trace McAllister slam the door behind him and felt the coach rock gently under his shifting weight as he settled himself inside.

41

"Seems to me a pretty young lady could think of a better way to get what she wanted than fighting," Noah mused aloud as he sat down beside Cassie.

"What're you talkin' 'bout? I ain't pretty. 'Sides, what diff'rence does it make how I get what I want, long as I get it?" she reasoned irritably, flicking the whip over the horses' rumps and starting the stage forward.

A low rumble of laughter issued from Noah's throat. "First of all, you are pretty — or you could be, if you weren't so busy trying to prove you're better than every man you meet."

"I ain't tryin' to prove I'm better than every man I meet!"

"Oh?" Noah asked, his eyebrows arched skeptically.

A mischievous grin suddenly split across Cassie's face. "Not *every* man." She giggled. "Most maybe. But not *every!*"

"But one of these days you're going meet the man you can't best in a yelling or shooting match, Miss Cassie. Then what are you going to do?"

"Well, I ain't met him yet!"

"I think you might be surprised, missy. I surely do think you just might be real surprised. . . ."

Chapter Three

Cassie and Noah helped Tom Newman into a seat beside Lovey LaRue, who had thrown herself into her nursing role with zeal, issuing orders and clucking protectively over her patient. "Careful of that shoulder now! Don't be so rough with him. He's been shot."

"That's a real nice piece of doctoring you did, Miss Lovey," Noah complimented as he stood back to admire her work.

"Ain't it!" Tom agreed, glancing down at his petticoat-bandaged shoulder. "Best doctorin' I ever had, I'll tell you that." He beamed an appreciative grin at Lovey.

"Oh, shoo. You're just saying that. I didn't do anything special. I was just doing my part as best I could," she preened modestly.

"That may be," Noah said, "but I do believe you might have missed your calling, Miss Lovey. I don't recall ever seeing a finer-looking bandage."

"I'll tell you a little secret," Lovey said, leaning forward conspiratorially. "At one time I did entertain the idea of becoming a nurse. Seems I've always had a knack for healing people. Of course, that was before I discovered my talent for making folks feel good with my singing."

Before Noah could respond, two Rangers came galloping up, their horses lathered and puffing, and everyone's attention was averted to them.

Expectant smiles on their faces, Cassie and Noah hurried to meet the horsemen, certain their gold had been recovered.

"We lost 'em!" the chief Ranger announced, taking off his hat and wiping the back of his arm over his forehead.

"You lost 'em!" Cassie cried, shock and disillusionment congealing into a sickening lump in her belly.

"They just disappeared, like they wasn't never there."

"What the hell did you expect?" Trace shouted at the Ranger. "You gave them a ten-minute lead! If you'd been here when they attacked like you were supposed to be, they wouldn't have had a chance!"

"Are you goin' to get my pa's gold back for me 'r not?" Cassie asked bluntly, the distrust on her angry face deadly.

"We're sure gonna try, miss. The California legislature authorized me to form this company to track Murieta down and capture him—dead or alive. And that's what we aim to do, Miss—uh?" He gave Trace a questioning glance.

"Cassie Wyman," Trace said with a scowl. "She had two saddlebags of gold on the stagecoach." He pointed at Noah. "And this is Noah Simmons. He had a trunk full of gold."

"I'm Harry Love," the man introduced himself, not bothering to hide his skepticism as he openly scrutinized the two unlikely looking rich people. Of course, these days you couldn't tell a man's worth by the clothes he wore. The most successful ones were usually the poorest looking. "And we're sure gonna do all we can to recover your gold for you. My men are still lookin' to pick up their trail again. We're not givin' up. Not when we're this close to makin' an arrest. In fact, today's the closest we've gotten."

"Close isn't good enough, Love!" Trace stormed. "You've bungled this whole thing! You were supposed to be here in time to stop the robbery!"

"Now, just you wait a minute, McAllister. We did the best we could!"

"If this was your best, then I guess these folks had better not look forward to seeing their gold any time soon!"

"You're askin' for it, mister," Love threatened. "I won't be talked to like that by one of my men."

"Well, that's no problem, Harry. Because I quit!" Trace dug a metal badge from his pocket and pitched it to the ground at Love's feet.

"Wait a minute!" Cassie interrupted, at last grasping what had happened. "You mean you knew we was goin' to be robbed?" she said to Trace, her stunned gaze jerking back and forth from Trace to his ex-boss.

"We knew Murieta was in the area and that this stage was carrying a lot of gold," Trace admitted sheepishly. "The plan was for the Rangers to be right behind the stagecoach so we could catch Murieta red-handed if he showed up."

Her sense of betrayal multiplying tenfold, Cassie wheeled on Love. "If you knew we was gonna be robbed, what in blazes took you so long to get here?" she asked in an accusing voice. "Do you know how long me 'n my pa worked to pan out that much gold? Four years! We dug and scratched 'n broke our backs for four years! Why wasn't you here to stop 'em?"

"We didn't want them to know the stage was bein' followed," Harry explained. "It might have scared

45

them off."

"That's a fine howdy-do, ain't it?" she said on a disbelieving laugh. "Our gold's halfway to Mexico by now, an' you're tellin' me you didn't want to scare them snakes off. Did you stop to think, Harry, that if he knew you was gonna be there, he might not've stopped this stage? An' me and Noah'd still have our gold!"

"But if we did it that way, we wouldn't catch Murieta. He's slippery. He just seems to disappear into thin air between robberies. Like he done today. We've got to catch him red-handed before he can hole up in his hideout."

"But your dumb plan didn't work, did it, Harry? Not only did you let him 'n his thievin' gang get away, but now me 'n Noah here don't have our gold neither!" Her voice cracked suspiciously on the last word.

Damn, she was going to cry. No one had seen her cry since she was a little girl. In fact, she couldn't remember the last time she'd cried. But no one was going to see her blubbering like a weak female now.

Cassie spun away from the stunned men and climbed up to the driver's seat on the stagecoach. "I'm takin' this here stagecoach on as far as Auburn," she called down, refusing to look at the Rangers and other passengers. "Then I'm gonna get me a horse 'n saddle 'n go after Murieta myself! So if anyone figgers to ride on this stage, you better get yourselves on over here. 'Cause as far as I'm concerned, I've wasted enough time with these sorry excuses for lawmen!"

Later, after riding in silence for over an hour, Cassie turned to the dejected man who sat beside her on the driver's seat, the shotgun resting across his lap. "What're you gonna do now, Noah?

"I really don't rightly know, Miss Cassie," Noah

46

answered, his pensive gaze staying riveted to the passing landscape, lush and green after the spring rains. "I just don't know."

Surprised by the despondent sound in Noah's voice, Cassie turned and studied him. She'd been so worried about her own gold and her own problems that she hadn't even given a thought to what losing his gold might mean to Noah Simmons. Ashamed, she touched his arm tentatively. "I got a idea!" she said cheerfully. "What say you 'n me team up 'n hunt down them polecats together? We could get our gold back, *and* the reward for Murieta's hide at the same time."

"It's not that easy, missy. I don't have time to go looking for Murieta. I need to be in San Francisco by the end of the month with $10,000 in gold."

Cassie whistled her surprise through her teeth. "Ten thousand dollars! What in tarnation could be worth that much money?" she choked.

"Salina," Noah said simply, his expression and voice softening. "Salina's worth that and more."

Cassie shook her head. "What's salina?"

Noah gave a cheerless chuckle at Cassie's lack of understanding. "Not a what, Miss Cassie. Salina is a who. She's a woman."

Cassie's brows drew together quizzically. "A wom—?" Then realization dawned on her and her eyebrows arched, her face turning a bright shade of pink. "Oh," she mouthed, nodding her head and forcing her embarrassed attention back to the road ahead.

"Not that kind of woman, Miss Cassie," Noah consoled, surprised he could still laugh.

Cassie didn't say anything.

"Salina's the woman I love and plan to marry. She's in San Francisco. Only I can't marry her until I give Cliff Hopkins ten thousand dollars for her and her mama. That's what I was planning to use my gold for—to buy Salina's freedom."

"Ten thousand dollars! Noah, don't you know there ain't s'posed to be slaves in California! This is a free state."

"It's not that simple, Miss Cassie. Her mama's still on Mr. Cliff's place in Georgia. And when he brought Salina out here, he told her that if she tried to leave him, he'd sell off her mama and make sure they never saw each other again. And he'd do it too. He's already sold off her two brothers and her sister. Her mama's the only family she's got left. That's why I have to get the free papers for both Salina and her mama, so we can go back to Georgia and get her. Because once we get back there, Salina's not free anymore."

"What about you, Noah? Have you got your papers?"

"I got my papers. I was born free."

Cassie's heart broke for the man beside her and for the beautiful bride he'd lost when his gold was stolen. "Are you sure he won't take less?" Cassie had heard prospectors who'd come from large plantations in the South talk about the cost of slaves, and she'd never heard of one costing anywhere close to ten thousand dollars. "I prob'bly could help you out with a little bit o' gold Murieta didn't know I had in my money belt."

"That's real nice of you to offer, Miss Cassie, but even with the two thousand I've still got—in *my* money belt—it wouldn't be enough. He wants the whole ten thousand or he won't let her go. Besides, he doesn't really want to sell her. He says he has big plans for her that are going to make him a rich man. She's the most beautiful girl you've ever seen, and he's going to build a gambling hall and pleasure parlor in San Francisco and force her to work in the rooms upstairs. He says men'll pay hundreds of dollars to spend a few hours with her."

48

Cassie's stomach roiled violently at the thought. Even she knew—or at least had a good idea—what women did in the upstairs room of saloons. "But how could he force her to do somethin' like that?"

Noah smiled desolately at Cassie's childlike innocence. For all her tough, experienced bravado, she had obviously been sheltered from the terrible things that went on in the real world. "Oh, there are ways, little girl. There are ways," he said, his wisdom making him feel twice his thirty years. Noah was silent for a long time, then went on speaking. "If Salina doesn't do as he says, he'll make her mama pay."

"Where'd you 'n Salina meet, Noah?"

"We met on the Oregon Trail when we all came out to California last year. And I loved her from the first minute I set eyes on her. We made plans to marry as soon as I could get enough gold to buy her and her mama free of Hopkins. And I thought I'd done it a couple of months ago. I got lucky and made a decent strike right off. I came up with a thousand dollars in gold, and I was sure it was enough. So I went to Hopkins and made him an offer. He turned me down flat. Said he wouldn't consider parting with her for less than ten thousand. That's when I found out what he was planning to do with her.

"I didn't know what to do. I was desperate. The only thing I could do was try to buy some time. I talked him into taking the thousand as a deposit and promised him another ten thousand if he'd give me his word not to do anything with Salina before I got back with the gold. I don't know if he thought I couldn't raise it or if the idea of getting his hands on that much gold without working for it was what convinced him, but I got him to agree to give me three months to bring the rest to him. But the three months is up two weeks from tomorrow."

Her own personal loss seeming minor compared to Noah's, Cassie had become emotionally involved in the tragic story of Noah and Salina. It sounded like a romantic play she had seen when a traveling troupe of actors had come through Goldville the year before. Of course in the drama, the hero had saved the girl, and there had been a happy ending.

But that was just pretend. This is real, she told herself with mind-swirling realization. There was every chance this story wouldn't have a perfect ending like in the play.

Cassie searched her mind frantically for a way to help Noah save Salina from the cruel, real-life villain who held her young life in his hands.

"There's got to be somethin' you can do!" she mused. "I know! Why don't you jus' go to San Francisco 'n snatch her out o' that fiend's evil hands? I could tell you 'bout lots o' places to get lost up there in the hills. Hopkins'd never find you!"

"That's what I'm going to have to do, now that I've lost my gold. But if I do, Salina's going to fight me all the way. She swears the only way she'll ever leave Mr. Cliff is if her mama is free. She'd never forgive me if I caused something bad to happen to her mama."

"Then, come after Murieta with me 'n get your gold back. 'Sides, if Hopkins ain't gonna do nothin' for two weeks, we got plenty o' time! We can get horses 'n gear in Auburn 'n head out in the mornin'. We'll have our money back in a coupla days. An' you'll be huggin' your Salina in a week!"

"I guess we could try it your way," Noah said, the weight on his heart lifting ever so slightly.

" 'Course we can!" Cassie laughed, suddenly feeling good enough to pop. Everything was going to be all right. She just knew it was. She and Noah were going to get her father's gold back, rid California of the dreaded Joaquin Murieta, *and* save Salina and her mother, all at the same time. That would certainly be something to tell her snooty relatives in Baltimore when she saw them again!

"Here you are, folks," Cassie announced, yanking open the door. "All safe 'n sound."

His mood little improved, Trace McAllister was the last to step off the stagecoach. Scowling, he started past Cassie without speaking.

"Well?" she said to him with a cheeky grin on her tan, lightly freckled face that said, *I told you I could drive this rig, didn't I?*

Ignoring her, Trace studied the people and the buildings along the street.

"Ain't you got *nothin'* to say to me?" Cassie hollered over the noise of the street, forcing Trace's attention back to her.

He looked down at her blankly. "Not that I can think of," he finally said, turning to leave.

Cassie ran after him and grabbed his arm, jerking him around to face her. "Ain't you goin' to 'pologize for sayin' that drivin' a stage was man's work?"

"No." He started walking again.

"No!" Cassie had to run to make her own long legs keep stride with Trace's even longer limbs. "I told you I could do it."

"So you did," he acknowledged, continuing to walk away from her.

"So, don't you think you owe me some kinda 'pology for sayin' I couldn't?"

"I didn't say you *couldn't* do it, kid. I was merely pointing out that the weaker sex's place was *inside* the coach where the stronger sex can protect her."

"Like you protected my gold? Why, I'll have you

51

know, I can outdrive, outshoot, 'n outmine any man in these parts!"

"Something to be real proud of, kid—if you were one of the boys, and not a bad imitation. Might be interesting to see how you'd measure up against ordinary females though," he challenged, his eyes deliberately directing her attention toward the Imperial Hotel where Barton Talbot was conversing with two attractive young women, one on each arm. "That's one contest I don't think you'd fare too well in."

Cassie stared at the frilly, large-skirted dresses and flowered hats of the two giggling women with Barton. Even from this distance, she could see that Barton was completely captivated by them, smiling his most charming grin and hanging on every word they said. Not like he'd been with her: a quick smile and then turning his attention to something or someone else.

"You might be the best shot and the best driver and the best miner in the state of California, kid"—Trace was unable to stop now that he'd started—"in the whole world, for all I know. But all the competing and wishing in the world isn't going to make you into a man. So where does that leave you? Because, as for being a female, not only do you not look or act like one, but you don't even *smell* like one!"

Trace was ashamed of himself before he was even through speaking; and if he could have inhaled the cruel words back into his mouth, he would have done it in a minute. But it was too late. His angry words had hit their mark with deadly accuracy and there was nothing he could do to reverse their stinging impact.

Cassie's brown eyes rounded with hurt and surprise. The corners of her perpetually smiling mouth turned down, her bottom lip tightening. And she just stared at him without speaking.

Trace felt like a cad of the worst sort, as though

52

he'd kicked that faithful Irish setter he'd had when he was a kid. Without thinking, he reached out to touch her shoulder and apologize. "Look, kid, I shouldn't ha—"

Shrugging away from his touch, Cassie spoke, the fire in her dark honey-colored eyes glimmering with held-back emotion. "I might not be pretty like them gals, 'n I might not have their fancy duds 'n manners; but I'll tell you one thing, Trace McAllister. I'm a good person, 'n I'd never—*never*—do nothin' to hurt a body who never done one thing to harm me. So I figger I'm a durn sight closer to bein' a lady than you are to bein' a gentleman!"

With all the control she could muster, she turned on her boot heel and stomped toward the livery stable to look for Noah, who was checking on the purchase of horses for their trip.

"Hey, kid, wait a minute!" Trace called after her. "I didn't mean what I said! It was just my mean temper flaring up."

"An' don't call me kid!" she shouted back over her shoulder. "I ain't no kid. I'm a full-growed woman!"

An hour later found Cassie sitting on a feather bed in a room in the Fremont House, her elbows resting on her knees, her hands clasped between them. Since it was too late to ride out tonight, she and Noah had decided to stay overnight. However, she still had an hour and a half until the dining room opened, so she continued to sit on the bed—thinking.

Thinking about what Trace McAllister had said about her not being much of a female; wondering about the things her mother should have—would have—told her about how to be a lady if she hadn't died when Cassie was twelve years old; and contemplating what she could do to make Barton Talbot look at her the way he had looked at those women outside the Imperial Hotel.

She eyed the washstand in the corner, studying the chipped washbowl and matching pitcher on it. Maybe if she washed up a mite, she decided, snatching the slouch hat from her head and tossing it onto the bed. Strands of reddish-brown hair, damp with perspiration, hung in limp curls around her shoulders. Taking off her dusty black coat, she pitched it in the same general direction as the hat. Next came the flannel shirt, boots, and jeans, until she was wearing nothing but her long johns.

Just as Cassie poured water from the pitcher into the white bowl, she was interrupted by an insistent knock on the door to her room. She turned and stared at the flimsy door, which was vibrating with every knock as though it would break apart any minute. "Who was it?" she asked, her voice a timid replica of her normal voice. There was something about being stripped down to her underwear that exposed more than just her shape.

"I got the bath you asked for, miss," a woman's voice called out.

Cassie snatched up her knee-length coat and hurriedly put it on over the long johns. "I didn't order no bath," she protested, holding the coat closed as she swung the door open wide.

There, with a confident grin on his arrogant face, stood Trace McAllister carrying a wooden washtub; and beside him, two young women were holding buckets of steaming hot water. "Just bring the water on in, girls," he ordered, shoving his way past the astonished Cassie with the wooden tub before she could react. The maids followed close behind him, darting curious glances toward the confused young woman.

"What're you doin' in my room?" she finally managed to croak out.

"That'll be all, ladies. I'll take care of things from here," Trace said, smiling at the maids and hustling them out the door without giving Cassie the slightest need. When they were gone, he turned to face her. "I've come to make amends."

Not certain what "amends" meant, but having been around men enough to make a pretty good guess, Cassie clutched her coat tighter to her, one hand at her throat, the other at her waist. She took an instinctive step backward. "You better get on outta here, McAllister! Or I'm gonna scream. You can go on over n' 'make amends' with one o' the gals over to the saloon. That's what they're there for."

Trace frowned. "What in the hell are you talking abou—" Understanding hit him with the impact of a slap between the shoulder blades, and a knowing smile spread across his face. He relaxed back against the door. "But I've got my heart set on making amends with you," he crooned, his voice deliberately seductive.

"Well, you can't. I ain't that kind o' woman!"

"Please," he begged, pushing away from the door and taking a step toward her.

"I'm warnin' you, McAllister. I'm gonna scream!" Her eyes wide with fear, she opened her mouth and took a deep breath. But before she could give sound to her protest, Trace was across the room and had a hard hand clamped over her mouth.

Cassie struggled against his hold on her, but his arm around her back and his hand on her mouth only tightened. "It's okay, kid. I was just teasing. You don't have to be afraid. I won't hurt you." As her struggling eased, he loosened his grip.

"You ain't gonna try to make amends with me?" she asked, her voice sounding very young to Trace's twenty-seven years of living.

"Well, yeah, but—"

Cassie opened her mouth again to yell for help. This time she succeeded, only to have her high shrill cut off by his hand again.

"Kid! Kid! Settle down. 'Amends' doesn't mean what you think it does! It means I want to make up to you for saying you weren't much of a female earlier. It means I want us to be friends. That's all." He slowly removed his hand from her mouth and released his hold on her.

"You mean you don't want to—?"

Trace shook his head, stunned that the thought wasn't as repugnant to him as it should have been.

"You jus' wanna be frie—?"

Trace nodded his head and grinned. "What do you say? Friends?"

"I s'pose it'd be better than fightin'," she said hesitantly. Then she remembered the bathtub. "But what'd you bring that for?"

"That's my 'amends.'" He walked over to the tub and removed a paper- and string-wrapped bundle and tossed it onto the bed. "I've decided I'm going to give you a few lessons on how to enjoy being a female. Lesson number one is a nice hot bath," he said, dumping the first bucket of water into the tub.

"You ain't givin' me no bath," Cassie decried with alarm, hugging her coat tighter around her.

"Then you'll give it to yourself." He dumped a second bucket of water in the tub.

"There's a chill in the air," she objected as he continued to fill the tub. She took another step backward, bumping into the washstand.

"There are plenty of towels to dry you off and keep you warm. Come on, off with those dirty clothes now!"

"I ain't takin' off my clothes. I'll catch my death!"

"Well, you can't take a bath with them on."

"It's too early in the year for a bath. An' I ain't takin' one!"

"Sorry, kid, but one way or another, you're going to take a bath. Now, are you going to take off that coat, or do you want me to do it for you?" He took a menacing step toward her.

"You get away from me, Trace McAllister!" She braced her feet apart and crossed her arms on her chest. "I'll take a bath when I'm good 'n ready, an' you ain't got no business comin' in here and tellin' me when I gotta do it."

Tempted to rip the clothes off her and throw her into the tub and scrub her until she was clean, Trace thought of another tack. He turned toward the bed and picked up the bundle he'd put there. "You didn't ask me what was in here."

"I don't care what's in there," she returned spitefully, though he noticed she craned her neck to peek around him for a better look. "Jus' take whatever it is 'n your bathtub 'n get on out' here."

"I can't take it. It's part of my 'amends.' " With torturously slow movements, he untied the string. "Besides, what would I do with a lady's dress?" He held up a lace-trimmed green gingham dress — not particularly stylish, but the best he'd been able to get on such short notice.

Cassie's eyes filled with awe. The dress was the most beautiful thing she had ever seen. "You bought me a dress?" she whispered. She hadn't had a dress since she had outgrown the last of the ones her mother had made for her when she was a little girl.

"And all the frilly things a lady wears under her dresses," he added with a taunting flare as he drew a white cotton and lace petticoat, drawers, and chemise from the package and displayed them for her approval. "That's how you tell a *real* lady—by what she wears under her dresses!"

"A lady?" she asked, stunned. It was her father's fondest wish to see her become a lady like her mother was, and she'd gone along with his plan for her to go to San Francisco to become one; but she had never dared to believe she could really do it. But here was this man—a stranger actually—telling her it was all possible. "Are they really for me?" She took a step forward and reached out to touch the clothes, her expression enchanted, her eyes sparkling with longing.

"Unh-uh!" Trace said, holding the beautiful clothing just out of reach and turning toward the door, confused by the unexpected twinge of shame that jerked through him. He'd already been party to a plan that had caused her to lose all her gold. Now what he was planning might be just as bad. And it might not even work. But if his suspicions were right and there was the slightest chance this could lead him to the stolen gold, he couldn't let himself worry about anything else.

He cleared his throat and wrenched the door open. "Bath first. Then the dress! I'll go to my room and clean up too."

His sharp words broke the hypnotic spell that had enveloped Cassie at the sight of the beautiful dress. She started to tell Trace to just take his dress and keep walking, but something stopped her.

Glancing at the tub of steamy water she would have ordered for herself if she hadn't needed all her cash to go after Murieta, she remembered the way Barton Talbot had looked at Lovey on the stagecoach and the girls on the street. Her gaze traveled longingly to the folds of green gingham and white cotton draped over

Trace's arm.

"Deal?" he asked.

Cassie hesitated. She hated to give in to Trace McAllister and his highhandedness. But she sure did want that dress—and to know what it felt like to wear beautiful clothes, just this once. Anyway, she'd been just about to bathe before he'd come into her room. And the tub would be a lot easier and more thorough than the pitcher and bowl she'd been going to use.

"Deal," she finally conceded. "But if I catch my death . . ." she warned, her threat going unspoken, but she just couldn't bear to let him think he'd bested her.

"I'll see you get a nice funeral," he chuckled. "Don't forget your hair and behind your ears, kid," he reminded her, disappearing through the door.

"I told you not to call me kid!" she hollered after him, watching the door to be certain he wasn't going to come back in.

"Your water's getting cold, *kid*," he called from the other side of the door, an annoying roll of laughter vibrating in his words. "I'll be back for you in an hour and a half."

Chapter Four

San Francisco

At the exploding sound of the front door crashing open, Salina's head snapped up from the mending in her lap. Barely daring to breathe, she watched the closed door of her tiny attic room, a distressed frown marring the smooth perfection of her *café au lait*-colored brow.

Apprehension darkened her brown eyes almost to black and rounded them even more than usual. *It's too early,* she worried, shoving her sewing aside and bolting up from her chair. *Something must have gone wrong with his plans for tonight.*

Knowing Cliff Hopkins would be in a violent mood if things hadn't gone the way he'd wanted, she hurried out onto the landing at the top of the attic stairs and waited, praying she was wrong and that he had just come home for something he'd forgotten.

As if in response to her thoughts, Cliff's voice shrilled up the two flights of stairs to where she stood, her body shaking with dread.

"Salina! Get down here!" he commanded in a voice that was too high to be considered anything but feminine.

Frantic to protect her only sanctuary in Cliff's large house from his sickening presence, Salina lurched into action and dashed down the stairs. Pausing for a moment on the landing of the second floor, she leaned over the banister for a view of the large marbled entryway below. Immediately she spied the balding blond head of Cliff Hopkins as he swiveled it from side to side looking for her. Seeing through the baby-fine hair on his head that the skin of his scalp was the apoplectic shade of pink she knew to associate with the "master's" temper tantrums and violence, she realized there was no point in holding out hope about what kind of mood he was in; and she fought the desire to turn and run back up to her room and lock herself in.

"Salina!" he screamed as he moved into the library. "Get your ass in here."

Her eyes burning with hostility and loathing, Salina drew her petite frame up to its full height of five feet three inches, and she released a resigned sigh of defeat.

Reaching up to check her hair to be certain all of her light brown curls were concealed, she adjusted her yellow bandana. She knew how Cliff hated any evidence of the white blood that coursed through her veins. As far as he was concerned, it was bad enough that her light tan skin served as a constant reminder that his father and hers were the same—though her mother was a slave on his family's plantation in Georgia, while Cliff's mother was a lady from an aristocratic Virginia family.

A hate-motivated smile curled Salina's lips for a moment as the temptation to leave some of her hair exposed nudged at her—just to annoy him further. But from the sound of his voice, he was already angry enough to rupture. So it would serve no purpose for her to add even more fuel to the fire with one of the "accidental" barbs about their common heritage she delighted in dropping whenever the chance presented itself.

But she vowed the day would come when she would openly throw their blood ties into her half brother's pasty face—even if she had to wait years for the opportunity. In fact, there were times when that goal was the only thing keeping her alive, that and the knowledge that Noah loved her and was working night and day to find a way to free her and her mother.

Slowly and deliberately, she made her descent, her mask of indifference carefully in place once more. "Did you call me, Master Cliff?" she said, speaking in low, expressionless tones as she reached the bottom of the stairs.

The pudgy young man whirled away from the bar, where he'd been pouring himself a glass of whiskey, to face her as she appeared in the entrance to the library. "You're damned right I called you! Where the hell have you been hiding?"

"I was in my room, mending the riding jacket you ripped the sleeve in last week." Her gaze remained leveled at his chest. She never looked him in the eye— not out of respect or fear, but out of the understanding that if she ever looked directly into his pale blue eyes, she would lose all control and reveal her true feelings for him. And until her mother was free, she wouldn't be free to take the risk. She couldn't even kill him, as she'd been tempted to do thousands of times. Not until he'd signed the emancipation papers for her mother. So she continued to play the subservient role she had been forced to play since her father's untimely death two years before—the role she would continue to play until her mother was safe. "Do you want some supper? I thought you would be out for the night, so nothing is prepared, but I can fix something."

"No!" he yelled, his voice rising to a screech. "I don't want supper." He threw back his head and tossed the whiskey down his throat, then turned to slosh another in the glass.

"If I can't get you anything, I'll return to my mending." She took a step back and started to leave.

"Stay where you are, bitch! You're not leaving until I say you can go."

The only indication that Cliff's words bothered Salina was the momentary narrowing of her eyes and the way her chin rose and jutted the barest fraction of an inch. But he didn't notice. He was pouring another drink down his throat.

"I want to know who your wardrobe is coming along. You know we open in two weeks!"

Two weeks! A streak of desperation cut a jagged path through Salina's stiffly erect body, but her face remained placid.

The Golden Goose was scheduled to open in two weeks, and still she'd received no word from Noah since he'd left San Francisco almost three months ago to find enough gold to buy her freedom. And though she tried to convince herself that raising $10,000 in gold in three months was not an impossible task, the closer the deadline drew, the more difficult it was to believe that Noah would arrive in time to save her from going to work in the Golden Goose.

"The seamstress was here today to fit me," she answered his question woodenly. "But when she learned you hadn't left a deposit for her, she went back to her shop in a huff."

"Damn!" he swore, slamming his half-full whiskey glass down on the bar, carelessly tipping it over.

"What's wrong with these California fools? First, I can't keep a carpenter on the job more than a week or two, because every time one gets enough saved up for a stake, he packs up and heads for the hills looking for gold. Now this temperamental seamstress. How California ever thinks it can survive without slavery is beyond me. Even my business partner has betrayed me tonight and seems to have found somewhere else to spend the evening."

So that's what has him in such a foul mood! Salina thought, finding a shred of pleasure in knowing that Cliff's business partner—and lover—had stood him up. Though she hadn't seen the mysterious business partner because she'd always been ordered to stay in her room whenever Cliff's "special guest" was expected, she'd heard the animal grunts and groans of heavy passion coming from her half brother's room and had often wondered what kind of woman could bring herself to submit to Cliff, whose pale, almost hairless flesh made Salina think of the fat on a freshly slaughtered hog.

She swallowed back the bad taste that filled her mouth and said a silent prayer of thanks that Cliff found sleeping with his half sister to his distaste.

"Maybe your friend was just late."

"Late is right!" he snarled, turning back to the bar and appearing to be surprised when he found the spilled whiskey glass. "Clean up this mess, Salina!" he demanded, reaching for a fresh glass and pouring himself another shot. "I waited at the Pot of Gold Restaurant for over two hours!"

"Maybe she's there now!" Salina tried to placate him, just wanting him out of the house.

"She?—oh, yes, she. Well, that's too bad. If she wants to see me, she can bloody well come to me! In the meantime, what about your dresses? I distinctly old that seamstress when I would pay her and it was perfectly agreeable. I warn you, I'm not going to put up with any more delays! Do you understand me, Salina?"

"It wasn't my fault," she protested. "I was here like I was supposed to be. I did everything you told me to, but she wouldn't do the measuring without some of the money up front. She said she's been cheated more than once by folks who say they have the money but are broke when it's time to pay her."

"Well, I'll take a little something by her shop tomorrow and send her back over here. But I'm warning you, you better be telling me the truth. Because if this is another one of your delaying tactics, I'm going to lay the whip to that black skin of yours!"

If she hadn't seen how sadistically brutal Cliff could be when he was angry with a servant, it would have been difficult to take his high-voiced, prissy-sounding threats seriously. But she had seen him whip a slave to death once in Georgia, and she would never again take his threats halfheartedly—though he had never physically punished her, because he didn't want to "damage his investment." It would be more his style to torture someone else for her "sins" and force Salina to watch.

"I swear to you, I'm not lying. It happened just like I said. But what difference does it make? When Noah comes with the gold he promised you, I'm going to be leaving. I won't need those dresses."

Cliff looked at Salina, his pale blue eyes simply staring in disbelief for the longest time. Then his mouth opened in a high giggle. "Do you really think that dumb buck's going to find that much gold? You must be as dumb as he is, if you believe that!"

"But you said . . ."

"I only told him that to get him out of San Fran-

65

cisco. I knew he didn't have a chance in hell of finding it. But if he does"— Cliff chortled mischievously — "he'll never get a chance to spend it. You didn't really think I'd let you leave me, did you?" He laughed sadistically. "Not for a mere $10,000! Not when you're going to make me ten times that at the Golden Goose!"

The taut wire that had contained her anger for two years suddenly snapped. "You bastard!" she shrieked. Acting on raw reflex, she picked up the whiskey bottle off the bar she was cleaning and banged the bottom of it on the marble ledge. Shards of glass splintered in all directions along with the last of her self-control. Waving the bottle before her, she took a menacing step toward him. "I ought to cut your—"

Cliff didn't flinch or move from where he stood, his round face splitting into a contemptuous grin. "Put that bottle down, Salina," he said as if speaking to a naughty, amusing child. "Or your mother is a dead woman—and I give you my word that her death will be a long and particularly imaginative one."

Salina froze in midstep, the broken bottle raised over her head in a threatening position. His words having interjected a degree of sanity into her brain, she lowered the bottle a few inches.

"You don't want anything to happen to your mother, do you, Salina?" he taunted in a singsong voice, sipping at his whiskey as though he were discussing the weather.

"You can't hurt her if you're dead!" she bluffed, her voice trembling.

His evil smile widened. "Oh, but I can. The details of my will are very exact. 'All slaves, with the exception of the female house slave known as Aretha, are, upon my death, to be sold immediately to the highest bidder. However, the slave known as Aretha is to be stripped and strapped on the rack, where every inch of her hide will be peeled—' "

"Stop!" Salina screamed, hurling the broken bottle across the room away from Cliff and clapping her palms up to cover her ears. "I'll do whatever you say. Just don't hurt my mama!" she pleaded.

Another malicious smile snaked across Cliff's face from fleshy jowl to jowl. "That's better," he said, turning his back on her to emphasize that he was not afraid of her in the least. "Now clean up this mess you've made and get on up to bed. It won't do at all for my star attraction at the Golden Goose to have dark circles under her eyes, will it?"

"No, Master Cliff," Salina answered obediently, falling to her knees to pick up pieces of broken glass, unaware of the reek of the whiskey as it soaked into her skirts. "It won't do."

Cassie stood up in the tub and sluiced a last pitcher of warm water down the length of her slender body. She released a sigh of sheer pleasure, which changed to sorrow as the last of the warmth streamed along her legs and back into the tub. She'd forgotten how wonderful a hot-water bath was. Usually, she'd been too tired at the end of a day to heat up enough water for a bath. So more often than not she had just stripped down to her underwear and taken a quick dip in whatever creek they happened to be panning.

Her body cried out to her to stay in the water just a while longer. And she was tempted. Really tempted. But Trace McAllister had said he'd be back in an hour and a half; and though she had no way of telling how much time had passed, she was sure the moment he would come bursting into her room again was danger-ously near.

The thought of Trace seeing her without her clothes on sent a shiver of embarrassment burning over her flesh, puckering the nipples of her full breasts into hard beads before concentrating itself in a dull ache in the most private part of her body. Shocked and startled by the unfamiliar reaction, she shot out of the tub, snatching a thick white bath sheet off the stool with a vengeance and winding it tightly around her.

The look on her freshly scrubbed face was only slightly less panicked once the towel was knotted securely over her bosom, Cassie reached for the hairbrush Trace had left on the dresser. "He could've at least left me the underthings to put on," she mumbled to herself as she dragged the stiff brush through her wet shoulder-length hair.

Just as she finished brushing the tangles from her hair and had it almost dry, the knock she'd been waiting for shook her door. Even though she'd been expecting it, when it came, she jumped, and a tingle of strange excitement set her heart racing.

"Are you out of the tub, kid?" Trace's familiar voice called.

Cassie glance down to check the knotted bath sheet and nodded her head in answer.

"Kid?" Trace said, a hint of tension beginning to build in the one word. "Are you in there? Kid!"

Before Cassie could regain her voice, the door flew open, slamming against the wall. "Hey, McAllister, what's the big idea!" She made a dash for the other side of the room, placing the bed between them. "Get outta here. You ain't got no right to come bustin' in here!"

Trace stood paralyzed in the middle of the doorway, his face frozen with amazement, his emerald eyes raking helplessly up the length of her, staying overlong on the spot where her breasts strained against the bath sheet as they rose and fell with her labored breathing. Shaking his head, he lifted his gaze up to lock with her tawny glare.

Under the heat of his stare, the same hot and cold tingling that had engulfed her for a moment before washed over her again. Only now, it was sapping the strength from her legs, making them feel as though they were turning to jelly. "You better get outta here, if you know what's good for you!" she shouted, her voice trembling as she steadied herself against the bedpost and reached for the gun in the holster hanging there. "I told you I wasn't interested in none o' your—"

At the sight of the statuesque goddess facing him, her hair curling in a riotous cloud of fire around her face, Trace's mouth dropped open and his eyes bulged. How could he have thought that "cleaning" Cassie Wyman up "might" make her passable? How could he not have noticed the way the light dusting of freckles that covered her skin called out to a man to taste them? And her eyes! How could he not have seen the passion that glowed innocently in the golden-brown depths of those eyes?

"I . . . uh . . . thought . . . uh . . . you were . . . uh . . ." he finally stuttered, too astonished to give the shaking revolver pointed at his middle any notice.

"Well, I ain't. I told you I wasn't that kind o' gal! Now get on out!" She waved the barrel of her gun away from her in a shooing gesture.

Regaining a modicum of his mental balance, Trace blasted Cassie with a sudden grin. "Is that what you're going to wear to supper?" He glanced down at the dress and petticoats draped over his arm. "Guess I'll just take these back to the emporium."

Cassie inhaled a wheezing gasp of air, and a fresh rush of color rose up out of the top of the bath sheet

69

to tinge her face and shoulders an endearing shade of crimson. "Leave the dress on the chair," she said, pointing the barrel toward the designated spot. "An' then get outta here."

"Maybe I'll just take them with me and give them to that cute little brunette who helped bring up your water. I bet she would show a thoughtful fellow like me a little bit of appreciation." He turned and stepped back into the hallway.

Cassie stared aghast as Trace's tall, broad-shouldered frame disappeared from the doorway. She'd had her heart set on wearing that dress and now he was taking it to some girl who probably already had a dozen dresses. Well, she wasn't going to have this dress!

"McAllister!" she bellowed. "You bring that dress back here!" Forgetting her modesty, she ran on bare feet around the end of the bed, across the hotel room, and out the door into the dark, windowless hallway, its only light coming from the window in her room.

"Say please," a deep voice answered from the shadows.

Cassie looked up to see Trace, not four feet in front of her, an arrogant grin on his face. Obviously waiting for her, he was propped casually against the wall between her door and the door to the room next to hers. His arms were crossed over his middle, the dress and slips draped tauntingly over them, and one leg was folded back to rest the sole of a boot against the wall.

"Over my dead body!" She wheeled back into the room. "I ain't beggin'." Let him give the dress away. What did she care? She didn't need it. *It probably don't even fit! 'Sides, I'll buy me a dozen prettier ones when I get my gold back.*

If you get your gold back, an irritating little voice

in her head suggested. *An' by then Barton might be gone.*

Cassie stopped just inside the room, her hand poised on the door where she'd gripped it with the idea of slamming it shut. Weighing her pride against an evening in the beautiful dress and the chance of having Barton Talbot see her in that dress, she decided she was willing to do just about anything to make her dream come true. Even if it meant saying "please" to the likes of Trace McAllister!

Her back still turned toward the hallway, she listened for sounds that Trace was still there. A rustle of movement told her he was there and shifting positions. "Please." Her voice was barely a whisper.

The rustling sounds stopped. "Did you say something?"

Cassie screwed her face into an infuriated grimace, but she tried again. "Please," she said, slightly louder, her breasts heaving with anger.

"What did you say? I couldn't quite hear you."

Cassie tightened her grip on the door and clenched the fist at her side. Oh, how she'd love to sink her knuckles into the cocky grin she could tell was on his face by the tone of his voice. "I said *please!*" she said scathingly, as she wheeled around to face the hall again. "Now give me the dress!"

"Of course, Cassie," he said unctuously, stepping away from the wall and coming to the door. "Here you go." He placed a large round box in the chair just inside the room and held out the dress and petticoats to her.

Cassie dropped the gun in the same chair and spun around, making a grab for the green and white folds being offered.

"Unh-uh," he said, shifting the gift so it was just out of her reach. "I didn't hear a thank-you, kid."

71

Cassie narrowed her eyes at him threateningly. "Thanks."

Trace tilted his head to the side and studied her thoughtfully. "Mmm, a little bit of sincerity would be nice . . ."

"You want sincerity!" she shrieked. "How's this for sincerity?" She reached for her gun.

But before she could lay her hand on it, Trace shrugged and tossed the clothing over her outstretched arm. "We'll work on the sincerity at dinner. I'll be back to pick you up in thirty minutes!" Wheeling around, he disappeared before she could respond.

Cassie stared at the dress in her arms for long silent moments. Then, as if she'd been spurred, she leaped into action. She banged the door shut with all her might, taking special satisfaction in the loud sound it made as it rattled in the doorframe. "Thirty minutes, huh?" She brought the wad of clean-smelling clothes to her nose and inhaled deeply. "Well, you can be here in thirty minutes, McAllister, but it ain't gonna do you no good. 'Cause I'm gonna be gone in twenty!"

Satisfied with her decision to have dinner alone before she would eat with Trace McAllister, Cassie laid out the clothing, picking through the underthings until she found a frilly white chemise. Dropping it over her head, she reached up and untied the bath sheet, letting it fall to the floor as she slipped her arms under the ribbon-decorated lace straps.

Unable to resist seeing how she looked in the filmy white cotton, she opened the wardrobe and gazed into the beveled mirror at its center. *There must be some mistake,* she thought as she gazed at the smiling young woman in the glass. "That can't be me," she said in an awed whisper. Her hands smoothed down the front of the chemise, the thought going through her mind that it was so beautiful it was a shame to cover it up with a dress.

Giggling at the thought of what McAllister would say if she met him at the door in the fancy undergarments and announced she was ready to go, she turned back to the bed and dug out the matching lace-trimmed drawers. She climbed into them hurriedly and stepped back to again admire herself in the mirror, front and back this time, before she straightened the chemise down over her hips and thighs.

"Petticoats next!" she said, surprised to see there were three in all, every one of them trimmed in the same lace as the drawers and chemise—even the stiff crinoline he'd brought.

Cassie's mood grew steadily lighter with each article of clothing she donned, and by the time she tied the strings on the final petticoat, she was humming a happy melody. Pirouetting to the bed, she whisked the green dress up into her arms, her anger with Trace forgotten for the moment. She held the dress up to her and stretched one sleeve out in a dance pose she'd seen the prospectors assume in the gold camps when, lonely for female company, they danced with each other for entertainment.

Not wanting to call extra attention to the fact that there was a real female in the gold camp, her pa had never let her dance with any of the men. But, watching from a safe distance, she'd managed to learn the steps, practicing when she was alone. "One-two-three. One-two-three," she counted out, whirling herself and the dress around the room in exaggerated dance steps to the imaginary waltz playing in her head.

"Jus' like Cinderella in the story Mama told me," she exclaimed, coming to a winded stop in front of the wardrobe again, her eyes glimmering with enchantment. Beside herself with excitement, she hurriedly worked the dress over her head and her arms into the sleeves. Quickly arranging the skirt over her billowy slips, she reached behind her to button the bodice in back.

"Damn!" The tiny, impossible-to-reach buttons running up her spine had just burst her fairy-tale fantasy with a rude explosion. "Just my luck. I wait twenty galdurned years for a fairy godmother. 'Stead I get McAllister! An' he brings me a ballgown I can't fasten!"

Contorting her arms and viewing herself in the mirror from behind, Cassie managed to close the top button and the bottom few, but left a gaping opening in the middle of her back. Frustrated, she gave up, deciding to ask one of the maids to help her on her way out.

Turning back to the mirror, she examined the overall look again. The dress was a perfect fit, and from the front it was impossible to see that she was exposed halfway to her behind in back. But something was still wrong, she realized. Something was missing.

Her forehead wrinkled with studious concentration, she leaned closer to her reflection. Maybe it was her hair, she contemplated, lifting the light auburn mane up off her neck. "Yeah, that's it," she told herself, pleased with the effect of the more sophisticated hairdo. But it wasn't just the hair. She still didn't look right.

Then to her horror, the answer to her question glared up at her from beneath the hem of her dress. Dropping her hands from her hair, she bent over and gawked at the floor. There, peeking out from beneath her skirt, were her toes. Ten bare toes!

"Shoes!" she exclaimed. "He didn't bring shoes!"

Her elation crashed to despair. She couldn't go out in her bare feet. She sliced a disappointed glance at her own muddy boots where they lay on their sides beside the bed.

Just as she bent to lift one of the ugly boots and put it on, a relieved grin split across her face. *The box!* she suddenly remembered. Trace had placed a round box in the chair by the door before he'd given her the dress.

"The shoes must be in there! Even a sorry fairy godmo—*father*—like McAllister wouldn't forget the shoes!"

She scurried across the room and tore the lid from the box. Inside, wrapped in white tissue paper, was another bonanza of feminine apparel: a beautiful flowered hat, which she plopped on her head askew to get it out of the way; white gloves, which she tucked under her arm; a beaded purse she set aside; stockings; garters; and . . . "No shoes!"

Flopping down on the bed, she didn't even care that she was dangerously close to tears. What good was a Cinderella dress if she didn't have the slippers?

Sniffing, she jerked a stocking up one long calf, then slid a garter on over it, with which she rolled the stocking to below her knee. Just as she poked her toes into the second stocking, an impatient knock sounded at her door.

Remembering what had happened when she hadn't answered him immediately, Cassie jumped up and hobbled over to the door, holding the stocking at her ankle with one hand, and the precariously placed hat on her head with the other. "Hold your horses, McAllister. I'm comin'!"

She tore the door open, still bending over and holding onto her stocking. "I ain't quite ready yet," she explained needlessly, her eyes roving up the length of the man filling her doorway. From her awkward vantage point he seemed even taller than she had remembered. *An' handsomer!* she noticed, as she took in the

75

clean-shaven, square-jawed face smiling down at her.

Don't laugh, Trace ordered himself as sternly as he could manage. Burying a polite cough in his hand, he pressed his lips together, making every effort to stifle the chuckle bubbling in his chest. "I can wait," he said through his strained grin.

Unfortunately, the imp of humor had taken complete possession of his funny bone; and the more he fought the innate need to laugh, the more demanding the need became—until finally he lost control.

First there was a rude snort as a burst of the suppressed laughter suddenly spewed through his clamped lips. Guilt coloring his face, he slapped his hand over his mouth in a last-ditch effort to contain it. But he was too late. Once the amused snicker vibrating in his chest had achieved the slight freedom, it immediately expanded into a full-fledged guffaw that shook his entire body.

Cassie stared at Trace, her eyes stinging with threatening tears. "What're you laughin' at, McAllister?" she asked with a bitter sneer, dropping her hold on the stocking and straightening her posture to glare at him. But suddenly she had no more fight in her. She just wanted him to leave. She turned her back to keep him from seeing the tears that were now rolling down her cheeks.

"I'm sorry," Trace chortled helplessly. "It's just that—"

"Well, it don't matter. I changed my mind anyhow, I ain't goin' to supper with you!" With an angry huff, she plucked the hat from the top of her head and pitched it toward the box, glad when it missed and toppled to the floor. Hopping toward the other side of the room on one foot, she snatched the ungartered stocking off her foot and tossed it in the general direction of the box too.

"So you can go on to supper alone!" She lifted her skirts and rolled the other stocking and garter off.

"Really, I didn't mean to la—"

"An' you can take this dumb dress with you when you go!" She contorted her arms behind her to struggle with the buttons. "An' this other stuff too! I ain't wearin' it! Give it to that gal you was talkin' 'bout."

Chapter Five

Shame and self-disgust conspired to knock Trace off balance and check his laughter with the same effect as being clobbered on the head by a board—which he knew was only a fraction of what he deserved. "I'm really sorry, kid," he apologized sincerely. "I didn't mean to laugh." In the mirror, he could see her lower lip trembling, and the stabbing remorse he felt twisted unmercifully in his gut. "Don't take it off. You look nice."

"Hmp!" she sniffed, her fingers feeling as useless as wood stumps as she battled the tiny buttons at the small of her back. "Ain't no need to 'pologize for tellin' the truth, McAllister. My pa always said, 'You can't make no silk purse outta no sow's ear.' An' he was right! I ain't got no business in these frilly clothes!" Her frustration with the obstinate buttons peaked. Letting a grunt, she dug her fingers under the open edges of the bodice and pulled.

"Let me do it," Trace offered, stepping up behind her and stilling her agitated actions with his gentle hands just in time to save the buttons.

Staggered by the bolt of electricity that jerked up her arms at his touch, Cassie's hands became para-

78

lyzed lumps of submission, which she allowed to be removed from the dress opening and lowered to her sides without protest.

Her startled eyes darted to the mirror. "Wh— What're you doin'?" she stammered dumbfoundedly, catching sight of the serious expression on his face as his black eyebrows drew together in concentration as he worked on the back of her dress.

"I'm helping you with these buttons! I can see how the damned things would make you testy." His long fingers slipped inside the dress.

The chemise might just as well have been nonexistent for all the protection it was from the jagged starburst of fire that radiated out from her spine, licking its way around her waist to caress her breasts, before settling in the vulnerable pit of her stomach. And though she knew she should move away from him, should turn and slap him for putting his hands on her in such a personal way, she didn't. Instead, she remained rooted to the spot, compliant and defenseless.

"Whoever made these tiny things ought to be strung up by his thumbs," Trace mumbled, his fingers more clumsy than he remembered them ever being before as he negotiated them up her back toward the nape of her neck.

When it became necessary to move the thick mass of her hair aside to take care of the upper buttons—which, except for the very top one, were in the wrong holes and out of line—he was suddenly overwhelmed with the impulsive desire to bend down and kiss the exposed back of her neck. Of course, the idea was too ridiculous to even consider!

"There you go," he breathed with a sigh of relief as he finished his task. Placing his hands on her shoulders, he turned her to face him, unprepared for the effect her golden-brown eyes would have on him.

"Thanks," Cassie said, her voice a hoarse whisper. Unable to move away, she raised her gaze to lock with his, which was oddly bewildered—and teeming with something she couldn't put a name to.

As if they had a will of their own, his hands glided along her shoulders to meet behind her neck. "You're welcome."

The black pupils in her eyes grew so large that most of the color of the irises disappeared. "What're you doin'?"

"Your hair," he answered, burrowing his fingers into the back and sides of the tousled mass of waves.

"What 'bout my hair?" Her question was whispered, her tone awed.

"It's pretty."

"It ain't!" she protested, disbelieving, yet glowing with definite pleasure from the compliment. If her hands hadn't been hanging uselessly at her sides, as they had been ever since Trace had put them there, she would no doubt have raised one and primped her hair. "It's way too wild 'n curly."

Trace shook his head to disagree. "I like it that way."

"You do?" What was happening to her? Why was she standing here like a puppet being held up by the puppeteer? Why didn't she tell him to get his hands out of her hair and stop looking at her like that?

Making a Herculean effort, Trace managed to regroup some of his own self-control. "Yeah, I like it. But if I don't want to fight off every fellow in Auburn, we'd better comb it into a style that's a bit more conservative." He was doing his best to bring a paternal—or a least fraternal—tone to his words. And he knew he was failing miserably.

"I've seen lots of ladies wear their hair like this," he said in a gruff tone. Awkwardly, he twisted the thick

80

hank of hair into a loose knot at her crown and held it there. "What do you think?" he asked, turning her face toward the mirror beside them.

Astonished to see the pretty, auburn-haired *lady* staring out of the mirror at her, Cassie couldn't speak. She nodded her head.

"Good! Let's get pins in it before I drop it," he said, dragging her to the dresser by the fistful of hair.

Not bothering to wonder why he was fixing her hair when he'd just undone her dress so she could stay in her room, Cassie stood patiently as Trace gave his full attention to securing her knot.

"How's that?" he finally said, expelling his breath in relief. He moved aside, putting some space between them—so she could see herself in the dresser mirror, he assured himself.

"How'd you learn to fix a lady's hair?" she asked, tilting her head at different angles and viewing herself with obvious approval.

A shadow of sadness masked Trace's expression for the briefest instant, then was gone as quickly as it had appeared. "I used to watch my older sister when I was a kid." His response was brusque.

Cassie studied Trace's reflection in the mirror. For some unexplained reason, the fact that he had a sister made her see him in a different light. It made him seem less intimidating, more human. "I didn't feature you as havin' no family. I kinda figgered you for a loner."

"Let's see how the hat looks with your hair fixed," he said, hurrying toward the chair and putting an obvious end to the line of conversation.

Cassie shrugged her shoulders. What difference did it make to her what kind of family he had. "I ain't gonna wear it, so why bother?"

"Just humor me." He whisked the hat up off the

floor, as well as the discarded stockings and gloves, which he shoved in his pocket. "Here, put it on."

"All right, but it's a waste o' time." She snatched the hat out of his hand and dropped it on her head, where it wobbled, dangerously close to falling. "See? One puff o' breeze 'n this thing'll fly off my head." She reached up to remove it.

"Wait a minute." Trace stepped up behind her and covered her hands with his, lowering them to her sides again. "There's a trick to keeping it on. You use one of these!" he announced. With dramatic flourish, he produced a long, pearl-tipped hatpin from the back of her hat.

Cassie's eyes widened and she covered her head protectively. "You ain't stickin' that in my head."

Trace chuckled. "I'm not going to put it in your *head,* kid. It goes in the hat and your hair." Without giving her a chance to protest further, he removed her hands again and secured the hat in her thick hair. "See, that didn't hurt, did it?"

She shook her head regretfully. The hatpin only served to remind her how much she didn't know, how much she would never know. And the longer she had these clothes on, the more it hurt to admit that she would always be a "sow's ear" and never a "silk purse." She reached up to slip the bodice of the dress off her shoulders, never giving propriety or modesty a thought. "Are you satisfied now? I humored you like you wanted. Now take these duds 'n go give 'em to that other gal. *She'll* know 'bout hatpins 'n such."

It was then she noticed the sleeve of her dress didn't budge. Wheeling around, she viewed her back in the mirror. "You done *buttoned* my dress 'stead o' unbuttonin' it!"

Trace gave her a sheepish grin.

"Well, it won't do you no good. I ain't wearin' it."

82

She presented her back to him. "Get me outta this thing!" she ordered.

"I'll help you get out of it after I eat supper." He turned away from her as if to leave.

"An' what the hell'm I s'posed to do while you're stuffin' your ugly face?"

"You could put on your shoes and stockings and come with me."

Cassie snapped angrily and snatched up her worn leather boots. "Now, won't these look just real fine with this fancy dress?"

"Wouldn't these look better?" he asked, picking up a box he'd placed unceremoniously beside the hat box when he'd come in the last time. He pulled out a pair of black ankle-high kid boots with pearl buttons up the sides, pointed toes, and two-inch heels. They were undoubtly the most wonderful boots Cassie had ever seen.

Jus' like the glass slippers! she said to herself, hypnotized by the shoes in his hand. "Where'd they come from?" she managed to ask.

"I brought them with me. I had more trouble finding shoes I thought would fit you than I did the other clothes. But I think these will come close." Without moving from the door, he held out the boots to her.

Could this really be happening? Could McAllister really be her fairy godfather?

'Course he ain't, she scoffed to herself. *Only a dumb little kid would b'lieve in fairy tales.* But her self-admonition did nothing to remove the enchanted expression from her face as she directed her steps toward him.

"Put on your stockings first," Trace ordered, retaining his grip on the boots and reaching into his pocket.

Her enthralled gaze never wavering from the boots, Cassie took the stockings and garters and sat down on

83

the bed to put them on. When they were both secured below her knees with the garters, she held out her hands for the treasure still in Trace's possession.

Sensing how important the boots were to her, though not understanding why, Trace knelt down beside the bed and lifted one of her slender feet. "Allow me, my lady," he said with exaggerated chivalry.

When he had used the button hook to close the shoes around her slim ankles, Trace stood up and smiled. "Perfect fit," he bragged, amazed at his luck.

"Perfect fit," Cassie agreed, holding out both of her booted feet and wiggling them to admire the soft kid from where she sat on the bed.

"Come on," Trace said, his own excitement hard to contain now. "Get your gloves on" — he handed her the gloves — "and let's take a look at the new you!"

Giggling, Cassie jammed her fingers into the gloves and held out her hands for Trace's approval.

He took her extended hands in his and drew her to her feet, bringing her closer to him than he had meant to. Their faces only inches apart, they stared at each other for long moments. Finally, Trace managed to speak. "You're lovely," he said, marveling at the delightful jewel he'd discovered beneath the rough miner's exterior.

The heat of his touch burned right through the gloves, and his words turned Cassie's face a bright shade of pink. "I'm more'n likely gonna fall on my face in these shoes," she said self-consciously, averting her gaze and removing her hands from his grip. "I ain't used to walkin' on my tippytoes all the time."

"You just hold on to me," he assured her, taking her hand again and placing it on his arm. "I won't let you fall."

She studied her white-gloved hand on his arm for a moment, then looked up to search his eyes for what he really thought about the way she looked. "Am I really all right? Are you sure folks ain't gonna laugh at me?"

A grin spread across his face. "See for yourself, Cassie!" He guided her to stand before the full-length mirror in the wardrobe. "Did I lie to you?"

Surprised by the sight of the tall, beautifully dressed young woman standing beside the handsome man, the top of her hat reaching just past his chin, her hand delicate on his arm, Cassie shook her head.

"So, what do you say we go eat supper? I'm starving. Besides, I want to show off the prettiest lady in Auburn."

"Do you s'pose we'll be likely to see Barton Talbot?" she asked, too fascinated with the vision before her to see the elation on the face of the man beside her slip into a confused frown.

Well, what the hell are you so upset about, McAllister? he asked himself caustically. *You're the one who thought it was a good idea to clean her up so you could use her to get close to Talbot!*

"Yeah, we'll see him. We'll make it a point to!" He turned her toward the door.

"Will he think I'm pretty?"

Trace stopped the angry reply that came to his lips as he looked down into the innocent upturned face that gazed hopefully up into his. His frown melted into a soft smile.

"Unless he's had both his eyes poked out since we saw him this afternoon!"

The street in front of the Gold Dust Hotel swarmed with people from every corner of the earth: Negroes from the southern United States, Frenchmen, Italians, Germans, Irishmen, Hawaiians, Chinese, Peruvians, Chileans, Mexicans, Australians, Jamaicans. And all of them seemed to be laughing and talking at once as they hurried or ambled from place to place. Adding to the cacophony and confusion of so many different foreign tongues were the baiting cries of the thimbleriggers, monte dealers, and string-game tricksters who lined the streets hawking their contests.

Intermingled with the prospectors, con men and gamblers were hucksters who haggled loudly with customers over price, auctioneers who rattled off their wares in a language peculiar only to them, and preachers who proclaimed the word of God from atop wooden crates and promised to be back for another sermon the next day — if there was no word of new diggings before then.

However, Cassie paid the raucous surroundings almost no heed as she glanced up at the front of the three-story Gold Dust Hotel.

Excitement boiled in her veins and her eyes glimmered with anticipation as she looked up at Trace. "Do you think he'll be here?" she asked.

"He'll be here," Trace drawled, hating the fact that Cassie's interest in Talbot was getting to him more by the minute. Disgusted, he tried to convince himself his only objection was that he didn't want the innocent girl to be hurt by the gambler. He remembered the way Talbot's eyes had lit up when he'd told him Cassie was the daughter of a wealthy miner who had found millions — and that she'd been wearing the outrageous disguise on the stagecoach to protect herself from murderers and highwaymen. *Yeah, the sorry bastard will be here. I'd bet my boots on it!*

"How do you know?"

"He mentioned it to me when I saw him earlier — before I came to get you." His words were impatient and irritable.

Suddenly, Cassie stopped in her tracks. She couldn't go through with this charade. In her hotel room when Trace had treated her like a lady and told her how pretty she was, it had seemed so easy to believe the fantasy was possible. But that was in the privacy of her room when she could pretend she was Cinderella or anyone else she wanted to be. This was the real world out here. And she just didn't think she could stand it if everyone—especially Barton—laughed when they saw her.

"Look, if goin' in here with me is gonna shame you, we can head on back to the Fremont House 'n eat. It don't make me no nevermind."

"Ashamed?" Trace repeated, astounded that anything he could have done would make her think that. "I told you, I think you look wonderful."

"Yeah, but you could just be sayin'—"

Trace sealed her lips with an index finger. "Stop it, kid. I'm proud to be with you."

"Then why you got that mean-lookin' frown on your face?"

Trace consciously unfurrowed the muscles in his forehead and smiled. He liked the way Cassie always cut through the crap and got right to the point. "I'm just thinking about the young swains I'm going to have to fight to keep you for myself," he said with a teasing grin.

Keep you for myself? Did I say that? Damn, McAllister, you're in worse shape than I thought. Keep saying dumb things like that and they're going to chain you to a tree with the lunatics.

Confused, now it was Cassie's turn to frown. Then her face brightened with understanding. Balling her fist, she punched him playfully on the arm. "You're joshin' me, ain't you, McAllister? You better be careful or one o' these times I'm liable to hold you to them words."

Trace managed a weak grin and covered her hand that still gripped him at the elbow. "I'll keep that in mind, kid," he promised dryly. "Are you ready to go inside?"

Cassie took a deep breath and held it for a moment, then expelled it on a chuckle. "I guess we might as well get it over with. Let's go give the folks a good laugh when they see me all gussied up in these fancy duds 'n wobblin' on these high heels!"

"That's my girl," Trace said, guiding her up the steps to the hotel porch.

Despite the false bravado she'd been able to affect outside, once Cassie and Trace stepped into the hotel dining room, she was assaulted by absolute panic. The color drained from her face. She froze. And her brown-gold eyes nearly doubled in size as she stared at the sight before her.

The noisy room was filled with people, mostly men, in all manner of dress, sitting at white-linen-covered tables, drinking, eating, chatting amicably, and arguing.

Her stomach lurched and she was certain she was going to be sick.

As though a signal had been given, a hush fell over the dining room—or was it just the fact that she couldn't hear anything over the deafening pound of her own heartbeat?—and everybody, male and female alike, seemed to turn their heads toward the entry where she and Trace stood waiting to be seated. They were smiling!

Any second now they were going to start laughing.

"Get me outta here, McAllister," she said through clenched teeth—not clenched because she didn't want anyone to hear what she said, but because every muscle in her body was so taut it threatened to snap.

Her fingers were digging into his arm so hard that he could feel her fingernails through his jacket sleeve. Trace searched her ashen face. Never in his life had he seen such stark terror.

Not questioning his strong protective feelings for this girl, his first instinct was to whisk her up into his arms and spirit her back to the safety of her room. But suddenly, he saw, really saw, Cassie for the first time.

It was so clear now. Without a doubt, he knew this was something she had wanted for a long time — maybe all her life. All the bragging and the masculine facade were just ways to hide the fact that she wanted to be something she didn't think she had a chance of being.

And he knew with just as much certainty that if he let her run away, she might never try again to make her dream come true.

"You aren't scared, are you, kid?" he challenged her, hoping her innate need to hide her vulnerability from the world would surface. But it didn't.

Cassie nodded her head and exerted more tugging pressure on his arm. "Let's go."

"Is this the Cassie Wyman who this afternoon was ready to take on the entire Joaquin Murieta gang single-handedly?" he asked, deliberately goading her.

When she didn't answer, he went on. "The gal who *says* she can outshoot, outride, and outdrive every man in the state?"

Still no answer. "I should have known you were all talk. Nothing but an ordinary weak female who needs a strong man to —"

"This here's diff'rent," she rasped through her teeth, her dry lips barely moving.

"How's that?"

"Look at 'em. They're gonna laugh. I know it."

Trace cocked his head to the side and listened to the low hum of conversation that filled the room. "I don't hear anyone laughing."

"They're fixin' to. Can't you see how they're starin' at me 'n grinnin'?"

Trace surveyed the dining room. "All I see is a room full of admiring faces, watching the prettiest lady they've probably seen in a long time, maybe ever."

"Miss Wyman!" a man called out before Cassie could argue any more.

Her head twisted around, bringing her face-to-face with Barton Talbot. *No!* a voice screamed in her head. She had prayed she could make an escape before the handsome gambler saw her. Cassie looked helplessly at Trace, her eyes pleading for him to get her out of this mess before Barton started hooting with laughter at her getup.

"McAllister told me how lovely you were when you shed your disguise," Barton babbled, taking her free hand—the one not gripping Trace's arm so hard he thought he might be losing the circulation in it.

Disguise? she repeated silently, certainly that if she spoke aloud she would say something that would make her look even more ridiculous than she already must.

"But I had to see for myself," Barton continued, bending gallantly to touch his lips to the back of her gloved hand. "And now that I have, I can see that his praise was greatly understated."

If possible, the amazed expression on Cassie's face became more agog. What was happening? Not only was the man of her dreams *not* laughing at her, but he was kissing her hand as if she were the Queen of Sheba or some other equally wonderful person. *If this is a dream, don't let me wake up,* she prayed, the corners of her mouth turning upward.

Smiling her thanks, she glanced up at Trace, who was glowering down at the top of Barton's head over her hand as if he would kill him at any minute. Cassie frowned her puzzlement.

Barton didn't notice Trace's glare, or if he did, he wasn't worried about it; nor did he seem particularly concerned that neither one of the people had said anything to him. He went on talking as though they were old friends. "Please, you must join me at my table." He took Cassie's hand and tucked it in the bend of his arm.

A radiant smile lit her face and she looked at Trace expectantly.

Though she couldn't be sure, she thought she heard what sounded like a growl, low and menacing, issue from Trace's throat. Her smile relaxed and she tilted her head questioningly. What was he in such a snit about? Hadn't he helped her fix herself up so she could impress Barton? Wasn't that why he'd chosen the Gold Dust for supper, because he knew Barton would be here?

"What do you say, McAllister? Will you share my table and this exquisite lady's company with me this evening?" Though he spoke to Trace, Barton never took his eyes off Cassie.

I'm going to either puke of blow his brains out if he doesn't get his hands off her, Trace told himself. "We planned a quiet supper alone," he said, not even questioning why he was changing his plans. He just knew there had to be a better way to find out if Barton Talbot was one of Murieta's men than letting the two-bit gambler maul Cassie. "Thanks anyway, Talbot."

Cassie shot Trace her sternest look. "What's the big—"

"Our table is ready," he said sourly, ignoring her protests and reaching across her to remove her other

91

hand from Barton's arm. He gave the waiter a nod and prodded Cassie forward.

"Why'd you do that?" she asked as they left Barton staring after them. "It was nice of him to invite us to eat with him."

"Don't act so eager, Cassie," Trace snarled out of the corner of his mouth. "A lady plays hard to get."

"She does?" Cassie said, casting a doubtful glance back at Barton. "Are you sure?"

"It's how she keeps a man interested. It's called 'being coy,' " he explained, holding a chair for her.

Cassie plopped herself down, relieved to be off her feet for a minute. They were killing her. Of course, it was no wonder, with her toes all scrunched into the pointed boots, then having to walk on them. Maybe being a lady wasn't all it was cracked up to be. "What's coy?" she wondered aloud, eyeing the table's elaborate setting curiously.

"When a lady is really interested in a man, she pretends as though she isn't," he went explaining. "She might even act as if she finds him company unpleasant."

"Sounds dumb to me," she mused, picking up a spoon and looking at her reflection in the shiny metal. "Why, if she likes the feller, don't she just tell him that?"

Trace rolled his eyes. Damned if he knew why women did what they did. And an even bigger mystery was why he was sitting here explaining it to this one instead of doing what he'd planned to do. Talbot had played right into his hands and he'd sent him packing. "I think it has something to do with the theory that men are supposed to want what they can't have."

"Oh!" Cassie said, her head bobbing up and down in understanding, though her expression told him she still didn't. "Only one thing, McAllister."

"What's that, kid?" he asked offhandedly as he studied the menu the waiter had given him.

"If a lady don't let on she likes a feller when she does, it don't seem likely there'll be too many *little* ladies 'n gents runnin' around, does it?"

Trace peeked over the menu at her.

Her lightly freckled face was split in an impish grin, telling him in no uncertain terms that she wasn't buying any of what he'd told her.

A loud laugh exploded from his throat. "Ah, kid, what am I going to do with you?"

"Well, first off, you can ask that fancy-dressed waiter—the one that's prettier than any female in here—to bring us some vittles. I'm right hungry."

"And then?"

"An' then you can invite Barton Talbot to our table so I can let on like I got no use for him some more. If I'm goin' after my gold in the mornin', I done already wasted enough time."

Trace's smile turned cynical. "Do you mind if I wait until we finish eating? I think I'll lose my supper if I have to watch him slobbering all over you while I'm eating it."

Chapter Six

Cassie's excited glance roved from the dark, scowling man on her left to the smiling, gaily chatting fair-haired man on her right. Never in her wildest fantasies would she have thought this night could be possible. In fact, she was tempted to pinch herself. But she didn't. If this *was* a dream, she didn't intend to take a chance on ending it.

Her beautiful clothes alone would have been enough to make this the most magical evening she'd ever imagined. But to be escorted into the Imperial Theatre on the arms of *two* handsome men. . . . Well, it was a dream come true.

She felt as if she were floating, suspended on a cloud, her new boots as light on her feet as down.

"I'm sure we're the envy of every man in Auburn," Barton said, bending his head down to speak softly into her ear.

The warmth of his breath wafted across her cheek and neck, sending an unpleasant shudder over her flesh. She had to fight the urge to lift a shoulder and rub her face against it. However, she managed a pleasant smile in response to whatever it was Barton had said. Though she had no idea what the exact words were, she was certain it had been another compliment. His conversation had been filled with nothing else from the moment he'd joined her and Trace at their table for dessert. At first, his flattery had been exciting to hear, but if she was honest with herself—which she usually was to a fault—his constant admiring words had become more than a little tiring.

Blanking out the drone of Barton's voice, she glanced up at Trace, wondering why he was in such a sour mood. He'd been like that—silent—since Barton had sat down at their table.

As though Barton wasn't still talking, she spoke to Trace, determined to include him in the conversation. After all, it had been because of him that this entire evening had been possible. "Have you been to the Imperial Theatre before, McAllister?" she asked him.

There it was again. That strange, low growl that seemed to have originated deep in Trace's chest, the growl she'd heard more than once since Barton had joined them. She frowned, wondering if Trace knew he did it.

His eyes grew hard like polished jade and glared into hers for a second, then wrenched away from her to focus straight ahead. "No, I haven't been to the Imperial Theatre before."

"I've been here," Barton announced smugly. "Many times. And believe me, my dear, you are in for a treat. But not nearly so grand a treat as everyone in the theater will receive when they feast their eyes on your loveliness."

Shit! What the hell am I doing listening to this crap? He was so adamant about sitting in that particular seat on the stagecoach, and I'd bet anything he raised the window shade as a signal to Murieta. But his hypocritical drivel isn't going to tell me anything. This whole thing has been a waste of time. I should've

95

gotten on Murieta's trail right away instead of staying here and trying to trap Talbot into leading me to their meeting place. Trace freed his arm from Cassie's hand with a rough shake.

"What's the matter, McAllister?" she asked, stopping to study Trace, her expression hurt and confused.

"I want to get an early start in the morning," he explained, a flash of guilt licking at his conscience at the thought of leaving Cassie in Talbot's hands. Shaking his head, he told himself he had no reason to feel guilty. *Who made you her guardian? She's a grown woman and if Barton Talbot's what she wants, it's none of your business.* Still he couldn't quite bring himself to look into her eyes. "I'm going to call it a night," he said, concentrating on a spot just beyond her. "You won't mind escorting Miss Wyman back to her hotel, will you, Talbot?" His request was more a sardonic statement than a question.

"It will be my pleasure!" Barton chortled. "Don't worry about Miss Wyman. I'll take good care of her."

I'm sure you will, you phony son of a bitch! Trace said to himself. But all he said aloud was, "Thanks."

Cassie's cloud of ecstasy seemed to dissipate, sending her spirits crashing to the ground without warning. "But I thought you wanted to hear 'The Lovely Lovey LaRue' sing," she protested, sounding very young and vulnerable.

Her words ate away at another layer of his conscience. "Yeah, well, I'll have to hear her another time. Right now, I just want to get some sleep." He wheeled away from the couple, who had remained arm-in-arm. It was bad enough seeing the gloating, cat-with-a-mouse look Barton focused on Cassie and not doing anything about it; but the hurt-little-girl expression on Cassie's innocent face really tore into his gut.

"McAllister!" she hollered, dropping her hold on Barton's arm and running after Trace. "I don't wanna go if you don't," she said out of the side of her mouth for his ears alone as she drew alongside him. Her voice had a slight quiver to it. "You gotta come with me."

Trace stopped and looked down at her, surprised at the thrill that coursed through his veins with the realization that Cassie might prefer his company to Talbot's. "I do?"

Cassie tossed an apologetic smile at Barton, indicating with her eyes that he should wait where he was. "Who's gonna watch to make sure I don't make a fool outta myself if you leave?" she whispered tersely, remembering how subtly Trace had lowered her napkin to her lap before anyone noticed she had started to tuck it under her chin. Thanks to him, she'd made it through supper without making any mistakes that were too terrible—like picking up her soup bowl to slurp the contents from it instead of using the round spoon to sip it. "I can't go in there alone."

"Sorry, kid, but I've done all I can for you. It's up to you now. Besides, you've got Talbot." His lip curled in a sneer when he said the other man's name. "That's what you wanted, isn't it?"

Cassie looked back at Barton, then returned to Trace. "Yeah, I guess so, but I don't want him to find out I don't really know what I'm s'posed to do. Maybe I got him fooled now," she confided, "but if you ain't there to help me, he's gonna figger out the truth. . . ."

So that was it. It wasn't his company she wanted. She just wanted him along to make her look good for Talbot. Trace leveled an angry glare in Barton's direction. "So long, kid. It's been nice knowing you. Believe me, you've got nothing to worry about. Your manners aren't what he's attracted to." He started walking again.

"McAllister," she cried, the last syllable dragged out in a frustrated plea.

"Let him go, my dear," Barton said, coming up behind Cassie and placing his hands possessively on her shoulders.

"But, he—"

"Shh," Barton soothed, turning her to face him. "He did us a favor. All evening I've been able to think of nothing but having you to myself."

Cassie watched over her shoulder as Trace was absorbed into the crowd that still milled in the street. "Yeah," she agreed with forced gaiety. "We don't need no stick-in-the-mud to ruin our evenin', do we?"

But he already had. Dammit! Trace McAllister had spoiled her fairy-tale night. And to top it off, her feet were hurting now. But she had no intention of letting anyone know. To hell with Trace McAllister. She didn't need him. After all, Barton was the one she'd set her sights on. Not Trace!

Determined to enjoy herself in the exciting atmosphere that surrounded them, she stepped inside the theater with Barton. But she could never quite regain the fairy-tale feeling she'd had as long as Trace McAllister had been with them.

And by the time Barton escorted her to her hotel two hours later, she was so tired of smiling and saying thank you to his effusive compliments that she found herself wondering what she'd ever found so fascinating about him. He really was a complete bore! It would suit her just fine if she never saw—or heard—Barton Talbot again.

"Well, thanks, Talbot," she said at last, extending her hand to him. It was the first genuine smile to cross her face for hours. In fact, she was so relieved to be able to say good night that Barton caught her off guard.

"It can't end here, Cassie, darling," he blurted out, suddenly grabbing her around her back and pulling her to him, trapping her hands against his chest. "Not when I've waited all my life to meet a woman like you."

Cassie's head reared back in surprise. She must have misunderstood. "What in tarnation's come over you? Get your hand off me!"

"Now that I've found you, I can't let you go." Before she could fathom what was happening, his mouth came down to crush her lips back against her teeth.

A wave of alarm washed over Cassie—not because she was being kissed, but because the kiss was wrong. Completely wrong. Kissing was supposed to be wonderful, exciting. All the dime novels she'd read over and over had promised that a kiss was supposed to make a woman feel like her head was spinning, and make her go all weak in the knees. And bells! Dammit! She was supposed to hear bells! Where were the bells?

Pushing at his chest with all her might and twisting her head to the side, Cassie struggled to free herself. "Cut it out, Talbot!" she ordered, gasping for air. "You're actin' like a madman. What's got hold o' you?"

"If I am mad, it is because your beauty has driven me wild."

Cassie shook her head impatiently. She'd dreamed of having a handsome man hypnotized by her beauty—it happened that way in the stories—but this fellow was carrying it way too far. She had to get away from him. "A good dose o' castor oil might help you," she suggested, taking a step away from him.

"Darling, please forgive me," he pleaded, moving close to her to again begin covering her face and neck with tiny kisses. "I don't know what came over me," he said between kisses. "No, that's a lie. I do know what came over me. It's you. You and your beautiful face. I love you. I want you to be my wife!"

"You what?" she choked, pushing his face away from her neck with one hand and wiping his wet kisses off her cheek with the other, an expression of disgust altering her face. "An' stop slobberin' on me!"

"I want to marry you, Cassie! Say yes. Say you'll be mine, and you'll make me the happiest man in the world. We'll travel. We'll go to Europe on our honeymoon. I'll buy you the finest jewels and furs and beautiful dresses."

"That's the craziest galdurned idea I ever heard," she said with a huff of disbelief.

"Don't send me away. You want me too. I know you do. I can see it in your eyes."

"Want you? What for? I already done had enough o' you to last me a real long time."

"You don't mean that, darling, Just give me a chance to prove how much I adore you. Let me come in for one sweet good-night kiss."

"You must think I ain't got a brain in my head 'cause I ain't got fancy manners 'n don't talk fancy. Well, you might be right. I might be dumb. But I ain't dumb enough to let the like o' you come in my room for no good-night kiss—or for no other reason!"

The color in Barton's face deepened radically. His lip curled with disgust. Who did this little hillbilly think she was anyway? "Why, you little . . ." He thought again about her father's gold and the fact that her father had no other living relatives. The gold would all be hers if anything happened to her old man. And if he intended to be on hand when she took over her inheritance, he'd better play the game. Even if it meant playing the game this coutry bumpkin's way. ". . . tease," he ended his sentence with that charming smile that had so taken Cassie on the stagecoach. "You don't need to play hard to get. It's not necessary, my love. You've already stolen my heart."

Cassie wondered why she'd been so taken with the smile before, and now only saw an artificial display of flawless white teeth. "I'm playin' *impossible* to get, as far as you're concerned, Talbot," she laughed, taking the key from her purse and inserting it in the lock. But before she could turn the key, the door was torn out of her hand.

"What the hell's going on out here?"

Both Cassie and Barton stared up at Trace, who loomed threateningly in the doorway. "Well, if it isn't Cinderella and Prince Charming." The distinct odor of whiskey permeated the air.

"So that's how it is," Barton snapped, flopping his hat on his blond head and turning on his heel to leave.

"Yep!" Trace hollered after him. "That's how it is."

"'What the hell're you doin' in my room," Cassie scolded, brushing past Trace, seeming not to notice—or care—what Barton Talbot had assumed. She was too startled by the thrill of excitement that flooded her bloodstream at the sight of McAllister. But damned if he was going to know it.

"Tut, tut, tut," he clicked his tongue, closing the door to her room and leaning back on it. "Careful, kid. A lady doesn't say, 'What the hell're you doin' in my room?' She says, 'May I ask what—'"

Cassie spun around to face him, cutting him off. "May I ask," she said with exaggerated hauteur, "what the hell you're doin' in my room?"

"Mmm," Trace hummed, tilting his head to the side and contemplating the difference. Damn, she was cute. "That's better, kid, but you still don't quite have the feel of it. A *lady* never, never, never says 'hell.' "

"Do you think I give a damn right now?"

He shook his head with emphasized disappointment. "She doesn't say 'damn' either."

"Will you stop it?" she squeaked, exasperated. "I jus' want you to get outta here to I can get some shut-eye."

"It would be a shame to let that go bad," he said, nodding his dark head toward the dresser as he shoved away from the door and crossed the room.

It was then Cassie saw a bottle of champagne cooling in a fancy ice bucket. "Where'd that come from?"

"The maid brought it up. Compliments of Prince Charming. Though I expect he planned on drinking it with you. Right here in this room," he said with a chuckle. "Just before he toppled you onto that bed and relieved you of your virtue!"

Cassie glared her irritation at Trace and sat down on the bed. Bending one leg at the knee, she propped her foot on the other knee, and attacked the buttons on her boot with a vengeance.

"Sorry to spoil his little surprise," Trace said. "Though not as sorry as Prince Charming is, I bet. You want some of this?" he asked casually, holding up the champagne bottle.

She nodded her head to the offer of a drink. "I'm gettin' real sick o' havin' you butt in to my business."

"I take it you didn't want me to protect you from the Big Bad Wolf. My apologies, Miss Riding Hood," he said, his tone anything but apologetic as he handed her a glass of effervescent wine. "You want me to go after him? He couldn't have gotten far."

She ignored his suggestion. "I got news for you, McAllister. I don't need your protection. I can take care o' myself jus' fine."

His eyebrows arched upward. "Oh?"

"I might not know 'bout what spoon to use on the soup 'n what one to stir the coffee with, but when it comes to other things things like scallywags 'n' weasels, I know what to do."

She took a gulp of the pale wine, wrinkling her nose at the tiny bubbles that popped playfully from her glass. "Mmm, that's right tasty." She quaffed down the remainder and held her glass out to Trace. "How 'bout another slug o' that stuff?"

The corners of Trace's mouth quirked up in a hesitant grin. "Have you had champagne before?"

"Can't say I have. But I drunk a bit o' 'Tarantula juice' once when my pa wasn't lookin'," she bragged. "And this is a lot tastier."

"Tarantula juice?" His face twisted into a wince at the thought.

"Home brew," she explained. "Pa 'n the boys usually got 'em a still goin'. So! You gonna pour me more of that stuff 'r not?"

"Well, I suppose one more won't hurt you," he said, taking her glass. "But you need to sip it. Don't gulp it. Besides the fact that ladies don't gulp their drinks, champagne has a way of sneaking up on you." He handed her the refill. "Sometimes it makes you do things you might not ordinarily do."

"You never told me what you're doin' here," she said, studying him. The champagne was already relaxing her and putting the unpleasant scene with Barton from her mind. She smiled. She really was glad Trace was here — and that he'd butted into her life.

"Uh . . . uh . . ." Trace stuttered, caught off guard. He couldn't tell her he hadn't been able to get her out of his mind or that the thought of Talbot's hands on her had torn his gut to shreds.

"I didn't figger to see you again."

"Your dress!" he exclaimed, relieved at the saving thought. "I promised to help you unbutton your dress!"

"Oh," she said, taking several consecutive "sips" of her drink as she tried to understand the disappointment she felt with his answer. True, she would need help with the dress. But a tiny ray of hope that he'd had another, more personal, reason had flared in her heart for an instant, and having it snuffed out hurt more than she ever would have expected. Seeing her glass was empty again, she held it out to him. "You sure that was your only reason?"

Trace took it from her hand and looked away from her guiltily. "What other reason would I have?"

She laughed. "Durned if I know. I just got to thinkin' you might've had a mind to do what Talbot had a mind to do. Crazy, huh?" She welcomed the refilled glass and grinned her thanks up into his stunned face.

As though someone had jabbed a hot poker into his belly, her smile seared right through him to his groin. And an overwhelming desire to tear her clothes off and make love to her shuddered through his strong body.

"Yeah, crazy," he choked, spinning away from her in a desperate effort to gain a semblance of control over his body's reaction to her. "Dammit, Cassie," he shouted suddenly, "do you think I'm cut of the same cloth as a man like Talbot?"

When she didn't answer, he wheeled back to glare at her. "Well, do you?"

Her automatic impulse was to say, *Hell, McAllister Barton Talbot couldn't measure up to your kneecap.* But she remembered what Trace had told her at supper about being coy.

"The way I see it . . ." She crawled to the opposite

side of the bed and set back against the pillow at the headboard. Tucking her skirt around her bent legs, she steadied her glass on her knees with both hands. "You're all pretty much alike."

"Alike!" Even he could see his indignant tone was overdone. He sat down on the bed, facing her. "Tell me, Miss Woman-of-the-World. How are we all alike?"

Cassie held her glass to her mouth and ran the tip of her tongue along its rim as she studied his face. Why hadn't she noticed before that he was so much more handsome than Barton Talbot? She sat up and leaned forward, her eyes focused on his well-shaped mouth. "I s'pose you kissed lots o' gals in your time, ain't you?"

Taken back by her change of subject, Trace coughed and answered hesitantly. "I guess I've kissed my share, but what . . . ?"

Disappointed with his answer, though she'd had no reason to expect it should be any different, Cassie leaned back again and took another sip of champagne. "That's what I figgered." She definitely didn't like the idea of Trace kissing another woman.

"What about you? Have you kissed a lot of fellows?"

"I kissed my share," she mimicked, not wanting to admit that tonight had been her first kiss and that it had been a total disappointment.

Trace cleared his throat uncomfortably. Something was happening he didn't seem to have any desire to stop. Of course, he had to stop it. Only a cad like Talbot would stoop to take advantage of such an innocent — especially one who'd just swigged down three glasses of champagne to boot! "So —" damn, his voice sounded like an adolescent teenager's — "it looks like we've both done our share of kissing."

She sat up straight, her eyes still on his mouth. "Yep, that's what it looks like. I don't s'pose you'd want to . . ." She shook her head and flopped back against the pillow. "Naw."

"Want to what?" he asked, leaning forward to lift her chin with a curved forefinger.

Tingles of something like tiny glass wind chimes jangled through Cassie's body. "Well, I was just wonderin' if you was of a mind to . . ."

"To what?"

"I mean, I was thinkin', since we both done our share o' kissin', I figgered we might jus' wanna kiss each other." Her brown eyes snapped up to search his expression for signs of amusement.

There were none, and relief washed over her, giving her the fortitude to continue. "I mean, since we're both leavin' in the mornin' an' won't be seeing' each other no more."

"Do you want me to kiss you, Cassie?" he asked, leaning toward her.

"Only if you're of a mind to."

Of a mind to? God, kid, if you only knew what your looking at me like that puts me "of a mind to"!

He wrapped his fingers behind her neck and drew her toward him slightly. "Sort of a good-bye kiss?"

The pink tip of her tongue poked between her lips to wipe along the soft pouting edges of her mouth, and the ache in Trace's groin tightened painfully.

"Sorta like that," she agreed in a husky whisper. Her lips pursing of their own accord, she leaned closer to him, as if she were being drawn to him by an invisible thread. Her eyelids fluttered helplessly downward.

"Damn, kid," he said with a tortured groan, "don't you know that giving an invitation like that to a man could get you into serious trouble!"

Cassie's eyes popped open. "You mean you ain't gonna kiss me?"

The mixture of indignation, confusion, and hurt he saw in her eyes combined to trigger a reaction in him that was based strictly on self-preservation. "Sure I am, kid," he said. His decision made, he took a deep breath and released it, then cupped the back of her head in his hand and brought her face to within an inch of his own.

His breath on her skin was a heady experience that warmed her entire body, not like Barton's, which had only irritated her. She breathed in deeply, her senses absorbing the smell of whiskey, bay-rum men's cologne, and shaving soap. Her head began to spin, and her limbs felt lighter than air.

Trace moved his lips so close to hers she could feel the heat from them radiating into her mouth, to tug at her deepest points.

Without warning, Cassie felt that wonderful warmth leave her lips and settle on the tip of her nose as Trace's mouth pecked her there with a big brother kiss. "And now, I'm going to help you unbutton your dress and then get out of here!" he announced, taking her lax body and twisting her around so her back was to him. It was a good thing she couldn't see what a strain that noble gesture had put on him—and in his trousers! "And you're going to go to sleep," he forced himself to say.

Hurt and embarrassment scalded their way through Cassie's blood as she bent her head forward to allow Trace to manage the tiny buttons. She'd made a bigger fool of herself just now than ever in her life. She couldn't speak.

His hands shaking, Trace removed each button from its hole. But as each of the round bits of pearl was freed, he was reminded of what he'd just turned down. And the ache in his loins grew proportionately. *Damn high price for chivalry,* he told himself bitterly, fighting the desire to caress her vulnerable-looking shoulders and kiss her bent neck. *She doesn't even realize I've done her a favor.*

"Is it because I ain't pretty?" she said softly. "Is that why you don't want to kiss me?"

Trace prayed for strength. Damn, did she have to say everything she was thinking out loud? "I told you I think you're very pretty."

"But you don't want to kiss me."

"I did kiss you."

"Not a real kiss."

Trace shook his head, his hands hovering a fraction of an inch from her shoulders. "Cassie, let it rest. In the morning you'll thank me for this."

"Why?"

"Because you'll see I was right. You'll realize it was for the best." God, he sounded noble. Downright priggish! What was it about this girl that made him want to protect her—even from himself? It was crazy. He was crazy! When had he ever turned down such an obvious offer?

She twisted around to face him, the hurt in her dark eyes making them glisten in the light of the oil lamp. "Why wouldn't you kiss me, McAllister?"

"Ah, kid," he said, his voice a low plea. His resolve was dwindling by the millisecond. "Don't do this."

"What's wrong with me?"

"Dammit! Nothing's wrong with you! Can't you get that through your head?"

In his intense desire to convince her that it was not her, he had inadvertently clutched at her upper arms and shaken her slightly. And now, as if her flesh were the magnet, his fingers steel, he could not find the strength to remove them.

"Then why?" she persisted.

He studied her upturned face, his baser self arguing with the part of him that had felt it was his duty to protect Cassie Wyman from men like himself.

"Why indeed?" he said, sliding his hands down her arms to lower her bodice as his mouth closed over hers in a searing, hungry kiss.

Chapter Seven

The instant Trace's lips came in contact with Cassie's mouth, he knew he was a lost soul. He could no more have turned away than he could have refused water after being on the desert for days without a drink. All thought of right and wrong abandoned him; and blind instinct assumed control of his actions with a need so basic that it would have frightened him if he'd been rational enough to recognize it for what it was.

And if anyone had tried to tell Cassie it wasn't the clanging of bells she heard, but simply the frenzied pounding of her own pulse, she'd have insisted they were dead wrong. For as surely as the flame of Trace's kiss blazed through her, weakening her muscles like so much melting wax, she heard bells. Loud, magical, glorious bells.

Her mouth fastened to his with joyous abandon, she didn't resist as he lowered her back on the bed and covered her upper body with his own. Nor did she resist when his tongue coaxed and prodded at her closed mouth, begging for — demanding — entry into the moist darkness.

She opened her lips to receive the welcome token of

his desire. It was as though her mouth had been created for just this moment. Never had she imagined a kiss could be this wonderful. The bells, yes. The books had warned her to expect them. And the weak limbs and racing heart came as no surprise—though her reaction was more incapacitating than the books had led her to believe. But it was the total feeling of fulfillment, of coming home, of at last being what God had intended her to be, that tossed her rational thinking asunder, rendering her a helpless bundle of longing.

Not thinking clearly enough to dwell on why the kiss meant so much more than she'd hoped for, Cassie gave herself over to it completely. She wrapped her arms around his rock-hard torso, her hands clawing at his shirt as they climbed his back in an instinctive effort to bring his body the rest of the way over hers.

His own body screaming for the feel of her beneath him, Trace fell to one side to reposition her, then rolled onto her gently undulating frame, melding their bodies together from mouths to knees.

Answering to instinct's promise of relief from the exquisite agony that throbbed deep in her groin, her thighs fell apart in a sensual cradle for his flanks. In reply to her invitation, he ground his hips against her and pressed even harder into the alcove she'd created for him between her legs.

Overwhelmed by his own passion and shamed by how dangerously close he was to taking advantage of the naive girl, Trace mustered enough strength to still his urgent movements on her. After all, defiling innocent virgins wasn't exactly his way of doing things. Dragging his mouth away from hers, he gazed down into her dismayed hazel eyes, now glazed dark with desire. His own forehead was furrowed with regret. "Look, kid . . . I . . ." His voice was a strangled whisper. "I better get out of here before—"

"Don't go," she whimpered, clutching desperately at his shoulders from behind and lifting her head off the pillow, her mouth aggressively seeking substance in his kiss. "Just one more kiss," she begged, her eyelids drifting closed as her lips reached their quarry.

Trace raised up and studied her dewy, slightly swollen mouth. "You don't know what you're saying, kid," he protested in a tortured plea. "Another kiss and I—Hell, kid, can't you see I'm already on the verge of—"

Cassie cut off his words with her parted lips, hot and insistent, on his. All she could "see" was that nothing mattered right then except relieving the unfamiliar craving coiling in the pit of her belly.

Trace released a defeated sigh, and his entire body seemed to relax on her as he finally succumbed to her invitation. Emboldened by his surrender and prodded by her own aching need, Cassie teased the rim of his lips with the tip of her tongue.

Beyond restraint, Trace opened his mouth to caress her tongue with his, languidly circling it, courting it.

As if her tongue had been groomed to take part in this special mating dance, it retreated coyly back into her mouth, bidding his to follow. Unable to resist the tempting invitation, he dipped once more into her mouth to continue the chase. Exploring the warm interior of her mouth, he mapped its every depression, discovering its unique textures and savoring its taste.

His lips, hot and wet, trailed kisses along her cheek to bathe her arching throat with fire. Jagged spears of lightning radiated haphazardly through her, and Cassie moaned her pleasure aloud, rolling her head to the side to give his lips better access.

With gentle actions, he lowered her bodice down to the bend in her elbows. The full mounds of her breasts strained against the delicate cotton of her chemise, her taut nipples jutting upward in a plea. His breath caught in his throat. Sliding his hands under her hips to fit her closer against him, Trace blazed a path of kisses from the curve of her shoulder to one of the enticing peaks.

Folding his lips back over his teeth, he nipped tentatively at the cotton-veiled bud, moistening it with his tongue until the delicate material of the chemise was molded to the pink-haloed tip in a glistening second skin.

"So sweet," he murmured against her breast as he moved his head to bestow the same loving treatment on the second rosy crest.

"That's nice," she said, her words slightly slurred—with sexual need and not from the champagne, he tried to convince himself.

Experiencing one last moment of hesitation, Trace levered himself up on his forearms and gazed into her lust-drugged eyes. She smiled and clutched him harder to her.

Hating himself for his weakness, Trace sucked in a ragged breath. He told himself he wasn't going to question the wisdom or morality of what he was doing any more. She was an adult and she obviously wanted this as much as he did.

As if he could exorcise the persistent threads of guilt from his mind, he brought his mouth down on hers with the urgency that had been building in him since the moment he'd seen her limber, towel-drapped body fresh from the tub earlier that evening.

Her head swirled from the champagne and the newly awakened storm of desire that raged through her veins, but Cassie felt no fear. Unable to sense the battle raging in Trace's thoughts, she returned his kiss with the same eagerness she'd given their lovemaking

113

from the first.

Resigned to his inability to leave her willing body, Trace removed the pins from her hair, pitching them to the floor beside the bed. "You smell good," he whispered, inhaling deeply and burying his face in the auburn-colored cloud framing her face. Desperate now to remove all the barriers of clothing between them, he pushed the lace straps of her chemise off her shoulders to ease it downward. Kissing a shoulder, he rolled to a sitting position, taking her with him.

Trust and the wine making her limp, she didn't balk when, one shoulder at a time, he caressed his way from her neck to her wrists, removing her arms from the dress sleeves and chemise straps. The garments fell away, exposing her breasts to his gaze. Before Cassie could voice her alarm, he dipped his head and latched onto a straining peak. And instead of crying out in dismay, she sighed her delight and tangled her fingers into Trace's dark hair, holding him closer to her, her own head lolling backward.

His need frantic now, he hurriedly divested himself of his shirt and boots, then, standing up, he drew her to her feet. Without giving her a chance to question what was happening, he undid her petticoat and skirt strings, letting them fall as one with the chemise and bodice in a billowy cloud at her feet.

Fascinated by Trace's naked chest, Cassie reached out a slender hand to curiously touch and experience the uniquely male feel of the dark hair curling over its breadth. With the tips of her fingers she idly traced the outline of his clearly defined pectoral muscles and flat brown nipples. As a blind person "sees" a piece of sculpture, she drew lazy circles over his taut skin, the wall of his flat stomach, the ladders of his rib cage, and especially the dark arrow of hair that piqued her curiosity as it disappeared into his trousers.

114

It was more than Trace could bear. "You're beautiful," he mumbled, toppling her over onto the bed and covering her with his body. Laving her face with kisses, he lifted his hips and fumbled with the buttons on his pants. But it was no good. He was too anxious to make his hands follow his commands.

He sprang to his feet and finished the task, whisking the pants and underwear down his long legs and off with his boots and socks in one swift action.

Cassie stared aghast. There, before her eyes, proud and erect, his manhood jutted out from a nest of dark curls. Her eyes widened. It was at once the most amazing and the most absurd thing she'd ever seen, the most desirable and the most frightening. She'd never seen a man naked before. Of course, she'd known they were different than females. After all, she'd seen animals mating. But somehow, that had not prepared her for this moment. She continued to stare in wonder.

Trace smiled in understanding and knelt on one knee on the edge of the bed. He reached down to cup her frightened face. "Don't be afraid, sweetheart. It's not as fierce as it might seem."

His hand on her cheek and his calling her "sweetheart," rather than "kid," combined to mellow the sudden turmoil that had gathered in her thoughts. She had nothing to be afraid of. This was Trace McAllister, the man who'd arranged for her to have her fairy-tale evening, the man who'd made her into Cinderella. *Her fairy godfather!* He wouldn't hurt her.

She smiled tremulously at him. "I'm not afraid." Dropping down beside her, he stretched himself along the svelte length of her. As though gentling a skittish young colt, he smoothed his hand over her flesh: her breasts, her rib cage, her stomach, her long legs, all

115

the while cooing assurances and adoring praises in her ear. When she had relaxed somewhat, he slipped his hand under the waistband of her drawers to stroke her softly rounded belly. When at last he reached the treasured point of his destination, he found she was moist with desire.

Cassie jerked violently as his fingers launched their invasion into the satiny folds of her womanhood. Her passion-lidded eyes popped open and she tried to sit up, shaking her head and muttering in surprise. "You're not s'posed—"

"Shh, it's all right," he whispered, stilling the movement of his fingers at the entrance to her body but not removing them from their intimate position.

"I can't let—"

He stopped the remainder of her words with an urgent kiss, filling her mouth with his tongue. His hand remained motionless on her as he remapped the sweet interior of her mouth. When he sensed she was once more at ease, he rotated the pad of his thumb ever so subtly on the sensitive tip of her sex. Then when he'd given her time to adjust to that intimate caress, he slipped a finger, then a second finger, barely inside her. Continuing to manipulate the outer nub with his thumb, he circled and prodded with the fingers inside her, quickly locating the protective maidenhead he'd known would be there, yet had prayed he wouldn't find. It would have been so much easier not to feel like a cad if she weren't a virgin.

Scissoring the two fingers sheathed in the heat of her gently rocking body, he increased the circular stroking of the exterior peak with his thumb, which found her dewy with the evidence of her passion.

Cassie felt as if every nerve in her body was being compressed into a tiny spring at the center of her soul, ready to leap free at any given moment and scatter in all directions. Then it was happening. And there was no more time for thinking. Only for feeling. An explosion riveted through her. Her hips bucked against his hand. And her insides seemed to burst in a shattering sensation that discharged from between in her thighs to every cell.

The involuntary muscles of her sex clenched tight around his fingers, and Trace took the opportunity to quickly plunge them deeper into her, swiftly tearing the virginal barrier with one quick jab.

Disguised in the spasms of ecstasy that shook her slim frame, the pinprick of pain went unnoticed by Cassie. Instead, she dug her nails into Trace's back and arched her pelvis harder against his hand in an attempt to relieve her need for more of him.

Ignoring the contractions of guilt he felt for what he'd just done, Trace removed his hand from her warmth and hurriedly peeled off her drawers. Refusing to think, he pulled her beneath him and positioned himself between her parted thighs, fitting his desire snugly inside her with one sure thrust.

"Oh," Cassie wailed, surprised by the wonderful sense of being whole that enveloped her the instant he was inside her. She'd expected pain, or at least discomfort, but not this . . . not this feeling of such completeness.

"Did I hurt you?" he asked, concern wrinkling his brow.

Cassie shook her head.

"Are you sure?" His fingers twined gently in the wild mass of her hair and he examined her face.

"Yes," was all she said before they simultaneously began to rock together.

Intrigued by the feel of his hair-roughened legs against her smoother ones, Cassie wrapped her long limbs around him and clung hard to his waist with her

117

arms. Raising herself off the bed to meet each of his thrusts, she reveled in the way her flesh molded itself to his, gripping him, squeezing him, almost releasing him as he withdrew, only to pull him back into her before he could escape.

Their tempo growing more urgent with each coming-together, they moved as one force toward their mutual summit.

Without warning, her world ruptured violently in a spray of color behind her closed eyelids. She was hurled into another sphere beyond rational thinking as Trace threw back his head and cried out his release.

His own desire spent, he collapsed on her with a final shudder, his skin slick with perspiration. His thoughts were rife with guilt. "Are you okay? Did I hurt you?" he rasped, his breathing labored.

"No." Touched by his concern, she suddenly found herself fighting tears pooling in her eyes.

Cassie shook her head, and laughed self-consciously. "I ain't hurt."

"But you're crying."

She reached up and rubbed at one eye with the heel of her hand. "No, I ain't."

"Then what's this?" He trailed a finger gently up from her temple to the corner of her eye and held it up for her to see.

Embarrassed, she sniffed and turned her head to the side to wipe her face on the pillow beneath her head. "I must 'a got somethin' in my eye."

"Cassie . . ." he said, his voice rising knowingly on the last syllable of her name. "Why are you crying if I didn't hurt you?"

She peeked up at him from the corner of her eye, then quickly averted her gaze again. "I don't know," she said, so softly he could barely hear her.

He cupped her jaw in his hand and forced her to

look at him. "What?"

Her teary eyes narrowed angrily. "I said I don't know!"

Certain she was already having second thoughts about what had just happened, Trace rolled off her and stared up at the ceiling. *Well, you bastard, how do you feel now? Like hell. That's how I feel.*

"It's not as if it was against your will," he said in his own defense. "I warned you, but you begged me not to stop."

Cassie's eyes grew large with indignation, her tears forgotten. Jackknifing to a sitting position, she glared down at the man beside her. "Begged you!" she gasped incredulously. "Why, you blowed-up bag o' hot air! I ain't never begged for nothin' in my life. An' I sure as hell ain't got to beg a feller for that. In fact, there's plenty who're beggin' me. Why, just tonight, Barton Talbot woulda give me the moon for just one more o' my kisses. Beggin'! Hmp!"

She snatched up the crumpled bedspread that had worked its way to the end of the bed and clutched it protectively to her breasts. Jumping off the bed, she stomped on bare feet to the dressing screen and slipped behind it.

"Are you trying to make me believe you didn't enjoy it just as much as I did?" Trace called, swinging his feet to the floor and shoving them into his long johns and pants. There was a disbelieving chuckle in his tone.

Cassie paused, her hand holding the water pitcher poised above the washbowl. A rumble of pleasant reminder shuddered over her as she remembered exactly how much she really had enjoyed it.

But she certainly had no intention of letting Trace McAllister know that! *That big head o' his is already swole up enough.* She shook her head stubbornly and resumed her toilette. "I ain't *tryin'* to tell you nothin', McAllister. I'm sayin' it right out. If you didn't get me drunk on that champagne, I'd 'a—"

"I knew it!" Trace pulled the fly of his pants together, then sat down on the bed—hard. "You may act and dress differently, but you're just like every other female!" He snatched up a boot and yanked it on his foot, not bothering with his socks.

"Oh, yeah?" she yelled, poking her head out from behind the screen. "What the hell's that s'posed to mean?"

Both boots on, he grabbed his socks in a fist and stabbed his arm into the sleeve of his shirt. "It means I never would have expected you to pull such an obviously female stunt as this."

"What stunt?"

"That's what makes this so funny. You're all alike. You do what you really want to do. Then you turn around and claim you were forced. You couldn't take it if someone found out you actually liked it!"

He slammed his hat on his head and stalked to the door, shirt unbuttoned, socks and gunbelt in his hand. "Well, kid, you can tell yourself whatever you want. If it'll make you feel better, that's fine with me. But there's no way you'll make me believe that what went on in that bed tonight wasn't exactly what you were asking for!"

"Askin' for?" she shrieked, drawing back the arm holding the clay water pitcher. "You're the one askin' for it, McAllister!"

She sent the pitcher hurling across the room toward him. Her aim was true and it splattered in the exact spot where Trace had been standing—the instant before he stepped out into the hall, slamming the door behind him.

* * *

120

Noah rose out of the lumpy bunk in the back room of the stable. It was no good. He wasn't going to sleep tonight. He might as well get up and make some plans for what he was going to do if he and the Wyman girl failed to find their gold.

He dug a match from inside his shirt and struck it on the sole of his shoe. Holding it to the wick of the stub of candle on the crate table, he stared at the flame until the match burned down to his fingers. "Damn," he cursed under his breath, shaking the match out.

Leaning back against the wall, he stared unseeing at the surrounding rough planks of the small room. What *was* he going to do if he couldn't get his gold back? If he'd been thinking, he would have gone after Murieta right away. But what chance would he have had alone in these mountains? He would have been lost within an hour off the road.

Anyway, he couldn't very well leave Cassie Wyman to fend for herself, which he had no doubt was her intention. Despite her tough ways, she was still a lady in his mind, and men took care of ladies. Besides, she probably knew the mountains better than anyone, since she'd lived here for eight years.

Thoughts of Cassie brought up another worry. Folks who saw him riding with her weren't likely to take too kindly to seeing the two of them together. If he wasn't careful, he could very well end up dangling at the end of a rope. *California may be a free state as far as the law's concerned, but a piece of paper can't change people's way of thinking,* he reminded himself, remembering a young teenager he'd seen hung by a mob for smiling at a white woman. No doubt about it, pairing up with Cassie Wyman could be dangerous.

121

Noah didn't pay attention to the restless horses shuffling and whinnying in their stalls — not until the sound of an angry curse word broke into his worried thoughts.

He sat up straight and cocked his head to listen. Maybe the owner who'd hired him to watch the stable in exchange for a bed for the night had come back early. Noah waited for the man to come in and take his place in the other bunk.

"Women! Who needs them?" he heard whoever was in the stable ask. "Hold still, horse!"

Noah picked his pistol up from the wooden crate table and pointed it toward the curtained doorway that partitioned the sleeping room from the rest of the stable. "Who's there?" he called out.

"It's McAllister, Zeb. I've come to get my horse. I'm riding out tonight."

Noah relaxed. He didn't particularly relish the idea of getting into a gunfight with a white man — horse thief or otherwise. "Mr. Zeb's out for the evening," he announced, pushing the curtain aside. "I'm watching the stable for him."

Trace spun around to face the voice. There, outlined by candlelight, was a man — a huge man whose giant frame blocked nearly the entire doorway. Only the smallest amount of candlelight escaped past him, giving his dark shape an eerie, unearthly glow. "Who're you?" Trace managed to ask the shadowy apparition.

"Don't you recognize me, Mr. Trace?" Noah said, stepping farther into the stable and bathing the area with more light in the moment before he dropped the curtain.

"Noah? Is that you? What the hell are you doing here? I was wondering where you disappeared to."

"We decided to get a good night's sleep tonight and

122

go after Murieta in the morning."

A frisson of apprehension sizzled through Trace's mind. He didn't want to hear the answer, but he had to ask. "We?"

"Miss Cassie and I are going after our gold. We don't hold out much hope on those Rangers finding it for us."

Trace blew out the breath he'd been holding and shook his head. "I don't blame you for not trusting them after what happened today, but you can't go looking for Murieta with her. She's a hotheaded little . . ." Trace closed his lips on what he'd been going to say. "You'll both end up getting killed."

Noah shook his head morosely. Trace wasn't saying anything he hadn't already told himself. "I don't see I've got any choice. I've got to find my gold but I don't know the country. She does."

"Then go with me. I'm going to catch Murieta if it's the last thing I do. I know the country. We'll find your gold—and hers—and bring it back here to her. A female's got no business out there looking for *bandidos*."

"I already gave her my word. I can't back out on her now. Anyhow, she'd just go by herself if I did. But we sure could use another man along. Why don't you join up with us?" Noah spoke enthusiastically. This might be the answer. If Trace was with them, folks would automatically assume the girl was with the white man and not with himself.

"You want me to team up with *her?*" Trace tossed a disbelieving laugh over his shoulder and resumed saddling his horse. "You've got to be insane. I'd sooner wrestle a bear in a pit of rattlesnakes."

Disappointment rained over Noah. "Sure wish you'd change your mind. I'd be glad for you to have my share of the reward if that's what's bothering

123

you."

"That's nice of you, Noah, my friend. But the only reward a man crazy enough to ride with Cassie Wyman is going to get is probably about six feet under. No thanks. I'll stick to riding alone. That is, unless you'll change *your* mind and leave her behind."

Noah shook his head and turned back toward the sleeping shed. "I'd better not."

"Well, I wish you luck. If I find your trunk, I'll leave it in the nearest bank and send a wire here telling you where it is."

"I surely do appreciate that, McAllister."

Chapter Eight

It was still dark when Cassie awoke — if you could call pitching and turning and wrestling with the covers all night something to awake from. And her mood was no better than it had been when she lay down a few hours before. Only now she had a headache.

"Oh, God," she moaned, spanning her forehead with one hand and rubbing her throbbing temples. "I never shoulda finished off that bottle o' champagne after McAllister left," she rasped, stretching an arm blindly toward the small chest beside the bed to grope over the top of it in search of a match. When she finally located the match holder, she wrapped her fingers around it, but did nothing about bringing it closer to her. She just lay there without moving in an effort to regather the strength that simple action had cost her.

She dragged the matches toward her. But the scrape of the holder on the wood top of the chest grated savagely through her senses. Her eyes winced closed more tightly and she cringed her shoulders. "Maybe I'll get lucky and be dead by noon." She slowly released her grip on her head and reached across herself to press her other hand to the table to stop its motion and the offending scraping.

Hearing her words brought a sudden vision of her father to her mind, and she couldn't help but see the irony here. Her mouth formed in a weak smile. But it even hurt to do that. Never again would she deliberately clang pots and pans so unsympathetically to waken him in the morning after he'd spent a Saturday night carousing with his friends.

She finally managed to raise up on one elbow and get a match out. She struck it — funny, she'd never noticed how much noise lighting a match could make. Squinting her eyes against the glare, she held it to the oil lamp wick.

As soon as the flame took hold, she replaced the glass chimney and shook out the match, then flopped back on her pillow. She needed to rest for another minute before she tackled actually sitting up.

A limp forearm thrown across her eyes to shield them from the light, she decided after a few minutes of silence that she might be up to moving again. Through sheer determination, she managed to roll to her side and hang her feet over the edge of the bed.

Satisfied that she was making progress, meager though it was, she propped herself up on one stiffened arm and prized open one gritty-feeling eye a fraction of an inch, then the other one. Glancing around the lamp-lit room, she located her coat near her feet on the floor. Not sure her head could take bending over to retrieve it, she sat up straighter and burrowed her toes under the heap of black material and lifted it with her foot.

Pleased with her cleverness, she arranged the coat

126

across her lap and poked her hand into a large inside pocket, bringing out the gold pocket watch her father had bought her for the trip. She had always dreamed of having a lady's lapel watch, but this had been all the traveling salesman had on hand at the time, so she'd settled for it. She snapped open the lid and examined the face.

"Four-thirty. Time to get movin', gal," she told herself, coming up off the bed in a momentary spurt of energy. "The sooner we put this town behind us, the sooner I'll forget that connivin' lowlife who—"

She stopped in midsentence and dropped her shoulders. How could she forget the man who'd made her feel beautiful and desirable for the first time in her life? How could she ever put the enchanted hours she had spent because of him out of her mind? And how could she forget the night when she had ceased being a girl and had become a woman?

Cassie shook her head in bittersweet resignation. To refuse to remember Trace McAllister would be to refuse to remember it all. And she couldn't do that. Despite the disappointing ending to the perfect evening, it had been something so precious and wonderful she would cling to its memory forever. She would never give it up.

"But that's just 'tween you 'n me, Lord!" she said, her voice edged with defensive stubbornness. "If I ever see that sidewinder McAllister again, he ain't gonna know I give it a thought."

Hurriedly bathing in the cold water left from the night before, Cassie pulled new jeans, a new red plaid shirt, and new long johns from her satchel. She'd meant to save the new duds for San Francisco, but since she wouldn't be going there until she located her gold, she decided she might as well spruce up a bit now. It might make her feel a little better.

A wave of sorrow darted across her mind. After a night of living out her fantasy of dressing up and being treated like a woman, would she ever be comfortable in men's clothing again? Had that one small taste of her birthright been enough? Or had it left her wanting even more?

"Well, it'll jus' have to be enough," she admonished with an angry stab of her fist into the sleeve of the shirt. " 'Cause I sure can't go after Murieta wearin' a hoopskirt." A picture of herself with a holster strapped on over the full-skirted green dress flashed in her thoughts. She chuckled and put her other arm in the second sleeve. "That'd be some sight."

Glancing down to button the shirt, she noticed for the first time that it fit her differently than her other clothes. She stepped in front of the mirror and examined herself. Instead of one of the baggy shirts she usually wore that would have fit a man twice her size, she saw a shirt that could have been made with her slim proportions in mind. The shoulder seams actually hit at the spot where her arm began, not halfway to her elbows as did the ones she was accustomed to.

"That stupid storekeep must 'a give me a shirt for a young'un," she said, trying to work up her annoyance, but too impressed with the becoming fit of the shirt to be very successful. She quickly buttoned the front and turned to the side, surprised to find that the red-checked material molded over her breasts, showing them off, rather than disguising them. It might be a shirt meant for a boy, but there would be no doubt in anyone's mind that a female was wearing it.

Pleased for a reason she didn't understand, she stepped into the new jeans. Again, the storekeeper must have made an error. The pants were snug rather than loose, fitting to her long legs and slender hips so well that they stayed up without suspenders.

Excited by her discovery, she quickly tucked her shirt in and twisted to view herself from behind. Her eyes zeroed in on the way the denim shaped itself to her bottom, detailing the separate cheeks in an embarrassing manner. "I can't go out in these," she said with a giggle. "I'd cause a scandal."

She quickly held up the other new clothes to her and discovered they were all the same. It was either wear the new things, and display her every curve to the world, or put on her old things. She glanced at the pile of clothes she'd worn the day before and wrinkled her nose. Facing the mirror again, she admired the way her long body nipped in at the waist, flaring gently into slender hips.

"I shouldn't," she said, her tone not at all certain. She looked at the old, familiar clothes again, then back to the mirror. "Maybe the pants won't look so tight if I have on my boots. She sat down on the stool and pulled on the worn boots, tucking the pants legs into the tops. She stood up and examined her reflection again.

Her face screwed into an expression of conflicting emotions. On the one hand, she was very pleased with what she saw and with the realization that she could look like a female without giving up the convenience and comfort of men's clothing. But, on the other hand, no one but a floozy would wear such a revealing getup.

She bent to pick up the shirt she'd worn the day

before. She stared at it forlornly for a long moment. Then, with stubborn resolve, she tossed it back to the floor. "Floozy or not, I ain't puttin' that old shirt back on!" she swore.

Before she could change her mind, she hurriedly stuffed her spare new clothes back into her satchel, deliberately leaving her old things on the floor where they lay in a discarded heap.

Next, she carefully folded her dress and fancy underthings and wrapped them up with the rest of the finery Trace had given her. She had no intention of leaving behind the only dress she might ever own.

She quickly brushed through her hair, then pulled it back to the nape of her neck and tied it with a piece of the string that had come on the package with her dress and slips in it. Strapping her holster to one hip and her bowie knife to the other, she surveyed herself one last time in the mirror. "Not bad, Cass," she told the decidedly feminine — despite her clothing — female in the mirror. "At least no one's gonna mistake you for no feller in these duds," she chortled, slipping into her long black coat — her one concession to keeping the old clothes. However, she vowed she was going to replace it the first chance she got.

Hefting her satchel, she gave the room a last quick once-over. Determining that she'd left nothing she hadn't intended to leave, she lowered the wick on the lamp and opened the door.

Funny, when she woke up that morning she wouldn't have given two cents for a chance to live another five minutes, but now she felt good.

With what might have been perceived as a triumphant chuckle, she left behind the room where Cassie Wyman, the girl miner who looked more like a man than a woman, had become Cassie Wyman, the *woman* who looked exactly like what she was.

Cassie held up her hand, signaling to Noah to stop. Leaping from her horse, she squatted down to examine the ground. "One of 'em has been by here not too long ago."

"How do you know?" Noah asked, dismounting and hunkering down beside her. They'd turned off the main road about an hour before, following a trail that seemed visible only to the girl, and still he couldn't see what was giving her clues.

"Fresh horse manure," she confirmed, indicating the line of droppings. " 'Member how the others we seen was starting to break up—like they been there since yesterday? This ain't been here more'n a coupla hours."

She rested her elbows on her bent knees and sat back on her calves, studying a large boulder that backed against the vertical wall of the wide coulee they'd been following. Noah nodded his head. "But you don't know it's one of them."

"No, but I'm pretty sure. Up till now, we been follerin' two groups o' riders. The first batch 'pears to be 'bout five 'r six men with rawhide pads tied on their horses' hooves—to protect their feet from gettin' bruised by the rocks, 'r to disguise their shoe prints. That'd be Murieta 'n his *bandidos*. Then on top o' those prints, it looks like 'bout fifteen horses, without pads, come by. That'd be those sorry Rangers. They was all ridin' fast."

Noah scrutinized the jumble of hoofprints on the ground. Damned if he knew how she could tell how many riders had gone by here. He shook his head.

" 'Cept that one," she said, pointing at a trail of

prints. Though their imprint showed they were wearing pads, they were deeper than the others. "That horse was walkin'."

"What makes you say that?"

"Look at the way the prints're spaced. The tracks o' the horses runnin' at a full gallop're seven to ten feet apart."

Noah shook his head with frustration and took off his hat to slap it on his thigh. The tracks all looked alike to him. How could she pick out one horse, much less measure the length of its stride?

" 'Cept that one," she said again, as if she were alone, seeming to be thinking aloud now. She pointed to the most distinct tracks. "Looks like he come along after all the hubbub was over. That feller was movin' like he had all the time in the world."

Even Noah could pick those tracks out. About two and a half feet apart, each of them appeared double, where the running tracks were each single imprints. "Like someone was coming to tell the bandits it was all clear?"

Cassie nodded her head and followed the tracks with her eyes as they disappeared up the path. "That's what I figger. If a body, say one o' them Rangers or someone from the stage was part o' their gang, Murieta 'n his boys could hole up somewhere till whoever he was brought 'em the all-clear. Then they could all ride outta here easy as you please."

It made sense, and Noah continued to be amazed by her cunning. If the bandits had some sure-fire hideout in these rocks and a prearranged meeting place, they could wait indefinitely for the signal that it was safe to come out.

"See, here comes the same horse back in this direction." She pointed to another similar set of tracks coming back toward them.

Noah bent over and examined both sets of tracks. Elated that he could pick them out as the same horse, he started trying to pick out other individual horses. "There's that walking one again, going up the trail again," he announced.

Cassie smiled and nodded her approval. "An' there he is comin' back."

"What's he doing?"

"I figger he's lookin' for somethin'. Maybe for a secret sign pointin' him to the hideout. I'd bet money, jus' up ahead's where those no-good Rangers lost them cagey varmints."

"What makes you say that?"

"Look," she said, pointing at the dirt. "Whadda you see there?"

Noah studied the spot Cassie was pointing at. Then his dark face split into a smile. "It's more tracks coming toward us! And they're moving at a full gallop!"

"How many horses?"

He squinted, beginning to enjoy this despite his worries about Salina and his gold. "Two!" he announced triumphantly.

"Right. Now, who do you s'pose those two riders was?"

"The two Rangers who came to tell us they'd lost Murieta and his men?"

"Right again!"

"How'd they lose them? Seems to me their trail would have been even easier to follow yesterday than it is today after the Rangers rode over it."

"If I 'member right, there's a spot 'round the next curve where two creeks cross each other. The *bandidos* coulda gone into any one o' them creeks 'n not

133

come out till they was far 'nough upstream 'r down-stream to be sure Love's men had give up."

"Is that what you think they did?"

"Could be," she mused, staring at the lone rider's prints again and following them with her eyes. "Or it could be Murieta jus' wants us to think they went into one o' those creeks. Could be they left the tracks to the creeks *before* the robbery. Then *after* they robbed the stage, they split off somewhere else along the way — even if it looks like they went on."

"Seems to me you would have spotted the place where they changed trails. You're very good at this."

Cassie shot him a discomfited grin. "Thanks. But sometimes 'good' ain't good enough. After the Rangers went through 'n confused their trail, only the best tracker probably woulda noticed where they lit out from if they was real good at hidin' it," she said, standing up and walking over to the large boulder at the side of the trail. "An' even that good tracker mighta missed it the first time 'round if he was busy followin' the obvious one like the Rangers done."

"Then what should we do? Double back and look again?"

"We could go on up to the creek crossin' 'n each o' us follow one branch to see if we can spot where they come out o' the water — if that's what they did after all."

"What if we're wrong and we pick the wrong ones to follow? We will have wasted a lot of time."

"That's a mighty strong possibility, 'n them no-good Rangers probably messed up any signs by now." She rubbed her hands over the boulder and looked up the length of it. It was about half again as tall as she was. Her actions seeming to have no

134

purpose, she worked her way around it.

Her freckled face split into a victorious grin. "Well, well, well," she said, "whadda you s'pose we got here?"

Noah joined her in time to see her pull some dead brush from between the boulder and the sheared rock wall. "Looks jus' about the size to 'commodate a horse 'n rider, now, don't it?" she asked, peering behind the rock into a crevice that led into the hillside.

"Is that where they went?"

"I wouldn't be a bit surprised. That's prob'ly why they robbed the stage where they did. They knew they had a guaranteed hideout."

"Then let's go after them," Noah said, his deep voice excited. There just might be a chance they would find his gold after all. He hurried back to his horse and mounted up.

"Tell you what," she said, bouncing into her own saddle and reining her horse toward the secret entrance into the mountain. "On the offhand chance I'm wrong, It might be a good idea if we split up for a while. You keep followin' the tracks we been followin' here on Fast Run Gulch, an' I'll check this way. I got a feelin' it leads to another gully that runs alongside to this one. If I'm right, we oughta meet up 'bout four miles on up the trail. In the meantime, you can be checkin' out the creek banks for tracks."

Worry wrinkled across Noah's brow.

"Go on, Noah. You won't get lost if you stick to the trail. An' if you see somethin' suspicious, fire your pistol twice and I'll come runnin'. If you don't, wait for me where the trail splits in two."

He knew her plan was the best way to cover the most area in the least amount of time, but he still

135

felt uneasy about leaving her—though so far she'd done more taking care of him than he had of her. "Are you sure you'll be all right?" he asked. "What if you come up on them?"

"There's five o' them an' one o' me. I figger that oughta make the odds 'bout even." She patted the heavy Colt on her hip and grinned.

Somehow, her confidence didn't make Noah feel better, but he didn't say so. "You be careful," he said, nudging his horse forward before he could change his mind.

"You do the same, Noah. I'll see you in a coupla hours. Sundown at the latest."

Cassie watched as the gentle man disappeared around an irregularly shaped rock that extruded up from the floor of the ravine. She rode her horse behind the boulder, dismounting long enough to replace the brush to conceal the entrance. When she was satisfied that no one would stumble on the secret passageway and come up on her from behind, she remounted and rode on.

The access she had discovered was like a long roofless tunnel, maybe a section of an underground river that had ceased to exist. And it gave Cassie the feeling of being in a place no man had ever been, even though she knew that was impossible if her theory about Murieta's escape was true.

Once she was fully inside the crevice, she found the split in the mountain wider than she'd at first suspected—maybe wide enough to accommodate three horsemen riding abreast. The sheer walls rose straight up from the sandy floor, curving in above her so the slice of brilliant blue sky she saw twenty feet overhead was not more than a few inches wide.

Suddenly aware of the way the sound of her horse's hooves echoed off the rock walls, she stopped and listened. Of course that would be the reason the bandits had put pads on their horses' hooves. They'd wanted to muffle the sounds in the passageway in case someone rode by while they were in here. It was almost as if they knew they would be followed by the Rangers.

The idea that one of the Rangers might have been in on the robbery continued to grow in her thoughts. Angry, she slipped from her saddle and fumbled in her satchel for something to put on her horse's feet. The best she could do was two pairs of wool socks.

"Well, it's better'n nothin'," she told the horse. The gray gelding swiveled an ear toward her in response to her voice. "We don't want no one to hear us comin', do we?" she asked, lifting one hoof and putting a sock on it. When she had finished tying rawhide thongs around each ankle to hold up the socks, she walked the horse forward to try out the improvised pads. "Not bad," she conceded, climbing back into the saddle.

Reaching the other end of the passage, she dismounted again and, with her revolver drawn, inched cautiously toward the narrow opening. Flattening herself against the shadowed wall of the entry, she peered out. It was just as she had expected, another gulch that ran parallel to the wider one she'd come from.

"So far, so good," she whispered to herself, daring to poke her head a bit farther outside the crevice. Giving her eyes a chance to accustom themselves to the sunshine again, she glanced up and down the secret alleyway. It seemed to begin not far from where she stood, stretching to the east farther than she could see as it wound deeper into the mountains. Its steep banks were layered with fir-covered shelves at different levels, and again Cassie had the feeling she was witnessing something untouched until now by mankind.

She dropped her reins on the ground in front of the gray, ground-tying him, and tiptoed out into the open. Thankful now for the black coat and its camouflage effect, she was careful to keep herself in the shadows of the fir trees and scrub brush that grew along the sides of the gulch. She wished now she hadn't given in to the impulse to go hatless rather than wear the felt slouch hat she'd left behind. All it would take would be one ray of sunshine on her auburn hair to turn her head into a warning beacon for anyone who might be watching from above.

She froze back against the sheer wall and visually searched from top to bottom every inch of the section of the gulch that was in her sights. With alert eyes honed to catch the tiniest movement that didn't belong, the barest hint of color that didn't blend with the rocks and trees, she looked for a sign that would send her darting back into the safety of the crevice.

The only thing she saw was a doe and her fawn as they flitted out from behind two trees, only to disappear almost as suddenly as they had appeared. She listened for sounds, but all she heard was the breeze stirring the brush and grass.

Deciding she needed to be higher up to get a better look, Cassie dropped to a crouch and began to creep along the wall. Ducking behind boulders and fir trees every chance she got and darting across spaces where there was nothing to hide behind, she made her way to the base of a cliff that rose about fifteen feet high to form a natural, tree-dotted shelf that seemed to run a good distance into the gulch.

Standing back, she studied the steep face of the rock. If she could just get up there, she might be able to determine if she was alone or if the bandits were still here.

Exploring the jagged rock with her hands, she decided there were enough hand- and footholds for her to climb it, and she began her ascent. Slowly and carefully at first, she discovered that the rock wall wasn't nearly as sheer as it had seemed from the ground, and she reached the top quickly. Securing her feet in solid places, she peeked over the edge of the cliff. No one was there. It was safe to go on up. She hurriedly scrambled onto the ledge and flattened herself on it.

Relieved, she paused a few moments to catch her breath. Then, staying against the inner line of the ledge where it made a sharp angle to rise higher, she crouched low and scurried to a place where she might get a better view of the gulch below.

Peering between the branches of a fir tree that grew precariously close to the brink of the ledge, she surveyed the distance. She decided there was no one down there and that it would be safe to go back and get her horse and ride on.

Just as she started to turn back, something out of the corner of her eye caught her attention. Her senses charged to alertness, every muscle in her body ready to spring into action. Holding her breath, she concentrated on the spot where she had seen the movement.

There it was again. As quick as the blink of an eye, a horse's tail had flicked at his flank. Someone was down there!

Her heart pounding with excitement, she searched for the man she was certain was with the horse. Then she saw him. At least she saw what looked like the tip of the crown of his hat as it caught a ray of dappled sunlight on it. She moved closer to the edge of the bluff in an attempt to see better. Yes, it was definitely a hat, only now she could see nearly half of it. Someone, probably the lone bandit, was hidden in the brush, evidently waiting for his partners.

And you're going to take me to the rest of those slimy bastards and my gold! she thought with a vengeful smile, turning around and scampering back to the other end of the bluff.

Jumping the last four feet rather than taking the time to climb the rest of the way down, she landed in a crouch and took off running toward where the man was waiting. As she neared the end of the ledge where it angled back into the alcove where the bandit and horse were, she dropped to her belly and began to lizard her way forward beneath the low branches of the fir trees.

There he was. He hadn't moved. She froze, lifting herself slightly on her elbows. Holding her gun on the man, she creeped out into the open, flattening herself against the rock. "All right, mister," she snarled, swinging out from the shadows and assuming a wide-legged stance. She held the gun with both hands to steady herself. "Come out with your hands up. I want to see who the yellowbellied traitor was that sold out the stagecoach to them *bandidos.*"

"What the hell are you doing here?" a masculine voice hissed from behind her as a strong hand clamped over Cassie's mouth. The edge of a second hand hit her wrist with a stunning blow that knocked the cocked pistol out of her hand. At the same time the revolver fired into the air as it hit the ground, she was slammed up against the wall of the cliff and pressed into it by a large male body flush against hers.

Fear and surprise running rampant in her brain, Cassie struggled against the grip on her, kicking at the man's shins, bending her knee in an attempt to injure him where it would really count. Twisting and writhing, she finally maneuvered herself so she could see the face of her captor. She went limp with surprise, her will to fight temporarily stunned.

No! she screamed inwardly, the feeling of betrayal so intense her vision blurred for a moment. *It can't be!*

Chapter Nine

"Damn!" Trace cursed, dropping his grip on Cassie and taking off at a run toward his horse.

Only knowing that she was free, Cassie didn't stop to wonder about his odd change of behavior. Instinctively, she dove for her revolver and came up with it cocked and aimed at his back. "Hold it right here, McAllister! Or I'll shoot!"

Trace stopped dead in his tracks and threw his arms up in defeat. He turned back toward her, a mocking grin on his face. "Have it your way, kid. It isn't *my* gold those *bandidos* are riding off with."

"What're you ta—?" Cassie broke off in midquestion as she became aware of the galloping thud of horses' hooves echoing off the canyon walls. They were growing more faint by the instant. Is that . . . ?" Her mouth dropped open and flapped voicelessly.

Trace nodded his head and shrugged his shoulders. "You're real quick, kid. They were taking a siesta, and I was just about to make my move when you crashed in here and scared them off. Nice work. Now that they know somebody's found their hideout, they're going to be hard as hell to find."

"Well, what're we standin' here for?" Cassie asked, stabbing her gun into the holster. "Let's go after 'em."

"I'll go after them," Trace said, lowering his hands and starting toward his horse again. "You go back to Auburn and wait for me there. I'll bring your gold when I find it." Snatching the reins, he bounded onto the horse's back.

"The hell you will," she shouted, running back the way she had come to retrieve her own mount. "I'm comin' with you!"

"No, you're not!" he yelled, kicking his bay horse harder than he intended to. The animal leaned back on his haunches and lunged forward to follow the escaping bandits. "I'm going alone!"

In record time, Cassie reached the deep cut in the mountain where she'd left the gray. Grabbing his reins up from the ground, she mounted at a run and took off after Trace. "Wait for me, you sneaky polecat," she called out, though he was probably already three quarters of a mile ahead of her.

Lying low over the gelding's neck she raced pell-mell up the natural corridor between the jagged hills, each of the horse's stretches for distance taking her deeper into the mountains. By the time she had ridden a mile at that undisciplined pace, her horse was obviously beginning to tire, and she was forced to bring him down to a slow canter.

It was then she realized that the sandy ground before her was free of any tracks. It was easy to see

143

no riders had passed this way recently. "Hell!" She sat back in her saddle and wheeled her mount around with a pull on the reins. "How'd I lose 'em."

With angry eyes, she scanned the rock bluffs on either side of her. Somewhere, there was another hidden passageway where they'd given her the slip. Well, she would just have to find it. She'd done it before, she would do it again. Besides, with Trace on their tails, Murieta's men wouldn't have had time to cover their tracks. It would simply be a matter of retracing her own steps until she met up with the bandits' trail.

Moving more slowly now, she made her way back down the ravine. Then a disconcerting thought occurred to her. Murieta could be up there somewhere, watching her, waiting for her to come within shooting range. A shiver of apprehension tentacled up her neck and around her shoulders, causing the fine hair on her nape to prickle and stand up. Though she saw nothing out of the ordinary, her eyes swept nervously over the towering rock cliffs surrounding her.

"I ain't scared o' that thievin' snake," she lied to bolster her courage, determined to shrug off the sensation of being watched. Her eyes raked over the hills again. Nothing! *There's nobody up there,* she chided herself.

She heard a soft rustle to her right the exact instant her horse's ears lay back with fright. Then, a split second later, before she could determine the cause of the horse's alarm, the animal squealed hysterically and reared back on his hind legs, his eyes bulging and his front hooves pawing the air.

There was no time for Cassie to brace herself for the fall and she was hurled through the air to land in a bone-bruising thud, her head and shoulders knocked against an outcropping of uneven rocks. Stunned, she lay there for a second.

Trace McAllister's voice was low and threatening, his expression grim, as he cautiously stepped from behind a group of large boulders eight feet away on the opposite side of the gulch. His revolvers, two of them, were pointed directly at her. "Don't move a muscle, kid, or you won't have much use for that gold you're set on getting back."

For once, Cassie had nothing to say. Now she knew why he had insisted on going after Murieta alone. He planned to find the gold and keep it for himself. Now, having failed to get her to go back to Auburn, he was going to kill her.

Anger and hurt and fear swirled through her head in equal proportions. But she was determined not to let Trace McAllister see in her eyes the fear squeezing at her heart. So she concentrated on her anger. "You bas—"

It was then she heard the chilling, ominous rattle directly above and behind her head. Her heart stopped for a long moment, then raced on at an irregular clip, so fast it seemed as if it would explode through her rib cage in order to escape the confines of her chest. Her first thought was of what she wouldn't give to have that ugly old slouch hat on her head for a little bit of protection. She knew that more than one seemingly infallible person had been killed by a rattler in these mountains. And she had no doubt her time had come.

145

"Just don't move," Trace said, inching toward her, his steps measured. His guns were directed at the coiled rattlesnake that had been sunbathing on the rock Cassie's horse had thrown her against. It wasn't more than a foot from her head.

Trace's own heartbeat was syncopated with terror, and he wasn't certain his hands were steady enough to get off an accurate shot at the snake. Under ordinary conditions, he could have easily put a bullet between the reptile's eyes from this distance. But with Cassie sitting so close, and his hands so unsteady, he couldn't risk it. "He's watching me. Don't do or say anything to call his attention to you. I don't want to take a chance on hitting you. I'm going to get just a little bit closer."

The seconds ticked by with agonizing horror for Cassie. Never in her life had she known such a frustrating sense of helplessness. She wished Trace would go on and fire. She'd rather he took the chance than leave her sweating out the seconds like this.

Perspiration trickled out of her hair to trail over her face, until her complexion was slick and glistening, and she wished she could take off the heavy black coat. What had been practical that morning, before the sun had risen to warm the air, had suddenly become a sweltering, suffocating oven.

Her head began to buzz. Her eyelids felt as if they were jumping in their sockets. Her mouth and throat were dry and parched. And her vision began to blur. She wasn't certain how long she could just sit here—waiting for the snake to strike the blow that would mean her death—without doing some-

146

thing to save herself.

As though he'd heard her thoughts, Trace answered her. "Not long now, kid. I'm almost there. Just hold on a minute more. Easy now. Eeeeeeee . . . seeeeeee," he said, drawing out the word as he gently cocked the revolvers, first the left and then the right. If he missed with the first shot, he didn't intend to waste any time getting off the second.

Cassie concentrated on the hard expression on Trace's face. But he seemed to be growing dimmer now, as though he were a character in a dream that was ending. She opened and shut her eyes several times in a vain attempt to clear her vision. If it just were't so hot!

Just shoot, dammit! she screamed inwardly. *I don't care if it goes straight through my head. Just put a end to it!* she pleaded, though he couldn't hear her.

But Trace did care where the bullet went. Virtually commanding his heart rate to slow and his hand to stop shaking, he forced himself not to think of Cassie as anyone who meant anything to him. Stopping in his tracks, he spread his feet apart and planted them solidly on the ground. He narrowed his eyes, tightened his grip on the triggers, hesitated the barest instant, then squeezed.

To his horror, Cassie pitched over in a heap at the base of the rock as blood and gore of the decapitated snake splattered on the vertical rock behind it.

"Oh, my God!" Stunned, he stared at the still form on the ground before him. What had he done? Was it possible he had hit Cassie and the snake with one bullet? Or had he been so tense that

147

he had fired the second shot and not even realized it? He held his spare gun to his nose and sniffed.

Terror blazing in his eyes, his legs suddenly jumped into motion and he ran to where Cassie lay on the ground, her skin pale and lifeless. Almost afraid to touch the freckles that seemed to rise out of her pallid flesh for fear of what he would discover, he pressed his hand against her cheek. She was cold and clammy.

"Oh, God, no! She can't be dead!" With shaking hands, he rolled her onto her back in search of the bullet wound he expected to find in her head.

Confused, he stared at her face. There was no blood!

His actions frantic now, he lifted her limp body and tore her coat off her shoulders to examine her chest front and back.

Nothing! No bullet hole. No blood.

"Shit," he sighed as realization filtered through the haze of his overwhelming fear. Releasing a hysterical chuckle, he sank back against the rock and caught his breath. "She fainted. I thought she was dead and she just fainted!"

He realized how close he'd come to losing Cassie and his hands began to shake for real. If he hadn't come back for her when he did . . . A shudder shook his large body.

He thought back to the moment when he'd realized she wasn't behind him anymore. He was sure she had missed the spot the bandits had angled off this ravine and headed back toward Fast Run Gulch. He had considered just forgetting her and going on after the bandits. After all, that was what he'd come here to do. And if she lost him, she just might get smart and head back to Auburn and let him do his job. Besides, she wasn't his responsibility, he'd told himself.

He remembered the anger he'd felt for being placed in the position of having to choose between catching the man he'd been after for months and a girl who'd caused him nothing but trouble from the moment he'd first seen her. But the thought of her lost and alone in the secret gulch had continued to nag at his conscience and he had given up the chase to turn back.

Then, when he'd seen the spooked horse throw her, he had been at once both relieved that he'd turned around and at a complete loss as to what to do. He'd felt so helpless. It had been in that instant, when he'd seen death hovering only inches away from her, that he'd known he couldn't bear the thought of anything happening to her. And it was in that same instant he realized that through some diabolical quirk of fate, Cassie Wyman had wormed her way under his skin!

That was when his hands had begun to shake so badly he hadn't been sure he could hit his target.

"Well, she can just worm her way back out!" he said aloud, lolling his head to the side to look down on the most hardheaded female he'd ever known in his life. He was surprised to see her staring up at him, her hazel eyes wide with childlike innocence. He was unable to stop the elated spurt his heart took at seeing her awake.

"It got me, didn't it?" she said, her tough, resigned tone not quite disguising the fear of dying.

149

"How much time you figger I got?"

His first instinct was to gather her in his arms and comfort her. But that wasn't exactly the best way to get a female out from under your skin. "No, it didn't get you!" he answered harshly. "But not because you didn't deserve it!"

"I ain't dyin'?"

Trace shook his head. "Don't worry, though. It's only a matter of time before one of your fool stunts gets you in a mess I'm not going to be around to get you out of. The way I see it, you're just living on borrowed time." He stood up and reached down to take her hand. "Can you walk or am I going to have to carry you?"

Surprised—and hurt—by the anger in his tone, Cassie jerked her hand out of his grip and struggled to sit up. "I can walk!" she said. "Using the rock behind her to keep from falling, she dragged herself to her feet.

Unable to stop from indulging her curiosity, she glimpsed at the remains of the rattlesnake smeared across the gray of the boulder. Her stomach roiling uneasily, she swallowed, forcing down the bile that rose in her throat.

"Wait here, and I'll go find your horse. Then we'll head back to Auburn," he said, his words stiff with pent-up anger.

"I'll find my own horse," she argued, pushing away from the boulder supporting her—which was a mistake, because her head immediately began to swim dizzily. "I don't need your help," she went on, despite the light-headedness. "An' I ain't goin' back to Auburn till I find my gold. I come this far 'n I

150

ain't goin' back without it!"

"Look, kid! Can't you just for once act like a female and let a man take care of things for you? I said I'd find your gold and bring it to you! Can't you be smart like Noah and just wait for me?"

"What?"

"I told Noah I'd find his for him, too, and you don't see him blundering in here and giving Murieta and his men a chance to get away just when I was on the verge of taking them all. Of course not. He's not some harebrained female who thinks she can do a man's work. He's got good sense. He trusted me. Why can't you?"

"First of all, I know what you're up to. An' second, Noah ain't waitin' for you in Auburn. Him 'n me're partners. Right now, he's followin' Fast Run while I check this gulch out. We're meetin' up at sundown. So put that in your pipe an' smoke it, McAllister!"

Trace frowned, then smiled. If she was with Noah, all he had to do was get the two of them back together and he could be on his way. It might slow him down a couple of hours, but not nearly so many as if he'd had to take her all the way back to town. Feeling relieved, he whistled for his horse.

The bay appeared from behind the same rocks Trace had come from a few minutes before. "Good boy," he said, mounting and nudging the horse into a fast gallop. "We'll be right back," he shouted over his shoulder as they headed in the direction the gray had disappeared.

"I told you, I'll get my own horse!" she called after him, secretly glad he didn't seem to have heard her. The rattlesnake incident had taken a lot more out of her than she cared to admit.

While she waited, she glanced around her, quickly noticing the horse tracks that disappeared into the boulders that Trace and his horse had appeared from behind. *That must be where I lost 'em,* she mused, making her way on shaky legs toward the rocks to investigate the possibility of another hidden passageway through the hill.

Sure enough, there it was. Long, and narrower than the first passage into this gulch, it wound into the mountain in what she determined to be the direction of Fast Run Gulch. Examining the jagged split in the hill by the light of the sun that filtered in from the narrow crack at its top, she realized she would have to be very careful. This passage had lots of layers and levels to its walls and could easily afford hiding places for one or more gunmen to ambush trespassers.

"Well, I'll jus' have to take the chance they've gone on," she said under her breath, spying a trickle of water spilling down the rocky wall into a small pool on a waist-high ledge, before falling into a tiny stream that disappeared into the hill again. Knowing she'd feel better if she could cool down, she pulled off her coat and dipped a bandana into the clear water. She quickly opened the top buttons of her shirt and washed her face and neck and underarms.

"What are you doing?" Trace asked, surprising her as he came up from behind.

Wheeling around to face him, one hand holding the damp bandana at the base of her throat, the other on the handle of her revolver, Cassie's retaliation was automatic. "If you know what's good for you, you won't go sneakin' up on folks like that, McAllister!"

Trace's astonished gaze fell from the wet handkerchief at her neck, to the patch of pale cleavage exposed by her unbuttoned shirt. His eyes roved downward over the slim-fitting jeans that clung to her like a denim skin, adhering to every curve and crease. He stared at the area at the top of her thighs, and he couldn't disguise his reaction. His eyes glowed with unbridled desire, darkening to a deep forest green, and he gasped aloud. He could actually make out the mound of her femininity in the tight jeans.

"Where'd you get those clothes?" His question was asked in a raspy whisper.

Her expression questioning, Cassie looked down at herself. Embarrassment rose from her exposed chest to color her neck and cheeks brightly. "Oh!" She grabbed the lapels of the shirt and held them together as she spun away from Trace.

Unfortunately, the rear view was just as revealing—and every bit as devastating to his rational thinking. The compelling need he'd succumbed to the night before throbbed in his loins and pounded in his blood. Dragging his tongue over his parched lips, he stared, hypnotized, at the curve of her bottom. His body screamed out to be pressed against that soft roundness, and his arms ached to wrap themselves around her slim waist to caress all the places the jeans clung to so snugly.

Her shirt rebuttoned, Cassie turned back to face

him, her embarrassment still evident in her high color. "Well, what're you gawkin' at, McAllister?"

On the verge of grabbing her and throwing her to the ground and making love to her, Trace tore his eyes away from her and whirled around. "I got your horse," he said, his voice a hoarse croak. He cleared his throat. "Where are you supposed to meet Noah? I'll take you that far and then you're on your own. If you're smart the two of you will head back to Auburn and wait there for me to bring you the gold."

"For your information, I'm meeting' him where Fast Run splits in half, and I don't need you or no one else to 'take' me there!"

"Yeah, well, since we're going in the same direction, I guess we're stuck with each other anyway." He whistled up his horse, who came immediately, followed by the gray, whose reins were tied to the bay's saddle. He mounted and waited for her to do the same.

She was tempted to balk even further at his high-handed manner; but as he'd said, as long as they were going the same way . . . "What the hell," she said, snatching the reins from his hand and jumping on her horse.

The pain that shot up her back as her rear end made contact with the saddle was a jarring reminder of the fall she had taken. And she didn't manage to disguise the look of surprise that washed over her face fast enough to keep Trace from seeing it — and knowing exactly what it meant. His face split in a taunting grin.

"Butt a little sore, is it?"

"What'd you 'spect?" she returned angrily, controlling the urge to rub her sore backside.

"What I ' 'spect' doesn't have very much in common with anything about you, kid."

"What's that s'posed to mean?"

"I'll tell you what I meant when you tell me what you meant when you said you knew what I was up to." He signaled to his horse with a click of his tongue and led off into the cut in the mountain.

"I was jus' sayin' it's plain as the nose on your face why you want to go after my gold alone." Her horse fell into step behind his. This gully wasn't quite wide enough for two horses to ride side by side comfortably.

"And why is that?" Though his posture seemed relaxed enough, his alert gaze continued to comb over the bluffs and ledges overhead. He was reasonably sure Murieta's men had gone on through, but he knew he couldn't be too careful. They'd had enough time now to send a man back to guard the passageway.

"I know you got your eyes on that gold. That's why you got me drunk last night — so I'd sleep late this mornin' 'n you could get a head start. All along you was plannin' on findin' them robbers and keepin' our gold for yourself."

Hurt for a reason he didn't understand, Trace turned and stared at her for a moment, then returned his attention to the danger points ahead. "If that's true," he said in a low, modulated tone that revealed none of the emotion he was suddenly feeling, "why do you suppose I didn't go after them yesterday as soon as I got to Auburn and collected

155

my horse and gear, instead of spending the evening with you? And for that matter, why—if I wanted to steal your gold—did I stop you from stumbling into that camp of outlaws and getting yourself killed? And if I wanted your gold so much, why did I just let Murieta get away and come back for you so I could save your ass when that snake was getting ready to cash in your chips for you?"

Cassie didn't answer right away. She had to think. "Why *did* you come back, McAllister?"

Trace's shoulders tensed, then dropped forward.

"Why didn't you keep on Murieta's tail 'steada comin' for me?" She studied his broad back, almost able to feel the strain knotting in his muscles.

"Damned if I know." He kicked his horse forward in a deliberate signal that, as far as he was concerned, their conversation had come to an end. *Damned if I know,* he repeated to himself. He refused to think about the possibility that the unfamiliar emotions he had experienced since he'd met Cassie could mean anything important.

Hell, there was nothing about her that he liked in a woman. She was reckless and muleheaded. She swaggered and bragged. She was loud. She was bent on showing a man up for being less than he was. Not to mention her grammar and the way she dressed! And she cussed like a sailor. *Not exactly the type of women a man takes home to meet his family, is she?*

However, despite the many reasons he didn't even *like* Cassie Wyman, he kept remembering things about her that were like no other woman he'd ever known—things he "liked" more than he wanted to admit. Her smile, her trusting friendliness, her way of saying whatever she thought, her honesty . . .

The way she fills out the seat of those jeans! he remembered with a stab of discomfort in his groin—which brought on an entire new list of things he liked about Cassie Wyman. The way she had thrilled to every new experience the night before, the way her eyes had glowed with excitement in the restaurant, the way there was no pretense about her, the way her breasts had felt pressed against his chest, the way her long willowy limbs had wrapped around him at the height of her passion, the way he'd felt when he was inside her, as if her body had been created for his, the way—

"Shit!" As though he could rid his mind of the unwanted thoughts, Trace gave his head a vigorous shake. This was ridiculous. He made another effort to concentrate on her undesirable attributes. *She acts like she knows everything.* His lips curled in disgust. *Though, she is a pretty good shot,* he conceded. *And evidently she's not a half-bad tracker or she wouldn't have found that hidden passage so fast.* Damn! There he went again, counting her good points!

"Can you cook?" he asked suddenly, certain a female with so many masculine talents would be found lacking when it came to *all* the important womanly qualities. It would be one more thing to hold against her.

"Sure I can," Cassie answered, surprised by the odd question after Trace's long silence. "How 'bout you?"

Irked, for a reason he still couldn't understand,

Trace leaped to the offensive. "The word is *about,* Cassie. Not 'bout!"

"I know it," she answered defensively.

"Then why don't you say it?"

"Saves time, I guess. 'Sides, what diff'rence does it make?"

"*Be*-sides, what diff-*er*-ence does it make?"

"*Be*-sides, what diff-*er*-ence does it make?" she imitated sarcastically.

A jab of remorse pierced through Trace's anger and frustration. "I'm sorry, kid. I shouldn't have said anything. It isn't your fault no one ever bothered to teach you the difference between the way a lady talks and the way a roughneck miner talks."

" 'Course they did!" she said, remembering with a pang of loneliness the constant grammar lessons her mother had insisted she practice almost until the day she had died eight years before.

Trace swiveled in his saddle and studied her. "They did?" he asked skeptically.

"Not that it's none o' your business, McAllister, but my ma was a lady from a rich family in Baltimore. She knew all that stuff 'n made sure I knew it too."

"Then why do you talk like you're uneducated?" he asked, confused by the new insight into Cassie's character.

" 'Cause in Californie, fancy talk 'n manners don't do nobody a bit o' good. An' it sure as hell never kept nobody alive. My ma thought it was all so important, and look how much good it done her. She died anyhow."

Trace was surprised at the bitterness he heard in

158

Cassie's tone, and his heart tightened with pity. He could imagine the little girl who'd felt so hurt and betrayed by her mother's death that she had turned her back on everything her mother believed in. "It wasn't your mother's fault she died, Cassie," he said gently.

Cassie leveled a glare at him, repelling the sympathy she saw in his face. "If she'd a spent more time learnin' how to live in the wilderness 'n less time worryin' 'bout piddlin' things like manners 'n talkin' right, she mighta still been alive. But she was always more worried 'bout doin' everythin' so proper 'n ladylike. 'Stead o' doin' her any good, it killed her, 'cause nothin' she knew made her tough enough to survive out here."

Trace turned back to the trail and kept his eyes focused straight ahead. "But you're tough enough, aren't you, kid?"

"Damned right, I am," she said over the lump in her throat. "Ain't no one tougher!"

Chapter Ten

Reaching the exit from the rocky passageway through the mountain, Trace held up his hand and pulled back on his horse's reins.

Cassie brought her horse to a halt behind his and waited for the signal to move out. Ordinarily she would have resented the way McAllister had taken command. But right now, she was just too tired to fight him. The drain on her emotions the last twenty-four hours had finally succeeded in exhausting her. It had all been too much: the robbery, the fairy-tale evening, the disillusionment with Barton, the champagne, the loss of her innocence, the rattlesnake, talking about and remembering her mother, and then getting so close to her gold and losing it again . . . Right now, she was content to sit back and let someone else take control. Once they met up with Noah, she'd take over again.

"It looks like they're heading toward Round The Hill Road," Trace said, breaking the silence between them that had lasted the past ten minutes. He pointed at the stretched-out horse tracks leading northeast up yet another gulch. "But the way they were riding those horses, they're going to need to hole up and rest them before long."

"This looks mighty familiar," Cassie commented, standing up in her saddle and twisting herself around to better view her surroundings. "Ain't this Fast Run?"

Amazed at Cassie's knowledge of the terrain, Trace nodded his head. "Mmm, just a little way from the split in the gulch, if my guess is right." He nudged his horse forward.

Cassie followed automatically, bringing the gray alongside now that the trail was wider. "Then Noah oughta be jus' ahead."

No sooner were the words out of her mouth than the gravity of the situation hit her full force. If Noah had a been waiting where she'd told him to, Murieta's men could have ridden right over him!

The expression on her face told Trace her thoughts were the same as his.

As though controlled by one brain, they both looked back down the gulch for Noah's tracks. At the same time, they spied the tracks of a lone rider coming from the south, before blending into the tracks of the escaping outlaws. Because the tracks were all so fresh, it was difficult to determine which had gone up the trail first: the group of riders or the single horseman.

Without the need to commune their thoughts aloud, they moved in unison. Kicking their horses' sides and hitting their rumps, they headed up the trail at top speed.

They reached the meeting place in a matter of minutes and drew the heaving horses to a halt. Neither Trace nor Cassie spoke their fears aloud as they each raked a worried gaze over the area. Noah was nowhere to be seen.

Cassie studied the tracks leading up the left fork, and she quickly determined Murieta and his men had gone that way.

Of course, that didn't mean they had seen Noah. If he had reached the meeting place before the stagecoach robbers did, he might not have even been here when they came by. A ray of hope jumped in her chest. It was very possible Noah could have decided to go check the right fork! Her gaze shifted anxiously to the other trail.

The optimistic expression on her face soured, leaving her staring forlornly up the second trail. There were no tracks leading off to the right.

Panic and guilt froze in Cassie's heart. She had practically forced Noah to go off alone so he wouldn't slow her down. Now, because she'd been in such a hurry, he might have met up with Murieta and been killed. "Noah!" she shouted, her voice verging on hysterical.

"Come on, kid. He probably came along after Murieta's men. And when he noticed their tracks, he just decided to follow them a little way while he waited for you. In all likelihood, we'll meet him coming back this way." Trace hoped he sounded more convinced than he felt. If the gentle black man had met up with the robbers . . . Well, he wouldn't think about that yet.

Cassie glared at him, her bottom lip trembling. "You know that ain't true," she finally said. "Somethin's happened to him, or he'd been here like we planned."

Trace wanted to gather her into his arms and comfort her. But he instinctively knew the tough

162

Cassie Wyman would reject any show of sympathy on his part as an insult. Instead, he pretended not to notice her miserableness and started his horse forward, saying, "Well, there's just one way to find out which of us is right."

Keeping the horses to a slow walk so they wouldn't miss any clues to the whereabouts of Noah Simmons, Cassie and Trace followed the tracks up the gully as far as Round The Hill Road, which was the main route between the mining camps of Ruff Diggins and Drexell. But by the time the sun began its descent, they still had found nothing to indicate what had happened to Noah, and they were forced to retrace their tracks to the meeting place on Fast Run Gulch.

"We're sure gonna feel dumb when we find him there waitin' for us," Cassie said with forced gaiety as they approached the fork in the mountain gap. "Noah prob'bly come along after we was there. Those tracks we seen might not 'a even been his!"

Trace smiled at her attempt to keep her own hopes up, but he didn't say anything.

By the time they reached the meeting place, it was nearly dark, but not so dark they couldn't immediately see that Noah wasn't there.

Cassie sagged in her saddle, her expression numb. "What're we gonna do now?"

"We might as well try to get some rest. We can't do much tracking in the dark. And who knows? He might still show up. Once it got dark, he might have thought you weren't coming and found a safe spot to sleep."

"Do you really think so?" Her voice held such a desperate need for assurance.

163

"Sure I do. In fact, since it looks like Murieta's headed on up toward Drexell, we'll just light a fire so Noah can see we're here."

They ate their supper of cold biscuits and dried meat in silence, then leaned back against the rock wall that edged their campsite and gazed into the fire. Cassie looked up at the sky, where fast-moving curd-shaped clouds streamed across the heavens, blocking out the stars and moon and giving the night an eerie translucent light. She pulled her coat tighter around her. "Looks like rain."

Trace looked up at the moonless sky. "It could."

"Or it might jus' pass us by."

"The clouds are moving pretty fast. It wouldn't surprise me if it cleared off in a couple of hours."

"Did Noah tell you why gettin' his gold back is so important?" she suddenly asked.

Trace shook his head and waited for Cassie to tell him what she knew about Noah.

"I promise you, McAllister," she said when she had finished her story, "if those bastards killed Noah, I'm gonna hunt down every one of 'em 'n make 'em pay—if it takes me the rest o' my life." She swallowed back the lump she felt forming in her throat. "An' then I'm goin' to San Francisco 'n get them free papers for Salina 'n her ma. No matter what it takes!"

"Let's not give up on Noah yet, kid," he said, standing up and stretching. "I've got a feeling he's okay." He walked over to their gear and pulled out the two bedrolls, pitching one toward her. "We'll get some sleep, then look for him first thing in the morning."

Certain she wouldn't be able to sleep, but liking

164

the idea of at least lying down, after spending all day in the saddle, Cassie agreed with him. She unrolled the bundle and put her saddle at the head of it. When she had taken care of her personal bedtime necessities, she flopped down on the blankets and stared up at the clouds.

Trace put his blankets beside hers, deliberately placing himself in the line of fire to protect her from any unexpected visitors who might stumble onto their camp. "Are you cold?"

When she didn't answer, he rotated his head to the side to look at her. Her eyes were closed, her mouth slightly open, and her chest was rising slowly. Trace smiled and raised up on an elbow to reach for her other blanket to cover her up. Then he lay back down, rolled over onto his side facing the fire, his gun in his hand, and fell asleep for the first time in forty-eight hours.

Five hours later, something jerked Trace from his deep sleep, snapping his eyes open wide. Not moving, he tightened his grip on the gun handle and swept his gaze over the area. The fire had almost burned itself out, leaving only a few tiny embers glowing in a bed of ashes. With the exception of normal night sounds and the occasional crackle and sizzle from the dying fire, he heard nothing, saw nothing.

But something had awakened him. He suddenly became aware of the warm pressure enveloping him from behind. It ran the entire length of him, from his back, curling around his buttocks and flanks to the bend in his knees. It even formed a pleasant band of security around his waist. Lifting his arm cautiously to peek down at his midsection, he saw a woman's arm thrown over him, and a feeling of pleasure flooded him. Evidently, in her sleep, Cassie had sought out the warmth of his body.

Not wanting the sweet feeling to end but needing to shift his own position, Trace turned to his back slowly, taking care not to move out of Cassie's unintentional embrace. He worked his arm under her, securing her head on the curve of his shoulder and pulling her closer. Aware he was only causing himself unnecessary discomfort, he couldn't resist. It had been a long time since he had slept with a woman molded up against his side. And it felt good, so damn good. He glimpsed up at the sky, noticing the clouds had cleared away and that the star-studded sky was brilliant. Then his eyes drifted shut again.

Cassie squirmed in her sleep to snuggle closer to him. Her arm across his belly tightened and inadvertently slid lower on his body.

As if she'd dropped hot coals on his bare flesh, Cassie's touch scalded him. His body's reaction was immediate and swift, jarring him fully awake.

He lay very still, almost holding his breath in anticipation, as he waited for her hand to move lower still. But she didn't move it again, leaving it just beneath his belt, mere inches from the unbearably tight throbbing in his jeans. Unable to stop himself, he lifted his hips slightly against the pressure of her hand.

"How'm I s'posed to sleep with you doin' all that tossin' 'n . . . ?" The realization of the fact that her head was on Trace's shoulder, his arm wrapped around her with one hand resting just beneath her breast, hit Cassie like a clap of thunder, sending knowledge ripping through her. The placement of her own hand seared into her sleep-numb consciousness. "What the hell?" she gasped, yanking her hand back and bolting to a sitting position.

Feeling like a kid who'd been caught giving in to a natural curiosity about his own body parts, Trace sat up, his back to her.

"Well, whatta you got to say for yourse—"

Before he could think of a saving explanation for what had happened, he heard a low moan from up the trail.

"Shh," he whispered, holding up a hand to silence her. "Did you hear that?"

Immediately alert, Cassie cocked her head and listened. "I don't hear nothin'."

"I'm sure I heard something." He stood and started up the trail toward the sound.

"Wait up," Cassie whispered, snatching up her gunbelt and hurrying to catch Trace.

"You wait here," he ordered, not looking down at her.

"I ain't gonna wait. If there's somethin' out there, I aim to be there when you find it."

"Why can't you ever do as you're told, kid?"

Another moan, a bit louder, came from a stand of fir trees off to the side of the trail. "Noah?" Cassie hollered, breaking into a run toward the trees.

"Dammit, kid. Don't go in there!" But Trace's warning was too late. She was already ducking beneath the droopy limbs of a large evergreen.

"Noah!" he heard her exclaim. "What happened to you? How'd you get here?"

In the dome created by the long, ground-sweeping

167

boughs of the tree, only the familiar bulk of Noah's giant frame was discernible as he dragged himself to a sitting position.

Trace hurried under the tree behind her. "Are we ever glad to see you, my friend! You had us pretty worried."

"It's a long story," Noah answered with a forced smile.

Stooping to help prop him against the tree trunk, Cassie bent close to see if his wounds were serious. "Where'd they get you, Noah? Can you walk out o' here if we help you? Where do you hurt? What—"

"Hell, kid, quit asking him so many questions." Trace draped Noah's arm over his own strong shoulders and wrapped his arm around the injured man's broad back. "Let's get him back to the fire first." With a strained grunt, and a bit of help from Noah, Trace heaved the heavier man to his feet.

Holding her curiosity and concern at bay temporarily, Cassie hurried to wrap her arm around the large man from his other side. Together, the three of them made it back to the camp, and while Trace settled Noah on a blanket, Cassie quickly gathered more firewood to build up the fire. When she was done, she turned back to Noah and Trace.

"It looks like he just got his scalp creased," Trace said, already swabbing at the injury with a wet bandanna. "It doesn't look too serious."

Relieved, Cassie squatted down beside Noah and looked at him more closely. "Are you sure that's all it is?" It was then she saw the enormous swelling on his forehead just above his left temple. "What happened there?" She reached out and touched it, bringing a wince from Noah.

"When I got to the meeting place and you weren't here, I decided to investigate a little farther up the two forks."

Cassie and Trace looked at each other with *we were right* in their expressions, but neither of them said anything.

"I went a way up the left fork. But when I didn't find anything, I started back so I could go up the right trail. But before I got to the split in the ravine, I heard riders coming toward me. Since there were several of them and only one of me, it seemed like the best idea to hide out until I could figure out who it was." Noah grimaced as Trace laid the wet bandanna over the swelling on his forehead.

"I remembered seeing those trees," he went on, "so I hightailed back to them. If I'd been a minute faster, they wouldn't have seen me." He shook his head in irritation. "But just as I turned off the trail, they came on me. And believe me, they were in a powerful hurry—"

"That's 'cause we was right behind 'em!" Cassie interrupted. "But what happened? If you was in the trees, how'd you get shot?"

Noah smiled and nodded his head. "Just as I rode into the trees, they got off a couple of shots at me. I guess when I fell over in the saddle they thought they got me, because they didn't take time to check if I was dead or not. Anyway, as they rode on by I sat up and looked back over my shoulder to make sure they weren't following me. And just as I faced front again, something hit me in the head and I was thrown off my horse. That's the last thing I remember, except waking up a few times during the evening and night. I must have run into a branch with my head!"

"I don't suppose you saw if it was Murieta or not," Trace said, wanting to make certain that they were still on the right trail.

"It was him. I'd recognize that big black horse of his anywhere."

"Are you up to riding for a few miles? Drexell's not too far ahead, and I think it'd be a good idea to get a doctor to look at your head."

Noah nodded. "I can ride, but my horse is gone. Must have run off when I fell."

"If we don't find him, the kid and I will ride double and you can ride her horse—that is, if you're not too weak to stay in the saddle."

"I'll stay in if I have to be tied in. I don't want to let them get any farther ahead of us than they already are. When I think how close I was to them, it makes me sick. We had them trapped between us and I let them get away!"

"It ain't your fault, Noah," Cassie said. "You didn't have no way o' knowin' it was Murieta comin' at you, or that we had flushed him out."

"Still," Noah said, lumbering to his feet, the expression on his gentle face set and angry, "I'm not going to make that mistake again. The next time I see those mangy dogs, I'm going to take care of them once and for all!"

"You're not going to be taking care of anyone until a doctor examines that head of yours," Trace said.

"A bump on the head like you took could be serious, Noah," Cassie offered, her worry about the change in the gentle man evident on her face. "You let the doc take care o' your head, 'n then we'll

170

decide what to do 'bout Murieta."

"I don't need a doctor. What I need is my gold back. And the faster I get it the faster my head will be just fine!"

"Well, since it looks like Murieta and his crew were headed toward Drexell, it won't hurt to stop and get your head looked at anyway," Trace offered. He pursed his lips and whistled for his horse, who'd been set to graze nearby with Cassie's gelding.

As they began to stomp out the fire and pack their gear, the horses appeared in the clearing.

"Will you look at that!" Cassie pointed toward three horses rather than the expected two. "Your roan musta smelled our horses 'n gone lookin' for 'em."

"That's a stroke of luck!" Trace said, patting his bay happily before slapping the saddle blanket over his back. "Now we won't have to ride double."

Irritated by the obviously relieved tone in his voice, Cassie slung her saddle on her horse's back. "I wasn't lookin' forward to ridin' with you either, McAllister."

Trace glanced over his shoulder at the touchy girl who had her back to him. He opened his mouth to explain that he'd meant they could go faster if the horse wasn't carrying double, but thought better of it. He didn't owe her any explanations! "You could have fooled me," he said out of the corner of his mouth for her ears alone.

Cassie stopped what she was doing and glared back over her shoulder at him. His green gaze locked to hers, holding her prisoner and sending a wave of feeling rocking through her. "Wha—" She cleared her throat nervously and started again.

171

"Whadda you mean?"

"Just that I'd have thought you'd like the idea of riding with me," he said, turning his back to her to continue saddling his horse.

Cassie returned her concentration to her horse, bumping him in the side with her knee to get him to blow out the air he was holding in his puffed-up belly, and yanking up on the cinch strap at the same time. "Where'd you get a dumb idea like that?" she asked with a grunt as she bent to tighten the strap even more.

"The way you were all cozied up to me when I woke up a little while ago made me think you were pretty fond of being close to me."

The only sound Cassie could make was a wheezing intake of air as she dropped her hold on the cinch and straightened her posture. Sputtering for a rebuttal, she spun around to face his back. "That was a accident!" she finally managed to get out.

"Didn't feel like an accident," he taunted unmercifully, taking special effort not to laugh.

"Well, it was—'n you know it! If I'd 'a known what I was doin', it never woulda happened! An' you ain't much of a gentleman for mentionin' it, neither!"

"I'm *not* much of a gentleman," he corrected, giving in to the devilish mischievousness in him that was demanding to be set free.

She'd heard her mother expound too many times on the word *ain't* to not understand what he was saying. But she had no intention of letting Trace McAllister know it. "You're right 'bout that, McAllister! You *ain't* no gentleman a'tall! An' I'm gettin' mighty tired o' your company!"

Grabbing her reins, she walked her horse to the other side of the campsite before she resumed saddling him. As far as she was concerned, she couldn't be rid of McAllister soon enough. She would put up with him until they got Noah to the doctor in Drexell. But that was it. They were definitely going to part company there. She would make it clear that she didn't need a bossy know-it-all to find her gold for her—if that was what he really intended.

Finished with packing her gear and loading it behind her saddle, Cassie mounted and waited for Noah to do the same, making a deliberate point of ignoring Trace.

Noah took hold of his reins and placed a worn boot in the stirrup, then paused. Before he could go further, Trace came up beside him and steadied the larger man. "Better let me help. You might still be a little dizzy."

"Thanks. I'm sure glad you two joined up together. With the three of us looking for them, we ought to be able to sniff out those *bandidos* in no time flat." He grinned, and glanced from Cassie to Trace, who protested in unison.

"I'm only staying with you till Drexell, then I'm going on alone."

"He's only gonna be with us as far as Drexell, then we're goin' on alone."

Glaring at each other, neither of them seemed aware of the astonished expression on Noah's face.

"That doesn't make much sense," Noah said, glancing from one to the other. "If we're all going after the same people, why split up?"

" 'Cause we don't need some know-ever'thin'

173

polecat tellin' us how to get our own gold back!"
She nudged her mount's sides and led out.

Trace watched her go, then turned to Noah. "I've
got an ax to grind with Murieta, and I've been
looking for him for a long time. I don't intend to
let some hotheaded little spitfire make me lose him
again." He swatted his horse on the rump and
moved out, leaving a baffled Noah to bring up the
rear.

The closer they got to Drexell, the more difficult
it was to discern the outlaws' tracks from all the
others on the frequently used road between Ruff
Diggins and the wild mining town. And they became increasingly discouraged.

When they found a site where someone had obviously made camp during the night, their hopes were
rekindled temporarily.

First, Cassie found a dirt-smudged handkerchief
of fine Irish linen. But the three quickly agreed the
handkerchief could have been dropped by anyone
who had come along Round The Hill Road that
day. There was nothing about it that would indicate
it belonged to one of Murieta's men. In fact, it was
of such fine quality material, the possibility seemed
unlikely.

Then Trace found a fragment of paper that
turned out to be an article carelessly ripped from a
newspaper. It told about a new two-volume novel
called *Uncle Tom's Cabin* by Harriet Beecher Stowe,
who was advocating the end of the Fugitive Slave
Law of 1850. On the back was half an advertise-
ment for prospecting supplies from Burke's Mercan-

tile in Coloma.

"Hardly something a Mexican *bandido* would carry in his pocket," Trace said, his voice rough with disgust. "We might as well face it, there's nothing here that proves this was Murieta's camp. In fact, it probably wasn't. It could have belonged to anybody." He wadded the scrap of newspaper in a ball and tossed it to the ground.

And with that careless, offhanded action, their luck changed.

Interested in reading the newspaper article for reasons of his own, Noah bent to retrieve it. As he wrapped his fingers around the paper, his nails clicked against something hidden in the dirt. Certain it was just a rock, but curious, he brushed away the dust to investigate.

Noah's eyes rounded in surprise, then gleamed with understanding as recognition set in. A wide grin split across his dark face.

Picking his find up, he rubbed it on his pants leg, then raised his pleased gaze to Cassie and Trace, who were only watching him with half interest.

"Look," he said, holding out a hand, palm up with a shiny bit of metal at its center. "It's a silver concho—the kind Murieta wears on his trousers!"

"That proves they was here!" Cassie squealed, making a dash for her horse. "Let's get goin'. He ain't gonna get away from us this time!"

Certain the thieves had worsened their own odds by stopping to rest, the three elated riders traveled at a full gallop the remainder of the distance to Drexell.

Now, as they stood on the rough-plank porch outside the sheriff's office, they stared in disillusioned amazement at the scene before them, all their hopes violently shattered.

"What're we gonna do?" Cassie asked, her gaze scouring desperately over the hundreds of men who moved up and down the only street in the rough mining town.

One in four of the passersby was a Mexican! And at least half of those were outfitted in large sombreros and tight black trousers. Besides that, they all wore jangling silver ornaments on their clothes or horses' bridles—exactly like the one they had found on the trail!

The three hunters were hit unanimously by the sickening feeling of defeat. They had lost Murieta.

Chapter Eleven

Making no effort to hide the bleak despair that warped her perfect features, Salina stared woodenly at the woman in the cheval glass. She looked like one of the "fancy" women she had seen back in Roster when she'd been allowed to go to town with her mother on shopping trips before the old master had died.

Salina closed her eyes on the bittersweet memory, recalling the way her mother had reacted when one of those satin-wrapped trollops had sauntered across their path and called out to men in the street.

"Hmp," Lizbet would always say, tightening her mouth into a disapproving line and tilting her nose higher in the air. "Gettin' so decent folks ain't safe on the streets no mo'!"

Then she would catch up Salina's hand and whisk her off the sidewalk into the road, rather than chance having her precious child come in contact with one of the painted ladies. "Cain't be too careful 'round dat kind," she would invariably say. "No tellin' what a body might catch!"

"I think they're pretty, Mama," Salina had voiced more than once. But her mother's reply was always the same.

"Dey's trash! An' my baby ain't never goin' ta have nothin' ta do wit' dat kind o' trash. You is goin' to be a lady."

"Mama, I can't be a lady," Salina would protest. "I'm not white."

"You hush dat kind o' talk, girl. Why do you think your daddy buys you all dem pretty dresses 'n' lets you learn your readin' an' writin' an' 'rithmetic right along with dat no good half brother o' yours? Your daddy done promised me when you is growed up he's goin' ta give you an' me our free papers. Den he's goin' ta buy us a nice little house in Atlanta 'n' set us up in our own dressmakin' business. An' you ain't never goin' ta have ta 'sociate wit' trash. My baby's goin' ta be able ta hold her head up every bit as high as dat uppity white wife o' yo daddy's!"

A lonely tear rose over the brim of Salina's eye and trickled down her cheek to splash on the exposed top of one breast. "But it was all talk, wasn't it, Mama?" Salina whispered to her reflection. "He didn't keep any of his promises, did he?"

"Pardonnez-moi," the puffy-featured woman kneeling on the floor beside Salina asked around the straight pins gripped between her teeth. The seamstress's fingers continued to pin a red satin ruffle to Salina's form-fitting dress at the knees.

As if noticing the presence of the seamstress for

the first time, Salina met the woman's eyes in the mirror. "I'm sorry, I wasn't listening."

Madame Felice—her name as phony as the French accent she affected—returned her attention to the ruffle. "You say something? You like the dress, *oui?*"

Salina nodded her head, knowing it would do no good to tell the woman what she really thought of the vulgar dress. The dressmaker hadn't become wealthy designing and making dresses for the most highly paid prostitutes and mistresses in San Francisco by worrying about what the women who wore them thought. It was the men who paid for the gaudy dresses whom she strove to please.

"The dress is fine," Salina said over a crack in her voice. "I'm certain my broth— I mean Mr. Hopkins, will approve," she told the woman. *It's garish and skintight. It exposes more of my breasts than it covers and it makes me feel naked. Cliff won't just approve. He'll love it! If only because he'll know how degrading it is for me to wear it!*

"But of course!" Madame Felice huffed, plunging a final pin into the ruffle and sitting back to examine her work in the mirror. "It is my most brilliant creation yet!"

Salina nodded her head, feeling as though she were seeing herself in the dress she would wear to her own funeral—for surely she would die if she had to wear it in public.

Oh, Noah! she cried silently, her vision blurring with tears that now streamed freely over her smooth brown cheeks. *Where are you? Why haven't you come back? Have you forgotten me?* She shook her

179

head vehemently. No, he hadn't forgotten. He would be here if he could. Something must have gone wrong. *Is that it, Noah? Has something happened to you? Has Cliff found a way to stop you from coming back?*

Then a crushing idea exploded in her mind, sending agony racking through her entire body. Cliff wouldn't be above having Noah killed to stop him from coming for her!

Oh, Noah! What have I done to you by putting my troubles on your shoulders? The guilt was more than she could bear, and she was no longer able to keep up any sort of facade for the dressmaker.

Covering her face with her hands, Salina rushed blindly from the room, the pain in her heart so excruciating she didn't hear the couturiere's indignant shrieks, nor feel the stabbing pricks in her knees as the pins holding the red satin ruffle in place pierced her tender skin over and over again.

"Someone musta seen them varmints come into town durin' the night," Cassie said, refusing to consider the possibility that Murieta hadn't even come to Drexell. "I say we get you to a doc, Noah. Then I'll start askin' questions 'round town. They're here somewhere. I feel it in my gut!"

"Forget the doctor. I'm fine. Let's check the stables first. Those thieves might be dressed like half the Mexicans in town, but they can't disguise that black horse. I'd be willing to bet there's not another one like it in the state. And if he's here, I'll—"

Suddenly, the effects of his injuries, and the fast

180

ride into town, caught up with Noah. Reaching out to steady himself against one of the posts supporting the porch roof, his eyes opened and shut sluggishly, and the expression on his face grew disoriented as he rocked back and forth where he stood.

Moving as one entity, Cassie and Trace closed in on Noah from either side, catching him around the chest just as his knees started to fold beneath him. "Tell us again how you don't need no doctor," Cassie said, her harsh tone failing to disguise her worry as they eased him down to a bench and waited for his dizziness to pass.

Releasing his hold on Noah, Trace straightened his back and cast a glance up and down the rutted street at the signs on the false-fronted buildings and tents that lined the thoroughfare. "Stay with him, kid," he finally said. "I'll go get the doctor."

"I can't stay here. I've got to find my gold," Noah objected, trying to stand back up. "I've got to . . ." But he immediately realized the futility of his efforts and was forced to surrender to his weakness. Defeated, he sat back down and leaned forward, his elbows propped on his knees. Holding his forehead in his hands, he swayed his body from side to side. "It's no good, Salina. He's beat me."

At a loss for words, Cassie sat down beside Noah and rested a consoling hand on his shoulder. Together they waited, each lost in his own worried thoughts.

Trace was back quickly with a frowning man who carried a leather saddlebag slung over one of his narrow shoulders. "Look, mister, I got reg'lar office

181

hours. And I don't take too kindly to bein' hauled outta my poker game for no ni—"

The cocking of a revolver hammer sounded threateningly, cutting off the medic's voice before he could complete the word.

The doctor's head jerked up, bringing him eye to eye with a tall young woman in a man's overcoat. Sweat popping out on his forehead, his gaze fell to the barrel of the Colt .45 aimed straight into his stomach.

"You was sayin'?" Cassie asked.

The physician continued to stare horrified at the weapon only inches from his middle. "I . . . uh . . . didn't mean nothi—"

"Just fix 'im up," Cassie ordered with a disgusted grunt, stepping aside so the man could get to Noah.

It took only minutes for the doctor to bandage Noah's head and proclaim that he would be fine after a few days' rest.

Noah bolted up from the bench, shaking his head. "I don't need rest. I need to find my gold!"

"Maybe you better listen to the doc, Noah," Cassie said. "I'll go ask 'round town 'n' see if I can find anyone who saw Murieta. By the time you're rested up a bit, I oughta know enough to figger out our next move."

Noah protested, but he didn't fight it when Cassie and Trace guided him toward the stable behind the sheriff's office, where Trace had made arrangements for Noah to rent a bed.

Once they had the wounded man settled, Trace and Cassie walked back toward the center of town. "Where do you s'pose we oughta go first?" she asked him, forgetting for a moment that this was supposed to be the end of her association with Trace McAllister.

"*We're* not going anywhere, kid. I want you to check into that hotel over there, and wait for me to get back to you. I'll let you know if I find out anything."

Cassie stopped in the middle of the street and wheeled on Trace. "We already been through this, McAllister!" she said, her fists balled on her hips, her face shoved up to his. "You must think I'm right dumb if you figger I'm gonna stand by 'n' let you get your hands on my gold!"

Trace blew out an exasperated sigh. "I told you, kid, I don't have any designs on your gold! I just want Murieta. And I'll find him a helluva lot faster without worrying about you being hurt or getting in my way!"

"Then, you got no cause to worry, McAllister. 'Cause I can take care o' myself jus' fine! I don't need you lookin' after me. I can outshoot, outtrack, outride . . ." Cassie stopped talking, realizing Trace wasn't paying any attention to what she was saying.

She turned her head to see what he found more important than their conversation, but the only thing she saw where his gaze was focused was the back of a buggy disappearing down the alley beside the Lucky Lady Saloon and Theatre. "What is it? Did you see somethin'?" she asked, still studying the street. "Was it Murieta? One o' his men?" Her voice was an excited whisper.

Trace shook his head as if coming out of a trance and frowned down at her. "It was nothing."

"Whadda you mean, nothin'? You was lookin' awful hard at somethin'. What was it?"

"For a minute there, I thought . . ." Trace shook his head and gave a forced laugh. "Never mind, kid. It wasn't anything. I just thought I recognized—" His puzzled gaze darted back to the alley entrance again. "—an old friend."

Not satisfied with his answer and confused by his distracted mood, Cassie persisted. "What ol' friend?"

Trace didn't answer. He was already moving away from her toward the alley entrance. "Listen, kid, you go on and do what you've got to do," he said with a pat on the back. "I've got some things to take care of."

"What things?" She ran after him and caught hold of his arm. "I got a right to know where you're goin' if it's got somethin' to do with findin' my gold!"

Trace glanced down at the slender hand gripping his sleeve, and a tremor of temptation shook through him. Maybe he should tell her. After all, it might not be all that disastrous for them to work together to find Murieta. It could even work out for the best if he could put the energy he'd been expending to fight with her to a more constructive use. Besides, that way he could see that she stayed out of trouble.

No! a voice bellowed in his head. *Don't you see what you're doing? You're just looking for an excuse to stay with her longer. Somehow she's gotten under your skin and the only way you're going to get her out of your system is to have nothing to do*

*with her. She's trouble! And the sooner you're rid
of her, the better off you'll be!*

"This has nothing to do with you or your gold,
kid," he finally said. "This is personal business." He
shook off her hand and quickly strode away before
he could change his mind.

Hurt by the way Trace had left her for reasons
she didn't understand, Cassie stared after his broad,
retreating back. The memory of that same hard-
muscled back — without the shirt and jacket —
streaked across her mind, settling in a pressing need
deep in her womb. Her palms tingled and her fingers curled open and shut with the remembered feel
of her caresses on his bare back.

Determined to fight the all-too-vivid recollections
that suddenly assailed her thoughts, Cassie hugged
her arms across her middle and tightened them as
she watched Trace walk into the alley beside the
Lucky Lady.

Her eyes narrowed angrily. "You ain't foolin' me,
McAllister. I know what you're up to." She broke
into a run to follow. "You saw somethin' an' you
think it's gonna get you to my gold first!"

Just as Cassie neared the alley, she heard voices
coming toward her. Reacting automatically, she
ducked behind the rain barrel on the corner of the
mercantile store next door and waited. She immediately recognized Trace's rich laugh, deeper and more
melodious than the woman's throaty laughter that
joined his.

"Tell me, what brings such a delectable piece of
masculinity to Drexell, lovey," a woman's husky
voice drawled in a silky English accent.

185

Surprised, Cassie peeked around the rain barrel.

"Your reputation precedes you, my dear," Trace said in a teasing tone, exiting the alleyway with a tall, overly endowed brunette on his arm.

Garbed in a mauve-trimmed gray alpaca dress that blatantly displayed her generous proportions, the woman wore a showy flowered hat and high-heeled half boots that made her nearly as tall as Trace.

"Well, you've come to the right place to be entertained, ducks."

So that's why he was so all-fired anxious to get rid of me! Cassie realized, her temper flaring in self-defense against the stab of jealousy that cut into her soul.

More than curiosity dictating her actions now, Cassie stood up slightly and peered over the top of the rain barrel to see the woman's face.

Damn, that silly hat hides her face!

"I'm glad I didn't miss you," Trace said, smiling at the woman.

Cassie stood up straighter, glaring at the couple's back as they moved arm-in-arm down the sidewalk toward the front entrance to the Lucky Lady.

"You almost did," the woman answered. "Tonight is our last . . ." Her voice drifted out of earshot as Trace entered the saloon with her.

Cassie did her best to convince herself that what she was feeling was disappointment because he hadn't found a lead to her gold. Not jealousy! It made no difference to her what he did with his time. As long as he stayed out of her way. In fact, she was *glad* the woman would be keeping him "en-

186

tertained" for a while. It would give her a chance to find out if anyone had seen Murieta without worrying about him butting into her business and telling her what to do.

"An' as long as you've got your doxy to keep you busy, you won't be sneakin' off to steal my gold for a while," she said to the empty boardwalk where Trace had been a moment before.

So, why wasn't she relieved? Happy? Why was she so miserable?

Well, she resolved, forcing her gaze away from the swinging doors of the saloon, *I just won't think about 'im anymore!* He was a slimy, no-good womanizer, and she wasn't going to let him interfere in her life again. He was the past. A foolish mistake made when her defenses were down and she'd been fooled into believing he was a decent sort.

She stomped off the sidewalk and looked up and down the street, determined to exorcise the feelings that continued to gnaw at her vitals.

She decided to start with the stables as Noah had suggested. He had said there couldn't be two horses like Murieta's. So, surely if the horse was in Drexell, she would recognize it, even though she was no expert on horses. Then once she found it, she would simply wait for the horse's owner to show up and lead her to the gold!

However, after checking several stables and finding no black horses, except for a couple of short, scrawny ones that could never be mistaken for Murieta's mount, her optimism was at a new low. So, when she spied a barn behind the Lucky Lady, she approached it with little enthusiasm.

Cassie paused just inside the doors, giving her eyes time to accustom themselves to the darkness before exploring further.

After a moment, when she was able to make out distinctive shapes in the dark, she became aware of a large caravan-type wagon in the center of the barn. On closer examination, she discovered it was decorated with fancy scroll carvings and bright paintings. The sign on the side of the wagon read, *The Traveling Witherspoon Family, starring Mrs. Mimi Witherspoon and her four beautiful daughters.*

"An acting troupe," Cassie said to herself with a frown. Forgetting her vow not to think about Trace McAllister again, she immediately wondered if the woman she'd seen him with was Mrs. Witherspoon herself, or one of her "beautiful daughters."

"What diff'rence does it make to me?" she scolded herself irritably, turning to check the six horses stabled in the nearby stalls.

Not surprised to find that none of them matched the description of Murieta's horse, she turned to leave. Though she hadn't really expected to find the big black horse here, frustration weighed heavy on her, causing her shoulders to droop.

Just as she was about to step back outside into the sunshine, she heard a muffled whinny from the rear of the barn. She looked inside again, squinting as she tried to figure out which horse it was. All six were quietly munching hay from the cribs in their stalls.

Laughing at herself for grasping at straws, she again started to step outside.

This time, when she heard the horse, it was louder. She stopped dead in her tracks. Now she knew why he neigh sounded muffled. It was because the horse calling out to the other horses wasn't one of he stabled horses at all. It was outside, on the other side of the rear wall of the barn.

She told herself the fact that someone had left a horse tied behind the building, rather than in it, didn't mean anything. But she couldn't keep her face from unfurrowing into an animated grin. Breaking into a sprint, her long legs quickly carried her around the stable, to where the rough-sawed lumber structure backed up to the bottom of a cliff, with just enough room between the wooden and rock walls to comfortably conceal a horse and buggy.

Cassie stared in amazement at the horse harnessed to the black, two-passenger buggy before her. Of course she had *hoped* she would find Murieta's horse, but she hadn't really believed it would be so easy. Surely, her eyes were playing a trick on her. This couldn't be the same horse.

But it must be! she said to herself. *Noah said there couldn't be two like him in the whole gold country!*

She glanced nervously around her. What should she do? "I gotta tell someone!" she said, her brown eyes clouding with worry. *But who?* Noah was in no shape to take on Murieta right now, and if Drexell had a sheriff to go with its sheriff's office—which she knew was unlikely since most mining towns couldn't keep one for very long—there was no guarantee he could be trusted. That left only Trace

189

McAllister.

And he was in the Lucky Lady with that woman!

"Well, that's just too damn bad, McAllister! You'll jus' have to do your whorin' some oth—"

Cassie was aware of a rustle of movement behind her only a fragment of a second before a mind-splitting pain burst from the crown of her head to vibrate along her spine with bone-dissolving destruction.

Her last thought as she pitched forward under the buggy was, *Got to find McAllister.*

Trace relaxed back in the overstuffed chair in the curtained-off dressing room in the back corner of the Lucky Lady. Propping his boots on a wooden crate and crossing them at the ankles, he took a long pull on a brown cigarillo and blew out the smoke slowly. "I couldn't help noticing that fine piece of horseflesh you've got pulling your buggy, Mimi," he said, idly watching the smoke as it curled toward the ceiling.

The stately woman raked her eyes hungrily over her handsome guest, lingering overly long on the generous bulge where his trousers stretched across his lean hips. A shiver of desire rippled through Mimi's body. What she wouldn't give to have him buried deep inside her. "The finest piece I've seen in these parts," she answered hoarsely, her gaze never wavering from below his belt.

Aware of the woman's double entendre, Trace made no effort to hide himself from her view. If her attention was focused on more basic things than

190

horses, she might slip and tell him what he wanted to know if she thought he shared her interest. "I don't suppose you'd want to sell him to me?" he said, taking another puff on the cigarillo. "It seems a shame to have him doing a nag's job instead of being ridden."

Mimi smiled and raised her eyes to see if Trace's choice of words was deliberate. With a sultry trip around the rim of her lips with her tongue, she moved closer to him. "Oh, I couldn't sell him. He was a gift from an admirer." She sat down on the edge of the chair, her hip flush with Trace's.

A feeling of revulsion bolted through Trace's strong body. And it took every molecule of strength he could muster to keep from standing up and throwing the actress away from him when she placed her hand high on his thigh.

Mimi leaned over his chest and smiled, her face close to his. "But you taking a ride is open to discussion."

The cloying smell of Mimi's heavy perfume caused the contents of Trace's stomach to churn, and an intense sense of panic he couldn't understand stormed over him. He had to get away from her!

Catching Mimi by the upper arms, he gently removed her. "Nothing I'd like better, Mimi," he said, his tone strained. "But it wouldn't be fair not to tell you I'm recovering from a little itch I picked up south of the border."

Mimi sat back and studied Trace, not bothering to hide her disappointment, even though she knew she should be relieved he had stopped her before it was too late. She knew she didn't have time to deal with the complications it would have created if he'd accepted her offer. "Yes, well, thank you for telling me, ducks," she said, standing up and walking to the mirror to fluff her hair and straighten her hat.

"About the black," Trace said, afraid he'd destroyed his chances of getting any worthwhile information from her, but determined not to give up. "How long have you had him?"

"Just a few months. An admirer presented him to me as a gift for a particularly wonderful performance."

Possibilities began to whirl in Trace's mind. "I don't suppose your admirer was a Mexican, was he?"

Mimi laughed, a low throaty chuckle. "Of course not. He was from Germany. Short, fat, balding, and the only man who ever gave me anything without expecting something in return. So you can see why I couldn't bear to part with the horse." She stretched her lips into an insincere smile that didn't reach her hard blue eyes. It was obvious to Trace that she was anxious to be rid of him now that she'd discovered he wasn't here for what she wanted.

Seems like you could've thought of something a little less drastic to get her off you than to let her think you've got the clap, he told himself, seeing no choice but to leave. He stood and picked up his hat. "Well, if you change your mind . . ."

"I won't. But now that I think of it, the other day I saw a Mexican riding a mount that could have been the twin to mine. If you want a black horse so

192

much, why don't you find the Mexican and make an offer on his horse. Besides, it would be a better deal since that one's broken to a saddle and mine's only good for pulling a buggy."

Trace spun to face her. "You saw a Mexican on a black horse like yours! Why didn't you say so? When? Where?" His fingers dug urgently into the fleshy part of her arm.

Mimi's eyes widened, then glazed as she again let herself imagine for the briefest instant what being with the strong man would be like. Damn shame about his itch. The chance would almost be worth the risk. *But not quite,* she told herself, shrugging off the strong hands.

"I've seen him several times since I've been in Drexell," Mimi went on. "As a matter of fact, I saw him ride past the Lucky Lady with some other riders late last night when I was leav—"

"Which way were they going?" Trace asked anxiously. "Do you know if they're still in town?"

She shook her head. "They were riding fast. It looked like they were heading out of town on their way west toward the Iowa Hill Road."

"Thanks, Mimi," Trace said, giving her heavily made-up cheek a pat. "You've been a big help."

"Always glad to help," she replied. "And if you ever get that little problem of yours cleared up, I hope you won't forget to look me up."

"I'll do that," he called out, making a dash through the smoke-filled barroom.

"I'll be looking for you, lovey," she said, holding back the curtain with one hand and watching as Trace strode toward the swinging doors. "Maybe next time, you won't be in a position to refuse my offer," she said, taking one last longing glimpse of Trace's buttocks as he left the saloon.

"Noah, wake up!" Trace whispered, giving the sleeping man a shake.

"What's wrong?" Noah asked, his words slurred with sleep.

"Nothing's wrong! I just wanted you to know I got a lead! I found someone who saw which way Murieta and his pals were headed."

Noah came fully awake. "What are we waiting for? Let's go after them."

"Hold on there, big fella. Remember what the doctor said. You need your rest. Besides, you've got the hard job. If I'm going to catch up with Murieta, I need someone to stay here and keep the kid out of trouble—and out of my way. Think you can do that?"

"I don't know. She's pretty set on going after Murieta herself."

"Just stall her for a day or two."

"She's going to wonder where you disappeared to. What'll I tell her?"

"Tell her anything. Tell her you haven't seen me. Or that I went back to where we found the silver concho. Or . . . I know! She saw me go into the Lucky Lady with Mimi Witherspoon. Let her think I'm still in there. But whatever you do, don't tell her where I've gone. Because sure as you do, she'll be on my rear end like a hound on a bone, and she'll foul things up again."

"I'll do my best, but it's not going to take her long to figure out what's going on. And when she does, she's going to be madder than a wet hen."

"Hopefully, by then, I'll be back with *your* gold and *my* prisoners!"

"And if you're not?"

"Don't worry about that. You just keep her here. One way or another, I'll be back."

Knowing instinctively he could trust Trace McAllister, Noah nodded his head. "I'll keep her here."

The two men clasped hands and smiled at each other.

The moment of silence was interrupted by a feeble knock on the door, transforming their smiles into questioning expressions.

Dropping Noah's hand, Trace drew his .45 from its holster and stepped quickly to the door. Taking a deep breath, he wrenched it open.

"Party over, McAllister?" Cassie mumbled, taking one wavering step into the room, then pitching forward into his arms.

Chapter Twelve

Trace stared down at the unconscious girl in his arms, the feeling of helplessness so overwhelming that he couldn't move.

"Put her here," Noah ordered, standing up and indicating the bed where he'd been sleeping.

Guided by Noah's hand on his back, Trace lowered Cassie to the cot and quickly opened her coat.

As her head touched the pillow, her eyes opened slowly to gaze in confusion up into worried green eyes, framed by a thick fringe of black lashes. An automatic smile spread across her face. "Hello," she said.

Then she remembered her vow to have nothing further to do with Trace, and her welcoming smile wrinkled into a frown. Fighting him, she struggled to sit up. "What're you doin' here, McAllister?" she asked in an angry tone, lifting a hand to rub the back of her head. "Ooh," she said, flinching when her fingers touched the lump she found there.

"What am *I* doing here! Trace pushed her hand out of the way and turned her face away from him so he could examine the spot she'd just touched. He found a large knot, damp and sticky with blood, and his heart raced with concern. "What the hell kind of trouble have you gotten yourself into this time?"

Cassie fought to move her head out of his reach. "If you wasn't so busy womanizin' 'stead o' lookin' for Murieta, maybe this wouldn't 'a happened."

"Womanizing? What are you talking about? I wasn't womaniz—" His dark brows raised in sudden understanding. "Oh, yeah, I forgot. You saw me with Mimi Witherspoon, didn't you?"

"Damn right I did! An' you was womanizin' if ever I saw a man womanizin'!"

"I wasn't 'womanizing'!" he protested impatiently. "I was questioning her about Murieta. But no matter what I was doing, you had no business spying on me. You were supposed to go to the hotel and wait for me. Now, spit it out! What the hell happened?"

"While you was 'questionin' ' Miz Witherspoon," she said with a snippy edge to her voice, slapping his hand out of her hair as she spoke, "I was findin' Murieta's horse!"

"You found the horse?" Trace couldn't hide the excitement in his voice. "Where?"

"He hitched to a buggy 'n' hid back o' the stable behind the Lucky Lady."

The excitement slid off Trace's face, but Cassie didn't notice.

"But before I could get help, some varmint clobbered me. Guess it was one o' Murieta's boys who didn't 'spect me to get so close."

"Let's go!" Noah shouted, revived by his short rest and the good news. Grabbing up his gun, he headed for the door. "They can't have gone far."

Trace stood up, the look on his face grim. "I've got bad news for you both. That wasn't the same horse."

Puzzled, Cassie and Noah glanced at each other, then back to Trace. "What're you talkin' 'bout. I seen 'im with my own eyes. Noah said there can't be two of 'em!"

"Well, evidently there are. That one isn't even broken to a saddle. He belongs to the Witherspoon woman."

"She's lyin'. I'm tellin' you, it's got to be the same horse! Why else would they 'a bopped me on the head."

"Someone probably wanted to rob you," Trace said with a regretful smile. "You should know better than to go off alone. It happens all the time to luckless prospectors who aren't more careful. You should count yourself lucky, kid. Murieta's men probably would have killed you."

Cassie's face reddened with alarm, and she dug her hands into the inside pockets of her coat. "Why, those no-good bastards. They got my money belt! Now I got nothin' left!"

Unsurprised, Trace nodded his head, but he had the good sense not to say *I told you so* or to point out the fact that if she'd done as he told her, she would still have her money belt. Instead, he chose to give her the one bit of good news he had. "I did

198

find out that a Mexican on a big black horse passed through town last night. So at least we know we're on the right trail."

"Then, what're we waitin' for? Let's go after 'em. We're wastin' time here!" Anger serving as the fuel for her energy and a momentary deadener for her headache, Cassie swung her boots over the side of the cot. But when she tried to stand, she couldn't. Her head swimming crazily, she collapsed back onto the bed.

"You're in no shape to ride, kid. I'll go after them alone and get back to you. Anyway, I have a better chance of catching them unaware if I'm by myself." Trace turned to leave.

"McAllister! You come back here!" She made a feeble attempt to pull out her Colt. "You ain't got no right to . . ." she started, unable to finish her order before slipping helplessly into oblivion.

Trace fought the desire to go to her. She really was something. A fighter. Like no other woman he'd ever known.

She'll be fine, he told himself. *Noah will take care of her. And it isn't as if I won't be back in a couple of days. It's for her own good I'm leaving her behind!*

"Keep an eye on her, Noah," he said hoarsely, ripping open the door.

"I'm going with you," the man said.

"Admit it, Noah, you're not ready to ride yet. And Cassie was right about one thing. We've already wasted enough time. Today's already over half gone as it is. Besides, we can't leave her here alone," he added sensibly. "And if I wait until

199

you're both ready to ride, we might lose them."

His own temporary surge of regained strength already beginning to wane, Noah nodded his head in resignation. "I'll stay," he said, sitting back down before he fell down.

Trace rode toward Iowa Hill slowly, his gaze focused on the ground as he tried to concentrate on picking up Murieta's trail. But no matter what he thought about, he couldn't get his mind off Cassie for more than a moment at a time. Every time he succeeded in putting her from his thoughts, she walked right back in—until finally he gave it up as a lost cause.

The fact was, he couldn't stop feeling guilty about leaving her behind, broke and injured. And he couldn't stop worrying about what she would do without him there to keep her out of trouble. Of course, Noah was with her. But that fact did nothing to ease Trace's mind. As big as he was, Noah was just as much a babe in the woods as Cassie. Anyway, what if Noah's injuries gave him trouble and he couldn't do anything for her? Who would take care of her then? Though Noah had seemed to be on the mend when they had parted, he could have a relapse any time. Or what if that lump on Cassie's head was more serious than he'd realized at first?

A million terrible things could happen to her. And every one of them played on his morbid imagination—in vivid, gut-wrenching detail.

She could be thrown from her horse again if she

tried to follow him—which he had no doubt she would do the instant she could get up. Or she could have a run-in with another rattlesnake. Or she could get lost. Or have her horse shot out from under her by Indians! Or what about the thousands of woman-hungry men who roved the gold country? What chance would she have against a gang of them?

Trace sat back in the saddle and reined in his horse. Twisting around, he studied the trail over his shoulder, cursing himself for a fool the whole time.

"Don't do it, McAllister," he warned, whipping around to face front again and nudging the horse forward. "She'll be fine. As long as she's got her gun, she can take care of herself better than most men."

But what if she loses her gun? a pessimistic voice in his head asked. *Or forgets to load it? Or someone gets the drop on her?*

A picture of Cassie blundering into Murieta's hideout and trying to take them alone flashed across his mind.

"Damn!" he spat, again pulling his mount to a halt. Shaking his head in disgust, he allowed himself another indecisive look back toward Drexell.

"No!" he insisted after a long moment of deliberation. "I'm not going back! I'm not going to lose Murieta again because of her interference. If she's stupid enough to try to take him, then let her! I'm not her keeper!"

His decision made, he sank his heels into the bay's sides with a vengeance, determined to put as many miles as possible between himself and Cassie

Wyman.

"Whatdda you mean, I can't leave?" Ignoring Noah, Cassie stood up and snatched her holster off the bedpost. "Just you try an' stop me. You might be dumb enough to fall for that hogwash McAllister's been handin' you 'bout findin' our gold for us. But I ain't! He jus' told you he'd be back to give hisself a better head start."

"But, he prom—"

"Promise don't mean nothin' to his type. He jus' says whatever it takes to get what he wants. It wouldn't surprise me one bit if he ain't already found our gold 'n' headed for San Francisco to spend in." She jerked her Colt and spun the cylinder to check it for readiness. "Fact is, now that I think on it, it wouldn't be no shock to me to find out he's the snake who hit me on the head and stole the rest o' my gold."

Noah shook his head. "You've got Trace McAllister all wrong, missy. He's a good man. He wants to help—"

"That'd be why he was so stymied when I showed up here," she went on, as though Noah hadn't spoken. "He pro'bly figgered me for dead. But he didn't count on my hard head. When I catch up to that yellow-bellied snake, I'm goin' to—"

A loud crash outside the door cut off Cassie's threat. She and Noah froze, staring at the door.

"All right! You win!" Trace burst into the room, his face dark with anger. "But we're going to get one thing straight from the beginning . . ."

202

"I told you he'd be back!" Noah said excitedly to the stunned girl who stared openmouthed at the scowling man filling the doorway. "I told her you wouldn't let us down," he said to Trace.

"I've decided we'll go after Murieta together," Trace went on, his eyes on Cassie. "But *I'm* in charge! You got that, kid? *I'm in charge!*" He narrowed his eyes to slits and bored his gaze into hers. "The first sign of trouble and I'm sending you back to town."

Cassie didn't answer. She was too astonished. What was McAllister doing here? Why would he give up several hours' lead time to come back?

Was it possible he'd been telling the truth all along and that he really wasn't trying to steal their gold for himself? Or . . . a spark of hope flared in Cassie's heart. Could he have come because he was worried about her?

Before it could ignite into a full flame of trust, Cassie immediately squelched the idea that Trace McAllister had come before she meant something to him. She shook her head firmly, the instinct for self-protection rising in her and hardening the expression in her eyes.

Whatever his reason for returning, she knew it was because he had something to gain, not to help her.

"What's the matter, McAllister? Did you get lost?" she asked snidely. Holstering her weapon, she turned away from him to retrieve her coat.

Trace released that funny little growl she'd come to associate with him, the one she didn't think he was even aware of. "I should have known better than to waste my time," he said. "It serves me right for thinking you might show a little gratitude."

Cassie's eyes bulged. "Gratitude?" she yelled, whirling around to face him again. "For what?"

"For caring about you!" he answered without thinking. "For giving a damn whether one of your hotheaded stunts gets you killed or not."

His words hung in the air between them for several long silent moments, catching both Cassie and Trace off guard with their disclosure.

Dumbfounded, Cassie was suddenly without a rebuttal. He had said he cared about her. The spark of hope she'd tried to douse exploded into a tiny flicker of excitement. Of course, she knew his words weren't exactly a declaration of undying love—or even "like," for that matter—but she couldn't stop the tiny smile that played at the corners of her mouth. "You care 'bout me?"

Trace hadn't meant to say that, but now that he had, he was forced to review his words to try to deny them one at a time. Did he care for her? No! Of course not! Well, he cared, but not any more than he would care about any human being.

So why weren't you just as worried about Noah as you were her? that damned nagging voice in his head asked.

I was worried about Noah! I was worried about both of them! he argued with himself.

Be honest, McAllister. Noah never really crossed your mind, except for what he could do for her. He needs you as much as she does. Maybe more. At least she knows the country. He doesn't even have that going for him.

204

A sheepish grin curled across Trace's mouth, which he quickly replaced with a harsh frown. "Sure, I care," he admitted gruffly.

"I'll go check on the horses," Noah, who they'd both forgotten, interrupted, making an exit before either Trace or Cassie could think to stop him.

"Why?" Cassie asked Trace, her eyes glittering more gold than brown with anticipation. Letting her coat slip from her fingers to the floor, she took an unconscious step toward him.

Uncomfortably aware of the way the plaid shirt stretched tightly over her breasts as they rose and fell with each of her breaths, Trace realized the small room had grown unbearably warm. He wished she'd wear her old baggy shirt and pants again. Or at least put her coat back on!

Trace wiped the back of his wrist over his upper lip. "Well . . . uh . . . You're not a half-bad tracker . . ." He improvised, not conscious of the way his upper body slanted toward her. "You might be some help."

Her smile faltered. "Is that the only reason you come back? 'Cause I'm a good tracker?"

His gaze wandered unwillingly to her lean, denim-encased hips at the tops of long coltish legs. And his body ached with the memory of those hips moving beneath his, those legs, tangled with his. "You're . . . uh . . . pretty good with a gun." His voice was a hoarse croak. "That could come in handy."

Disappointment flooded through her. She'd been right. He had just realized he couldn't go after Murieta alone. The only reason he cared if she lived or died was because he needed her gun and tracking talent. Her gaze dropped from his, but her feet stayed rooted to the wood floor.

The hurt expression that had dulled Cassie's dark eyes knifed ruthlessly into Trace's heart, and the only thing he could think of was removing that injured look from her face. Acting with an instinctive will of its own, his hand lifted and lay along her cheek.

"And I wanted to see your smile again," he said softly, caressing his thumb over her lips as though drawing the smile back on her face.

Her surprised glance raised to blend and lock into his green eyes. "My smile?" she asked, hypnotized. Her mouth twitched into an embarrassed, disbelieving grin.

Trace nodded, beyond rational thinking now. He caught her other cheek in his free hand and held her face between his palms. "It was the first thing I noticed about you."

"Honest?"

"Honest," he answered, bending his head to bring his mouth within inches of hers. "You smile with your whole face. It's the kind of smile that can light an entire room and make a man feel warm all over."

Cassie leaned forward and raised up on her toes, moving even closer to his magnetic presence. Her gaze a willing prisoner of his, she parted her lips in an unstudied invitation. "I ain't been smilin' much the last coupla days, have I?"

A touch of sadness clouded Trace's eyes. "I know, kid. And I'm sorry. I guess that's the real reason I came back. It's my fault you quit smiling—because of what happened back in Auburn. It never should have happened. But it did, and I can't erase the fact that it did. But I can at least make sure you're not hurt again. I owe you that much."

Her eyes flitted to his mouth, only a scant inch from hers now, then back up to his eyes, her expression injured. Was he saying that he was sorry the most magnificent night of her life had happened? The fact made a jagged rip in her heart.

"You don't owe me nothin', McAllister," she bit out. "I don't hold no grudge for what happened. So, if that's the reason you—"

Trace's mouth closed over hers before she could tell him she didn't want him to stay. And a feeling of relief, so warm, so absolute, washed over her. Thank God he had stopped her before she could send him away!

Without a moment for second thoughts, she stepped closer, wending her arms around his neck and returning his kiss. Her heart danced with the feeling of coming home, and she wondered how she could have lived for the past two days without his kiss—how she had lived her whole life without him, for that matter. It made no difference why he had come back. He had, and that was the only thing she knew. That, and the fact that she was where she belonged.

Moving his mouth hungrily over hers, Trace wrapped his arms around her waist, crushing her hard against him. Though her mouth yielded willingly under his fiery possession, she was not docile. Instead, she pressed her mouth greedily against his, meeting his tongue with hers time and again in an erotic duel for dominance.

Her knees weakened and she sagged against him, her head beginning to swirl crazily. "Ooo," she sighed, burying her face in the curve of his neck when the kiss ended, and planting a series of small pecks along the strong column of his throat. "I figgered it was the champagne that made me so dizzy the other night," she said with a smile against his skin, skin that was rough with the dark stubble of day-old whiskers and pricked her lips in a pleasant reminder of the differences in their bodies.

Disgusted with himself that he'd let his desire assume control of his actions again, Trace stepped back to look down at Cassie, his apology written in his expression. She smiled up at him. His heart turned over in his chest. "Look, kid," he said, unable to resist basking in the warmth of her infectious grin for just a moment more before he pushed her away from him. "I didn't mean for that to happen."

Happiness spilling through her veins, Cassie's smile broadened. "Me neither, McAllister. I figgered next time we met up we'd be shootin' at each other!"

"Shooting at each other?" he said, astonishment on his face. "You didn't really think I would ever shoot you, did you?"

Ashamed to admit that she had thought he was responsible for hitting her and stealing the last of her gold, Cassie smiled guiltily and shrugged her shoulders. "To tell the truth, I didn't figger on givin' you the chance before I shot you."

"And now?"

An impish smile split across her face, disclosing her sudden good mood. Suddenly, everything was going to be all right. "Now, I figger I'll give you a chance."

Relief spread across his worried brow, and he returned her smile. "So, have we got a deal? Are we going to team up and go after Murieta together?"

Cassie stepped closer and lifted her face for another kiss. "We got a deal."

Trace lowered his head, bringing his mouth close to hers in the automatic response of a thirsty man to water. But good sense and conscience brought him up short. If they didn't stop, there was going to be a repeat of the other night. He couldn't let that happen. Cassie Wyman was definitely the type of girl who would take making love again as some sort of commitment. As much as he wanted her, he had no intention of getting involved in a situation where he'd be trapped into making that commitment to any woman.

"If we're going to be partners, there can't be any more . . . of that," he said stiffly, every cell in his body screaming out in protest as he shoved her away from him with superhuman resolve and turned his back on her. Damn her! Why'd she have to look at him that way? He couldn't bear to see that hurt in her eyes!

Cassie stared at Trace's back in astonished surprise for several seconds before she was able to regather her composure. "What's the matter, McAllister?" she asked, her tough-woman facade in place again. "You 'fraid I might think a coupla kisses meant we was gonna get hitched?"

209

Startled by her ability to know what he was thinking, Trace turned to study her, his expression guilty. "What makes you think that?"

Their gazes locked for a long moment. Then Cassie had to break away. It was that or cry. And she'd die before she'd let him know how much his rejection had hurt. She stooped to retrieve her coat from the floor, speaking as she did, though she didn't look at him. "Don't worry 'bout it. McAllister. I ain't got no 'designs' on you or no other man. An' when I do get a itch to go to the parson with a feller, it ain't gonna be with no driftin' bounty hunter like you."

Surprise at her words overriding the twinge of wounded ego that contracted in his chest, Trace frowned. "You think I'm a bounty hunter?"

"Well, ain't you?" She stabbed her arms into her coat, desperate to hide her vulnerable femininity beneath its bulk and ugliness.

Trace thought for a moment. Maybe he should go on and tell her why he was so determined to be the one to bring Murieta's reign of terror to an end. It might help her to understand why he didn't want anything — or anyone — to get in his way.

No, it would only complicate things, he told himself. The less she knew about him, the less chance there would be for her to get caught up in some young girl's romantic notion that their physical desire for each other was anything more than just that.

Trace nodded his head and turned toward the door. "Yeah. And bounty hunters prefer to travel alone."

"Then, why'd you decide to team up with me 'n Noah after all?"

"I decided I was better off knowing where you were and what you were doing than I was riding with one eye on the trail ahead of me looking for Murieta and the other over my shoulder waiting for you to pop up behind me." He wrapped his hand around the door latch and stared unseeing at it.

"That's the only reason I said I'd go with you too!" she lashed out at his back, glad he couldn't see the tears that blurred her vision. "So I could keep a eye on you!"

"Yeah, well . . . As long as we both know where we stand, we ought to get along fine." He plucked open the door, hesitated a moment, then turned back to face her. "By the way, kid, that stuff about your smile . . ."

Please! Don't let him take that back too! "I know. It was just talk. I knew all along you was funnin'. You didn't think I believed you, did you?"

Fighting the urge to cross the room and grab her by her stiffly erect shoulders and spin her around so he could hold her one more time, Trace said, "I was going to say, I meant what I said. You do have a pretty smile. And one of these days the right man is going to come along and he's going to be knocked out flat by it — and by you."

Cassie's shoulders sagged slightly, then straightened as she won the battle over her emotions. "Whadda you want from me now, McAllister?"

Trace took a deep breath and exhaled it slowly. "Nothing, kid. I just wanted everything to be straight between us before we set out."

211

"Far as I'm concerned, it's straight. You want Murieta and the reward money, and I want my gold back; and we're gonna be a team for as long as it takes to get the job done. Then we're goin' our separate ways. That 'bout cover it?"

"Yeah, that covers it," Trace said, unable to understand the reason for his disappointment in her easy agreement to their new arrangement.

"Then, let's hit the trail so we can get this partnership over with as soon as we can."

"We'll leave when we've all had a decent meal and a good night's rest."

"Why wait till tomorrow? We still got at least a hour o' daylight left. We already give Murieta more lead than we should."

"Don't forget who's in charge, kid. And I say we'll leave in the morning. Besides, I've got a feeling Murieta didn't go too far. He's probably holed up somewhere on the road to Iowa Hill. From what I saw, too many stagecoaches and freight wagons use that road for him not to hit again before he leaves the area."

"All the more reason to go after him today."

"Come on, kid. Let me get you settled in the hotel. Then after I get a bath and a shave, we'll all go have a nice steak dinner."

"You musta forgot, McAllister. I ain't got no money!"

"This one will be on me, kid. And while I'm getting my bath, I want you to go buy yourself some different britches—and maybe a couple of new shirts. Some like you were wearing when I first met you might be better."

"What's wrong with my britches? They're brand new."

"Brand new or not, get some different ones. I don't intend to spend the next few days fighting off every female-starved male in these parts."

Chapter Thirteen

By noon, the temperature was increasing rapidly and the three riders traveling southwest on the road to Iowa Hill had begun to feel the heat of the glaring sun. When she could stand it no more, Cassie blew out a defeated sigh and took off the new, wide-brimmed hat she'd bought with Trace's money, and waved it in front of her face. Though the hat stirred a slight draft, it wasn't enough to bring any relief. Setting it back on her head, she shrugged out of the new gray overcoat she'd purchased at the general store next to the Lucky Lady. It was perfect for cool nights, but right now it was too heavy. Carefully folding her new possession, she twisted around to tie it with her other gear behind her saddle.

Just as she was finishing her efforts, a shiver tripped unexpectedly up her spine. Someone was watching her! Goose bumps popped out on her arms. She could feel eyes on her as surely as if she'd been physically touched by someone's hands. Controlled by the compelling energy that bored into her, her head jerked up, bringing her gaze level with angry green eyes that glared at her with unrelenting ire.

Cassie raised her chin defiantly and affected a look of innocence. "What's the matter with you, McAllister? Don't you like my new coat?" Of course, she knew the answer to her question, but she had no intention of admitting it.

Trace rode his horse alongside hers and spoke out of the corner of his mouth so Noah, who'd gone on ahead, couldn't hear. "The coat's fine, but I told you to get new britches and shirts that didn't flaunt your every . . ."

Cassie grinned daringly. "Every what?"

"Don't bat those eyelashes at me, Cassie Wyman. You know exactly what I'm talking about. Why didn't you spend the money I gave you like I told you to? Those pants you're wearing are entirely too tight. As a matter of fact, they're downright indecent! They make you look like a . . . like a . . ."

"A female?" she asked, her sandy-auburn eyebrows raising as she completed his statement. "That the word you're lookin' for, McAllister?"

Trace sputtered helplessly, then cursed. "Dammit, kid! Don't you know what seeing you in those pants will do to men?"

"I don't see they done nothin' to you—'cept maybe make your normal ugly mood even uglier," she said, deliberately baiting him with a wiggle of her bottom in the saddle.

There it was again: that low, almost indiscernible growl that signaled to Cassie she was getting to him.

"My mood's not the question here, kid!" he snarled, his color deepening.

"Then, what is, McAllister?" She leveled her hard

215

gaze on him, enjoying the uneasiness he couldn't disguise. "What 'xactly don't you like 'bout these britches?"

"It's not the pants!"

"But you said—"

"It's the way you look *in* them!"

"How *do* I look in 'em?"

"Like a female, dammit!" he grumbled irritably. *A desirable, beautiful female,* his inner voice protested as his eyes inadvertently dropped to the place where denim-hugged thighs separated to wrap intimately around her saddle. A surge of painful longing cramped in his groin. His fingers squeezed with knuckle-whitening tenseness on the reins, setting his horse to a nervous, sidestepping prance.

The horse's sudden skittishness forced him to realize what he was doing, and he relaxed his grip slightly, though he continued to bite down on the inside of his lip in a herculean display of restraint.

"Well, that's what I am, McAllister. You was the one who told me in Auburn that I didn't look or 'smell' like one 'n' that I should stop tryin' to be a feller. You need to make up your mind."

"That was before I . . ."

Cassie's breath caught in her chest. She'd been deliberately goading him, wanting to repay him for his rejection. But suddenly she was overwhelmed by a need to hear him admit he was sorry he'd put an end to what had started between them the day before in the back room of the barn. She wanted to hear him say he wanted her—just so she could tell him she was no longer interested and that he was too late, of course. "Before you what?"

Hating himself for his inability to stave off the attraction to Cassie that had plagued him almost

216

from the beginning, Trace moved his gaze hungrily over her from the crown of her new hat to the shiny toe of a new riding boot, lingering overlong on her breasts that pushed temptingly against the fabric of her blue-checkered shirt.

His eyes widened in alarm and he felt as if his own temperature were on the rise. He could swear he saw her nipples harden and thrust outward under the heat of his gaze. Clearing his throat, he squirmed uncomfortably in his saddle and wiped the sweat from his upper lip with the back of his wrists. Then, using every ounce of self-denial he could muster, he dragged his gaze away from the tempting sight.

This was ridiculous. He was acting like a teenager about to explode just from looking at a picture of a naked woman. How Cassie Wyman dressed shouldn't make any difference to him, he told himself sternly. *And it doesn't!* he maintained with resolve.

Then a wave of self-disgust rocked over him as he faced the truth. It was true. What she wore really made no difference to him. She still got to him. He still wanted her like no woman he'd ever known. Even the baggy overcoat she'd worn all morning hadn't made him able to forget what was under it, hadn't been enough to blot out the memory of the way her slim curves fit so perfectly against the harder, more angular planes of his body.

Seeing that Cassie was still waiting for his reply, he scrambled for an excuse. "Before I . . . uh . . . Before I said we'd be partners until we catch Murieta," he said, spitting out the words defensively, still refusing to look at her.

"Know why I figger you're makin' such a *conbob-*

beration 'bout my britches, McAllister?" she asked, her voice taunting as she deliberately used prospectors' slang to bait him.

"No, but I'm sure you're going to tell me." He pulled out his pocket watch and flipped it open, first studying it, then squinting up at the sun.

Undaunted by his obvious pretense, Cassie went on. "I figger you think I'm right *ripsniptious* in these britches. An' it's givin' you a fair case o' the *peedoodles* thinkin' some other feller's liable to come 'long an' like lookin' at me in 'em—as much as you do," she added with a deliberately testing rise to her voice. "That's it, ain't it? You're nervous as a long-tailed cat under a rockin' chair 'bout my britches 'cause you're scared some other feller's gonna beat your time with me!"

Stunned by how close her observation was to the truth, he shoved his watch back into his vest pocket and pretended to survey the surroundings. "That's the most ridiculous thing I've ever heard," he said with a forced laugh. "What you wear and how you look in your clothes is no concern of mine," he went on in a strained tone of pretended boredom. "I just don't want to be attracting every horny male in these hills when I'm trying to concentrate on finding Murieta and your gold. Three *men* riding together won't draw any special attention. But the minute someone sees we've got a female with us—a young, pretty one at that—they'll be all over us like flies on honey."

Cassie's heart did a flip in her chest. Trace had just said she was pretty. Maybe he really did like her! Then she thought about what he'd said, and her heart dropped with a thud to the pit of her stomach.

His reason made perfectly good sense, she had to admit, and it had nothing to do with liking her. But damn, it hurt to realize he was just being practical and wasn't in the least bit jealous of other men who might like her—or who she might like better than him.

"Well, whatever the reason, I can't do nothin' 'bout it now. I pitched out my old duds before I left Auburn. All 'cept the coat, 'n' I got ridda it before we left Drexell. These new jeans 'n' shirts're all I got with me. 'Cept the dress you bought me, o' course. But I don't figger it'd be much good for hidin' the fact that I'm a female, do you?" Her tone carried more than a tinge of bitterness.

"You can put the coat back on."

"Too hot."

"I've got an idea!" More concerned with protecting himself for the rest of the day from the tempting view of her round bottom molded to the saddle than he was about who else might be treated to the same view, he shucked his vest and hurriedly unbuttoned his own shirt.

"What're you doin'?"

"I'm giving you the shirt off my back," he answered with a sarcastic chuckle as he shrugged out of it and shoved it toward her. "Here, put it on. It'll fall past your fanny and make the truth less obvious—at least from a distance."

Cassie stared at the outstretched forearm, tan and corded with muscles beneath a sparse dusting of dark hair. Unable to stop herself, she moved her gaze along the rock-hard contours of his biceps to the bulging curve of his shoulder. Mesmerized, her study roved over and along his shoulder in a lazy caress that moved hungrily down his broad chest, which glistened with a sheen of a perspiration that made the swirls of black hair covering it flatten and separate in damp curls. Remembering the salty taste of his skin, her tongue flicked out to wet her dry lips, and her knees tightened inadvertently around the horse's barrel in an instinctive response to the ache that settled deep and heavy between her thighs.

"I can't wear your shirt," she protested, her voice not much stronger than a hoarse whisper. "What'll you wear?"

He wondered again how he'd ever thought for the briefest instant that she wasn't a woman, or that she wasn't particularly good-looking—when just the opposite was true. Flushed as she was now from the heat, she was the prettiest, most feminine woman he'd ever seen—or wanted. And a whole new storm of reaction was set off in his body. He had to look away. "You said it yourself. It's hot. I'll be fine. When we stop to rest the horses, I'll get another one out of my pack."

Unable to think of anything else to say, Cassie reached out to grasp the shirt. Her fingers accidentally grazed the edge of Trace's hand, and a shock of electricity stormed up her arm, setting every cell in her body ablaze with light. As though their hands were magnets irresistibly attracted, their flesh stayed in contact longer than necessary, actually strained toward each other.

It was Cassie who finally managed to break the connection. "Thanks," she said, barely aloud, the breathy voice she heard unfamiliar to her ears.

"It's nothing."

Cassie noticed his voice didn't hold its usual deep steadiness either. But she was sure it was her imagination. Her hearing was obviously distorted by the thrum of blood in her ears.

Holding the shirt up to herself with the intention of slipping it over her own shirt, Cassie was given no reprieve from the relentless assault on her senses. Without warning, her nostrils were filled with the distinctive odor of bay rum and leather—the familiar scent of Trace McAllister.

Her head grew light. Like a starving man attacks a plate of food, her breaths came in rapid pants in an attempt to sate her desire for the masculine bouquet.

But her addiction to the tantalizing scent of him could not be satisfied with the short whiffs. Her lungs were screaming to be filled with the powerful masculine fragrance that clung to the shirt.

Inhaling, she gorged herself on his essence, drawing it deeply into her soul. She held her breath, determined to hoard his musky aroma in her lungs next to her heart, determined to keep it inside her until every cell in her body could be brought to life by its sweetness. But, alas, she had to free it. Begrudgingly, she released the air amassed in her lungs, blowing it out slowly.

"Are you all right, kid?"

Trace's words brought Cassie back to the present with a thud. She blinked her eyes and studied him for a moment, her expression drugged, her pupils so dilated that her eyes were more black than brown. "What?"

"Are you okay?"

Her mood mellow, Cassie snapped out of her daze with an embarrassed shake of her head. "I'm fine!" she protested angrily, poking first one arm and then the other into the sleeves of the shirt.

"For a minute there I thought you were about to pass out—"

She looked at him, her features hiding none of the longing she was feeling. "Trace . . . I was jus' . . ."

Trace studied her in surprise. It was the first time she'd ever called him by his first name. And he liked the sound of it on her lips. In fact, he realized with panic, he liked it a lot. A lot more than was good for him. "Just what?" he asked gruffly, his resolve tested to the limit.

His tone was the sobering blow that freed her from the intoxicating trance that had taken hold of her. Thank God, his disposition had saved her from making a bigger fool of herself than she already had. Cassie shook her head and concentrated on regathering her composure. Wouldn't he have howled if she'd finished telling him what she'd been thinking? Well, he'd never know now. Never know how close she'd come to telling him how she felt. Never know how she longed for him to touch her, hold her, kiss her, love he—

"Nothin'," she spit out with disgust. "I just felt kinda crazy for a second there. Musta been from the bump on my head."

"Yeah, that must have been it," he said, frowning inquisitively at her. Funny, her answer disappointed him. He'd obviously been reading something into her look that hadn't been there. And he was relieved to realize his mistake! Well, wasn't he? Of course, he was. He didn't need any lovestruck girl mooning over him. He had Murieta to settle with. Then he had a life to get back to, and there was no place in his plans for a wife. Wife! How could the word *wife* and Cassie Wyman come to mind in the same thought? If the whole idea weren't so ludicrous, it would have been scary!

"A bump on the head can cause you to do some very strange things," he commented, wondering what his own excuse was.

Just then, Noah came riding toward them from up ahead. His dark face was radiant with excitement. "We're still on their trail!" he shouted. "They're not more than an hour ahead of us!"

Both relieved to have something new to think about, Cassie and Trace hurried to meet the rider. "What makes you say that?" Cassie called out, knowing that if Noah was basing his information on tracks he'd spotted, he could easily be wrong.

"I met a Drexell-bound stage about half a mile up the road! Murieta and his men robbed them earlier this morning."

"Were they sure it was Murieta?" Trace asked, his optimism beginning to grow.

"It was them all right. Right down to the black horse!"

"What'd they get?"

"Not much! Just a few personal belongings. The stage is full of prospectors going to the fields with not much more than a few supplies and some equipment."

"Which way'd they go?" Trace asked, looking down the road ahead.

"Just like we thought. They're headed toward Iowa Hill."

"Then, let's ride," Trace hollered, hitting the bay's rump with the end of a rein. "They evidently don't know we're behind them if they took the time to rob the stage!"

"Or they ain't got sense enough to spit downwind," Cassie gloated, bringing her horse to a quick gallop. "With the headstart we give 'em, they coulda been in San Francisco by now 'n' all they are is a hour ahead o' us!"

However, during the next week, after searching every coulee and side road from Drexell to Sacramento, Cassie was forced to eat her words. In fact, she came to the conclusion that Joaquin Murieta and his band of desperados were either the smartest outlaws ever to rob a stagecoach — or the luckiest. But whatever they were, it wasn't dumb. And the prospects for finding them and the gold grew more bleak by the mile.

Even though she and Trace and Noah continued to find evidence that indicated they were still on the right trail, the gang had managed to evade them at every turn. There had been false trails that had sent the threesome doubling back on their own trail for one wild-goose chase after another into mining camps and towns all along the way. And each time the results were the same. No one had seen the Mexicans.

Then, when they had lost so much time following a false lead that there seemed to be no chance of catching up to the *bandidos,* they would hear that Murieta had robbed another stagecoach or freight wagon not more than one or two hours ahead of them. So they would resume the chase, checking every clue they found — even the ones they knew were deliberately left to throw them off the trail.

"Well, I guess that's it," Noah said dejectedly as they rode into Sacramento. He took a long worried glance around the busy street. "We'll never find them here."

"Don't be too sure, Noah," Trace said, his tone

distracted as he cast a disturbed glance over the new town to get his bearings.

An expression of sadness fleeted across his features. Everywhere he looked, there were people and animals and wagons. He couldn't help remembering that when he'd been through here in November of 1848, there hadn't been a single house or building on the spot where Sacramento now stood. In fact, it hadn't even been called Sacramento then. And the only sign that civilization had reached the fork where the American and Sacramento rivers came together had been a beached riverboat that was used as a trading store and warehouse. The rest had been wilderness. Beautiful, untainted wilderness.

Even now, he realized, the wilderness wasn't all gone. In fact, it grew right up to the hastily laid-out and erected town of over 10,000 people that served as the main supply center for emigrants who'd come from around the world to hunt for placer gold on the hundreds of creeks and streams that fed into the American, Yuba, and Feather rivers. He'd heard more than one story of grizzly bears, cougars, and black wolves that had left tracks right up to the edge of the city of tents and rough plank shanties.

But it's sure not untainted, he remarked to himself bitterly as a gust of wind forced him to remember the deep swamp on the north side of town where cattle were constantly getting lost and sinking into the mire to die. The particularly vile stench of the swamp combined in Trace's nostrils with the odors of animal waste, fried foods, open fires, garbage in the streets, and unclean humanity; and he closed his eyes for a moment to silently mourn the lost splendor that had been California before gold had been discovered here.

225

"You got any bright ideas what we're gonna do now, McAllister?" Cassie asked, defeat bitter in her tone.

Continuing to scrutinize the town with a frown on his face, Trace shook his head. "Don't give up yet, kid. We'll find your gold. Something tells me Murieta's right here in Sacramento."

Cassie's head swiveled anxiously as she searched the crowd for someone she recognized as Murieta. "Where? Did you see him? One of his men? Why do you think he's still here?"

"Just something about this whole thing strikes me wrong. It's as if it's a game with Murieta so he can show us how clever he is. He's had a hundred chances to lose us, but every time he does, he dangles another carrot under our noses to tell us which way to go next. You just wait and see. He's not through with us yet. He'll give us another clue." Trace continued to rake his alert gaze over the area.

Astonished, Cassie squinted and tried even harder to recognize someone. "You mean he's been *lettin'* us foller 'im on purpose?"

He nodded his head. "I wouldn't be surprised if he was watching us right now."

Noah's brown eyes narrowed angrily at the thought of being so near his quarry and his gold, yet unable to get to it. "Right n—"

Trace acknowledged Noah's words with a smile as he dismounted and tied his horse to a hitching rail. "So until he decides to let us know what he's doing, we might as well check into a hotel and get a decent night's sleep in a bed instead of on the ground." He started working his way across the congested street toward the City Hotel.

"I ain't gonna just sit 'n' wait for Murieta to

make the next move!" Cassie protested, running after Trace and matching her long-legged stride with his as best she could. "We gotta keep lookin'."

"You got any suggestions where, kid?" he asked offhandedly, never slowing his step a bit.

Cassie stopped walking, the look in her brown eyes perplexed. "We can't just do nothin'!"

Trace didn't break his stride. "I don't know about you, kid, but I won't be doing 'nothin'." I'm going to get a bath and shave. Then I intend to get the first good meal and entire night's sleep I've had in more than a week. And if you're smart, you'll do the same thing."

"Can't we just ask around town to see if anyone knows anything?" she called after him. "I could check the stables 'n' stores while you go into the dance halls & saloons," she suggested anxiously, unable to control the despairing tremor in her voice.

"I'll have them hold the key to your room at the desk," he tossed back over his shoulder as he stomped onto the porch of the hotel. "But don't stay out too late, kid. I want to get an early start in the morning."

"I'll stay out as late as I damn well please," Cassie assured herself as she stared at the door where Trace disappeared into the hotel. "An' you can take your hotel room key and—"

"Well, this must be my lucky day!" a cheerful baritone voice crooned in Cassie's ear at the same time the sweet, pungent scent of men's cologne assailed her nostrils.

Cassie pivoted around, her right hand on her Colt, her left hand going for her knife. "Not if you don't step back, it ain't!" she threatened, her tone daring the man to make a move so she would have

227

a reason to turn the anger quivering inside her into action.

"Don't shoot! It's me! Barton Talbot!" the man protested, taking a step backward and holding his hands out in surrender.

"Barton Talbot!" Cassie said, her face breaking into an embarrassed smile. "What're you doin' in Sacramento? I thought you was—"

"When you left Auburn without so much as a good-bye, my heart was broken." He affected a pouting moue in an obvious play for sympathy. "I worked the gambling halls there for a few days, praying you would return to me. But, alas, my heart was not in the game and I didn't do well. So when it seemed I had lost you forever, I came on to Sacramento, though I knew I'd never smile again," he said, his straight white teeth gleaming in his charming smile. "Now you've come back into my life and I'm going to do my best to see that you stay. Will you do me the honor of having dinner with me? I haven't been able to eat a bite since you left me."

Cassie grinned at the gambler's obvious fib. But it didn't matter if his line was one she knew he had given to a dozen women before. It felt good to have a handsome man happy to see her and smiling at her, instead of alternating between ignoring her and complaining about the way she dressed or acted. And it was certainly nice to feel desirable and wanted for a change.

Yes, Barton Talbot might be just what she needed to bolster her ego. After the past week with Trace, she felt about as appealing as a wet dog at a parlor social. Maybe she'd give Barton another chance. "You don't need to fill my head with fancy words,

Talbot. I'd be pleased to share supper with you," she answered, her freckled face happy. "But I can't go nowhere in these duds. First, lemme go on over to the hotel and take a bath 'n' change clothes. I'll meet you in the lobby in a hour."

Cassie was flattered by the way Barton seemed to heave a sigh of relief, as if he'd been holding his breath waiting for her answer. Maybe she'd been wrong about him. Maybe he really meant what he said. Maybe he really did care for her. At least his reaction was a confidence booster after all the glowering she'd been subjected to the past week.

"One hour!" he said with a jubilant laugh, spinning away from her and starting down the street. "I'll be there! Don't be late!" he called back over his shoulder as he disappeared around the corner.

"I won't," she promised, adjusting her saddlebags on her shoulder and hefting the bundle with her dress and hat in it. "I don't guess he noticed I had such a load to carry."

A minute later, Cassie stood in front of the registration desk in the City Hotel, speaking to a young man not much older than herself. "I'm Cassie Wyman. Trace McAllister was s'posed to leave a key to my room here."

"Oh, yes, Miss Wyman," the desk clerk said with a surprised smile. This girl certainly didn't look like the type to be . . . Well, it was none of his affair. Wiping his hand over his heavily pomaded hair, he turned and removed a key from a box and handed it to her. "Here you go. Two-twenty-two. Upstairs and to the left. You need any help with those bags?"

"No thanks. I toted 'em this far. I guess I can carry 'em the rest o' the way."

When she entered the room, she was surprised to

find a bathtub had already been filled with hot water and was waiting for her. Thrilled by McAllister's thoughtfulness, she didn't take time to wonder why he was suddenly so concerned about her comfort. She could worry about that later. Right now, all she was going to do was sit in that tub and soak.

Slamming the door behind her, she made a bee-line for the steaming water, tossing her belongings on the bed as she passed by and shedding her clothes as she crossed the room. By the time she reached the tub she was naked and had left a trail of discarded clothing from the door to the bath.

"Oh! That feels good," she sighed, settling into the water "This makes me forgive him for just about anything!" Sighing regretfully because she couldn't take the time to just soak, she picked up a cloth and lathered it with soap.

When she had scrubbed herself clean from head to toe, she stood up, again regretting that she had accepted Barton's invitation to dinner. After a week on the trail, she could have easily lolled in the tub for another hour.

The sound of a lifting door latch clanked into Cassie's euphoric mood. One foot in the tub and one out, her head jerked up. Paralyzed, she stared at the door to the room as it swung open, revealing the shape of a man.

Frozen where they were, the two startled people spoke in unison.

"What're you doin' in my room?"

"What the hell are you doing in my bath?"

Chapter Fourteen

Instinctively crossing her arms over her breasts, Cassie dropped back into the tub with a splash. "*Your* bath?" she shrieked.

"*Your* room?" Trace yelled at the same time, crashing the door shut behind him, his freshly-shaved face crimson with rage. Slapping a bottle of whiskey and a glass down on the bureau, he strode across the room and glowered down at her, unable to tear his gaze away from her slim body. God! How he wanted her. In self-defense, he yanked up a bathsheet and shoved it toward her. "Out!" he ordered.

Shrinking deeper into the water in a futile effort to escape the heat of his gaze, Cassie shook her head. "You're the one who better get out, McAllister! Or I'm gonna scream bloody murder!"

Trace opened his mouth to tell her go on and scream. Then a thought occurred to him and his face broke into a knowing smile. "What're you doing in my room, Cassie?" he asked, dropping the towel on the stool and starting to unbutton his shirt.

"This ain't your room. It's mine. The clerk gave me the ke—" Her eyes glittered with a mix of horror and excitement as she watched him shake his muscular torso out of his shirt, then reach for the top button on his fly. "What're you doin', McAllister?"

"You can cut the innocent act, kid. I know what you had in mind when you climbed into my bathtub, and I wouldn't want it said that I couldn't give you what you want!" He sat down and tugged off his boots and socks.

"McAllister, stop it!" she gasped as he stood up again and tucked his thumbs into the waistband of his trousers.

"You're the one who started this." With no pretense at modesty, he peeled the denim down his lean hips and long legs, revealing his blatant arousal to her thunderstruck gaze. He took a step closer to the tub. "Move over, kid."

"Wait a minute! I'm through! I'll get out! You can have the tub! I don't want it any more!" Her words were thrown out in a frantic rush as she stood up and tried to exit the tub on the opposite side.

"Not so fast, kid." Without hesitation, he stomped into the water and snaked out a long arm, wrapping it around her waist before she could make good her escape.

"Uhh!" she grunted in a startled gasp as she was jerked back into the tub and pressed to him. Paralyzed by the searing heat of his manhood straining against the roundness of her hip, Cassie's struggles

:ased.

"That's better," he said, dipping his head to kiss he tantalizing spot where her neck curved into her ;houlder.

An involuntary moan escaped her throat as the ;iss shuddered throughout her body, turning her imbs to jelly. Of its own will, her head fell to the ;ide to give his lips better access.

"There's no need to pretend any more, hon. I understand why you're here."

Cassie stiffened in his arms, his words sending a :hill over her. True, this was what she wanted, had been on the verge of begging for all week long; but that wasn't why she was here. She had to make him understand that she hadn't deliberately come here for this.

"The clerk said it was my room," she tried to explain, ducking her chin to her chest so he could move her hair aside and kiss the nape of her neck. "He gave me the key."

"Shh, we'll talk about it later. Right now, the only thing that matters is that you're here and want me as much as I want you." He caressed his hands up her torso to hold her breasts, massaging and kneading them until their peaks thrust and burned into his palms. "This week's been pure hell," he sighed against her ear.

"I know," she agreed breathlessly, all the resistance gone. Helplessly, she leaned into his kiss. "You didn't have much use for me, did you?"

Trace released his distinctive growl, then laughed in disgust. "Trouble was, I had so much use for you, I couldn't concentrate on much else. And the way you kept wiggling your bottom in those tight jeans didn't help a helluva lot." He slid a hand down her body to cup the mound of her femininity and draw her closer to him. "I couldn't keep my eyes off you."

The syncopated rhythm of Cassie's heart skipped a beat, then raced haphazardly, pounding wildly and making her chest heave as if she'd been running. Trace didn't hate her! He wanted her—had wanted her all along!

Unable to remember why she had needed to escape from him, she turned in his arms and splayed her hands over his chest. "I couldn't stop lookin' at you either," she admitted, ruffling her fingers through the dark hair that tickled her palms. " 'Specially when yo—"

Her words were cut off as Trace's mouth fell on hers in a kiss that contained all the pent-up passion he'd struggled so valiantly to contain during the long, torturous hours of the last week. And Cassie opened to him, her reaction making no secret of the fact that she was every bit as hungry as he was.

Releasing her lips, he burned a trail of kisses over her jaw and down her neck. Cassie's head fell back as he sank to his knees in the tub, raining kisses over her breasts and belly as he lowered himself into the water.

He sat back on his calves and pulled her to him. Digging his fingers into the roundness of her bottom, he buried his face in the downy softness at the apex of her thighs.

Lightning streaked in every direction with the touch of his tongue and lips, and her knees collapsed. Held standing only by his rough hold on her, she sagged against his mouth as his intimate kiss hurled her to a rapid climax.

"Come here," he ordered, lowering her down to

traddle his lap. "Do you know how many times during the last seven days I've watched you sitting in that saddle and imagined having your legs wrapped around me like this?" he asked, his voice hoarse as he lifted her upward, then thrust his hardness inside her. "I was jealous of that damned horse!" he admitted with a husky laugh.

"Oooh." She moved impatiently on him to deepen his possession, the muscles of her sex still contracting helplessly with the erotic spasms he'd incited with his tongue. "I thought about it too," she whispered, burrowing her fingers into his hair and bringing his mouth to hers. "But I figgered you didn't like me no more."

Then it was happening again, that urgent ascent to the top of the universe, and there was no more conversation. There was only the labored breathing of the man and woman and the sloshing splash of the bathwater as their starving bodies slammed together, then pulled apart, then came together again. Over and over, harder and harder, the compelling need growing more demanding by the instant.

When they would have delayed the finally moment for want of just a few seconds more in the special heaven their desire had created, the inevitable explosions came simultaneously, shaking them both to the very tips of their toes.

Trace fell back against the edge of the tub, carrying her with him. "That sure beats the hell out of fighting over whose tub this is, doesn't it?"

"Mmm," she hummed, sprinkling his chest and shoulders with kisses. "It sure does."

"I'm glad you decided to come to me. I don't know how much longer I could have stayed away." He combed his fingers through the freshly sham-

235

pooed riot of her hair.

"The clerk gave me this room. So you're the one who come to me," she said, sitting up with a smile. "But it's okay. I'm glad you did."

"Well, whatever the mixup was, the fates must've been looking out for me. I feel better than I've felt in days!"

"Me too," Cassie said with a grin, so happy she didn't care if Trace's pride wouldn't let him admit to being the one to come to her first.

"Let's finish up *our* bath and get dressed and go have some supper," he suggested, picking up a bar of soap and lathering her arms and breasts. "Then we can come back here for *dessert*." His smile was mischievous.

Cassie nodded her agreement and smiled. Then her expression changed to one of horror. "Supper! Oh, no! I told Barton Talbot I'd meet 'im in the lobby 'n' go eat supper with 'im! What time is it?" she asked, grabbing a washcloth and rinsing herself hurriedly. Giving modesty no thought, she exited the tub at a run and snatched up a towel.

"Talbot?" Trace said, exploding up out of the water. "You're kidding, aren't you?" He bounded out of the tub, oblivious to the rush of water sluicing down his magnificent body to the floor.

"No. I saw 'im in the street 'n' promised I'd go." She hurriedly toweled herself off and opened her satchel, donning her drawers and chemise as she pulled them out.

"Well, you can't go now!" he yelled.

"I gave 'im my word."

"That was before we, uh—" He glanced over his shoulder at the bathtub, then reached for her.

Tempted to return to his arms, Cassie shook her

head with a regretful smile. She really would rather stay here with Trace. "It'd hurt his feelin's if I didn't show up. 'Sides, I owe it to him." She wheeled out of his reach and began rummaging through her packs. "He was nice to me when I was feelin' mighty low."

Trace blew out a rude snort. "You don't owe him anything. He's only after you because he thinks your daddy has made a huge killing in the gold fields, and he wants to get his hands on your money."

Cassie straightened and pivoted to face Trace, her skirt and petticoats clutched to her chest, her expression confused and hurt. "An' jus' why would he think that?"

Guilt and irritation with himself for his thoughtless words played across his features, and Trace suddenly busied himself with drying off. "I—uh—" he stammered, searching for a way out of telling her the truth.

"Why, McAllister? Why would Barton Talbot think I got a lot of money?"

"It's just a feeling I have," he lied, stabbing his arms into the sleeves of a fresh shirt. "His kind is always after something."

"It's more'n a feelin', ain't it?" she said woodenly, turning away from him and stepping into her skirt and petticoats, desperate now to be gone as soon as possible.

Trace coughed nervously. "What're you talking about?"

"You said what you said 'cause you can't believe a feller might jus' like me for myself. Ain't that it?"

"No! That's not it!" he protested.

"Well, don't go puttin' your sneaky intentions on

237

Barton. It might int'rest you to know he wants to marry me! He ain't like you at all. He ain't jus' nice to me when he wants somethin' or has a itch. So, McAllister . . ." She fastened the top button on her bodice and dropped her hat on her head as she headed for the door. "Put that in your britches and scratch it."

Outside in the hallway, Cassie's indignant facade deserted her, and she fell back against the wall, burying her face in her hands. *He's right. What man's gonna like a tall, skinny, freckled female like you if he ain't goin' to get somethin' from it?* Still, it hurt—not hearing that Barton•might be after money she didn't have, but knowing how Trace thought of her. He'd done it to her twice now, filling her head with pretty words and making her believe she was beautiful and desirable so he could get what he wanted, when all the time he hadn't changed what he thought of her from that first day.

Well! she thought, pushing away from the wall with a determined shove. *There won't be a third time!*

A semblance of her pride restored, though her self-image continued to waver on the thin line between low and nonexistent, she checked to be sure her bodice was tucked into her skirt, straightened her hat, tugged on her gloves, then hurried to find a hotel maid to help her with her buttons and hair before her meeting with Barton Talbot.

Salina choked back the tears that had threatened to cascade down her cheeks from the moment she'd first entered The Golden Goose an hour before. Hearing Cliff talk every day about the progress be-

238

ing made on the four-story gambling casino on Portsmouth Square had been just that. Talk. It hadn't been real. Half the time she hadn't even heard what he was saying.

But now, standing beside her half brother in the center of the eighty-foot-long room, she could no longer fool herself into believing Noah would arrive in time to save her. The saloon was completed, the red velvet drapes had been hung from thick gold rods over tall, eight-foot-high windows, and the gilded walls, painted in fresco, were lavishly decorated with ornamental paintings. The entire room breathed with elegance.

All along the wall opposite the bar were couches and lounges of green, gold, red, blue, and purple velvet, each piled high with plush cushions. Scattered between the divans and chairs were marble tables displaying costly Bohemian glass and alabaster vases and porcelain jars. The only thing left to be done was stock the bar, bring in the gaming tables, and hire the musicians, dealers, and bartenders who would work there.

"Well! What do you think?" Cliff asked, his walk a positive strut as he showed off the plush room.

Salina didn't trust herself to speak. The best she could do was nod her head as she glanced around.

"This bar's the longest one in San Francisco," he volunteered, directing Salina's gaze toward the ornately carved and gilded bar that ran the length of the room. "And no other gambling casino in California has mirrors like these. Not the El Dorado or the Bella Union or Parker House. None of them," he bragged with a histrionic sweep of his hand that took in the marbled mirrors covering the wall behind the bar.

"I'm sure they don't," Salina managed to say, refusing to give him the praise he obviously expected. She knew that despite the way he had resented her existence all her life, for some strange reason he needed to impress her with his achievements — as if by gaining her approval he could prove their dead father had been wrong about his only son. But no matter what he did to her or forced her to do, she would always withhold it from him. She would clean for him, bow down to him, even whore for him if it came to that, but she would never give him the thing he wanted most from her.

"That's the musicians' gallery," he pointed out proudly, calling her attention to an elevated stage halfway up the far wall, its gold railing draped with red velvet like that on the windows.

Salina pretended to stifle a yawn.

"I had the chandeliers brought all the way from Paris, France," he said, his tone growing slightly anxious. "No expense has been spared to make this the finest gambling establishment in northern California."

"I thought you were going to put rugs on the floors," she commented dryly, glancing down at the plain plank floor beneath her feet. "Bare wood seems rather incongruous with the extravagant decor, don't you think?"

Cliff frowned his displeasure. Damn her. Incongruous, indeed! Leave it to her to find something to criticize. Just once, he'd like to have her show a little admiration for something he did. But no, just like his father, she always made him feel as though he'd fallen short.

Well, let her ask her disapproving little questions with that superior sneer on her face. Soon now, he'd make her sorry. He would wipe that look off her face once and for all. She was beaten. She'd respect him all right! And never again would he fall prey to that scathing condemnation that brought back ugly memories of a father who preferred the bastard daughter of a slave over his legitimate white son. Yes, he was going to bring her down. Before he was through he would have her kissing his boots with admiration.

"The private game rooms upstairs have covered floors," he answered irritably. "Here in the main hall, with spilled drinks, muddy boots, and hot cigar ashes to destroy them in a matter of days, rugs would be the incongruity, my dear—not boards that can be swept clean daily and washed down!"

"I suppose that makes sense," she told him, though her expression said something else.

"I don't know why we're wasting time down here. What does a slave know about grandeur anyway?"

"I'm no longer a slave, Cliff, but I will always be your sister," she reminded him, taking pleasure in the flush of anger that rose to color his pale cheeks. Even his scalp beneath his thin blond hair was a vibrant shade of pink. "And just like you, our father taught me to appreci—"

Salina's words were cut off by the loud crack of a backhanded slap across her left cheek, sending her head reeling. "Shut your mouth, bitch! I told you never to say that!" Cliff shrieked with a second blow to the other cheek.

Her slight weight inadequate to withstand the power of his blow, Salina flew backward, landing in a sprawl on the floor that had started their argument.

A plan to gain more time ignited in her brain.

241

Hauling herself to a sitting position with labored effort, she forced herself to smile. "That's it, isn't it, *brother* dear? Our father loved me more—"

Livid, his temper out of control, Cliff fell on her, straddling her lap and cutting off her words with two rapid slaps, snapping her head from right to left.

"Our father—" she slurred through lips that were already beginning to swell. Success numbing her pain, she managed a triumphant smile as she saw her half brother ball his fist and draw it back.

"Shut up!" he screamed.

"—loved me best," she goaded, just an instant before his violent punch made contact with her jaw and gave her the blessed escape of unconsciousness.

"I must say you had me fooled," Horace Gilbert said as, uninvited, he drew up a chair and sat down with Cassie and Barton at their table beside the window that looked out on the street. "When you got on that stagecoach last week, I never would have guessed what a lovely young woman you are. But I suppose that was your intention, wasn't it? It was an excellent disguise."

Cassie stared, surprised, at the traveling salesman who'd accosted them minutes after they had sat down at their table in the restaurant. He was different than she remembered, more sure of himself, more aggressive. His clothing even looked nattier, newer. Ignoring his comment about her "disguise," Cassie changed the subject. "You look like the boots-'n'-work-clothes business's been right good lately, Gilbert," she commented frankly.

"I do?" he said, his smug expression making no

pretense at not being pleased with her observation. "That must be because it has!"

"Oh?" Barton said, the expression on his previously annoyed countenance suddenly becoming animated and alert. "How's that?"

Frowning, Cassie turned and studied Barton. It was then she noticed for the first time that his starched white shirtfront was showing signs of age and the sleeve edges of his black coat were beginning to fray. Of course, they were probably that way when she'd first met him. She'd just been so blinded by his good looks and smooth manner that she hadn't seen it. "Yeah, tell us your secret, Gilbert," she said, turning back to Horace.

The salesman looked from side to side and leaned toward them, his forearms resting on the table. "Maps," he said in a secretive whisper.

"Maps?" Cassie and Barton asked together, inadvertently dropping their voices too.

Gilbert nodded his head and sat back in his chair. "I'm making a killing," he bragged.

"What kind o' maps?" Cassie asked.

"Do you realize how many greenhorns arrive in California every day?" he asked, pulling forward a piece of paper from his breast pocket. "Thousands." He spread the paper on the table in front of him.

"Yeah?" Her voice held a suspicious ring.

"They've come from all over the world to strike it rich in the gold fields, but when they get here, they find they've got a problem. That's where I come in."

Understanding dawned on Barton's handsome face. "You not only sell them their supplies but you sell them—"

"Maps!" Horace finished for him. "Maps of the

gold country with all the places gold has been found marked!"

"Lemme see that," Cassie grabbed the map to her for closer scrutiny.

"How much are you getting a piece?" Barton asked, his tone obviously intrigued.

"Fifty dollars in paper, twenty-five in gold."

"These places you got marked was all played out a couple years ago," Cassie interrupted, shoving the map back to Horace and indicating a group of *X's* on the south fork of the Yuba. "You're stealin' from those poor folks who come out here with their hearts full o' dreams!"

"Don't be foolish, my dear," Barton said. "It appears to me that Mr. Gilbert is merely an enterprising businessman."

"I would never willingly cheat someone out of their hard-earned money," Horace said with an injured sniff. Whipping out his handkerchief, he dabbed delicately at his nose. "I don't guarantee they'll find gold. I just tell them how to get where others have found it. Where they choose to go is their business." He snatched up his map and stuffed it back into his pocket. "I can see I was wrong to share my enthusiasm with—"

"Don't leave, old man," Barton said, catching the other man's sleeve before he could get away. "Miss Wyman just doesn't understand the intricacies of business as you and I do. Sit back down and we'll talk about it some more. Say, why don't you have dinner with us?"

"Well, I suppose . . ." he conceded with a questioning look in Cassie's direction. "But you must let me buy your dinner."

"I wouldn't hear of it," Barton protested, though

244

Cassie was sure she detected a nervous relief in his tone. "I invited you."

"But I intruded on your evening. If you won't allow me to make restitution, I can't possibly stay."

Barton sat back in his chair and lifted his hands out to his sides in defeat. "Well, if you insist. But next time it will be on me. And I won't take any arguments. Now, tell me more about your maps. Have you ever thought of expanding your operation? Say, taking on a partner?"

"What are you getting at, Talbot?"

"Just that I've been thinking of making a change of occupation, and your ingenious idea may be exactly what I'm looking for."

"I have been toying with the idea of increasing my territory," Horace mused. "But a partner? I'm not sure I'm ready for that. Do you have something specific in mind?"

Cassie's disgusted gaze sawed from man to man as the two hucksters, head to head, each obviously bent on besting the other, connived a scheme meant to relieve twice as many innocent people of their money. She was completely forgotten — which was fine with her. But she had no desire to sit here and listen to them.

"You fellers don't need me for this, so I think I'll head on back to my hotel," she said with a disapproving snort as she opened her bag and drew out her gloves. She pushed her chair back and stood up. "G'night."

Barton glanced up at her, an apologetic expression quickly disguising the annoyance she saw flit over his face. "I'm sorry, my dear. We didn't mean to be rude. It's just that I'm so fascinated by the possibilities of this that I forgot my manners. Will you forgive me?" He lifted her hand and held it to his mouth. "Please, don't be angry." He raised his dazzling blue gaze to her, his eyes pleading.

How could a look that she would have died for a week ago mean so little to her now?

Cassie pulled her hand out of his with the same distaste she would have shown if she'd accidentally stepped barefoot into the muck of the Sacramento swamp. "To tell the truth, I ain't got much appetite right now. Good seein' you both again."

Without giving either of them a chance to try to stop her, she whirled away from the table and out the front door, her head held high, her smile relieved.

Outside on the porch, Cassie looked from left to right, wondering what to do now. She'd lied about not being hungry, so she needed to find something to eat. Besides, she couldn't go back to her room. Trace might still be there, since she hadn't been gone long enough to be sure he'd had time to straighten out the room situation and get moved to his own room. Yes, eating alone was the answer.

Pausing, she opened her purse to see how much money she had. There ought to at least be enough left from what Trace had given her for clothes to buy an inexpensive supper for herself.

Coming up with a bit more than two dollars, she bit her lip thoughtfully. Maybe in Goldville it would be enough to buy something to eat, but it wouldn't pay for a decent meal in Sacramento. She would just have to go without—because she had no intention of returning to Barton Talbot's table, and she refused to ask Trace to pay for her supper. Her stomach voiced its protest to her decision with a wrenching spasm.

"Don't think about it!" she ordered herself as she stepped off the porch, suddenly aware that it was almost dark. "I'll just look around a bit to give McAllister time to get to his own room. Then I'll head on back to the hotel." Unfortunately, her stomach needed more convincing.

Across the street, on the end of the porch of Lee's Exchange, Sacramento's largest gambling house, a loud cheer suddenly erupted from the crowd of men gathered there. Curiosity getting the better of her, Cassie hurried toward the crowd, for the moment forgetting her hunger—and that she was no longer safely disguised in baggy miner's clothing.

Chapter Fifteen

Stretching her neck and standing on her toes, Cassie strained to see what all the fuss on the porch was about. She glanced at the miner beside her, then back ahead. "What's goin' on?"

"A feller jest took Lucky Bill Thorington fer a clean hundert," the whiskered man answered.

"Who's Lucky Bill?" Cassie asked, still trying to see.

"Who's Lucky Bill!" The prospector's voice was animated with amazement. "Why, he's jest the best thimblerigger in the whole durned gold country. That's all."

"Hmp," Cassie grunted with a disapproving frown. "A thimblerigger. I thought somethin' int'restin' was goin' on. I've seen a thimblerigger. You see one, you seen 'em all." She started to turn away.

"You ain't seen one the likes o' Lucky Bill, little gal. No one can beat him." The prospector was an obvious fan of the thimblerigger.

"Someone just did." As if in answer to her argument, a disappointed moan rose from the crowd around the hustler.

"Lucky Bill was jest playin' with 'im. He sometimes takes it easy on a feller first time 'round and don't move the cups too fast."

Cassie slowed her retreat and turned back to the miner. "Oh?" An idea for a reprieve from her temporary dilemma flashed through her brain. "Does he really?"

"You bet! Ever' time a feller wins, he gets cocky 'n' greedy 'n' bets again. That's when Lucky Bill shows 'im his real stuff. Then, folks oughta call him 'Lightnin' Bill.' His hands're that fast. He al'ays gits his money back—'n' then some!"

Not if the bettor only plays that first time, she told herself. As though urging her on, her stomach gurgled loudly in support of the idea.

She hesitated for a moment, then shrugged her shoulders. "I don't believe anyone can be that fast," she said to the miner. "I'd like to see this for myself." She tapped the man in front of her on the shoulder. "Excuse me, sir, I can't see." Her "lady" voice was even better than it was in her imagination. Maybe she remembered more of what her mother had taught her than she thought.

Surprised to see her, the man smiled and moved aside. "Get out o' the way, ya lowlifes," he bellowed. "Give the little lady some room. She cain't see."

"Thank you," she said, tossing in a bat of her eyelashes for good measure. "You're—you are very kind."

Her bearlike protector blushed to the roots of his bushy black beard and hair, and in that moment Cassie realized the power she held at her disposal but had never bothered to use. It was a heady sensation.

Straightening her spine, she moved gracefully — well, as gracefully as she could in her high-heeled boots — through the pathway cleared for her.

"Better luck next time," Lucky Bill was saying to the big winner/loser as Cassie took over the disappointed man's vacated spot at the shell game. Spotting Cassie, the huckster's ruddy face split into a wide grin. "Ah! What have we here?" A female at his game would bring even more spectators — and suckers. "Has the little lady come to try her luck?" The entire time he spoke, his hands busily moved the shells around the table, lifting the one with the ball under it periodically to show the onlookers how easy it was to pick the winner.

"I don't know," Cassie said. "I don't know very much about gambling."

"Gambling? Not at all, little lady. This is just a quiet little game of challenge. In fact, it's recommended by the clergy for its wholesomeness. Anyone who ain't blind can win."

"How does it work?"

"You see these three little wooden cups and this little ball." He held up the ball between his thumb and forefinger for all to see. "I simply place the little ball under one of the cups." He slipped the ball under the middle cup and started exchanging the positions of the shells — very slowly. "Then, after I move the cups around a couple of times, I bet you can't tell me on the first guess which one the ball's under. That's all there is to it!" He lifted his hands off the containers and indicated with his palm upward that she should try to pick one — just for practice.

Cassie held her fingers to her chin and studied the table. "Oh, dear," she sighed, enjoying herself more by the minute. "I just don't know. Is it that one?" she said, pointing at the left shell.

Lucky Bill lifted the cup to expose the ball. "Oh, oh. The lady's got the eye. Or she's awful lucky. Either way, it's a good thing for me we didn't bet on that. An eye like yours could end up takin' every bit of gold I've scraped together over the last two years."

"Really?" Cassie asked, her eyes widening with excitement as she looked from side to side. "Do you mean if I put a coin on the table, you will give it back to me with a matching amount if I can find the ball again?"

"You bet!" he said, using the gold country's most commonly repeated phrase for affirmation.

"In that case, maybe I'll try it—just once—for money" she said, digging into her purse and bringing out two coins. "Is two dollars enough?"

Bill, who'd been watching the crowd grow since the girl had gotten there, smiled. "Two dollars it is!" he said, displaying the ball for her to see, then ostentatiously tucking it beneath a shell. Moving the wooden cups with much less than "lightning speed," he switched them around, bringing them to a stop in a straight line.

"That one!" Cassie cried, pointing out her choice. Of course, she was right, and Bill had to pay off. "I win!"

"You're just too quick for me," Lucky Bill said with exaggerated regret. "How 'bout givin' me another try?"

"I'd like to, but I'd better not. No doubt it was just good luck on my part, and I don't want to risk

251

losing my supper money," she said, turning to leave. "But thank you so much for letting me play your game."

Bill's face twisted in an obvious play for sympathy. "You're not going to leave without givin' me a chance to win back my money, are you?" He didn't care about the two dollars, but he wanted to keep the attractive young woman at his game so the others would stay. The better the "scenery," the bigger their bets would become.

"How 'bout if I stake ya, little gal?" the miner who'd made room for her at the front of the crowd said, digging into his leather pouch as he spoke. A cheer rose from the men around her.

Cassie looked up at the bearlike man and shook her head. "I couldn't. I would feel terrible if I made the wrong choice and lost your money."

"You let me worry 'bout that, miss," he said, plunking down a gold nugget.

Before the man could change his mind, Bill whisked up the nugget and dropped it in one side of his pennyweight scale, quickly matching the weight in the other side with gold of his own.

"Well, if you're sure," Cassie said, stepping back to the table and examining the cups Bill moved tantalizingly under her nose.

Bill stopped, a hush fell over the crowd, and Cassie pointed out her choice. She knew before Bill even removed the cup that she had been right. He'd made it easy for her again, obviously to raise the miner's bet.

"Yea!" the crowd cheered as her backer became *backers* when three more prospectors joined the first in laying down bets.

Excitement pounding in her ears, Cassie concentrated on the shells as Bill began his spiel again, switching the small cups much more rapidly than before.

Cassie bit her lip and looked at each of the hopeful miners who had money on her. "That one," she said positively, pointing to the shell on her left. A groan rose from the bettors. They could all see it was the one on the right, not the left. But Cassie knew she was right. Lucky Bill had just wanted her to think it was the one on the right.

And Bill knew she was right—*and* that he was in trouble!

When, against his will, Bill lifted the cup Cassie had chosen, the miners' excitement rose to frenetic proportions. Everyone laughed and cheered and slapped someone on the back. Everyone except Lucky Bill Thorington.

"Can she do it again?" was circulated through the crowd.

"An ounce'll get you two says she can't."

"You got a bet."

"Come on, little lady, let's see you do it again!"

"It's about time someone showed Bill a thing or two!"

Knowing he didn't dare pull out when the girl was winning, the frown on Bill's face deepened as he studied Cassie's expression. He refused to believe he'd been set up. As many hustles as he had pulled off in his life, he could surely spot it when it was happening to him. *She's just lucky,* he told himself with conviction. Her uncanny luck was a fluke. That's all. It wouldn't last. It couldn't.

The bets down on the highest-stakes thimble game ever played in Sacramento, Bill stared hard at Cassie and her army of supporters. Sweat beaded on his forehead. *It's not a hustle. It's not!* Wiping his damp hands on his pants, he took a deep breath and began.

Holding the ball up for all to see, he slapped it under a cup, then began to move the cups, slowly at first so it was easy to keep the correct one in sight. Then, in as long as it took to blink an eye, he exchanged the shells three times, making it impossible for the keenest observer to keep up with the ball.

He held up his hands and smiled directly at Cassie. "Go on, little gal. It's up to you."

Cassie smiled back at him, studying him rather than the identical cups. Then she acted. "That one," she said, pointing without hesitation.

The confident grin dissolved off Bill's face. After two years of lining his pockets with the hard-earned gold of the miners, his bank had just been broken!

A cheer rose from the crowd as, his skin pale with shock, Bill lifted the shell to expose the ball that meant his downfall.

Though she could have felt guilty for what she'd done to the thimblerigger, she wasn't, in the least. First of all, she knew she hadn't truly broken him and that he would just set up his game again tomorrow and win back what he'd lost in no time. Secondly, she'd seen too many men lose literally everything they owned to the professional gamblers and conmen who abounded in the gold country. And it made her feel good to be able to give some of it back to them—even though most of them would probably lose their winnings before the night was out.

An hour later, when she had finally relieved her hunger in a small restaurant a few blocks from the

254

hotel, Cassie hurried along the boardwalk toward the hotel, her mood high. But a block away from the City Hotel, for no reason she could put a name to, her elation suddenly dipped ominously into anxiety and fear—as if she'd been touched by something evil.

Though for the most part women were amazingly safe on the streets at night because they were so respected by the almost totally male population, she suddenly felt very vulnerable.

Clutching her purse protectively to her chest, Cassie cast her glance from side to side. The street was much quieter now than it had been before, but she had the most eerie feeling she was being watched.

Everyone who'd seen her win from Lucky Bill Thorington knew that her purse contained over ninety ounces of gold dust and nuggets, which had been given to her as tips by the miners she had won money for. And anyone who knew what was in her bag could be planning to rob her. A shudder of apprehension washed over her, and her grip on her purse tightened.

"You're actin' like a baby," she said to herself, her eyes shifting from left to right. But the feeling of being stalked persisted.

Stopping dead in her tracks, she spun around, determined to catch whoever was following her off guard and confront him. But no one was there. The way behind her was empty!

"Your imagination's playin' tricks on you," she scolded under her breath as, quickening her step, she resumed her stroll toward the hotel. Passing the Eagle Theatre, she noticed a placard advertising the fact that Mrs. Witherspoon's company had performed there tonight. And a moment of regret dashed across her mind. It would have been nice if she'd gotten to see a play while she was in Sacramento. But the thought was not enough to relieve her uneasiness, and her temporarily distracted concentration raced back to the immediate fact. She was scared! Unable to deny it a moment longer, Cassie broke into a dead run to pass the alley and building between the theater and hotel.

When she reached the hotel without mishap, she felt foolish for letting her imagination run away with her the way she had. Able to laugh at herself now that she was safe, she grabbed the porch rail and paused to catch her breath. She'd made it! And there was nothing to be afraid of any more. Taking a deep breath, she straightened her shoulders and lifted a foot to step onto the porch.

Just as her foot would have come down on the plank stair, a black-gloved hand shot out of the dark walkway that ran alongside the hotel. Clamped suffocatingly over her mouth, the hand was immediately joined by another around her waist, and she was jerked off her feet and into the shadows.

"So, *señorita*," a man's heavy Spanish accent hissed into her ear from behind. "We meet again."

Murieta! her mind screamed.

"You did not think I would forget our last meeting, did you?" His grip tightened and he pulled her farther into the shadows.

Panic whirling crazy in her thoughts, Cassie didn't know what to do. She shook her head.

"Did I not tell you that anyone who draws the weapon on Murieta does not live to talk about it?"

The cold, hard pressure of a knife point dug into her neck just beneath her jaw — where she could feel

256

her pulse pounding frantically against it.

"Answer me, *señorita!*" he whispered, his words sounding as if they were being strained through his teeth.

Cassie nodded her head.

"But I have decided to make the exception in your case," he said in the same hoarse wheeze.

Cassie relaxed slightly.

"If!" he said with extra emphasis, "you give to me the gold you won tonight and—"

"Kid? Is that you?" Trace McAllister's voice boomed, accompanied by the echo of heavy boots running along the hotel porch toward the shadowy passageway between the hotel and the building next door.

Taken off guard by the interruption, Murieta's head jerked up and he pulled her deeper behind a packing crate. "Do not make a sound." His words against her ear were so quiet that she felt more than heard them.

Removing the knife from her neck, he whipped out one of his silver pistols. Holding it alongside her face, he aimed it at the entrance to the walkway and cocked the hammer. "Your *amor* is a dead man."

The click twisted ruthlessly through Cassie. And fear such as she had never known consumed her thinking, leaving her with only one terrible thought. Trace was going to be killed.

Desperation raged through her blood, making the terror she had felt with Murieta's knife at her throat seem minimal. And she knew she had to do something. Even if it meant giving her own life, she had to stop Murieta. She wouldn't lose Trace!

Acting on impulse, Cassie tightened her hold on

257

her purse, which she still held clutched to her breast, and lowered her hands. The purse was heavy — over five pounds heavy. Without taking time to consider the consequences, she kicked out at the man behind her as she brought the concentrated weight of the gold up to crack him on the side of the face.

The instant the bandit released his hold on her to grab at his cheek, Cassie dove for cover, screaming, "Trace! Look out! It's Murieta!"

Cursing her, Murieta fired two rapid shots into the bush she had sought refuge behind, then squeezed off two more at the male figure that appeared in the walk entrance, the light of the hotel porch outlining him perfectly.

Trace had seen Cassie from where he sat in a chair propped back on two legs against the wall of the hotel — he'd been watching her, on the verge of going after her just before she had appeared. He hadn't wanted her to know he'd been concerned about her whereabouts, so he had turned his head in the opposite direction the instant he saw her, planning to act surprised when she walked past him.

However, when Cassie hadn't appeared in the next minute, he hadn't been able to stop his head from swinging back to the end of the porch. He was disconcerted to find that she had completely vanished from sight. Panic storming through him, he had not been able to keep up the facade of nonchalance any longer. He had exploded out of his chair and run toward the spot where he'd seen her the moment before.

When he had heard her scream out her warning, he had been certain he knew the real meaning of the word fear. But when he heard the gunfire discharge from the walkway alongside the hotel, he realized he'd never known true terror until that very moment.

Horror and rage tunneling his vision and coloring it a blistering red, he jerked his gun from its holster and propelled his large frame into the entrance. He knew he was a sitting duck. But it didn't matter. All he knew was he had to get to Cassie!

No sooner had he appeared in the open than two more shots were fired. Though both were wild and off target, he was forced back to the hotel porch.

His heart beating a frantic tattoo against his ribs, he flattened himself against the wall. Holding his revolver over his left shoulder, his thumb on the hammer, his forefinger curved over the trigger, he turned his face toward the path and listened intently.

"Are you okay, kid?" he called out, needing some sign that the first shots hadn't killed her.

Cassie didn't answer. And Trace's erratically beating heart plunged with sickening weight to the pit of his belly.

"So help me, Murieta," he warned, the threat in his tone not quite disguising the tremor, "if you've hurt her, you'll wish for death before I'm through with you."

A malicious giggle echoed from between the buildings. "Have I not yet made it clear to you that you will never find me, *gringo*?"

By the sound of the voice, Trace surmised Murieta was against the building next door, about a third of the way back from the street. Deliberately aiming high so he wouldn't hit Cassie, he stepped into the opening and fired, then ducked back to the protection of the hotel.

His shot was answered by Murieta's bullet. Splinters of wood showered to the ground from the corner of the hotel wall, only inches above Trace's head.

Using the fire-and-duck method again, Trace managed another high shot into the walkway. This one was not answered. Could he have hit Murieta? He waited, his chest heaving with apprehension. But he heard nothing except his own labored breathing and . . .

Footsteps! Running footsteps fading down the walk toward the alley behind the hotel. Murieta was getting away!

Making a deliberate target of himself, Trace stepped into the open and raked his gaze over the dim path.

"Ohhh . . ."

"Oh, my god! Is that you, kid?" he called out, knowing it was. Forgetting that Murieta could still be there, he rushed to the bush from which the voice had sounded.

Gut-knotting dread twisting at his vitals, he dropped to his haunches beside the crumpled figure on the ground, knowing without doubt that Murieta had shot her. What if she died? How would he live with himself?

Gathering her half-conscious body into his arms with desperate urgency, he clung to her tightly, as if his hold could stave off death. In his head, he knew he had to get her to a doctor, should check to see where she'd been hit; but all he could do was squeeze her harder to him.

"Cassie," he wailed, covering her face and hair with kisses. "You can't die on me!" he demanded, is voice breaking, then becoming a plea. "Please don't die."

When Cassie opened her eyes and saw Trace bending over her, his handsome face twisted with despair, a blessed warmth enveloped her. Trace was alive! He was alive and she was in his arms, where nothing could hurt her.

Melting like ice under the summer sun, the hard shell of pseudo-independence she'd hidden behind the past eight years suddenly evaporated, leaving her emotions naked and vulnerable, and cracking the dam on her tears that had held since the day of her mother's funeral when she was twelve years old.

"Oh, Trace," she wept, wrapping her arms around his strong back and clinging to him, her tears spilling uncontrolled over the rims of her eyes. "I was so scared. I thought he was goin' to kill you."

Her tears wrenched at his heart, and her concern for him, rather than for herself, brought a strange moisture to his own eyes. Embracing her even more, he kissed her wet cheeks and eyelids. "Don't cry, sweetheart. It's all right now," he soothed between kisses. "You don't have to be afraid any more. I'm never going to let anything hurt you again. I promise. And I swear I'm going to kill that bastard who shot you if it's the last thing I ever do!"

"Shot?" she asked, a dreamy mental fog of well-being disguising her memory of the moments before she had slipped into unconsciousness. "Did I get shot?"

Her question brought a fragment of rationality back to Trace's emotional behavior. He relaxed his hold on her and drew back, his forehead furrowed in a frown. "Weren't you?"

Forcing herself to conduct a mental check of her

body, Cassie struggled to a sitting position and shook her head in confusion. "I don't think so — unless my head . . ." She dug her fingers into her hair at her crown.

"Your head!" His voice was rife with panic and guilt because he hadn't examined her immediately. Without waiting for her to say more, Trace shoved her hand aside and frantically began to search her scalp for the wound.

When he found none, he blew out a loud sigh of relief. "You must have bumped it when you fell. You've got quite a goose egg, but there's no blood."

"I guess that's what knocked me out," she said thoughtfully, bending her arm so she could see her elbow and determine the reason it was stinging. It was then she saw the blood. And the dam on her tears burst anew. "Ooooh," she wailed, staring in horror at the sight of her bloody elbow protruding through a long rip in her sleeve.

Forcing himself not to give way to panic again, Trace gently cradled her arm in his hand and began to carefully probe the wound. Not only was there no evidence of a gunshot, but she didn't so much as flinch when he touched the skinned joint, though her sobs grew louder and more forlorn with each breath she took. His expression questioning, he said, "It's not shot, sugar. You just skinned it. It'll be fine in a couple of days."

"That's not why I'm cryin'," she sobbed, a hiccup between each syllable.

"Then, why? Do you hurt somewhere else?"

Cassie shook her head and sniffed. "My dress," she admitted tearfully. "My pretty dress is ruined."

"Your dress?" Trace repeated, his tone disbelieving.

Cassie nodded her head.

Trace stared at the sobbing young woman in his arms for a full minute. Then the impact of the fact that Cassie had not been shot hit him square in the chest. And he felt more alive than he had since the day he'd buried his sister a year before.

The laugh started as a chuckle deep in his chest, growing until it rumbled into as roaring guffaw. Relief and happiness doing flips in his heart, he threw his head back and laughed. "Cassie, Cassie, Cassie," he said. "Do you know you're one in a million! And I lo—"

"Are you laughin' at me?" Cassie interrupted with an indignant sniff, certain he was making fun of the fact that she was crying.

He shook his head and made every effort to stifle his laughter—though he couldn't quite disguise the amusement in his eyes. Scooping her into his arms as though she weighed nothing, he stood up. "I'm not laughing at you, love. It's just that I was half out of my mind with worry about you and"—his expression suddenly sobered—"I thought I had lost you, Cass . . ." His voice cracked.

Her hand moving of its own accord, she placed her palm on his cheek, caressing his smooth chin with her thumb. "I was afraid I'd never see that ugly face o' yours again," she said with a tremulous smile.

"Well, you don't have to worry about that any more. From now on, I'm not going to let you out of my sight until Murieta's dead!" he promised, clearing his throat several times. "And, as for your dress, I'll buy you a dozen more—every one of them prettier than this one."

"There'll never be a dress prettier'n this one,

McAllister. It's the first grown-up dress I ever had
'n' that's special. Even when it's old 'n' patched up,
not good for much more'n dust rags, I'm gonna
love this dress. Just like I'm always gonna love the
ma—" Her eyes burned with shock.

Cassie felt the muscles in Trace's arms tighten as
he waited for her to continue. And she knew he
wasn't ready to hear that she loved him—yet. But
he would be, she promised herself. And the minute
he was, she would be there to complete her declaration
. . . *Just like I'm always gonna love the man who gave
it to me.*

Chapter Sixteen

Cassie looped her arms around Trace's neck and rested her head against his shoulder. "I s'pose you could put me down an' let me walk since I ain't been shot after all," she said. When he tightened his grip on her and started toward the street, she smiled contentedly. "A bump on the head 'n' a scraped elbow ain't 'xactly a reason to—"

"Tell me what happened, Cassie," he said, totally ignoring the subject of releasing his possessive hold on her. "Did Murieta give you any clues to how he keeps just one step ahead of us? Did he say how he knew you'd be passing the walkway just then?"

"He musta been who was followin' me from the restaurant where I ate supper," she surmised.

A fresh spurt of fear erupted through Trace's brain. She'd been out there all evening with Murieta watching her, waiting for a chance to attack her.

"What the hell are you doing out here alone? Where's Talbot been? What if I hadn't been on the porch waiting for you when Murieta grabbed you?" The horrible possibilities for a different ending to the situation assailed him with unrelenting viciousness. "That does it," he announced with passionate resolve. "From now on, I don't want you going *anywhere* without me or Noah with you. Is that understood?"

His dogmatic tone and her own natural tendency to resist orders burst the bubble of happiness she'd been content to luxuriate in until then. "You ain't gonna tell me wh—"

"Cassie! You've got to do what I say or you're going to get yourself killed. Can't you see I'm trying to look out for you?"

"I don't 'gotta' do nothin', McAllister. An' I don't need you 'r no other man watchin' over me every minute. I'm a grown-up woman, 'n' I can take care o' myself."

A low, almost inaudible growl vibrated his chest against her shoulder, a warning that was quite familiar to Cassie. "Like you did tonight? Just once, can't you do what I tell you without an argument?"

"No," she said with a stubborn lift of her chin. Another growl rattled behind his ribs. "Why not?"

"Somethin' 'bout takin' orders just makes me swell up like a poisoned pup 'n' gets me madder'n a peeled rattler every time."

Another growl. "Well, kid, 'peeled rattlers' and 'poisoned pups' be damned, this time you're going to do what I say if I have to hogtie you."

"We'll just see 'bout that, McAllister. We'll just see!"

Both of them too angry to care about the curious stares they got as Trace carried her into the hotel and up the stairs to the second floor, neither spoke again—until they entered the room. Then the silence was broken.

"What's your gear doin' here? You was s'posed to move to a diff'rent room!"

"When I pointed the error about our rooms out to the desk clerk, he apologized, then told me all the others are taken," Trace explained, dropping her in the middle of the bed and turning back toward the door.

Inside, Cassie was secretly thrilled with the idea of sleeping all night in a bed with Trace, but pride and anger would never allow her to confess it. "That's a likely story, McAllister. Admit it. This is what you had planned all along, ain't it?"

"No, but now that it's happened, I can't say I'm unhappy about it."

Cassie's eyes lit with joy, and just a trace of a smile twitched at the corners of her mouth. "You ain't?"

"It'll make keeping an eye on you easier. So it's just as well it worked out like it did."

Her expectant smile slid off her face. "Is that the only reason?"

Trace hesitated before answering her. Hell, no, it wasn't the only reason! In fact, it was no reason at all. It was just an excuse to do what he'd fantasized about doing every night on the trail when they had spread out their bedrolls for the night. "What other reason could there be?" he asked, his back still to her.

Her dissolving smile deteriorated into a frown. "Well, it better be, 'cause if you got any ideas 'bout us sharin' this bed, you got a right big surprise comin' to you, mister!" There! That ought to show Trace McAllister he couldn't treat her like a woman when he had a hankering for one, then like a pesky kid the rest of the time.

"Believe me, kid, you're safe from me. I'm not even going to be here. Right now, I just want you to get into that bed and get some rest. And while you do, I'm going out to see if Murieta left any clues before he got away. I'll be back later."

"I told you, I don't like bein' called *kid!*" Cassie said, sitting up straight and tugging her bodice down to neaten it. "An' I ain't gonna be here neither. I'm goin' with you. I got my own score to settle with Murieta."

"You can't. I work better alone." He crossed to the door.

"I thought you wasn't gonna let me out o' your sight. Who's gonna 'look out' for me if you're gone?" Her voice contained a spiteful ring.

"You'll be okay. No one can get to you in here. And I won't be gone long. Besides, I doubt Murieta would chance coming into the hotel." With an angry yank on the door, he opened it, then turned back to Cassie, a knowing grin on his face. "And don't get any bright ideas about leaving after I'm gone, because I'm locking the door," he said, banging it closed behind him.

Cassie stared aghast at the barrier between her and the outside world. The sound of the key turning in the lock clamped around her lungs and squeezed the air from them as surely as if two hands had done it. Gasping, she ran toward the door and tugged on it. "You come back here, Trace McAllister! Unlock this door! I can't breathe in here!" But her only answer was the sound of foot-steps clumping down the stairs. "I can't breathe," she said again, her chest rising and falling rapidly as she turned back to the room and sagged against the door. "Please," she whimpered, sliding down to the floor and hugging her knees. "I can't breathe with the door locked."

Her eyes frantically searched the room for a means of getting out. Hope was reborn as she spied the window, its curtain fluttering softly as the evening breeze came in through the scant inch it was opened. "Leave me locked in a room, will he?" She sprang up from the floor and made a desperate dash for the window.

With more effort than was necessary, she ripped away the extra piece of mosquito netting that had been tacked to the window frame and flung the window open the rest of the way.

Leaning outside as far as possible, she sucked in great gulps of night air, the entire time telling her-self that she had to get over her fear of locked doors. In her rational mind, she knew there was no less air in a room with a locked door than there was in an unlocked room. But, unfortunately, thinking about her problem logically was only possible when she was able to get enough fresh air into her lungs.

The picture of a weeping ten-year-old girl flashed across her mind. She was kneeling on the floor, her thin body slumped against the door, her small hands above her head and clinging to a door han-dle. *Don't leave me,* the little girl cried in her mem-ory. *Mama! Papa! Please don't leave me!*

"Don't leave me!" Cassie pleaded aloud, though no one heard her.

Slowly, as her lungs filled with fresh, life-supporting air, Cassie regained her ability to act rationally. Bringing her head back inside the room, she took a deep breath and stared out the window. She knew what she had to do.

Without giving thought to what Trace would do when he found her gone, she hurriedly changed into her jeans and strapped her holster around her slim hips. "There's more'n one way to skin a cat," she told herself as, taking a last glance around the room, she hiked a long leg over the window edge.

Straddling the sill as she would a horse, she studied the ground below, then glanced upward. The third story had a balcony all the way around. But this wasn't the third floor. It was the second. And there was no balcony on this level—except across the front of the hotel. From this room it was a straight drop to the walkway where Murieta had accosted her. No wonder Trace had thought she wouldn't be able to leave. Well, she'd show him.

Working her way to her knees on the window ledge, her bottom exiting first, she hooked her fingers over the inside sill, then eased herself, one leg at a time, out the window. When she was dangling on the side of the building, her long arms and body stretching their full length, she peeked back over her shoulder at the ground to gauge the distance she would have to drop. From here it looked a long way down. But fortunately, her toes were at least five and a half feet closer to the ground than her eyes were.

Bolstering her courage with one last gulp of air drawn into her lungs and held there, Cassie released her grip on the windowsill and dropped to the ground. Expelling her breath as her boots touched the ground, she agilely folded her body into a crouch to absorb the initial shock of the fall.

The back door leading out to the alley behind the Eagle Theatre opened suddenly, startling Trace. Acting automatically, he ducked into the shadows of the acting troupe's wagon and waited cautiously. He didn't have any particular reason for not wanting to be seen by whoever was coming out of the theater—once more Murieta had slipped from his grasp without leaving a trace—but still he didn't move. Call it gut instinct, a hunch, wishful thinking, he only knew he should stay hidden.

Listening intently to the murmur of two voices, one decidedly feminine, he tried to determine who it was. If he could just make out what they were saying.

Careful to stay hidden, he inched his way a little closer to the door, which opened outward and blocked his view of the two people. He immediately recognized the feminine voice as belonging to the buxom Mimi Witherspoon. But it was the man's voice that caught his attention. It sounded vaguely familiar, though it continued to be so low and intimate that he couldn't make out the words the man was saying.

"Don't worry, lover," he heard Mimi say, her voice husky with sexuality. "It won't be long. I'll see you in San Francisco on Friday just like we planned." There was a long silence as the man and the woman must have been kissing. "There, that ought to hold you till then," she said with a suggestive chuckle.

The man's low reply went unheard by Trace, who was too busy kicking himself for getting caught in such an awkward fix. Now that he found himself the unwilling witness to a lovers' good-night kiss, he would have liked nothing more than to just walk away. But he couldn't suddenly appear from behind the wagon and act as if he hadn't been there all along. He had no choice but to wait until the two had finished their farewells. Then he could sneak away unnoticed.

Feeling like a perverted eavesdropper, he tried to block out the private conversation going on a few feet away by using the time to retrace his actions since he had left Cassie. How could Murieta just appear and disappear the way he did? And how could he have gotten in and out of Sacramento without anybody seeing him?

The man in the doorway said something, then laughed. And it was in that instant that Trace recognized who Mimi's lover was. *Murieta!* a voice in his mind shouted—just as a skull-crushing blow made solid contact with his head and sent him into oblivion.

Sticking in the shadows, her hat pulled low, her hand poised on the butt of her Colt .45, Cassie made her way through the alleys and stables of Sacramento. She knew she wouldn't find Murieta in the saloons or on the streets. No, his type skulked in dark alleys and back rooms, waiting to attack unsuspecting passersby. If he was still in town, he'd be back here with the rats and pigs rooting through the garbage thrown into the alleys.

"I might as well go back to the hotel 'n' get some rest," she said to herself with a disgusted snort for the wasted hour she'd spent. She hadn't even turned up one clue!

She had talked to one old man who had caused her hopes to sail when he'd said he might've seen Murieta. But then in the next breath, he had whipped a whiskey bottle out of his pocket and, between swigs, said, "But then, them Mexes all look alike to me. Like those fan-tan-playin' Chinamen do."

When Trace awoke, he was in what seemed to be a very small room. Though it had no windows, the cramped space was lit by a glass-chimneyed lamp on a small table beside the velvet couch where he lay. All around him, in trunks on the floor, and from pegs on the walls, were hats, props, wigs, and brightly colored costumes of a dozen different styles.

"Ah, I see you're awake," a feminine voice cooed from above his head. "How do you feel?"

"Mimi?" Trace asked, tilting his head back and looking up at her. "Where are we? How'd I get here? Where's Murieta?"

Mimi laughed. "There, there, luv. Always in such a hurry." She caressed his cheek with a large but graceful hand. "Relax. You've had a nasty blow on your head. You shouldn't try to talk now."

Tossing her hand away from his face, he sat up. "I can't wait until later. I need some answers now! Where's Murieta?"

Seeing there was no putting him off, Mimi sighed and sat down beside him. "*Joaquin* Murieta?" she asked innocently.

"Of course, Joaquin Murieta! You were talking to him! Where is he?"

"You must be confused, ducks. Where did you ever get the crazy idea I was talking to the likes of him?"

"Cut the act, Mimi," Trace said, standing up. "I heard you."

"Oh!" She looked worried, then quickly masked it behind her heavily made-up eyes. "You *heard* us? Didn't you *see* who I was talking to?"

"I didn't need to see him. I recognized his laugh."

Trace was sure he detected a flicker of relief in Mimi's expression. "Well, it's too bad you didn't get a look at him. He may have a laugh like your Mexican bandit's, but believe me, that's the only similarity. Not only is my dear Maxwell older, grayer, lighter complected, and heavier than Joaquin Murieta, but he has a thick German accent."

"How do you know what Murieta looks like? I thought you told me before that you've never seen him," Trace said, watching her suspiciously as she toyed with the fringe on a nearby costume.

"I've seen the wanted posters," she came back quickly. "They all describe him as under thirty, slim, and having black hair."

"If you were talking to Maxwell and not Murieta, why was I hit on the head before I could see him?"

"That, I'm afraid, is Angel's fault."

"Who's Angel?"

"One of my girls. She was in the wagon and heard you lurking outside. She thought you were coming to rob us, so she hit you with one of these." Mimi held up a heavy brass candlestick holder. "I am sorry, but a girl can't be too careful these days. Besides, it was your own fault. You really had no business being there, did you?" Her mouth spread and her eyes narrowed in an insincere smile.

274

Knowing that arguing with Mimi Witherspoon any longer would be a waste of time, Trace shook his head. Besides, maybe she was telling the truth. Maybe he was just letting his imagination run away with him. Either way, it might be better if he seemed to believe her story about her German suitor.

"I feel like a fool," he said, managing to look properly shamefaced. "I guess having Murieta keep giving me the slip has gotten me so frustrated that I'm starting to make things up! Maybe I ought to just give up and admit he's too smart for me." He headed for the door. "Apologize to Angel for me for scaring her, will you?"

"Are you sure you're all right to leave? You know you're welcome to stay here tonight," Mimi said, catching his arm in her hand and giving it a squeeze, then gliding her hand upward.

Why being touched by this woman repulsed him so much he didn't know, but it was all he could do to hide the shiver of distaste that tore through him. "I'll sleep better in my own bed. But thanks anyway." He slammed the door to the wagon open and bounded to the ground rather than use the stairs.

"If you change your mind, the offer's still open!"

"Yeah, well, I'll keep that in mind. Thanks for taking me in."

"Any time, lover. Any time!"

Cassie stared dumbfounded at the woman silhouetted in the doorway of the theater wagon and at the man looking up at her from the bottom of the stairs. *So that's why he was in such a all-fired hurry to lock me out of the way!* Well, she'd show him that Cassie Wyman wasn't a woman to take being two-timed so lightly!

"Howdy!" she shouted, her friendliness disguising the hurt and rage that pulsated through her veins with the intensity of Indian war drums as she stepped out of the shadows, a forced smile pasted on her face.

Trace jumped back from the wagon door, his expression as guilty as if he'd been caught in a truly compromising situation. "Cassie! What're you doing here? I thought you were in the—"

"Looks like you figgered wrong, don't it?" She walked over and stood beside him, her companionable smile directed to Mimi. "Ain't you gonna introduce me to your friend, Trace? Never mind," she said, holding out her right hand. "Name's Cassie. An' I guess you're the famous Mrs. Witherspoon."

"Why, yes, I am," Mimi said, obviously flattered that she'd been recognized. "How did you know? Have you seen me perform?"

Her friendly smile never faltering, Cassie shook her head. "Heck no! I just figgered the 'four beautiful daughters' on the sign would be much younger than you."

"I see," Mimi said, her pleased expression falling. "In that case, you must come see us perform while you're in town. We'll be here one more night. I can arrange a ticket for you."

"Why, that's right nice o' you. Ain't it, Trace, honey?" She hooked her arm in his and smiled. "We just might take you up on your offer. Mrs. Witherspoon—that is, if we stay in Sacramento another night."

Trace stared in astonishment at Cassie. Then his astonishment turned to anger. Who did she think he was, coming here and acting like she had some claim on him?

Mimi looked at Trace questioningly, as if to say he found it hard to imagine him with such a country bumpkin as Cassie. "We?" she asked with raised eyebrows.

Recovering from the shock of seeing Cassie strolling toward him a moment before, Trace's minimal control of his anger gave way. Shaking off her proprietary hold, he grabbed her upper arm tightly. Yeah, 'we,'" he growled, never lifting his glare from Cassie's grinning face. His fingers dug into the muscle of her arm and he gave her a prod forward. "Come on, kid! *We* have some business to take care of, don't we?" He gave her another shove.

"Looks to me like you already took care o' your 'business'!" she said under her breath for his ears alone. "I'd say you 'n' me got no more business 'tween us!"

"Thanks, Mimi!" Trace called over his shoulder to the woman, who continued to stand in the wagon doorway and watch them. "Now! Suppose you tell me what you're doing here?"

"I was tendin' to real business, not *monkey business* like some folks I ain't gonna mention!"

"Stop it," he ordered through his teeth. "What I was doing with Mimi or not doing with Mimi is no concern of yours. I want to know how you got out of that hotel room and what you've been up to—besides spying on me."

"I was lookin' for Murieta, not that it's none o' your business. An' I got lots more interestin' things to do with my time than spy on you 'n' your floozies!"

"Once and for all, Mimi Witherspoon's not my

277

'floozy'!"

"Hmp! You don't 'spect me to b'lieve that, do you? If she ain't your floozy, what was you doin' comin' outta her wagon just now?"

"It doesn't make any difference to me what you believe, kid. All I care about is putting Murieta in jail and getting your gold back from him, so I can wash my hands of you and this entire mess. I never should have agreed to this crazy partnership in the first place. I must've been out of my mind!"

Trace's words slammed into Cassie's gut with brute force, almost doubling her over in pain. He couldn't wait to be rid of her!

Self-disgust and embarrassment flooded her every cell. It was bad enough that she'd fallen in love with him. But what was even worse was that she had convinced herself he felt something for her too. Well, she didn't intend to hang around and continue making a fool of herself.

"As far as I'm concerned, we can call off the whole deal right now. In fact, that's what I come to tell you. Partners are okay for some folks, but not for me. I figger things'll work out better if I ride alone from here on out."

Unable to resist admiring Cassie's spunk and pride, Trace's anger mellowed. He knew he'd hurt her by saying what he had said, and he was ashamed of himself. But dammit! What the hell was he supposed to do? Why'd she have to be such a handful? Why couldn't she be like an ordinary female? Dress and act like she was supposed to? Females were supposed to do things to please a man, make his life more pleasurable, not obstruct and defy him at every turn. A woman was supposed to let a man take care of her and make decisions for

278

her, not try to best him on everything.

But if she wasn't like she is, she wouldn't be Cassie, an inner voice pointed out with anger-dissolving clarity. *And I probably wouldn't be in love wi —*

Trace's eyes filled with alarm as the gut-knotting thought ricocheted through his body.

Of course, it wasn't true. It had just been an accidental slip, he placated himself. He wasn't in love with her—or anyone else, for that matter. But when he did fall in love, it wouldn't be with someone like Cassie. His ideal woman would be a woman he could put on a pedestal, a woman he could worship and protect, a woman who would listen to him and respect his word, a woman who would be happy to be at home waiting for him at the end of a weary day.

But no matter how many reasons his brain managed to manufacture for why he couldn't be in love with Cassie, his heart would supply a logical argument: *She's foolhardy—She's brave . . . and she's smart!—Too smart. She thinks she knows everything. And if just once she considered the consequences before she acted, I'd be shocked—But she's honest. And that's rare—If you call being tactless and not thinking before she blurts out whatever she wants "honest," I guess she is—She is fun to be with—If she just weren't so opinionated and unpredictable and . . .*

When Trace didn't respond to her suggestion that they break up their partnership, Cassie's heart slipped another degree. *Well, what'd you expect? You didn't think he was gonna fight you about it, did you? He didn't want you along in the first place. And he jus' told you he can't wait to wash*

279

his hands o' you. What more do you need, girl?

"I'll just get my gear out o' the room 'n' be on my way," she said, unable to look at him for fear she would burst into tears if she did, a condition she'd found herself in a lot since she met Trace McAllister.

"What're you talking about?" Trace asked, looking as if he had suffered a grave shock and had just realized he wasn't alone.

" 'Bout me goin' on after Murieta by myself," she said over an annoying break in her voice.

"I don't know where you get these harebrained ideas you come up with, but you're not going anywhere."

Confused, Cassie stopped in her tracks and looked up at Trace, despite her vow not to. "Says who?"

"Says me!"

"Yeah? You 'n' what posse? We ain't partners no more, so you can stop tryin' to order me 'round. I'm sleepin' in the stable tonight 'n' gettin' a early start in the mornin'. Alone." She wheeled on her boot heel and broke into a run down the walk that stretched alongside the hotel.

"Hold on there," Trace said, his long legs making it possible for him to overtake her in a couple of strides. Grabbing her by the shoulders, he spun her around to face him.

"Let go o' me!" she grunted, twisting against his hold on her.

"Not till we settle this."

"It's settled. You wanted us to split up 'n' that's what we're doin'!"

His patience dropping to an all-time low, Trace released one of his almost-indiscernible growls, bent

280

forward, and grabbed Cassie around the knees. In one efficient motion, he slung her over his shoulder, straightened his posture, and started walking.

Stunned to find herself in such a position, Cassie kicked ineffectively at the air and flailed his hard back with her fists. "Put me down, you whorin' son of a—"

Her unladylike insult was cut off with a resounding slap on the denim-covered roundness of her aptly positioned bottom. "I've told you I don't want you talking like that!"

Cassie sucked in a squawking gasp of air. He had spanked her! Just who the hell did he think he was? Her fight for freedom resumed with revived determination. "You bas—"

Whack! The distinctive sound of another stinging blow to her backside reverberated through the darkness. "Keep it up, kid, and tomorrow you'll wish you could ride standing up!" His stride carried him rapidly toward the front of the hotel.

"Go to he—"

Smack!

"Dam—"

Thwack! "Are you through?"

"You no-good, yellow-livered, so—"

Cassie sensed, rather than saw, Trace's hand poised above her buttocks in preparation for the next wallop. "All right," she grunted, the fight suddenly drained from her, "you win. I won't call you no more names. Just put me down."

"Sorry, kid," he said, the apology in his voice not the least bit genuine. "But I don't trust you."

Adjusting her weight to a more secure position on his shoulder, he tightened his grip on her thighs. Then, refusing to recognize the true reason he'd been unable to let her leave him, he exited the walkway and stormed onto the front porch of the hotel—oblivious to all the smirks and wisecracks for the second time that day.

Chapter Seventeen

Salina straightened her shoulders. "It's useless, Noah," she said, her large eyes watery with tears. "You tried, but he's won."

"No," Noah protested. "We can't give up! I'll find a way. I will!"

Shaking her head, Salina released a sad little laugh. "We were fools to think we could beat him. He has everything on his side. Money, power, color. He has it all and we have nothing."

"Don't say that. We have our love!"

"Before he's through, Cliff will destroy that too!"

"Never! He can't take our love from us!"

"He will. You'll grow to hate me."

"No!" he said, pulling her into his arms and hugging her possessively.

Rather than give in to the embrace, Salina pushed Noah's chest and said, "Yes, Noah, he will."

"No," he moaned.

"Will you still want me after I've worked in the upstairs rooms of Cliff's gambling hall, Noah?"

"I'll always want you! Always!"

"You may think so now, but after I've whored for Cliff and been used by other men, how will you feel?"

The tears were running freely down her golden brown cheeks now. She reached up and cupped his dark cheek in her small hand. "I could never do that to our love, Noah. I could never come to your bed dirty."

"You wouldn't be dirty if you had no choice. I wouldn't care what's happened in the past."

"It's no use, my love. You tried and I'll always remember how hard you tried. But now it's time for you to forget me and let me do what I have to do."

"Noooooo!" Noah cried, but she was already backing away from him, growing smaller and smaller. "Don't do it, Salina. Wait for me. I'll find a way for us to be together."

"Perhaps in another place and another lifetime. But not in this one, my love. We can never be together in this life! Good-bye, Noah. I'll always love you!"

"Don't leave me, Salina," he pleaded, reaching out to her disappearing form. "I'll find a way."

"There's no more time, Noah." Her voice was fading. "Forget about me. Cliff has won."

Her words were growing more difficult to hear and he started to run after her. But his feet wouldn't obey his brain's command. He couldn't make them move. He looked down and found his legs were buried up to his knees in sticky, gluelike mud. He struggled against the hold the goo had on

284

him, but it was no good. The more he fought, the deeper he sank into the mire. Panicked, he shouted, "Come back, Salina. I'll find a way! I will!"

"It's no use!" the fading voice called from so far away that she was only a tiny figure on the horizon now. "Cliff has won!"

"Sa-leeeeeen-aaaaa" Noah wailed, bolting upright in the bunk where he slept in the back of a Sacramento stable. "He won't win! He won't!"

"Wake up, boy," the gruff user of the other bunk ordered, giving Noah's hard shoulder a good shake.

Noah opened his eyes and stared glassily at the older man. A dream. It had just been a dream. There was still time!

"You all right, boy?"

"What's the date?" Noah asked wiping the beads of sweat from his brow. "How long until the end of the month?"

Frowning, the man squinted at a tattered feed-store calendar on the wall. "Looks like the end o' the month's 'bout a week away yet. Today's the twenty-third."

"Seven days," Noah shouted, his face breaking into a relieved grin. "I've still got seven days!"

Jumping up from the bunk, he set his hat on his head and shrugged his arms into his shirt. "I'm sorry I woke you up, mister. Will this cover the inconvenience?" he asked, digging a gold coin from his pocket and handing it to the surprised man.

The man looked down at the coin in his hand and nodded his head. "Yeah, it'll cover the in-con-ve— Say, anybody ever tell you, you don't talk like no ni—"

"Can you take a message to my partner first thing in the morning?" Noah interrupted, fishing paper and pencil from his saddlebag. "He's staying at the City Hotel." Noah was already writing.

"Sure," the man answered, his expression impressed at the sight of a man of color who not only spoke fancier than most white men he'd met, but could actually *write!*

"His name's Trace McAllister," Noah said, handing the man the folded note and a second coin. "Don't forget. Trace McAllister, City Hotel. And I've told him to give you something extra for bringing this note to him."

"You can trust me to get it to him, boy." He tucked the note in his vest pocket and bit down on the coin. Finding it was genuine, he dropped it into a sadly empty pouch.

By the time they reached the locked room on the second floor of the hotel, Cassie's ears were ringing and most of the fight had left her.

"Now," Trace said, letting her down on her feet with a less-than-gentle drop, "get out of those clothes and into bed before I really lose my temper. We're leaving early in the morning and I don't want you holding me up. I know where Murieta's going to be at the end of the week and I plan to be waiting for him when he shows up."

Her ears roaring from being upside down, Cassie's vision swam crazily as she assumed her natural upright position. "You really know where Murieta is?" she asked with a drunken slur to her words, swaying helplessly the instant Trace released her.

"Yeah," he admitted, catching her as she leaned forward. Scooping her into his arms again, this time cradled against his chest, he carried her to the bed. "At least, it looks that way." He took off her hat and pitched it toward a chair. Seeming not to notice the cascade of riotous red-gold hair that spilled to her shoulders as he lay her back on the pillow, he began to unbuckle and remove the holster around her waist. Then he started on her shirt.

Her dizziness made it difficult to concentrate on his words *and* what his hands were doing at the same time, so Cassie didn't resist his gentle actions. "Where is he? How'd you find out?" she asked, lazily shutting her eyes. Certainly if she rested them for a moment or two her head would clear. "Are you sure it's him?"

"I can't be until I'm actually face to face with him, but it's the best lead we've come up with," he said. His deep voice broke as he became uncomfortably aware of the gentle rise and fall of her breasts against the outside edges of his hands as he worked on the shirt buttons. His fingers froze on the button between her breasts, and his gaze rose helplessly to meet hers. All thoughts of Murieta were magically erased from his mind. And suddenly all the fight left him too.

Face it, McAllister! You're in trouble. Cassie Wyman may not be what *you want, but she's who you want!*

He shook his head in hopeless resignation. "Cassie, Cassie, Cassie," he said, his gaze roving over her trusting face and down to where his fingers had just opened her shirt to expose the beginning swell of her breasts.

"What?" she asked, frowning at the feeble smile on his face. Her head and vision were clear now, but she found she had no desire to move.

"What am I going to do with you? I keep telling

287

you that you're going to get killed if you aren't careful, but you keep doing these crazy things. What can I say to you to make you understand how dangerous this all is?"

Her hands acting of their own volition, Cassie sandwiched Trace's unhappy face between her palms. "Don't say nothin'," she whispered hoarsely, lifting her head off the pillow to meet his lips as she brought his face toward hers.

Trace hesitated an instant, his mouth a scant inch from hers, so close the warmth of their breathing united in a sweet cloud of oneness that left him weak. He knew that if he had a shred of sense, he would get up that very minute and run like hell. But he knew just as certainly that if he were facing a threat of death for kissing Cassie, he would have willingly given his life for that one last kiss before he died.

The reflection of the lamplight changed his green eyes to feverish gold and he knew there was no turning back. Expelling a low, hungry growl, Trace closed the unbearable space between their mouths.

Cassie's trembling lips opened to welcome the possession of his tongue, and she burrowed her fingers into the dark hair at his temples to clutch him harder to her. A tiny voice deep in her conscience scolded her for not resisting him. After all, hadn't he told her he couldn't wait to be rid of her? And hadn't he humiliated her unforgivably when he'd carried her up to the room just now, slung over his shoulder like so much excess baggage?

But a need, more urgent and more demanding than the loudest of voices, screamed out, telling her not to listen to the torturous advice of her mind. And she didn't. Couldn't!

His mouth on hers was so warm, so right, and all she knew was that as long as she lived, she would never have enough of it, or of him. If he didn't want her after tonight, then so be it. But for now, she would not deny herself the chance to know paradise one last time. And afterward, when he left her, she would not be sorry, for her memories of their brief moments together would remain with her the rest of her life. And that would be enough for her.

Disentangling himself from her frantic grip, Trace hurriedly tore off his clothes, then stretched his long frame out beside her. "Oh, honey, do you have any idea what you do to me?" he moaned, moving his hardness against her as he tried to manipulate his shaking fingers to finish unbuttoning her shirt.

Cassie smiled at his sudden nervousness and closed her hands over his on the buttons. "I'll do it," she offered softly.

Trace nodded his head and removed his fingers from the buttons. Dragging his tongue along the perimeter of his mouth, suddenly gone dry, he propped himself up on his elbow and watched her fingers, which were shaking only slightly less than his, slip one button, then another, from their respective holes.

Slowly, deliberately, her gaze locked with his, she moved her hands down the row of buttons, seductively exposing a bit more flesh with each unfastening.

"Oh, my god," he groaned, unable to deny himself the view of more of her chest than just the pale strip between the opened shirtfronts. His entire body trembling now, he rose up on his knees and slipped his hands inside the shirt, spanning her waist from side to side with their breadth. His touch caressed its way upward along her rib cage and over her breasts, peeling the shirt back from her shoulders to at last reveal the desirable mounds to his ravenous gaze.

With the groan of a starving man at the sight of food, he stared entranced for a long moment, as if he could not believe he wasn't going to die after all. Then, as the reality of her loveliness sank into his brain, he bent his head to taste the delectable manna of the hollow between her breasts. Cradling his face greedily in the softness, he squeezed the firm mounds together against his cheeks. His thumbs rotated over her nipples, working them to hard pebbles. "You taste so good," he said, licking up and down the length of the deep crevice he had created.

His words and moist breath against her flesh were hot, scalding, yet they sent a storm of goose pimples storming over her skin. "Must be all the baths I been takin'," she murmured, holding his head tighter to her.

Her words taking him off guard, Trace reared his head and stared down at her, certain she was making a joke. He was surprised by her serious expression. She hadn't been teasing. She had merely been stating what she believed to be a fact. A smile twitched at the corners of his mouth, but he couldn't allow himself to laugh. Their relationship was still too fragile. "Must be," he said, his voice rasping as he swallowed back the chuckle that continued to bubble in his chest. "So there's something good to be said for them, after all, isn't there? Even if you do hate them."

Cassie smiled lazily, raising her arms and rubbing

290

her hands over his broad shoulders, now slightly damp with perspiration. "I'll tell you a little secret. I don't hate baths. I like 'em."

"You could have fooled me, the fuss you put up about that first one."

"I just don't like bein' told to take one."

His ardor cooled only slightly by the brief conversation, Trace slid his fingers inside the waistband of her jeans. "I wonder—" His heated gaze scorched over her body. "—do you taste so good all over?" To answer his own question, he ducked his head and trailed his tongue along the narrow line where the denim of her jeans pulled away from her belly.

Her stomach muscles contracted in an erotic spasm as the torch of his tongue inflamed her flesh from hip to hip.

"Mmm." The sound vibrated against her belly. "Delicious." He sat up and reached for the top button on her fly. His fingers suddenly nimble again, he hurriedly slipped the button from the buttonhole, then bent to taste the pale vee of white lawn drawers he had exposed. Another button, another kiss, until there were none left to undo.

Trace could no longer hold back, could no longer deny himself the view of the feminine treasure hidden behind the translucent material of her undergarment. "Stand up," he commanded, drawing her to her feet.

With agility born of desperation, he stripped the shirt the rest of the way off her and tossed it aside, unconcerned when it landed a foot short of the chair he had aimed for. Dropping to his knees before her, he lifted one foot, then the other, and removed her boots and socks. Looking up the length of her statue-still body, he wrapped his fingers around her legs at the ankles and slid his hands up the long limbs. Spanning the narrow width of her hips with his hands, he pressed his thumbs along the crease at the tops of her legs until they met at the center of her body and burrowed into the hot division.

"Oooh," she sighed, rocking the mound of her femininity toward the pressing, exploring thumbs.

His actions instinctive and urgent, Trace hurriedly completed the journey of his hands to her waist where he inserted his fingers into the waistband of her jeans. His impatience evident, he dragged the pants and drawers downward.

Her own urgency as great as his, Cassie steadied herself by gripping his shoulders and lifting her feet one at a time so Trace could remove the last of her clothing.

Trace rested back on his haunches and turned her around slowly, his gaze assessing her willowy proportions with lazy approval. "Mmm." He stopped her pivot and leaned forward to kiss the defenseless creases behind her knees.

Flames of fire raged up her thighs to the moist center of her sex as his light kiss quickly became hungry nibbles moving up the backs of her legs. Moaning her pleasure aloud, Cassie sank helplessly to her knees, catching her torso on the edge of the bed.

A fiery trail of kisses burned over the roundness of her buttocks to the sensitive hollow at the base of her spine. She lurched forward as if she were attempting to crawl away from the exquisite torture.

Insinuating his knees between hers, Trace gripped her hips in strong hands and covered her back with his body. Gently biting her shoulder, he dug his fingers into the susceptible folds of her pelvis and dragged the mounds of her buttocks into the curve of his own hips.

Succumbing to the demand that pressed into her, Cassie widened the space between her knees and, instinctively arching her hips to make herself more available, strained back toward the probing hardness of his manhood.

"Yes," he groaned, entering the hot satin sheath of her femininity with a hard thrust as he caught the bud of her desire in his fingers.

"Uhh," she ground out, her own fingers frantically clawing at the bed linens as he carried her closer and closer to the edge of sanity with his twisting caresses and the penetrating motions of his body.

Their rapid breathing growing more labored by the instant, he plunged deeper into her welcoming heat with each stroke.

Holding her breath, Cassie bit back the cry of ecstasy that surged in her throat. In an effort to retain her hold on reality, she buried her face against the wadded blanket she clutched with desperate strength. But it was no use. She was too far gone. Too far removed from the awareness of anything but the building volcano that was threatening to erupt within her.

Then it was happening, and all she could do was ride out the explosion. She was no longer in control. Rearing her head, she released a long cry of ecstasy as the muscles of her desire convulsed in shuddering spasm after spasm.

His own fulfillment imminent, Trace tensed, then slammed into her with a final burst of passion as her body seized him and wrung his rapture from him with its tight, frenzied possession.

Her chest heaving, Cassie buried her face in the rumpled bedding, and Trace dropped his forehead against her back, now damp with a dewy sheen of perspiration.

After long moments, when their breathing had resumed a slight semblance of normalcy, Trace slowly withdrew from her while raining a line of nipping kisses across her shoulders. "Let's go to bed," he whispered against her neck.

"Are you gonna stay?" she asked breathlessly. The other times they'd made love, it had been wonderful too, but they'd had fights afterward and one of them had ended up storming out of the room both times. She hadn't dared to let herself hope this time would be any different.

"I told you, Cassie, neither of us is going anywhere." He drew her to her feet and threw back the covers on the bed. "We're partners," he said, guiding her onto the mattress. "So whether you like it or not, you're stuck with me. And no matter what you say or do, I'm going to take care of you until I know Murieta can't hurt you."

He blew out the lamp and climbed into the bed beside her, pulling the covers over their naked bodies. Settling himself on his pillow, he wrapped his arm around her shoulders and brought her head to rest on his chest. "Now, what do you say we get some sleep? I have a feeling this partnership has only begun to test my strength."

Afraid to trust the glorious feeling of security that enveloped her, Cassie snuggled against his side and wrapped her arm over his chest. "Trace?"

"Mmm?" he answered drowsily.

"When Murieta's took care o' 'n' we ain't partners no more, where you gonna go?"

Trace was silent for so long that she thought he must be asleep. Then he spoke. "Home, I guess."

"Home?" She'd never thought about Trace McAlister having a home. He had just seemed like a man with no roots, a wanderer. "Where's home?"

"My family's in Los Angeles," he said.

Family? Panic and hurt squeezed at her heart. It had never even occurred to her to ask Trace if he was married. She had just assumed he wasn't. "Your family?" she asked, her hand on his chest tightening in a tangle of dark hair.

"What there is left of it, anyway," he said bitterly, catching her hand in his and bringing her fingertips to his lips. "Thanks to Murieta, there's only my grandfather and me now."

Feeling guilty for the excited rush of relief that washed over her at his words, Cassie relaxed. He wasn't married! "Murieta?"

Trace sucked in a labored breath, then released it slowly, as though debating whether or not to tell her. "About six months ago, the stagecoach my sister and my grandmother were traveling on was topped by Murieta and robbed. But the bastard wasn't satisfied with just stealing. He had to have his fun. When he'd taken everything of value off the stage and from the passengers' purses, he fired shots over the backs of the horses to deliberately frighten them. In their blind panic, they stampeded and ran off the road into a deep gully. The driver managed to jump just as the coach went over the edge. But the people inside weren't so lucky. They were all killed instantly," he added with a shudder that Cassie was sure was a sob.

Compassion and love for Trace clutched painfully at her heart, and she burrowed her face into the curve of his neck. "I hope he roasts in hell for what he done."

"Not a day has gone by in the last six months that I haven't said the same thing. And I plan to be the one to put him there. That's why I joined up with Harry Love and his volunteers. I wasn't getting anywhere on my own and thought they might help. But you see how much good they did me."

"An' if you hadn't o' been workin' with them sorry lawmen, you wouldn't 'a got yourself saddled with me neither." She rolled onto her stomach and, resting her chin on his chest, studied his face for his reaction.

Trace didn't answer for what seemed like an eternity. Then a sad smile curved his mouth as his glance moved over her face. "Being 'saddled' with you is probably the best thing that's come from this whole thing."

Cassie's heartbeat accelerated and her eyebrows raised hopefully. "It is?"

"Until you came along, I'd forgotten how good it felt to smile. But from the minute I saw Tom Newman's mouth drop open when he found out you were a female, you've made me smile."

"An' feel good?"

Trace released a defeated chuckle and nodded his head, remembering all the times he'd been so frustrated and angry with Cassie. "Better than good, sugar. Keeping up with you has made me feel alive again. For the first time since my sister and grandmother were killed, I've thought more about keeping someone alive than I have about killing Murieta."

"Does that mean you're glad we're partners?" she asked, relaxing her head on his shoulder again and squirming to snuggle closer against his side.

"Yeah, I guess that's what it means," he admitted with an affectionate squeeze. "Though I never thought I'd hear myself say it out loud," he said drowsily.

"I'm glad too. Since my mama died, no one's ever wanted to take care o' me. Not even my pa. I was the one who done the takin' care of. To tell the truth, it's kinda nice havin' you worry 'bout me—even if you're awful bossy 'bout it."

When Trace's response was a soft snore, Cassie smiled to herself and rose up on an elbow for one last look at his handsome face. Funny, he looked younger and more vulnerable than she'd ever noticed. And Cassie knew in that instant that he needed her just as much as she needed him. "Good night, sweet Trace," she whispered and kissed his lips lightly.

"Ga-night, love," he mumbled. "Sleep tight."

And for the first night in many years, Cassie went to sleep feeling protected and loved and needed.

"What's it say?" Cassie asked, peeking around Trace's broad back to see the message the old man had just delivered to their room. "Who's it from?"

"Noah's decided to go on to San Francisco," Trace said. "He's worried we're not going to find Murieta soon enough to save Salina. So he's decided to go after her, gold or no gold."

"But if he does that, Salina will never forgive him for putting her mother in danger!"

"He says he's willing to take that risk. But I'm more worried about what's going to happen to him. No matter what the law says, there's still a fierce prejudice against black men. And if he looks at someone the wrong way, he's liable to find himself arrested on some trumped-up charge and dangling at the end of a rope before he's been in San Francisco twenty-four hours."

The thought of the big, gentle man hanging gathered in a sickening knot in Cassie's belly. "We gotta stop him!"

"According to the old man, he left about midnight. That gives him at least a seven-hour head start on us."

"Well, what're we waitin' for. Let's go after him!" Cassie said, tossing aside the towel she'd been drying herself with when the knock announcing the messenger had interrupted her bath.

Admiring Cassie's lack of false modesty—and the view of her bottom as it disappeared behind the dressing screen, Trace shook his head and frowned. Who'd have thought they would ever be working together like this, rather than fighting each other all the way? This partner thing could get to be a habit that might prove hard to break. But for now, he couldn't think about that. He had to concentrate on Noah.

"I just hope we're not too late. From the sound of the mood he was in when he wrote this note, if we ride into San Francisco seven hours behind him, it'll all be over but the cheering when they string him up!"

"Knowing the way Noah follows a trail," Cassie said, peeking out from behind the screen, "I wouldn't be surprised if we overtake him halfway there!"

"I hope you're right, kid. But I've got a feeling we're dealing with a different Noah than we've known in the past."

Chapter Eighteen

Oblivious to the workmen who scurried past where he stood in the main salon of the Golden Goose, Cliff Hopkins studied the letter in his hand. His lips moving silently, he reread the message, his face staining a deep crimson. With an angry growl, he wadded the paper and tossed it to the floor. "They're not going to get away with this, you know," he said to no one in particular. "I'm opening a week from tomorrow, and no one's going to stop me!" He stormed over to where Salina was polishing mugs and arranging them on glass shelves behind the bar. "Aren't you about through here?"

Salina turned her bruised face to her half brother and smiled, her crooked smile accentuating her swollen lip. "What's wrong?" she asked, deliberately ignoring his question.

"That's right! Smile! You'd like it if they forced me to shut down before I even opened, wouldn't you?"

Rather than tell the truth, Salina answered his question with one of her own. "Is someone trying to close the Golden Goose?"

"Don't give me that innocent look. You know the other gambling casinos on Portsmouth Square have banded together from the very beginning to try and stop me."

"What makes you say that? They've been very friendly. Just this morning the manager of Parker House came by to—"

"Of course they make a show of welcoming me, to my face. Their type prefers to sneak around behind a man's back."

And you certainly do understand that kind of person, don't you, brother dear? Salina asked silently.

"But I know they're behind all the delays and problems I've had: getting shipments on time, keeping workmen on the job . . . and now this latest ploy. Well, it won't work! We're opening next week with or without their good wishes!"

"What ploy is that, Cliff?" she asked, turning her back to him and resuming her work. She'd grown very tired of hearing her half brother rant and rave about the way all the big casino owners were in cahoots to put him out of business.

"That policeman just brought me an order saying I can't open for business until I have some sort of license to operate a gambling establishment! Hmp! I'll tell you what they can do with their license!"

"Aren't you making a mountain out of a mole-hill?" she asked with disgust. "Why don't you just go get the license?"

301

"I would if I thought it was legitimate. But you mark my words, as soon as I pay the license fee, they'll just manufacture another trick to stop me. The crooks at City Hall are all on their payrolls. So if the big-money boys want me out of the way, City Hall's going to back them all the way. But they don't know who they're dealing with here. They're not the only ones who can play games." He spun away from the bar and snatched up his walking cane and hat.

"What're you going to do?"

"I'm going to City Hall and make a few friends of my own!" he sneered over his shoulder. "And when I get back, you be through there!"

"Yassuh, Massa Cliff," she mumbled with a sarcastic curtsy to his back. "Ah'll sho 'nuff do dat, Massa Cliff!"

Returning her attention to the crate of glasses at her feet, Salina squatted down and began to unpack them one at a time, her movements slow and careful. Then, as the full impact of her hopelessness hit her, the fragile rein she'd managed to keep on her emotions broke.

With a long shuddering moan, she made a sweep of her hand, knocking over a whole row of freshly unpacked glasses and shattering them. Bursting into tears, she buried her face against her knees and sobbed.

Salina had no idea how long she stayed like that, crouched behind the bar, surrounded by splintered glass and crying the pent-up despair she felt. So when she heard the front door open, she assumed it was Cliff returning from his mission to City Hall.

302

Drawing on a last reserve of will, she grabbed her apron hem and wiped angrily at her tearstained face. He'd never seen her cry yet, and damned if he would now. He may have won, but she would never give him the satisfaction of hearing her admit it or seeing her defeat on her face. Taking a determined sniff, she ripped the packing paper from a glass and stood up, her aloof expression once more in place, though her eyes were red and swollen. "What did they sa . . . ?"

Her eyes grew large with shock and her mouth fell open in a loud gasp. "Noah?"

"Salina," the giant man said from where he stood just inside the casino doorway, his eyes not yet acclimated to the indoor light. "Is that you, honey?"

"Oh, Noah!" she cried, dropping the glass from her hand and running out from behind the bar. "You came! I was so afraid!" she said through renewed tears as, arms outstretched, she raced toward him.

"I told you I would." Noah caught her small body to him and lifted her off the floor.

"I know you did." Laughing and crying, she held his face in her hands and covered it with kisses. "But I was afraid Cliff had done something terrible to stop you. He told me he had people watching for you—and that you would never get here in time. But you did! Oh, Noah, you came!" She resumed her kisses over his face, which was also wet with tears, his own as well as hers.

"Salina," he said, his deep voice breaking as he put her from him. "Honey, there's something I've got to tell you."

Apprehension shook through her petite body, and cold, clammy fingers of inevitable doom raked jagged nails over her skin. She didn't speak.

Unable to look at her, Noah threw his head back and stared with unseeing eyes at the gilded ceiling of the Golden Goose. "I don't have the ten thousand dollars to buy your free papers, Salina," he announced gruffly, his feeling of failure coloring his tone.

All the faith she'd found a moment before drained from her. They really were defeated. Cliff had won. Her shoulders melted into a conquered slump, her chin dropping forward to her chest. "Then, that's that, isn't it?"

His gentle heart splitting in two, Noah grabbed her by the shoulders and clutched her to him. "Oh, baby, I'm so sorry I failed you."

"You didn't fail me, Noah," she said against his rock-hard chest. "Cliff admitted he didn't intend to give you the papers even if you found that much gold. I had just hoped that if he was actually confronted with the ten thousand dollars, he might relent and—"

"Don't give up, honey. It might be too late for me to buy your mama's papers from Cliff Hopkins, but it's not too late for you. Come away with me now."

Salina rolled her head from side to side. "I can't come with you, Noah. I have to stay as long as there's a chance I can keep my mama from being—"

"Do you think this is what your mama would want for you?" he shouted, making a wide sweep with his hand. "Don't you know she would die if she knew what you were willing to do to protect her?"

"Well, she won't know," Salina said, her spine stiffening as she pushed away from him as far as his intense embrace would allow. "As long as I do what Cliff tells me, she never has to know."

"Please, Salina! Come with me. I'll find a way to get your mother's papers! I swear, I won't give up until I do. But it'll take me longer than a week. And I have to know you're safe now. Come with me."

Salina took a step backward and looked up at Noah's anguished features. "I can't, Noah. My place is here until my mama is free and safe."

It was then Noah noticed the bruises and cuts on the right side of her face. In that one moment, every instinct for generosity and understanding he'd ever possessed disintegrated, like paper in a blazing furnace. "Who did that to you?" The rage burning inside him was so intense that he could barely speak.

Having forgotten her face in her excitement at seeing Noah, Salina's hands flew to cover her mouth and cheek and eye. "A fall!" she blurted out, afraid for the first time of what Noah would do. "I fell down the stairs!"

Noah didn't hear her lies. He released a long yell of total despair, his cry like that of a fatally wounded bear. "Where is he? I'll kill him!"

Remembering the details of Cliff's will regarding her mother should he die, Salina screamed, "No! Cliff didn't do this. I tell you, I fell!"

But Noah's blind wrath had pitched him beyond

rationality, and her protests fell on deaf ears. Not knowing where he was going, he whipped her off her feet and started for the door.

"Noah! Put me down," she cried. "He'll be back any minute, and if I'm not here when he comes, he'll—"

"I'm going to make sure Cliff Hopkins never lays a filthy hand on you again!" Noah raged as he crashed out the door onto the plank sidewalk.

"Well, well, well!" Cliff said, quickly overcoming his surprise at seeing Noah coming out of the Golden Goose. "Aren't you a bit premature, boy? I believe there's a matter of ten thousand dollars to be taken care off, isn't there?" Cliff stuck out his hand as if expecting Noah to pay him right then, though his expression gave away the fact that he knew Noah didn't have the gold.

Noah stared at the extended hand.

"Well? Either give me my money or put my property down and get out of here."

"You bastard. I'm going to kill you!" Anger and frustration ruling his actions, Noah put Salina aside and tore at Cliff Hopkins. Unaware of the crowd that had gathered, his fists pummeled furiously at the smirking white face.

No sooner had Noah flown at Cliff than the surrounding crowd of white spectators dove at Noah. With attackers hanging on each of his arms, one clinging to his leg, and another riding his back, Noah managed only to grab Cliff's lapels and sink a fist into his face several times before the mob could drag him down.

"Get him out of here!" Cliff shrieked, his voice

unusually high-pitched, even for him. Wiping at his bloodied nose and mouth, he staggered to a bench and sat down. "I'll see you hanging from a rope for this, you black bastard!" he screamed as the crowd dragged Noah, who was proving to be a handful even for the six of them, off the porch and into the street. "Do you hear me? You'll hang for this!"

"Let him go," Salina pleaded, running into the street after Noah and his captors. "He didn't know what he was doing! He didn't mean it!"

"Shut up! And get your ass back inside, bitch!"

Salina recognized the unspoken threat in Cliff's tone and stopped in her tracks. "Please, Cliff," she begged, turning back to face her half brother. "Tell them to let him go. I'll do anything you want. Just don't let them hang him."

Cliff threw back his head and released a high giggle. "You'll do what I want whether he swings or not! Have you forgotten? I own you, girl. Body and soul. And don't you forget it!" He hit the door to the Golden Goose and stepped inside. "Now get in here and clean up this blood." He moved his pudgy fingers down the length of his nose. "If he broke my nose, so help me I'll—"

Salina ran inside behind Cliff and grabbed at his arm. "Where are they taking him? You've got to stop them! Please! I won't fight you any more about working upstairs. Just tell them to let him go."

Cliff looked down at the café-au-lait–colored hand gripping his sleeve. "Get your hand off me."

Dropping her hold on the black sleeve of Cliff's coat, Salina continued her protest. "What about

Noah? Are you going to press charges against him?"

"No," Cliff answered, watching her face, then laughing at the relief that washed over her features. "You are!"

"Me? You're crazy. I won't do it!"

"Of course you will, my dear. Because if you don't testify that he was taking you against your will, I'll press charges. It's your choice. No one's going to hang him for taking you—it's not as if you were a horse or anything valuable, is it? He'll just spend a while in jail. On the other hand, if you don't make the charge, then . . ." Cliff shrugged his shoulders and released a demented little giggle. "Well, what can I say? He won't be the first buck to hang for assaulting a white man, now, will he? In fact, when they hear my testimony, I wouldn't be the least bit surprised if they aren't so outraged by his audacity that they hang him this very day. Save the city the cost of feeding him."

"You vicious swine. I loathe you!"

"Now, is that any way to talk to the man who, out of the goodness of his heart, has just given you the opportunity to save your lover in exchange for the complete obedience you've promised me? Just say the word, and I'll take back my offer. As a matter of fact, you've hurt my feelings. I think I'll go on down to the police station and—"

"No!" Salina cried, running after him. "I'll do it. I'll do what you want! I'll press charges against Noah."

"And follow my every order cheerfully and without argument?"

Salina's lip curled as if she were barely holding back an angry retort. But she nodded her head. "And willingly?"

"Yes," she whispered, the word forming a painful lump in her throat.

"Then, let us be on our way to do our civic duty and see that one more dangerous criminal is put behind bars."

"Put that gun back in your holster!" Trace hissed, clamping his fingers around Cassie's wrist and forcing the drawn revolver downward.

"They're gonna hang Noah!"

So much for getting here in time to stop Noah from doing something dumb, Trace thought with disgust as he watched his struggling friend being dragged toward the jail. "They're not going to hang him. That is, not if you don't do something stupid—like trying to take his captors on all by yourself!"

"You heard what that man said. He wants Noah hung!" she protested. "We gotta do somethin'."

"We will." His answer was terse as he squinted his eyes and studied the street from where they stood in an alley. "I've got a plan."

"Just what kind o' plan if you won't let me use my gun?"

"You've got to learn how much better—and safer—it is to think before you act, kid. If I let you go after those men with your gun blazing, you'd probably get yourself killed, or at least arrested. And Noah would still be a prisoner. Is that what you want? How much help do you think you'd be to him then?"

Cassie's mouth twisted into an irritated line. She knew he was right. Impulsiveness was her worst fault, but it irked the dickens out of her to admit it. And she didn't intend to. Not to Trace McAllister, anyway. "Well, what's this big plan o' yours if we're not gonna shoot him outta this mess?"

When Trace didn't answer, but just kept staring after Noah, Cassie's expression grew more alarmed. "We are gonna break him out, ain't we?"

Trace glanced at Cassie out of the corner of his eye and smiled. "It's time you learned the art of making plans and carrying them out, kid. Come on," he said, grabbing her arm and dragging her toward the harbor. "We've got a man to see."

"But what 'bout Noah?" she sputtered, running to keep up with Trace's long-legged stride.

"Believe me, kid, Noah's not going anywhere."

Cassie and Trace stepped out of the entrance of an abandoned ship that had been beached and converted into a store along the waterfront. Since buildings and building materials were at such a premium in San Francisco, it wasn't the least bit unusual to see the bow of a ship protruding from between two more conventional storefronts. And it was much more practical than leaving the ships to rot in the harbor when passengers and crews alike had deserted them to go look for gold.

"This is crazy." She ran her fingers up under the black knit cap covering her hair, and scratched her mple. "I still don't see how wearin' this is gonna elp Noah."

Trace directed a one-eyed leer in her direction and ached up to check the black patch hiding his left e. "Jus' trust me, mate," he said with the accent assie recognized as that of a seaman. There were ousands of them in northern California, men ho'd spent their lives at sea and had given it all up seek their fortunes in the Sierras.

"I trust ye, all right, old salt," she returned. 'Bout as far as I can hoist ye!"

"Say, you do that pretty well," he praised her, his pression surprised and pleased. "Can you do any ther accents?"

Blushing under his compliments, Cassie nodded r head and said, "A few," then changed the sub- ct. "Just tell me how these sailor duds're gonna ep Noah from gettin' his neck stretched?" She quirmed uneasily in the black peacoat and ratched under the hat again. " 'Cause the sooner I t in my own, the happier I'm gonna be. Some- in' tells me whoever wore these last forgot to take few o' his six-legged pals with him."

Trace smiled at Cassie's grumblings, then decided e'd left her wondering long enough. "Every time a ew ship anchors in the bay, most of the crew imps ship, and the owner has a hard time hiring a ew for the return trip."

"So?" Cassie was growing impatient.

"So, they get their crews wherever they can. And uying them out of the jails is a real good place — hen the pickings on unsuspecting lads fresh from e farm are slim. Which reminds me . . ." He

311

paused and cuffed her playfully on the chin. "You
better stay close to me. In those clothes, you'd
make a perfect target for shanghaiers. And I don't
think you want to take any unexpected sea voyages
right now."

"Just let 'em try." Cassie patted her belt where
she'd tucked her pistol.

Trace sent a prayer for patience heavenward and
went on explaining his scheme. "In these clothes,
we'll simply buy Noah out of jail."

Cassie's face lit up with understanding. "Oh, I get
it!"

Trace grinned and nodded his head. "And doesn't
it beat getting shot at? It's perfect and there's abso-
lutely no risk. It's amazing what a little bit of planning can do, isn't it?"

Cassie had to admit his idea sounded like it
would work—at least to herself. But never to him.
He was already too pleased with his own cleverness.
"Don't get too cocky, McAllister. Your fancy plan
ain't done the trick yet. Noah's still locked up. An'
if this don't work, we're gonna do it my way."
Without giving him a chance to answer, she started
in the direction she'd seen them take Noah.

Catching up with her, Trace pulled the knit cap
lower on her face and wrapped his fingers around
the back of her neck and squeezed it affectionately.
"It'll work, kid—if you don't do something to give
us away."

Indignant, Cassie stopped and planted her fists
on her hips. "Me?"

Trace looked from side to side, hoping no one
had noticed her decidedly feminine gesture. Knock-

ing her hands off her hips, he gripped her arm and hurried her along. "Just keep your head down so no one sees your face. And let me do all the talking. You might have a sailor's accent down pat, but your voice is a dead giveaway."

"Hmp." She wrenched her arm free of his hold. "Don't you worry 'bout me."

"And for God's sake, forget you've got that gun!"

"Have you got it straight?" Cliff asked Salina as he hurried her toward the jail.

Salina nodded her head, her expression that of a trapped animal. "I'm to tell them I don't have any idea who he is and that he broke into the Golden Goose looking for money."

"But when he found there wasn't anything in the cash box, he grabbed you instead," Cliff finished for her.

Salina looked up at her brother, her tearful eyes wide with uncertainty. "You promise he won't hang if I do what you want?"

"Of course."

"Say it, Cliff! Let me hear you say it."

"I'll see that he doesn't hang if you press charges against him."

"Swear it!" she commanded. "Look me in the eye and swear on our father's soul."

Cliff dug a finger into his shirt collar and rotated his neck uneasily.

"If you don't swear on his soul, our bargain is over."

"All right! I swear it. I swear on Papa's soul that

313

I'll make sure your buck doesn't hang for assaulting me. There, are you satisfied now?"

Salina didn't answer, but simply resumed her walk toward the jail where her love was waiting.

Trace let out a loud whoop as he and Cassie slipped Noah into a small room behind the Happy Moon gambling hall on the east side of Dupont Street in the Chinese quarter. "Didn't I tell you we'd get him out without using guns, kid?"

Her right cheek quirked up in a conceding grin. She felt too good to keep up the argument. "All right, I give up. You was right. Your way was better'n mine." Trace's face split into a wider grin and she couldn't resist adding, "This time."

"How do you feel, Noah?" Trace said, tearing his gaze from Cassie. He guided the man to a cot in the corner and sat him down. "You haven't said much since we got you out of the hoosegow. Are you hurt?"

Noah shook his head and buried his face in his hands. "It doesn't matter. Nothing matters now. I ruined everything."

"Maybe not," Trace said encouragingly, and sat down beside Noah. "What would you say if I told you I've got an idea that will not only put Hopkins into a position where he'll give you the papers for Salina and her mother, but will put an end to Murieta too—and maybe even recover your gold at the same time?"

"I'd say that's a mighty tall order for one idea. Even one o' yours," Cassie said with a teasing sniff

314

of disapproval. "If you ask me, success has gone to your head more'n a little bit. Why don't I just amble over to that Golden Goose and hold this here 'equalizer' " — she whipped her revolver from her waist and spun the chamber around to check the bullets — "to the bastard's head? He'll sign the papers all right."

Trace shook his head and released a low growl. "I was beginning to think there was some hope for you, kid. But you just don't learn, do you? If we do what you want, he'll sign papers all right — on your death warrant. Don't you realize that once Cliff Hopkins finds out Noah's not safely behind bars, he'll have so many bodyguards around him, you'd be dead before you got two feet with those papers."

"Well, then, what's this big idea o' yours?" she asked, disgusted with the way he always made her look like a hotheaded little kid without a lick of sense. And the fact that he was right — again — didn't help her disposition either.

Noah's posture straightened, and he looked at Trace eagerly, desperate hope lighting in his dark eyes. "I'm willing to try anything. I've got to get Salina away from him before it's too late."

"It's going to require patience — especially from you, Cassie. Are you up to it?"

She gave him a you-think-you're-so-smart-don't-you wag of her head and said, "Just tell us your idea, McAllister."

"Actually, you're the one who gave me the idea," he began.

Cassie's dour expression lightened. "Me? When?"

"It was something you said when we came out of the store in these sailor clothes."

Her brow furrowed as she reran their conversation through her mind. "I don't 'member sayin'—"

"When I asked you if you could imitate any accents other than a sailor's, you said you could."

Confused, Cassie crossed her arms over her chest and said, "Will you just get to the point, McAllister?"

Trace let a chuckle. He'd baited her long enough. "All right, all right. First of all, my plan involves your imitations."

"You mean you want me to stay in these duds? You're gonna have to think o' somethin' else, McAllister!" To emphasize her resolve, she tore the knit cap from her head and tossed it into the corner.

"You don't have to wear those clothes any more. As soon as we get Noah settled here, we'll go fetch our gear and you can get out of them."

"Then, what's the plan?" Patience had never been one of Cassie's virtues, and he was testing the little bit she had to the limit.

"You told me your mother was a lady from back East, didn't you?"

"Yeah, but what's that go—"

"Do you think you could imitate her?"

Remembering her lady act when she had tricked the thimblerigger in Sacramento, she nodded her head. "I s'pose I could. But I don't see how that's gonna help Noah—or flush out Murieta."

"Hopkins is going to be expecting Noah to come crashing into the Golden Goose after Salina again. So, he'll be on the lookout for him. Noah couldn't get past the front door. On the other hand, he would never suspect a rich man and his beautiful wife from back East as being in his casino for anything other than gambling, would he?"

Cassie squinted her eyes suspiciously. "Are you sayin' you 'n' me're gonna be that rich man 'n' his wife?"

Trace nodded his head enthusiastically. "Right. Cliff Hopkins hasn't ever seen either of us, and with some new clothes and a few review lessons on the grammar your mother must have taught you, we'll be 'close friends' with the owner of the Golden Goose in no time—especially since we're going to have something he's bound to want."

"Whadda we got he wants?" she asked, her curiosity getting the better of her and bringing an excited light to her eyes.

"Nothing. But Cliff Hopkins doesn't know that. He's going to think we do, and that's what counts."

"Oh!" she exclaimed, nodding her head and grinning knowingly, then frowning. "I don't get it."

"What am I going to be doing?" Noah asked at the same time.

Answering Noah first, Trace said, "Well, it's obvious you can't go near the Golden Goose for a while. But that's where my plan for Murieta comes into play. In Sacramento, I overheard Murieta telling Mimi Witherspoon that he'd see her in San Francisco on Friday. That's tomorrow. All we have to do is find out where her theatrical troupe is going to be and watch the place until he shows up. Cassie and I can't do it because Mimi would recognize us, and she knows I'm looking for Murieta.

317

But she's never seen you, has she, Noah?"

"Not that I know of. Still, I feel like I ought to be doing something for Salina."

"You will be," Cassie said, sitting down on the other side of Noah and taking his hand in hers. "Trace's plan makes good sense, Noah. Maybe it's time you an' me tried it his way. 'Cause, far as I can see, neither one o' us has got too far 'actin' b'fore we think.'" Glancing across Noah, she directed a shy smile at Trace, whose mouth had dropped open in amazement.

"Well, we gonna hang 'round here all day jawin', or are we goin' after those two scoundrels."

"We're going after those scoundrels!" Trace and Noah answered in unison, covering Cassie's hand on Noah's with his.

"Then, let's do it!" she laughed, placing the final hand on the friendship pact. "Let's go show 'em what happens to folks who tangle with us."

Chapter Nineteen

"Did he get away?" Salina cried, her hands flying o her mouth to cover an excited gasp.

"What do you mean, he's not here?" Cliff hrieked at the same time. Leaning over the desk, ne shoved his flushed face toward the man on duty. "He assaulted me and tried to abduct my maid, and now you tell me he's free? What kind of law-enforcement organization are you running here?"

Ignoring Cliff, the policeman raked a leering gaze over Salina's curvaceous frame, lingering insolently on her breasts. "For someone who was bein' taken ginst your will, you're mighty het up, gal."

Cliff shot Salina a warning glare and jerked her to his side, his fingers digging cruelly into the fleshy part of her upper arm. "She's afraid he'll come back again."

The burly man in charge heaved a bored sigh and azed back in his chair. Propping his boots on the desk, he crossed his ankles and stuck a toothpick between his teeth, his gaze never leaving Salina. "If that's the case, you don't need to worry 'bout that buck no more. He ain't 'xactly on the loose. By now, he's chained in the hold o' some ship that's gettin' ready for a trip back East."

"No!" Salina gasped.

"What are you talking about?" Cliff asked impatiently. "What ship?"

The policeman scratched his stubbled chin and blew out a disgusted snort. "How the hell should I know? All I know is, a coupla sailors come in here lookin' for likely crewmen. An' when they saw that big, strong buck you're askin' 'bout, they figgered him for doin' the work o' two 'r three men. That one-eyed first mate didn't even quibble 'bout the two-hundred-dollar bail. He jes paid it 'n' whisked that prime out o' here so fast I didn't even need to lock 'im up."

"Bail? Who set bail?"

The lawman swung his feet off the desk and stood up. His face twisting into a malicious grin, he said, "I did." Balling his fists, he planted them on the desk and leaned forward on stiff arms, daring Cliff to challenge his authority. "You got a problem with that, mister?" When Cliff didn't answer right away, he nodded his head. "Now, if there ain't nothin' else . . ."

Cliff sputtered at the man's rude dismissal, then spoke. "I'm warning you, sir. If we're ever bothered by that criminal again, you will pay. I'll have your job!" Pirouetting on his heel, he started for the door. "Come, Salina!"

320

"You prissy little fart," the lawman muttered to himself, dropping back into his chair and propping his feet back up on the desk. "I'm jes real scared," he laughed, pulling his money pouch from his pocket and bouncing it triumphantly in his hand.

"You don't think Noah'll get itchy 'n' decide to go after Salina again, do you?" Cassie asked as she entered the dimly lit hotel room ahead of Trace.

"He'll be fine. That tea Mai Lin brought him before we left will make him sleep through the night like a baby. He's not going to know a thing before morning." Trace shut the door and slid the bolt into the lock.

The sound crashed into Cassie's spine, as if she'd been shot. "Don't do that!" she demanded, wheeling around and springing toward the door.

Confused by the sudden change in her, Trace stared at Cassie. "Do what?"

"I can't breathe in here if the door's locked." She grabbed at the bolt and hit it out of the lock. Her chest rising and falling rapidly, she turned back toward the astonished Trace and sagged against the door. "That's better."

"Cassie, San Francisco is filled with thieves and murderers." Trace reached over Cassie's shoulder and resecured the door. "We need to lock the door—unless you want to wake up dead in the morning."

Managing a feeble smile at the thought of "waking up dead," Cassie shook her head in protest. She knew he was right.

"Now," he said, wrapping his arms around he
and gently removing her from her position at th
door, "what's all this nonsense about not being abl
to breathe if the door's locked?" He sucked in
deep breath and blew it out loudly. "See? There'
plenty of air in here."

"I know it," she spit out angrily, her own breath
ing rapid and agitated.

"Then, why do you think you won't be able t
breathe if we lock the door?" He sat her down i
an upholstered chair and hunkered down before he
Taking her trembling hands in his, he searched he
frightened brown eyes. "Tell me, Cass. Why are yo
afraid of a locked door?"

"I ain't afraid!" she answered defensively, he
posture stiffening. "It's jus' that . . ." She slouche
back in the chair and shrugged.

" 'Just that' what? Come on, Cassie. Tell m
what you're afr— I mean, what *bothers* you abou
locked doors. Maybe together we can work it out.

Cassie looked up, hope glistening in her expres
sion, then dissolving into embarrassment. Sh
dropped her chin to her chest and shook her head
"It's nothin'."

"You've never lied to me before, Cassie. Don
start now. What is it?"

"You'll think I'm loco."

"No, I won't. I promise." He lifted a hand t
stroke her cheek, then crooked a finger under he
chin and raised it so he could see her eyes. "Te
me."

"I know in here"—she tapped her temple with
slender forefinger—"there's as much air in a locke

322

oom as in an unlocked one. But here"—she clapped
her hand to her chest—"it feels like there ain't.
When I hear a bolt slide shut, or a key turn in a
lock, it's like somethin's squeezin' the breath right
out o' me." She twisted her mouth in a silly half
grin and drew up her shoulders. "See, I told you
I'm loco."

Trace smiled and shook his head. "You're not
loco, honey. Everybody has a quirk or two. Did I
ever tell you I'm afraid of snakes?"

Cassie cocked her head to the side and eyed Trace
suspiciously. "You're pullin' my leg."

He shook his head and chuckled. "I'm not. Just
thinking about a snake gives me chills." As if to
prove his statement, he shivered and grimaced.

"But when that rattler was 'bout to take a nip
outta my neck, you didn't act like you was scared o'
snakes."

"No, but you sure didn't see me pick him up and
make a hatband out of his skin, did you?" he
laughed.

Cassie smiled, her breathing slowing slightly.
"Now that you mention it, I don't guess I did."

"And you won't. But that doesn't mean that every
time I see a snake I can let myself go berserk."

"I guess I'd be buzzard meat right now if you
did."

"That's the whole point. We all have fears that we
can let control us. Or we can face them head-on
and learn to function in spite of them."

"But how do I do it?"

"You've already made a start by talking about it
to me. By the way, do you realize we've been having

323

a rational conversation in a locked room for several minutes now and neither of us is having the least bit of trouble getting enough air?"

Panic shot from Cassie's eyes, and her gaze made a frantic jump toward the door. Her breathing grew more rapid.

Catching her cheek in his palm, he turned her face back to him. "Trust me, sugar." He stood and scooped her into his arms, then sat back down cradling her in his lap. "Just trust me and together we'll face it."

The soothing, hypnotic sound of his voice flowed into her, easing the tension that stretched her every muscle taut, and she relaxed against his shoulder. "How?"

"Maybe it would help if we knew what caused you to dislike locked doors so much. Have you always felt this way?"

Cassie nodded her head, then shook it. "I guess I never give 'em much thought before—"

"Before what?"

She straightened and glanced nervously at the door. "Before we come out here from Baltimore nine years ago."

Trace tightened his hold on her and guided her head back down to his shoulder. "What happened when you came to California."

"It was before we left Baltimore. I told you my ma was a lady, didn't I? Well, I didn't tell you that when she married my pa, her parents was fit to be tied. Said she'd married b'neath her. They disowned her. Told her they didn't want nothin' more to do with her.

"My folks went to live in New York City after ʌat 'n' didn't see them for several years. That's ¹here I was born. But Ma thought it wasn't fair to ʌe or to her folks not to know 'bout each other, so ʌe talked my pa into movin' back to Baltimore. I ʌink she was hopin' things could be all right 'tween ʌr 'n' her folks again.

"But when they heard 'bout me, 'stead o' forgivin' ʌa 'n acceptin' Pa, they did everythin' they could to ʌt my folks to give me to them to raise. They ʌromised they'd give me the prettiest clothes 'n' the ʌnciest school. They even said they'd arrange the ʌst marriage for me — 'when the time come.' " Cas-ʌe's lip curled in distaste. "Can you see thinkin' ʌose things was more important than bein' with my ʌwn folks?"

"No, I can't." Trace wasn't sure what the story ʌad to do with her fear of locked doors, but he ʌnsed Cassie's need to talk, so he rubbed her arm ʌacouragingly and said, "Go on."

"After a few years o' battlin' over me 'n' bein' ʌld over and over how worthless Pa was, my folks ʌecided to move to California to prove they was wrong ʌout him."

Cassie heaved a sigh and went on. "But then the ʌghtin' really got bad. They offered my pa money ʌr me, 'n' when he wouldn't take it, they made all ʌrts o' trouble for him. When nothin' they tried ʌorked, they finally paid a judge to sign papers ʌyin' my folks wasn't fit to bring me up and sent ʌe law to take me away from Ma 'n' Pa 'n' bring ʌe to 'em."

Trace had all sorts of questions he wanted to ask

about the fantastic story that was unfolding, but h
didn't dare interrupt Cassie's outpouring of words

"The minute the policeman put me down in th
front hall o' my grandmother's fancy big house,
kicked him 'n' run out the door. But there was to
many of 'em, 'n' I didn't even make it to the stree
before they caught me 'n' carried me back inside.

She looked up from her hands in her lap an
grinned mischievously through the tears that wer
starting to trickle down her cheeks. "Bitin' 'r
kickin' 'n' screamin' all the way."

Trace returned her smile and kissed the tip of he
nose. "Somehow, I don't have any trouble picturin
that."

"I told 'em they couldn't make me stay there.
swore I was gonna run away. But they jus' ignore
me 'n' paid off the policemen. Then my grand
mother had a servant carry me up to a bedroom o
the third floor.

"I'll never forget the look on that old woman'
face when she come into that room. 'You are en
tirely too much like your father, child,' " Cassi
said, mimicking her grandmother's Eastern accen
and stern manner. " 'And I will not tolerate anyon
in this house who reminds me of him. So, you wi
stay in your room until you decide to behave in
manner befitting your position and the Dariu
name.' "

Darius! a voice shouted in Trace's head. *My goc
I remember reading about her. She's Cassandra Da
rius Wyman, the missing heiress to the Harley Da
rius fortune. Why didn't I make the connectio
before?*

" 'Your meals will be brought to you on a tray,' "
Cassie went on. " 'And a maid will attend to your
personal needs. But otherwise, you will see no one,
and no one will speak to you until you are able to
show us that you have changed.' Then, she jus'
walked outta the room 'n' locked the door behind
her."

Cassie's tears were flowing freely now. "I'll never
forget the way that key sounded turnin' in the lock.
Everythin' got so quiet. Like a coffin. I couldn't
breathe, 'n' I was sure I was gonna die in there. It
was like someone was holdin' a big pillow over my
face."

"It's no wonder. What kind of monster would do
that to a little girl? How'd you get away from there?
Did your parents come for you?"

Cassie shook her head and grinned. "Ma always
said I was part monkey, 'n' I guess she was right. I
got out the same way I got out o' the hotel in
Sacramento. I climbed out."

"From the third story?"

She nodded. "It wasn't easy—my legs were a lot
shorter then—but by droppin' to a narrow strip o'
roof from the second story that stuck out under my
window, then scootin' over its peak 'n' halfway
down the other side, I could reach the limb of a big
oak tree. From there, it was easy. I jus' crawled
along that limb, then shimmied down the trunk. As
soon as my feet hit the ground, I took off runnin'
for the place my ma had told me to go if I got
away before they could come for me. An' I ain't
never been back to my grandmother's house or seen
her since."

"Or been able to breathe in a locked room," Trac
finished for her.

Cassie's head twisted around and she studie
Trace's concerned face. "Or breathe in a locke
room," she confirmed.

"Don't you see, Cassie? It's your grandmothe
you're afraid of, not locked rooms. The locke
rooms just remind you of her and how helpless sh
made you feel. But you don't have to be afraid o
her any more, do you?"

Cassie glanced nervously at the locked door an
shook her head, her expression not totally cor
vinced.

"Of course, you don't. As for your grandmothe
have you ever thought about going back and facin
her?"

"That's what Pa 'spected me to do with the gol
Murieta stole. He wanted me to buy some fanc
clothes 'n' get someone to teach me how to act lik
a lady so I could go back East 'n' show th
old biddy how wrong she was 'bout him neve
amountin' to nothin'. An' I always told Pa I'd do
when we got us a good nest egg stored up, but I—

"But your were afraid, weren't you? You wer
afraid your grandmother could hurt you again."

Cassie bristled at the word *afraid* and opened he
mouth to deny it. Then she relaxed and nodded he
head. "Yeah," she admitted.

Trace gave her an approving hug. He knew wha
that admission had cost her. "But you don't have t
be afraid of her. Don't you see, when you were
helpless little girl and there was nothing you coul
do to protect yourself, you still managed to beat he

328

and escape. What kind of chance do you think she would have against the grown woman you are now? You father's right, Cassie. You need to go see her—not to prove anything to her, but to prove to yourself once and for all that she can't hurt you."

Cassie took a deep, shuddering breath and smiled weakly. "Maybe I will one o' these days . . ."

"That a girl."

"I ain't makin' no promises," she quickly amended. "But I guess it won't hurt to think on it."

Trace released a hearty laugh and stood up, taking her with him. "In the meantime," he said, placing her unceremoniously onto the bed, "we better get some sleep. Starting in the morning, we've got our work cut out for us if we're going to convince Cliff Hopkins we're rich Easterners before the week's over."

Suddenly feeling more free than she'd felt in years, a sprite of playfulness bubbled in Cassie's heart. "What if I ain't sleepy?" she asked, swinging up to her knees and catching her fingers in Trace's belt.

"Well," he said with a grin as he allowed himself to be drawn closer to the edge of the bed. "I suppose we could begin our lessons tonight."

"That sounds like a in'erestin' idea," she said, playing her fingers across the buckle of his gunbelt and looking up at him, her grin naughty. She quickly undid the belt and dropped it and his holster to the floor. "Where we gonna start?"

Fascinated by this new side to Cassie, Trace did nothing to hurry her along—or to stop her. His hands hanging loosely at his sides, he waited for her to make the next move. "I suppose grammar and word pronunciation would be as good a place as any. They're dead giveaways to a lady's background."

"You sure there ain't somethin' 'sides grammar 'n' the way I talk on your mind right now?" She grazed her hands over the front of his trousers, which were already becoming uncomfortly tight with his desire.

"Not that I can think of," he answered, his voice rough. His endurance was fast approaching its limits. Grinding out a low growl, he covered her hands with his, holding them still on his belly. "First of all, a lady never says 'ain't.' It isn't considered proper."

Her eyes twinkled lightheartedly. "It ain't?" she said, wiggling her fingers free from his loose grip on them and running a forefinger up the row of buttons to the bandanna on his neck. "S'pose you tell me 'xactly what's 'proper.' "

His mouth twitched helplessly as he struggled to hold back the chuckles threatening to burst from his throat. "*SUP-pose* you tell me *EX-actly* what is proper," he corrected.

"Me?" She walked toward the edge of the bed on her knees and kissed his Adam's apple, "You're *SUP*-posed to be the teacher here. *AREn't* you?" Though her voice was husky, her pronunciation and inflection were perfect.

His expression incredulous, he held her off and took a step back to study her face. Surely he wasn't that good a teacher.

Cassie arched her eyebrows in a deliberately artificial look of innocence. "What's the matter, Mr. McAllister? *Haven't* you ever heard a lady speak?"

Then the laughter Trace had tried so hard to contain escaped in a low rumble. "Why, you little faker!" he laughed accusingly.

"I beg your pardon?" Her higher-pitched giggles joined the rich base tones of his as she relaxed back on her calves.

"You've known what was correct all along, haven't you?" With a playful lunge, he toppled her over on her back and covered her with his body. "It was all an act."

Cassie smiled at Trace, a warm cozy feeling stealing through her at the pleasure she'd brought him. "Maybe at first, it was," she said, enunciating each syllable carefully in an effort not to make a mistake. "I was so mad at my mother for leaving me and Pa alone. And I wanted to spite her. So I decided I'd get even with her by forgetting all the things she thought were so all-fired important. But it's got to— got*ten* to be a habit now. I ai— I'm *not* sure how long I can keep it up without screwin'—"

Trace's brows arched in teasing disapproval.

Cassie winced and wrinkled her nose. "I guess ladies don't say things like that, do they?"

Trace shook his head, his expression that of an excited little boy who's just found a bicycle under the Christmas tree when he was expecting coal and sticks in his stocking. "Don't worry about it. It'll all come back to you. Why, I wouldn't be surprised if in a few days, we'll have you speaking so perfectly that you could sit down to tea with Queen Victoria herself!"

331

Cassie blew out an unladylike snort. "Don't go gettin' too carried away, McAllister. 'Member—"

"*Re*member.

"*Re*member," she said with a what-did-I-tell-you shrug, "I've been drinkin' my coffee out of a saucer for a lotta years now. My table manners ain—Dammit!" She shot him an embarrassed glance. "—Aren't too good. They might need a lot more work." Then, hating the idea of displeasing Trace, she added, "But I'm sure as hell gonna try—Oh!" She slapped her hand over her mouth.

"Cassie, Cassie, you're one in a million," he laughed and hugged her tight. "And trying is all anyone can ask of another person."

The warm contented feeling wending its way around and through her began to settle in her womb. But now, instead of warm contentedness, it began to burn and pulsate into demanding restlessness. "Is my first lesson over?"

He nodded. "I guess so."

She knocked him on his shoulder and flipped him over onto his back, quickly covering his chest with her upper body. "Then, do you s'pose we can stop talkin' and do somethin' else?"

"I surely do, sweetheart. I surely do!" He dug his fingers into her thick hair and pulled her down to cover his mouth with hers.

Like a morning glory kissed by the first rays of the sun, her mouth flowered under his, opening and blossoming for him alone, so he could taste the special life-supporting nectar that only she could supply.

"Sweet, sweet Cassie. I'm so glad I found you,"

332

he said, working his hand between them so he could unbutton her shirt. "You've brought the light back to my life."

"And you've brought light to mine for the first time," she whispered, her eyes tearing as her fingers nimbly finished opening his shirt and helped him out of it. "I love you, Trace McAllister."

A bolt of panic shot through Trace's veins at Cassie's words. Everything in his body cried out for him to tell her he loved her too, but an old hurt shouted out a warning. He couldn't love her. He'd lost every woman he'd ever loved—his mother, his sister, his grandmother—and he knew now that he couldn't bear to lose Cassie too.

Tossing her shirt aside, he hauled her against him and latched onto a breast with his mouth, sucking and nursing her as his hands kneaded her buttocks, rocking her roughly on him.

"Oh," she groaned, her legs falling apart to straddle his hips so the pleading ache between her thighs could press closer to the hard ridge in his jeans. "—please. I want—"

"What, Cassie? What do you want?" He pushed his hardness up against her. "This?" he asked, taking her hand and placing it between their bodies. "Is this what you want?"

Her mouth dry and open as she gasped desperately for air, she nodded her head and fumbled with the buttons that kept her from having what she wanted.

Catching her wrist in his fingers, he stilled her hand, though he continued to move tauntingly against her palm. "Say it, Cassie. Tell me what you want."

"I want you," she rasped. "I want you inside me."

A strained smile on his face, he released his hold on her hand and clasped his hands behind his head.

Cassie looked up, confused.

"Well?" he asked.

Her desire was so demanding she didn't have to be told a second time that she'd just been granted free license to explore his body as he had explored hers. Quickly lifting herself off him, she made short work of the rest of his clothes, then hers.

He watched her lazily as she lowered herself beside him again.

Beginning with his mouth, she covered his face with kisses, her hand making swirls on his chest. She moved her lips to his ears and neck, and her fingers filtered through the arrow of hair that ran down the center of his body from his navel.

"Oh, God!" he gasped, lifting his hips in invitation to her caress.

As impatient as he, Cassie wrapped her fingers around the satiny staff and dipped her head to play her tongue across and around a flat male nipple, which immediately hardened into a tiny pebble at the center. Moving her lips lower, she followed the path her hand had taken. And soon her lips were pressed to that same alluring arrow that pointed the way to the heart of his manhood.

She flicked her tongue in and out and moved her head from side to side as she traced and retraced the trail, each time getting closer to where her hand was moving up and down with squeezing caresses, but never quite traversing that final few inches.

Then, though it had never occurred to her before that she would have the desire to do such a thing, the need to kiss all of him, taste and know his every subtle nuance, overpowered her.

Ignoring the little voice that said, *A lady would never do such a thing,* she brought the tip of him to meet her kiss. "Ahhh," he cried with a hiss of indrawn breath at the touch of her lips. His head rocked from side to side.

A feeling of power crackled through her. "Do you like that?" she asked, tickling her tongue over him before her lips parted to take him into her mouth.

Then, he was no longer able to lie there letting her make love to him. Without warning, he snapped Cassie upward and settled her on him, slamming his rigid member deep inside her before he could lose control to her intimate kisses.

"You're a witch," he panted, unable to hold back his climax. He pushed up into her with his hardness one last time, then suddenly went limp under her. "I'm sorry, honey. I didn't mean to go so fast."

Disappointed in spite of herself, and still painfully aware of the throbbing pressure between her thighs, she said, "It's all right." She started to slip away from him.

But instead of allowing her to leave, Trace caught her under the arms and lifted her upward to delve into her femininity with his tongue. Catching the bud of her desire between his lips, he tugged and twisted until Cassie, crying out her ecstasy, shuddered spasmodically against him.

"Is that better?" he asked, his warm breath disturbing the curls as he turned her over onto her back and lay his cheek on her belly. "Because if it's not . . ." He opened her and resumed his kisses.

Her body twitched defensively as his mouth touched her again. "Nooo," she pleaded.

But he didn't listen, and soon she was holding his head tight to her and crying out her rapture a second time.

336

Chapter Twenty

Cassie scrutinized the front of Cliff Hopkins's house from across the street and glanced impatiently at the new watch adorning her lapel. "Almost eight o'clock," she murmured to herself, the watch calming her restlessness somewhat.

Smiling, she lovingly wrapped her fingers around it and remembered when she'd first seen it. Trace had just finished paying for their purchases the day before when he had spotted her eyeing it enviously in the case. Realizing how much she wanted it, he had insisted on buying it for her.

Because she knew the right image was necessary to carry out their plan, she hadn't objected when Trace had spent their pooled resources to buy her three beautiful dresses with matching gloves and hats, instead of just one outfit. But the lapel watch

337

was the last thing they needed to make their scheme work, and she had thought it was wrong to spend their limited money on it. So, she had protested vehemently.

But Trace had bought it anyway.

With a pleasant rush of warmth, she recalled how he had shushed her protests and shoved her hands out of the way so he could pin the coveted time-piece to her collar, telling her in no-uncertain terms, "No more arguing, kid. You've worked hard these past few days and you deserve a reward. Besides, that smile on your face is worth it. We'll cut corners somewhere else."

It had been the most wonderful moment of her life, receiving a treasured gift from the man she loved. Well, one of the most wonderful moments, anyway. Actually, the past six days had been an ecstatic blur of wonderful moments. And except for the fact that Trace hadn't told her he loved her—though he had shown her in a hundred ways that he did—she was sure she could never be any happier.

The door to Cliff's house cracked open slightly and Cassie jumped to attention. The door opened wider, just enough to allow a petite female figure to slip through it before closing behind her.

Taking care not to show any recognition, Cassie raked a cursory glance over the street, then started walking away from the spot where she'd been stand-ing. Salina moved along a parallel course on the opposite side of the street.

When they reached the market area, each woman strolled idly among the stalls and carts, fingering merchandise, even buying a few items. It was th same routine they had followed each morning since Cassie had first contacted Salina and told her Noah was safe — and still in San Francisco. After several minutes, when they were certain no one was paying particular attention to them, they came together at the entrance to the alley beside the Chinese gambling den owned by Mai Lin. After furtively glancing both ways, Salina, then Cassie, hurried down the alley and ducked into the back room where Noah and Trace waited for them.

Giggling their relief in spite of the seriousness of the situation, the two young women fell into the arms of the waiting men. "I ain't had so much fun in all my life!"

"You *haven't* had so much fun," Salina, Trace, and Noah corrected in unison.

"I keep forgetting," Cassie said with an embarrassed wince. "But don't worry. It only happens when I'm not thinking about what I'm saying." She placed deliberate emphasis on the *g* in each *ing* to prove her point. "I promise, when we meet Cliff Hopkins tomorrow night, I'll be on my toes every second."

Trace lifted her feet off the floor and swung her in a circle. "We're not worried. You're perfect. We know you won't let us down." He set her feet back on the floor, but kept his possessive hold on her as he turned to the embracing couple across the small room. "So, are we all set for tomorrow night?"

"All set," Salina said, turning in Noah's arms. She heaved a deep sigh, her expression not nearly as convincing as her words, and added, "I hope!"

"Are you sure you're going to be all right?" Noah

339

asked her.

The tiny woman reached up to pat his cheek "Don't be afraid. I'll be just fine."

"Okay, let's go over it one more time," Trace said "We don't want any mistakes. Salina, do you hav any questions?"

She shook her head, "My part's easy. But Cliff going to be furious," she said with a hunch of he shoulders and a grimace that was more mischievou than dreading. "I can't wait to see his face."

"Furious but helpless," Cassie offered with a wr grin. "And there won't be anything he can do abou it. Because you sure won't be in any shape to worl at the Golden Goose."

"At least not doing what he has planned."

"Once we have you taken care of, Noah goes t the theater and watches for Murieta, while Cassi and I go into action at the Golden Goose. Sound good. Have we forgotten anything?" Trace arche his dark eyebrows and glanced around the room.

Noah frowned. "I still feel like I should be doin more."

"We've been over that, Noah. Your size alon makes it too risky for you to get anywhere nea Cliff Hopkins before the right time. We don't wan him to know you're still in the city. Besides, sinc Murieta hasn't shown up at the theater to see Mim yet, I'm hoping he'll come tomorrow. I just assume the Friday she was talking about was last week. Bu it could just as well have been this week. An tomorrow's Friday, so someone needs to be there i case he shows up. If there's any chance to get you gold back, we don't want to miss it, do we?"

340

"I know you're right," Noah admitted begrudgingly. "It's just that I—"

"Come on," Cassie interrupted, tugging on Trace's sleeve. "Let's go finish Salina's shopping so these two lovebirds can have a few minutes alone before she has to go back."

Noah and Salina sent grateful looks to her. "Thank you, Cassie," Salina said, handing her the shopping list and a pouch of gold to pay for the purchases. "I know you've both put aside your own plans to help us, and I want you to know that no matter how this all turns out, we'll always remember what good friends you've been to us."

Cassie hugged Salina and Noah as one. "Listen to you! You'd do the same of us if we were in trouble," she insisted, her eyes misting suspiciously. "Now look what you've done," she accused Salina. She stepped back and delicately dabbed at her tears with a lace handkerchief, then sniffed—not quite as delicately. She turned and made a dash for the door. "I'm gettin' outta here before you start me blubberin' like a baby."

No one felt inclined to point out her temporary lapse that time—if they even noticed. They were too busy wiping their own eyes, or coughing self-consciously, or clearing their throats.

Trace blew out a long breath. "Well, kid, this is it. If we're not ready now, we never will be."

Taking a nervous last-minute glance in the mirror, Cassie smiled at the lovely green-velvet-clad lady she saw there. "Look at that, Trace McAllister!" She

341

pointed to herself in the mirror.

"What's wrong?" He came up behind her and wrapped his arms around her waist. Smiling appreciatively, he rested his chin on her shoulder and studied their reflections. "You look great."

"That's the whole point. Do I look like someone who should still be called 'kid'?"

He scrutinized her from head to foot, his expression serious. "Now that you mention it, I don't guess you do." He dropped to one knee and grabbed her hand to kiss it. "Can you ever forgive me for being such an unobserving lout, my lady?"

Her smile radiant with love, Cassie bopped him on the head with her folded fan. "Get up off the floor, lout. You're forgiven."

He stood up grinning. "Thanks — kid!"

"I give up. You're impossible." She turned back to the mirror, patted her hair, and picked up her purse. "I'm ready, Mr. McAllister. Are you?"

"Just one more thing," he said, digging into his coat pocket. "If we're going to do this right, you'll need this, *Mrs.* McAllister." He held out a plain gold band for her to see.

Cassie gasped, doing her best not to show how much she wished this wasn't all pretend. "How could I forget the ring?" she asked, reaching for it.

"Let me."

Before she could jerk her hand back to avoid another reminder that they were just playacting, he took the fingers of her left hand in his. Slipping the ring on her third finger to the first knuckle, he asked, "Will you marry me, kid?" His voice was suddenly hoarse and she was certain she felt his

…and trembling.

Cassie searched his face for a sign he meant the proposal, and was not still playing games, but she saw nothing that would give her any insight to his thinking. "You mean, just till we get Salina free — don't you?"

Trace frowned, his expression stunned, then embarrassed, then breaking into a baiting grin. "Of course, just till we get Salina free. What'd you think I meant?" He shoved the ring the rest of the way onto her finger and wheeled away from her. "We'd better get going," he said gruffly, taking a watch from his pocket and studying it. "The sooner we get there, the sooner we can get this over with."

What had she said? Was he angry because he thought she was asking for a real proposal? Cassie looked down at the ring. Hot and foreign on her finger, the band was a reminder that once more she'd let her imagination run away with her. She'd let herself believe that because they enjoyed a physical relationship, he would want to spend the rest of his life with her. What a fool she'd been not to have remembered that underneath the fancy new clothes, she was still the same skinny 'kid' she'd always been. Why would a man like Trace want to marry her?

"I wasn't askin' you to marry me, McAllister!" she blurted out defensively. "I just wanted to make sure you weren't getting any crazy ideas." She sensed, more than heard, the low growl that vibrated in his chest.

He reached for the door, but he didn't open it. "Is it really such a crazy idea?"

343

Cassie froze, her brown eyes wide with anticipation. "Isn't it?"

Trace nodded his head. "Sure it is. I mean, we' both be out of our minds to even consider it Wouldn't we?"

"Out of our minds," she agreed, the expressio on her face giving away her hopefulness.

"We'd probably wind up resenting each other i we got married."

"Probably so."

A fleeting shadow of hurt crossed over his face "On the other hand . . ."

"Yes?" she asked expectantly. She took an anx ious step toward him. "On the other hand . . . ?

Trace's face brightened in a disbelieving smile "We actually make a pretty good team, don't we?

"Uh huh." She wrapped her arms around hi neck. "And it's kind of nice having someone t cover your back when you get in a fix, isn't it?

Trace's hands stole around her waist and h pulled her to him, his mouth open as though h was going to say something.

Then, as though an invisible hand had slappe his face, his expression suddenly soured and h clamped his mouth shut. Turning away from her, h said, "We'd better get going or we'll forget wha we're here for."

Salina smoothed her hands down the front of th yellow satin dress. Releasing a frustrated growl, sh tugged at the black lace-trimmed neckline in a vai attempt to raise it. But the corseted bodice of th dress had been designed to push her breasts upward to the point that only a fraction of an inch of fabric covered her nipples. So her angry gesture was wasted. In fact, she realized, if she wasn't careful, she might tear the lace. Then, even that meager protection would be lost.

"How can I let anyone see me in a dress like this?" she asked herself in disgust. The thought of leering gazes on her breasts sent shivers of revulsion crawling over her skin.

Determined not to let her depression gain any better hold on her than it already had, she blew out the lamp on her dresser and answered her own question. "You do what you have to do."

Stepping out of her room, she leaned over the banister and listened. The drone of male voices reached her ears from Cliff's room, and she heaved a sigh of relief. Obviously, he was talking to his manservant and was still in his room dressing.

"Take your time, brother dear," she said under her breath as she reached back inside her room to pick up a shawl and a small wash bowl with a cup towel draped over it. Covering the bowl and towel with her shawl, she scurried down the stairs on light feet.

She paused only a moment outside Cliff's room to make certain she was still safe. Then, on tiptoes, she made the final dash across the second-story hall and down the main stairway.

When she was nearly to the bottom stair, she stopped, took a deep breath, and let a bloodcurdling scream. Then, knowing speed was of the essence, she ran the rest of the way down the stairs, bumping the wall as she went.

Her insides quivering with apprehension, she dropped to the floor and dabbed the towel in the washbowl — which contained blood from the chicken she'd killed for dinner that day. Her face twisted into a grimace, she splashed the blood on her face and head, spilling the rest on the floor and one of her arms.

"What's going on down there?" she heard Cliff holler from his room.

"Ohhh," she cried loudly, hurriedly shoving the telltale bowl and cup towel into the narrow space beneath a hall chest. Giving the heel of one shoe a hard twist, she fell back on the floor, assuming a position she prayed looked like the result of a fall. "Ohhh, my head!" she groaned.

The instant Cliff appeared at the top of the stairs, she snapped her eyes shut and held her head in her hand. "My head, my head," she wailed.

"What the hell happened?" Cliff asked, pausing at the top of the staircase, his voice registering his shock.

Salina smiled inwardly. She knew the sight of blood made her brother ill. In all likelihood, he wouldn't come any closer now that he'd seen it. And that served her plan well.

"Miss Salina's done took a fall," she heard Joseph, the manservant, announce in horror, to the sound of running footsteps descending the stairs. "It looks right bad, Mr. Cliff."

"She can't have taken a fall!" Cliff shrieked from his safe distance. "We're due at the Golden Goose in less than an hour. Help her to her room, and for

346

God's sake tell her to hurry up and change."

Salina felt Joseph stoop beside her, glad just this once for the old man's poor eyesight.

"Miss Salina, can you hear me?"

"What happened?" she asked, rolling her head so she could direct a disoriented gaze into the concerned face. She hated doing this to the man who'd been with her father since his own youth, but she knew she had no choice. "I can't remember."

"You done took a fall, chile. Mister Cliff, it looks bad!" he called upstairs. "We better be sendin' for a doctor before we move her. She might have broken somethin'."

"Nonsense, she doesn't need a doctor. Just get her up to her room."

"Ohhh," Salina moaned, lapsing into "unconsciousness" again.

"She's gone again! Oh, lordy, Mister Cliff, she's bleedin' bad. You gotta let me get her a doctor!"

"All right," Cliff muttered in disgust. "Go for a doctor. I'll finish dressing myself." He wheeled away from the railing and headed to his room.

"You just hold on there, Miss Salina. I'm goin' for help!" Joseph quickly draped the bloody shawl over her exposed bosom—for which Salina was very grateful—and hurried out the front door. But before he had gone more than a few steps, he realized he didn't know where to begin looking for a doctor.

" 'Xcuse me, suh!" he called out to a man strolling by. "We need a doctor. Right away. Somebody's been hurt. Do you know where I can find one?"

The man stopped and glanced up and down the street. "I believe there's one over in the next block—

347

name's Dr. Rondale, I think."

"I beg your pardon," a tall blond man interrupted. "I couldn't help overhearing your conversation. I'm Dr. Seifert. Can I help you?"

Joseph glanced down at the black bag in the man's hand and his old eyes watered with relief. "Thank you, Lord!" he praised, looking up at the sky. "It's Miss Salina! She fell down the stairs! She's bleedin' somethin' terrible." He took the taller man's arm and tugged him toward the front door. "I didn't move her. I thought you ought to see her first."

"You did the right thing. You never can tell about falls. I've seen cases where moving the patient has caused more problems than the accident itself."

Joseph nodded his head. "Yessuh." He opened the front door as quickly as his arthritic hands would allow and led the stranger into the entry, where Salina lay, still "unconscious."

"How long ago did this happen?" Seifert asked, rushing to her side and examining Salina's head. Without waiting for an answer, he opened his bag and took out a roll of white bandage.

"Just a few minutes."

"Mmm," the doctor hummed, winding the bandage around her head. "She's lost a lot of blood. Has she regained consciousness at all?"

"Woke up just for a few seconds, then went back to sleep. She ain't gonna die, is she, Doc?"

"I don't think so," Seifert assured him, picking up Salina's "wounded" wrist and bandaging it too. "That is, if she receives good care and gets lots of rest the next week or so, she won't. Of course, with

348

head wounds you just never know."

"Ohhh." Salina tossed her head from side to side. "What happened? Who are you?"

"I'm Dr. Seifert, and you evidently took quite a spill down those stairs. How do you feel?"

"I feel dizzy, and everything is blurred. I see two of you."

"Double vision. That's not unusual in these cases. But if you stay in bed and get plenty of rest, it ought to clear up in a week or so."

Cliff reappeared at the top of the stairs, fully dressed for the evening. "That's out of the question. She can't go to bed for a week! She has responsibilities!"

"Well, whatever they are, I'm sure they aren't as important as her life. With head injuries like this, she could get up too soon and kill herself. No, I'm afraid, she'll have to put off *all* activities for at least a week—if not longer." He lifted her leg to examine it for injuries and exclaimed, "Aha! There's your culprit!" He took off her high-heeled slipper and held it up for Cliff and Joseph to see. The heel was breaking away from the shoe. "I can't tell you how many sprained and broken ankles these fool things cause." He wrapped her ankle and foot quickly, then scooped her into his arms and stood up. "Where's her bed?"

Realizing Salina was in no shape to work at the Golden Goose tonight, Cliff begrudgingly pointed upstairs. "Third floor, top of the stairs," he instructed angrily, pushing past the doctor and entering the library. "Joseph, fix me a drink!" he ordered, leaving the doctor to take Salina to her room.

Alone in Salina's room on the third floor, the doctor and patient broke into silent laughter as he set her down on the bed. "You were very convincing. Are you really a doctor?" she asked, taking extra care to keep her voice low.

The man winked a blue eye mischievously. "I've been called a lot of things in my life—Doctor's just one of them. And you were pretty convincing yourself. It's a good thing the sight of blood doesn't bother this *doctor!*"

"You saved my life tonight, and I'll never be able to thank you enough."

"Don't worry about it. I owed McAllister one. Now, I better get out of here so you can get undressed and in bed before we ruin the whole thing." He opened the door and peeked outside, then stepped onto the landing. "Now, remember what I said, young lady," he boomed loudly, loudly enough to be heard downstairs. "Complete bed rest for at least a week!"

"Thank you," she mouthed, her gratitude gleaming in her dark eyes.

"Good luck," he whispered, then winked and was gone.

Telling herself she'd wash off the bloodstains after Cliff was gone, Salina hurriedly undressed and slipped her nightgown over her head, then slid beneath the covers.

No sooner had she pulled the sheet up to her chin than she heard heavy boots ascending the stairs to her room. She squeezed her eyes shut.

"Well, well, well," Cliff said, crashing through the

door. "You're pretty happy now, aren't you? Well, don't think I don't know what you're up to! I know you threw yourself down those stairs to spoil my opening for me. But, don't get too comfortable in this bed. I'll give you one week, but if you're not at the Golden Goose by the end of that week, I'll bring your customers here to you—bandages or no bandages!"

Cassie had regained her composure by the time she and Trace arrived at Portsmouth Square, which glimmered brightly with lights from all the gambling casinos bordering its four sides. After all, saving Salina was more important than her own happiness right now.

"I hope I don't give us away," she said breathlessly, squeezing his arm as they strolled along the board sidewalk toward the newest casino on the square.

The protective instinct that had plagued Trace from the moment he'd first seen Cassie automatically rose to the occasion. He covered her hand with his. "Don't worry. I'll be right beside you the whole time. Besides, it's been so long since most of these miners have seen a real lady, they won't notice if you make a mistake or two."

Cassie's excited gaze rose to meet his. "But Hopkins has seen lots of 'real' ladies. Are you sure he's not going to know I'm a phony right away?"

"Shh," he commanded, sealing her lips with the pad of his forefinger. "First of all, you're not a phony. And Cliff Hopkins may've seen more than

351

his share of ladies in the past, but not since he's been in California—and never one as pretty as you are."

Cassie's face split in a self-conscious grin, and color tinged her cheeks pink. She stopped walking and pulled back on his sleeve. "Thank you, Trace."

Surprised, he stared down at her and asked, "For what?"

"For all of it. For the clothes, for reminding me I was a female, for making me feel pretty, for not laughing because I was afraid of locked rooms, for the watch—just for all of it. The past couple of weeks have been the best time I've ever had in my life."

"You're talking like I'm someone you're never going to see again, instead of the man you're going to spend the next week or so with."

"I just wanted you to know—in case."

Trace grinned and tweaked her nose. "Well, you're welcome—in case." He patted her hand on his arm and resumed his gentlemanly stroll along the walk. "But we'd better talk about it later. Right now, it's time for you to go into your act. You ready?"

She sucked in a deep fortifying breath, tightened her grip on his arm, and nodded her head. "As ready as I'm going to be."

"Then, let's go."

The instant Cassie and Trace entered the casino, heads turned to stare in wonder at the handsome couple framed in the entrance. With the exception of the professional gamblers, most of the men in the noisy hall were wearing ordinary work clothes, so Trace stood out, tall and regal in his immaculate

352

ening clothes. And while the few women who adorned the room were eye-catching in their heavy makeup and low-cut, bright satin dresses, Cassie's natural, clean beauty and classic features made the others all pale in comparison.

At the far end of the hall, the musicians' gallery exhibited an orchestra that was already competing with the clashing sounds that filled the hall: men shouting and talking in different languages, women laughing shrilly, chips and coins clinking as money changed hands, and the ever-present drone of the dealers as they encouraged bettors to raise their wagers at the faro, roulette, and monte tables throughout the room.

"Come in, come in," a pudgy balding man who also wore evening clothes sang out as he hurried to greet the newest arrivals to the Golden Goose. "Welcome! I'm Cliff Hopkins, the proprietor of the Golden Goose."

Cassie's eyes lit and her mouth split in a sultry smile. "Mr. Hopkins," she cooed, taking Cliff's arm. "It's such a pleasure to meet you. I was just telling my husband how I admire your lovely establishment."

"T.C. McAllister," Trace said, holding out his hand to shake with Cliff. "And this is my wife, Cassandra. Your saloon is quite nice, old man—for San Francisco, that is. Of course, in New York . . ."

"Don't be such a tease, T.C. You know the Golden Goose is exquisite and just the thing I have in mind for us."

"Oh, do you intend to open a casino in San

353

Francisco?"

Trace shrugged his shoulders. "Actually, it's on of Cassandra's little whims. Nothing definite ha been decided."

Cassie poked out her bottom lip and looked up a Trace, her brown eyes wide with threatening tears "But you promised."

Trace looked helplessly at Cliff, then lifted Cas sie's chin and smiled into her pouting face. "O course I did, darling." His tone was coaxing an coddling. "And if you want a casino, I'll build yo one."

Her face brightened. "As nice as this one?"

"If that's what you want, then you shall have i But let's not talk about it now. We came here to tes our luck at our charming host's tables. What strike your fancy tonight, my sweet?"

"Monte!"

"Monte it is," Cliff said, starting toward the nea est game.

As Cliff parted the crowd at the monte table t make room for his guests, Trace's gaze landed o the dealer. *Barton Talbot! That's just great!* H caught Cassie's attention with a subtle touch on he arm.

Cassie looked up at him, her smile in place though her eyes were questioning.

Trace tilted his head and shifted his eyes towar the monte dealer.

Cassie followed his gaze, her own zeroing in o the familiar profile only an instant before Clif Hopkins would have called the dealer's attention t the new players. "I've changed my mind. I'm not i

354

e mood for monte, after all." She batted her yelashes beguilingly at Cliff and pivoted away from ie table, taking him with her. "Maybe faro would e better."

Certain she was going to break out laughing any noment if she looked at Trace, she directed her aze toward the faro tables and asked, "Is that greeable with you, darling?"

Trace came up beside her and wrapped his hand round her waist, giving her a secret squeeze of pproval. "You know that I'm happy as long as ou're happy, my sweet."

"Then, faro it shall be," Cliff announced mag-animously. With a flourish, he guided them to a aro table and pulled out a chair for Cassie. "Mr. IcAllister?" he said, offering Trace a chair.

Trace shook his head and waved his hand. "I on't play. I'm just along to carry my wife's 'win-ings,' " he explained with a wink in Cliff's direc-on and an affectionate caress of Cassie's shoulder.

Cassie covered his hand on her shoulder and atted it. "Just you wait and see, my darling. One f these days you're going to regret your cruel :asing." Her face glowing with excitement, she eyed ie faro layout in front of her—a long green board nameled with pictures of thirteen cards of the pades suit. "Who knows? It just might happen. 'm warning you, I'm feeling very lucky tonight."

"I've heard those words before," Trace laughed, xtracting an envelope from his breast pocket and anding it to Cliff. "Will the usual thousand dol-rs' worth of chips be enough to bring about this iracle, love?"

"You don't believe I'm going to win, do you? Well, I'll show you. I'll only need three hundred in chips."

"But you always start with a thousand," Trace protested.

"Three hundred is all I want," she said, scooting to the edge of her seat. "My chips, please, Mr. Hopkins."

Cliff directed a questioning glance at Trace, who lifted his shoulders to indicate his helplessness and nodded his consent. "Whatever makes her happy. Give her three hundred—though, for the life of me, I can't imagine why she wants an unlikely amount like three hundred."

"Three's my lucky number," she explained, holding her hand palm upward for her chips as she continued to look over the layout and observe where the other bettors at the table were placing their wagers.

Examining the one-thousand-dollar bank note Trace had handed him, Cliff turned to the dealer, "Give Mrs. McAllister her chips, Clyde." Then smiling at Trace, he said, "I'll need to go into the office to get your change."

Trace looked apologetic. "If I'd known, I would've had the bank issue them in smaller amounts," he explained sheepishly.

"Don't worry about it. I'll be right back. You just go on and enjoy yourselves." He hurried away.

"You heard what the man said, sweetheart," Trace said against her ear as he bent to kiss her cheek. "You're doing great so far."

Cassie beamed under the compliment and picked

p three twenty-dollar chips. "I've only just begun," he laughed, placing the chips, one at a time on the three.

Chapter Twenty-one

"All bets down," the dealer announced, dropping a new deck of shuffled cards face up into the dealing box. He removed his hand, exposing the top card—a three of hearts.

Since the top card, called "soda," was automatically discarded, Cassie's chances of winning with her three bet were immediately lowered. "Three's your lucky number, huh?" Trace goaded her.

Cassie shot him a perturbed glare, but said nothing, her complete attention on the dealer's finger perched on the dealing box, ready to remove the soda card and expose the first card of the game.

He glanced from player to player, waiting for the nod indicating they were ready. When he was satisfied that no more bets were going to be played, he disclosed the first card—the two of diamonds. "Two loses," he announced, slipping that card from the box and revealing a six of clubs. "Six wins." A miner at the end of the table voiced his disappointment as the dealer raked in the chips bet on the two o win. No one had bet on the six and all other bets stayed. "Place your bets, gentlemen—and ma'am."

Cassie left her chips on the three and put three more on the nine. Then, as an afterthought, she tossed three chips on the six. "To lose," she said, placing a six-sided "copper" on top of her bet.

"All bets down?" The dealer removed the last card played, revealing the six of spades. "Six loses," he announced in the same disinterested voice.

"I told you!" Cassie shrieked, exuberantly clapping her hands together.

His wooden expression never changing, the dealer removed the six, showing the nine of hearts. "Nine wins."

Screaming excitedly, Cassie grabbed for her winnings. "Two in a row! I picked two in a row! I knew my luck was going to change today! I just felt it in my bones!" She stacked three additional chips on her three-bet and dropped three on the queen. "Ready," she announced, shooting a disconcerted grin at Trace.

He leaned down to kiss her cheek. "You're supposed to be losing," he whispered against her ear. "How're we going to prove what free spenders we are if you keep this up?"

She returned his kiss. "I'm trying," she said softly. Studying the layout again, her expression serious, she picked up three chips and put them on the nine with a copper—to lose.

"Nine loses," the dealer announced, laying it aside and exposing the next card. "Seven wins."

Cassie glanced over her shoulder and gave Trace a sheepish grin. At least she hadn't won on both of the cards!

Cassie released an excited squeal for her audience
as the dealer paid off her nine bet. Her expression
thoughtful, she considered the casekeeper, an abacuslike device that kept track of the cards dealt.
Chances of a nine or six coming up right away were
slim. "Four to lose, king to win," she said decisively, placing her chips accordingly.

The dealer exposed the king of spades. "King
loses. Four wins."

"Lucky night, huh?"

Cassie glared at Trace and stuck out her tongue.
"Are you happy now?" she asked him peevishly.

"Don't be too upset, sweetheart. It's just one
hand. And after all, the important thing is that you
enjoy yourself."

"For your information, I don't ever enjoy losing,
even one hand."

"All bets down," the dealer instructed in that
same droning voice that showed no excitement or
interest in the game.

"Go on," Trace encouraged her. "Don't worry
about winning or losing. Just have fun."

At that moment, Cliff showed up with Trace's
$700 change from the bank note. "Are you enjoying
yourself, Mrs. McAllister?"

"I was until the last hand," she said petulantly.

"She's all upset because she lost on a couple of
cards. But I told her not to worry about it." Trace
caressed her upper arms lovingly. "It's only money,
isn't it?"

He smiled at Cliff and took the pouch of gold
the casino owner had for him. He bounced the

360

ouch playfully in his hand, then dropped it into his pocket, not even bothering to make certain he hadn't been shortchanged or been handed gold that had sand mixed into it — a detail Cliff took particular interest in. In California, no one trusted anyone when it came to gold. Yet this man . . .

"You're right!" Cassie exclaimed, and patted Trace's hand on her arm. "It's only money, and I shouldn't take it so seriously. I should just play for fun and shouldn't worry about winning or losing." She turned back to the dealer. "Maybe if I change the size of my bets my luck will turn. One hundred dollars on the jack to win, two hundred dollars on the ace to lose," she announced loudly, removing her other bets and placing all but a few of her chips on those two numbers.

Whisking the top card from the box, the dealer resumed the game by showing the next two cards in quick succession. "Six loses. Ace wins." He retrieved the house winnings. "Put down your bets."

"Drat! What's gone wrong? Why can't I pick them right?"

"Oh, you're picking the right numbers, love. You've just got your winners and losers mixed up." He laughed cheerfully in Cliff's direction, his expression saying, *Isn't it something what we men will do for our women?*

Watching her $200 disappear from the ace on the table, Cassie experienced a moment of serious regret. She shook her head unhappily. She sure hoped Trace knew what he was doing, because ignoring a winning streak and deliberately losing like this was hurting her a lot more than she had expected it to.

361

Besides, if her luck held she might even be able to get the $10,000 they needed that way. In fact, she had already suggested that to Trace. But he had reminded her that Cliff had told Salina he hadn't ever intended to let her go at any price. No, the only way they would be able to deal with Cliff Hopkins would be to force him into a position where he was desperate for money.

Still not completely convinced her plan wasn't the best, Cassie sneaked an uncertain glance at her "husband" from the corner of her eye. "Are you sure about this?" she asked.

"Go on, love. Don't worry about the chips. I'll buy you more." To Cliff he added, "Looks like I'm going to be giving this back to you pretty quick." He patted his pocket that contained the gold.

Cassie played her last three chips—on the nine to lose.

"Four loses, nine wins." The dealer raked in the last of her chips.

"Guess we need some more chips," he told Cliff with a smile behind Cassie's back. He reached into his pocket for the pouch. "Might as well make it for the whole seven hundred."

Cassie held up her hand to stop him. "I don't think so," she sighed, pushing away from the table and standing up. "I want to go somewhere else."

His hand froze in midair over Cliff's extended palm. "Are you sure? I thought you liked it here."

"I do. I just think I'll be luckier somewhere else tonight."

"Maybe you'd be more fortunate at the roulette table," Cliff offered enthusiastically. "I understand 's been paying off very well tonight."

Cassie stared at the crowd around a roulette table nd thought for a moment, then shook her head. No." She looked up at Trace. "Maybe my luck will e better at the Bella Union." She started for the loor.

Trace shrugged his shoulders and shoved the urse back into his pockets. "I'd like to stay, but — vell, you do understand, don't you?" He pitched a 50 gold piece to the dealer, threw out an off-anded, "Thanks," and started after Cassie.

His disappointment showing on his face at letting uch an obvious free-spender get away, Cliff fol-owed him, nodding his head. "Of course I under-tand. But I do hope we'll see you at the Golden Goose again soon."

"I'm sure that by tomorrow night she will have lecided she feels 'lucky' again and will want to ome back," Trace said at the door, giving Cliff a eassuring pat on the back. "I guess one of these lays, I'm going to have to buy her that casino she vants, after all. Maybe then she'll be happy to do ier gambling in just one place." Trace laughed and :upped his hand over the side of his mouth, direct-ng an aside remark to Cliff. "In fact, now that I hink of it, she's probably lost enough in the past /ear to buy a couple of casinos!"

"Come on," Cassie prodded. "I've really got the 'eeling I'm going to win big at the Bella Union!"

Trace winked at Cliff and pressed his lips together n a this-I-gotta-see smirk. "I'm coming. Nice meet-ng you, Hopkins. Thanks for the hospitality. We'll ook forward to seeing you again."

363

"And I'll look forward to seeing you again, too," Cliff called after Trace, who was already hurrying across the square to catch up with Cassie. "Not to mention your money," he added to himself as he turned back to the casino. An idea on how he could recoup the exorbitant cash amounts he'd been forced to lay out to open the Golden Goose was already beginning to germinate in his mind.

He was still contemplating the best way of carrying out his plans for the McAllisters an hour later when Sam Seifert ambled into the Golden Goose. "Doctor, what a surprise to see you here," he said, his greeting guarded. "I hope you haven't come to give me more bad news."

"Who me?" Seifert asked, staring at Cliff as though he couldn't quite place him. "Have we met?"

"Earlier tonight. You were at my house to attend to my housekeeper. She had fallen down the stairs."

"Oh, yes. Good to see you again," he responded, his attention on the crowds around the gaming tables, rather than on Cliff. "Nasty fall." He glanced around the casino with interest. "Nice place you have here. You own it?"

Cliff nodded his head. "Then, you aren't here about Salina?"

Seifert shook his head and chuckled. "I'm just here for a quiet bit of gambling—" he followed the swaying movements of a golden-haired beauty's hips as she strolled past him, her smile suggesting something other than gambling to him, "or whatever other entertainment strikes my fancy. It was just getting too depressing over at the Bella Union. I go

364

sick of watching."

Cliff's eyebrows rose with interest. "Sick of watching what?"

The doctor shook his head in disgust. "There's a little gal over there playing faro who must've lost three or four thousand dollars. They ought to be ashamed taking her money like that — she was close to tears a couple of times."

"What did she look like?"

"Pretty, tall, kind of reddish-colored hair. Early twenties, I'd say."

"I don't suppose you got her name, did you?"

"Naw, but she was with her husband, and I got the idea she does this pretty regularly. Someone said she lost a bundle at the El Dorado last night. They'll probably make it over here one of these days."

"No doubt you're right," Cliff said, his expression distracted as his plan knitted more tightly together in his thoughts. "Now, what's your pleasure, Doctor?"

"To tell you the truth, I missed supper. I think I'll just grab a bite at your buffet first. Then I'll decide." His gaze swept up and down the length of a bosomy brunette who had struck a pose at the bar.

"Help yourself," Cliff said, making a sweep with his hand toward the array of free food meant to entice customers away from his competitors. "I'm sure you'll enjoy our delicious cuisine. Our chef has worked in the finest restaurants in the world, you know."

"Looks great," Seifert said, popping a hard-boiled egg into his mouth and chewing loudly as he filled

365

a plate.

Eyeing the man, cheeks puffed out with food and smacking, Cliff gave him a strained smile. "Then, I will leave you at your own discretion. If you need anything, anything at all . . ." He glanced pointedly up to the balcony that bordered the casino in time to see a woman and man disappear into a room up there. "I'm certain one of my lovely 'hostesses' will be able to take care of you."

"Mmm," Seifert grunted with a nod, stuffing two oysters into his mouth. "Been a pleasure."

"Yes," Cliff said, wheeling away before he became ill at the sight of his elegant table being attacked by the boorish doctor with the table manners of a pig.

"Are you sure no one went in or came out the back door of the theater besides Mimi and her daughters?" Trace asked Noah.

Straightening from his crouch behind a packing crate in the alley at the back of the theater, Noah shook his head regretfully. "I've been right here from before the time they arrived to do their show, until they came out and walked toward the hotel." He raised his hands over his head and stretched. "I don't think he's going to show up."

Cassie, her skirt bunched up around her knees to keep it from getting dirty, stood up too and looked at Trace. "I hate to say it, Trace, but I think Noah's right. It doesn't look like Murieta's coming."

"I guess you're right," he agreed with a disappointed shake of his head. "Damn! I was so sure."

366

"Maybe something happened to him. Maybe he's been caught already and that's why he didn't come."

"That's probably it," Noah agreed. "I read in the paper the other day that a posse had some Mexican they think is Murieta holed up in a cave in the mountains."

"Yeah, I read that too. But I can't get rid of the feeling that he's right here and somehow got past us."

Cassie patted his arm and tugged him away from their hiding spot. "Maybe he went in the front door."

Trace shook his head. "He'd be too easy to spot."

"Not if he knew someone was looking for him at the stagedoor," she reasoned. "All he'd have to do would be wear different clothes and he'd look like any other Mexican in San Francisco. But there's no use worrying about it any more tonight. Everyone's left the theater, so we might as well do the same and go back to the hotel and get some sleep."

Trace stared at the theater's back door, as if he could see the answer there if he looked at it in just the right light. "I guess he could have spotted Noah watching the back entrance, couldn't he?"

"Tomorrow night, after we put on *our* show, at the Golden Goose for Cliff Hopkins, why don't we go see the Witherspoons' show?" Cassie said. "Maybe we'll spot him in the crowd."

"If he hasn't already been here and gone," Trace grumbled, balling a fist and pounding it into his palm.

"You said you felt like he was still here, and so far your instincts have been pretty good," Cassie

367

consoled him. "Why don't we give it a few more days? Besides, ever since you got me to wear a dress, I've been hoping to see some actors doing a play. I saw one a couple of years ago and liked it a lot."

Trace gave Cassie an enthusiastic hug. "I'll just bet you did! You're quite a little actress yourself! You should have seen her, Noah. She was perfect as the pampered wife of a rich man."

"I'm not surprised."

Blushing under his praise, Cassie stomped her foot and planted her fists on her hips indignantly. "Are we going to stand here all night, or are we going to get some sleep?" she asked in her spoiled-brat voice.

"We might as well call it a night," he chuckled, taking a swipe at her butt. "And tomorrow night we'll try your idea about the front door."

Cassie's face brightened. "You mean you think I had a good idea?"

Trace hunched his shoulders, crinkled his upper lip and waggled his head, as if to say her suggestion was only so-so. "I mean, it can't hurt anything, can it? And, as you said, you have been wanting to see a play."

Cassie's smile fell. "Why can't you just once admit somebody besides you might have a good idea?" Her voice shook slightly, the excitement and tension of the evening suddenly getting to her. She wheeled about and strode angrily down the alleyway, her ladylike demeanor discarded. "I'm gonna get me some shut-eye!"

Trace looked at Noah, his expression stunned.

368

"What'd I say?"

Noah shook his head and clicked his tongue. "For someone as smart as you are, you're sure dumb. When are you going to learn to give that girl a little credit?"

"I give her credit!" Trace defended himself, studying Cassie's retreating figure as it disappeared around the corner. "Didn't you hear me tell her how well she did tonight?"

"Oh, you give her credit when she's following through on your orders—like tonight. And I'll bet you tell her she's pretty when she's wearing clothes *you* picked out for her."

"What's your point?"

"When was the last time you agreed with an idea she had? Or told her she was pretty in something she picked out?"

With a cringe of guilt, Trace remembered the way he had carped on her about the tight pants. "Well, you have to agree, those britches she insists on wearing are too tight. And I told her we'd go to the theater tomorrow night. That was agreeing with her. What do you expect me to do?"

"Sure, you agreed to take her to see the play. But you couldn't admit her idea might be just as good as ours, could you? Maybe even better?"

Trace didn't say anything. His mind was too filled with memories of all the times he had tossed off Cassie's suggestions as useless.

Seeing that Trace was feeling guilty, Noah laid a hand on his friend's arm. "Can't you see she's bending over backward to be what you want her to be, man?"

Trace nodded his head. "What should I do?"

"Just learn to bend a little yourself. It won't be that hard, and you won't even have to bend that much. Just every once in a while, let her know how smart she is and that you respect her ideas. Even give in now and then."

"Thanks, my friend. You've given me plenty to think about."

Cassie slammed the hotel-room door behind her, and without thinking, locked it. When she heard the bolt click into place, she realized what she'd done and paused, a feeling of panic grabbing her. Her hand flew back to the lock to undo it. But Trace's words stopped her. If she was ever going to conquer her fear completely, she had to face it head-on—and alone.

Her chest rising and falling rapidly, she dropped her hand away from the lock and stared at it, waiting for the smothering feeling to consume her as it always did. But nothing happened. She was breathing almost naturally now.

Frowning, she pursed her lips, and sucked in a tensing gulp of air. And her lungs filled easily with oxygen. There was no squeezing feeling in her chest, no lightheadedness. Nothing. It was just like being outdoors.

Slowly, breath by breath, the panic ebbed from her chest, and realization penetrated her thoughts. She had fought her fear and defeated it. She had won! She stared at the lock in amazement. It was really over.

A loud knock shook the door, and Cassie jumped back in surprise.

"Trace!" she called out, forgetting her anger with him in her excitement to tell him about her triumph. "I did it!" she exclaimed. Sliding the bolt from the lock, she flung the door open wide. "I locked the door and I could still br—"

Her excitement exploded into alarm. "Barton! What are you doing here? How did you know where to find me?"

"So, it is you!" he accused, hitting the door with the heel of his hand and barging into the room. He spun around to face her, kicking the door shut. "When I heard the faro dealer talking about McAllister and his wife, 'Cassandra,' I was sure there must be some mistake." His angry gaze zeroed in on the gold band on her left hand. His eyes narrowed and he grabbed her hand for a closer examination. "But I see there's been no mistake."

He went further into the room. "Tell me, Cassie—or Cassandra—or whatever your name is, what kind of con game are you and McAllister trying to pull?"

"I don't know what you're talking about," she said, wrenching her hand from his and turning her back on her uninvited guest lest he see the lie in her eyes. "And you'd better leave before Trace comes. He'll be angry if he finds you here."

" 'Angry'?" he mimicked. "What happened to the little country bumpkin who'd have said, 'madder'n hell'? Tell me, what did yo hope to gain by leading me on with that diamond-in-the-rough act of yours?"

"Leading you on? You're insane! I didn't lead you on! Now get out of here." She crossed to the dresser and tore open a drawer. "And if you don't leave, I'll be forced to—"

Before she could wrap her fingers around the handle of her revolver, Barton hurled himself at her. He knocked her away from the table and onto the bed, landing on top of her.

"Barton! Get off me!" she demanded, struggling beneath him. "Trace will—" Her words were cut off by Barton's mouth over hers.

"What will Trace do?" a deep, controlled voice asked from the doorway.

Barton's head bobbed up, and he and Cassie stared in horror at the man propped nonchalantly in the doorway, his arms folded over his chest, one ankle crossed over the other.

"This isn't what it looks like, old man," Barton babbled, scrambling to stand up, doing his best to straighten his clothing as he did.

"Thank goodness you came," Cassie cried, leaping off the bed. She ran to Trace and threw her arms around his waist, so relieved he was there, she didn't notice that he wasn't returning her embrace.

Not even looking at her, Trace unfolded his arms and removed her from the path between him and Barton. "What are you doing here, Talbot?"

"She was going for a gun to shoot me!" he explained excitedly, pointing to the dresser drawer. "I had to knock her away from it. In the struggle, we fell on the bed."

"It's true!" Cassie interrupted. "He burst in here accusing us of being crooks and me of leading him

372

on and . . ." Cassie stopped, realizing Trace was watching her with an amused expression on his face. Cold and amused and disbelieving.

"Go on."

She hesitated uncertainly. He was looking at her so strangely, as if he were seeing her for the first time, and a chill of foreboding rippled through her. "An' . . . And . . . I told him to leave. When he wouldn't go, I went for my gun. But I wasn't fast enough and he—"

Trace nodded his head. "You don't need to tell me the rest." He pushed away from the doorframe and stepped the rest of the way into the room, closing the door quietly behind him. "So, what do you think I should do about this?" He shoved back his coat, exposing his holster.

Sweat glistened on Barton's forehead and upper lip. "It was all a mistake. Let's just forget it happened." He held out his hand to shake with Trace.

Trace made no move to take the extended hand. With a sneer, he laughed, the sound anything but cheerful. "It might be a bit difficult to forget walking into a room and finding you in my bed on top of my wife."

Barton threw out his hands in a posture of surrender. "All right. I give up. I know I had no business coming here, and I apologize. But when I heard you married her right out from under my nose, I went crazy for a minute or two. Can't we just forget this happened?" He held out his hand again. "After all, you won the entire package, didn't you?" He winked conspiratorially.

"What did he win?" Cassie interrupted. "What

package?"

Startled by her voice, both men turned and gaped at her.

"Somebody tell me what you're talking about."
Trace grabbed the gambler's extended hand and shook it. "Apology accepted," he said, the words exploding from his mouth as he clapped Barton on the back and prodded him toward the door. "Just don't come sniffing around Cassie again. She's taken."

Barton tilted his head questioningly at Trace. A knowing smile spread over his face and he looked back at Cassie as if he had something to say. His mouth opened, he took one last peek at Trace, whose angry glare dared him to go on.

The gambler's mouth clamped shut on a surrendering smile, and he shrugged his shoulders. "What the hell? You can't blame a fellow for making one last stab at success, can you?" He hit Trace on the back and smiled as if they were old friends. "No hard feelings?"

"No hard feelings," Trace agreed halfheartedly as he shoved Barton the rest of the way through the door before he could say anything else.

The instant the door closed behind Barton, Cassie ran to Trace and spun him around to face her. "What the hell was he talking about?"

Trace raised his eyebrows in a reproachful arch at her choice of words. "You're slipping, Cassie. But we'll let it pass this ti—"

"You better tell me what Barton meant, McAllister! Or I'm going to do more than slip. I'm goin' to go after him and make him tell me."

374

Trace walked past her, loosening his tie as he went. Damn! Why had he ever made up that ridiculous story about Cassie being rich? After what he'd found out about her past, she would never believe that hadn't been his ulterior motive all along. "It was nothing, Cassie. He was just trying to make trouble."

"Then, why are you actin' as nervous as a whore in church?"

"I'm not acting nervous. I'm just tired and want to get some sleep." He threw his jacket on a chair and sat down on the bed, patting the spot next to him. He looked up at Cassie and gave her his most charming smile. "Really, that's all it was. He's jealous and was trying to make trouble between us. Come on, let's go to bed."

Cassie shot an indecisive glance over her shoulder at the door, then back to Trace. Relaxing her stiff posture, she crossed the room and disappeared behind the privacy screen. "Okay, we'll drop it," she said, her tone indicating that the subject was anything but dropped. "But sooner or later, I'm going to find out—one way or the other!"

Chapter Twenty-two

Cassie stepped out from behind the screen, dressed for the night in a gown. Glaring at Trace's back from the corner of her eye, she snatched up a pillow and the spare blanket folded on the end of the bed. "You take the bed tonight. I'll sleep in the chair," she said, dropping into the stuffed chair in the corner and arranging the blanket over her lap.

"What the hell do you think you're doing?"

She socked her pillow several times and placed it behind her head. "Just because we're actin' married in public, don—*doesn't* mean I have to sleep with you, does it?"

The low growl. "Don't be ridiculous! You can't sleep in the chair." He stood up and walked toward her.

As though she hadn't heard him, she yanked the pillow out from behind her head and slapped it onto the arm of the chair. Giving it a severe plumping, she dropped her head onto the pillow and squirmed herself into a ball, trying to ignore the fact that her long legs were half off the seat of the chair. She closed her eyes and burrowed down into the blanket.

"Cassie. Get up and get into the bed!"

"Tell me what Barton Talbot meant and what those funny looks you two were exchanging meant."

He turned away from her and began unbuttoning his shirt. "We didn't exchange any funny looks."

"Good night, McAllister."

"All right, dammit! If you insist on continuing with this ridiculousness, I'll sleep in the chair. You take the bed."

"No thanks," she muttered. "This is fine." Sitting up, she jerked on her pillow and plopped it onto the other arm, where she again went through the twisting gyrations of curling herself into a comfortable position—her feet and lower legs still hanging off the chair.

His familiar growl tripped up her spine, bringing her very little satisfaction as he turned back to the bed. "Fine," he yelled, stripping back the bed quilt angrily. "Be stubborn." He blew out the lamp with a frustrated puff of air, leaving the room in darkness. "Go on and wake up with a crick in your stubborn little neck. Don't say I didn't warn you. But once and for all, I'm telling you he was just trying to make trouble."

She heard the sounds of him removing the remainder of his clothing and then the creaking of the bed as the ropes supporting the mattress strained under his weight. "G'night, kid."

Refusing to acknowledge him, Cassie sat up and punched her pillow again, then rearranged her long body, in yet another attempt to find a satisfactory position for sleeping. When she finally found one she hoped would let her relax, she squeezed her eyes shut and started counting sheep.

One . . . Two . . . Three . . . Why won't he just tell me what Talbot was talking about? she asked herself forlornly. *If it's got something to do with me, I've got a right to know!*

Don't think about it, Cassie! You're supposed to be thinking about sheep!

One . . . Two . . . Three . . .

I really thought he was starting to love me, but if he doesn't trust me enough to be honest—

Stop it! Right, sheep. One . . . Two . . . Three.

I don't know why I ever thought I could make him love me, anyway.

Realizing the futility of sleeping, she rolled to a sitting position and stretched her coltish legs out in front of her, crossing them at the ankles. In the dark, she could make out the shadowy shape that filled the length of the bed, and she could hear the slow, steady breathing of someone in very deep sleep. Her anger rose to irrational proportions. Furiously seizing her pillow, she hugged it to her chest and rested her chin on it.

Listen to him. Sleeping like he doesn't have a worry in the world! She squeezed her pillow tighter and scrunched her face into a glare. *Who does he think he is? He leaves me wondering and then he sleeps like he's completely innocent!*

She stared at Trace for long, silent minutes, willing him to wake up, fall out of bed, get a sudden itch—anything to disrupt what looked like his perfect slumber. But he only answered her "hexes" with a soft snort as he turned over on his side and faced away from her.

Then an idea occurred to her. Who was she punishing by spending a miserable, sleepless night in a chair when he was lounging comfortably in the bed? And only using half of it at that! Why should she be the one to suffer while that empty half was unused? What was stopping her from getting a few hours' sleep in that soft bed? Anyway, since she always got up before he did and could get back to the chair before he woke up, he wouldn't even know where she'd slept!

Pleased with her idea, Cassie uncrossed her ankles and inched her feet out of their sprawled position, then dragged them slowly under her. Easing her bottom to the edge of the chair, she held her breath and waited a full minute to see if Trace knew she had moved. His breathing stayed the same, slow and rhythmic. He was sound asleep.

Blowing out a sigh of relief, she cautiously maneuvered her way out of the chair, her concentration on the sleeping man's back the entire time.

Still clutching her pillow, she pointed the toes of one foot toward the bed, then paused. Trace didn't move. So far, so good. Carefully letting down her heel, she shifted her weight to that foot. She stopped again and waited another few seconds before she felt secure enough to move the next foot.

Toe, pause. Heel, pause. Shift weight, pause. Toe, pause. Heel, pause . . . until she was beside the

379

bed. Now, if she could just get into it without disturbing him.

Moving carefully, each motion measured and slow, she put the pillow on the bed, then lifted the covers and slid between the sheets. Taking care not to touch Trace, she sank back, luxuriating in the feel of the soft mattress around her. With a silent *Ah,* she settled the covers over herself and closed her eyes.

"It's about time."

Cassie's eyes snapped open, her fingers stiffened on the blanket, and her head jerked to the side. "You're awake!"

"Uh huh." Trace flopped over onto his back. "How could I sleep with you making all that noise tiptoeing across the room like that?"

Doing her best to stop the snicker that popped unexpectedly from her throat, Cassie threw back the cover and sat up, swinging her feet over the side of the bed.

Trace reached out and tangled his fingers in the back of her nightgown, cutting her escape short. "You've come this far, don't you think you might as well stay and get a decent night's rest?"

"I thought you were asleep."

"Do you think I could sleep, knowing you were all wadded up and miserable in that chair?"

Cassie stopped straining against his hold on her gown. "I'm not going to forget," she warned.

Trace heaved a defeated sigh. "Let's just get some sleep," he said, releasing his hold on her gown and flopping a bent elbow over his eyes. "Maybe in the morning you'll be able to see how silly this all is."

380

Looking over her shoulder at the bare-chested man, Cassie was faced with indecision. Her stubborn pride told her to go back to the chair, but intelligence reminded her why she'd left the chair in the first place. She lay back down and stared up at the dark ceiling, her arms limp at her sides.

"Trace?" Her voice was a testing whisper. "Are you asleep?"

"No."

"Oh." Now that she had his attention, she didn't know where to begin.

"Still can't sleep?" His hand on top of the covers in the space that separated them ached to reach out and cover hers, only two inches from his. But he didn't.

"Unh uh. How 'bout you?"

"No."

"You want to talk a while—just till we get sleepy?"

"What about?"

"You never mention your parents. Where are they?"

"Dead."

"Oh, I'm so sorry."

"That's okay. It happened twenty-two years ago, so I don't remember much about them. I was only five at the time. My father was a Scottish ship-owner, and he met my mother on one of his trips to Los Angeles. My grandmother told me it was love at first sight. Anyway, they hated to be apart, so she often went with him on his trips around the Cape to the East Coast. But the last time, their ship broke up coming around the Cape."

"Was it a storm? I've heard stories of ships that had to endure hundred-knot winds for days at a time off Cape Horn."

Trace nodded his head. "The trip's particularly bad in the winter."

Cassie's heart twisted with compassion. She'd always felt sorry for herself because she'd lost her mother. But at least she'd had both her parents for twelve years and could remember more about her mother than just what someone else had told her. *And* she still had her father. Trace had no one but his grandfather. Poor lonely little boy. But he didn't have to be lonely any more. He had her now, and she would see that he never felt alone again.

Cassie reached out and covered Trace's hand with hers. "I'm sorry, Trace."

"You don't need to be. My grandparents were good to me. My sister and I were really very lucky."

"I mean I'm sorry I was making such a fuss before about what Talbot said. I know I was being 'ridiculous' and 'silly.' And I know if it's important, you'll tell me when you're ready."

Trace didn't answer. Then after long, silent moments, he said, "Did I ever tell you how much I like you?"

Cassie's heart thumped rapidly in her chest. Like was getting pretty close to love! "You 'like' me?"

Trace chuckled softly. "Now that I think of it, you really caught me with my defenses down. It just never occurred to me that a gun-toting female prospector would worm her way into my heart. But you sure did. I never even had a chance once you flashed your smile at me and I saw those—"

"Those what?"

"Those freckles. I really like your freckles."

"Now, I know you're crazy." She fell back on her pillow in a pretended huff. "And I was just starting to believe you'd all of a sudden gotten halfway smart!"

Trace worked an arm under her head and around her shoulders, then pulled her snug against his side. "You really don't know how pretty you are, do you?"

"For a speckled string bean maybe."

Trace covered her lips with his fingertips. "Stop that kind of talk. Didn't you see how every man in the Golden Goose looked at you tonight? Do you think a 'speckled string bean' would turn heads like that?"

Cassie thought for a minute and smiled against his neck as she wrapped her arm around his waist and snuggled closer. "I guess we did make a nice sight all decked out like we were."

"You were the nice sight," he said, turning on his side to face her and reaching down to ease her nightgown upward. "Do you really need this thing?' he asked.

"I thought I might get cold sleeping in the chair." She lifted her hips slightly so he could work the gown up to her waist.

"You're not in the chair."

"You're right, and now that I think about it, I'm not cold either." She lifted her upper torso and let him draw the gown up over her breasts.

"In fact, it's hot in here," he whispered huskily, leaning forward to mouth and tease a peaking, swollen breast.

"Oh, Trace, that feels so wonderful," she moaned, falling back, the nightgown bunched up under her arms making her back arch and lift her breasts up to meet his kiss.

His mouth traveled between her breasts, working each tip to a hardened nub, then traveled downward, shoving the blanket out of the way as he went.

Her insides were pulsating with desire. Erotic chills exploded over her belly, their electricity radiating to between her legs. Cassie writhed under the shower of wet kisses, her senses all focused on the unbearable craving he had created in her.

Raising up on his knees, Trace turned and knelt at her side. He reached behind him and grabbed his pillow. Lifting her undulating hips, he shoved the plump padding beneath her. Delving between her thighs with his fingers, he spread her legs wide, opening her to receive his kiss. Then, as a bee is drawn to the nectar of a rose, he bent to taste her.

The caress of his tongue sent flames raging through her, and she thrashed her head and shoulders from side to side. Her passion pounding wildly out of control, she bent her knees and dug her heels into the mattress and levered her hips higher.

His erotic tonguing was at once gentle and rough, shy and bold, taunting and praising. Never in all their times together had Cassie felt so thoroughly loved. Never had she imagined the heights the flames he was stoking in her body could reach. And never had she dreamed such ecstasy could exist. She prayed it could last forever.

Then, it was happening. The pressure inside her was screaming for release. Every muscle in her body grew taut. Her toes and fingers curled into the sheet beneath her. Her neck arched, and she threw her head back, letting a low animal moan as her hips bucked and jerked against him.

Her body still spasming helplessly as he continued to sip at and court the dewy softness of her, she reached out for him. She wrapped her fingers around the solid strength of his manhood, twisting and turning her body so that she could pleasure him as he had her. Touching the tip of him with her tongue, she brought her head to the side, surrounding him with her lips, slowly, lazily, before taking him into her mouth.

"Oh, God," he pleaded against the inside of her thigh as his hips rocked in rhythm with the movements of her hand on his manhood. "I can't . . ." he protested, ". . . take much of . . . oh, God, it's so good."

Suddenly, as though it were the hardest thing he'd ever done, he wrenched himself from her caress. Moving like a man half crazed, he turned around and stabbed his pulsating passion into the fiery warmth of her body. He slammed into her, each thrust harder and more desperate than the preceding one.

Bracing her feet on the mattress, she lifted her hips off the bed, welcoming his greedy possession eagerly. "It's so good," she wailed, gyrating wildly beneath him. "Now!" she cried, her nails digging into the tautly stretched skin of his back and shoulders. "Fill me now!"

385

"Oh, Cassie!" he panted, his face twisted into a straining grimace as he spilled the fluid of his passion deep, deep inside her.

Letting her bottom relax back against the pillow, Cassie wrapped her legs around Trace's jerking hips and locked her ankles together. Tears of joy sprang into her eyes. "My sweet, sweet, love."

"Another superb performance, my darling wife," Trace said the next night as, arm-in-arm, they made their way along the plank walkway toward the theater where the Witherspoon company was playing.

Cassie responded with a grin and a quick curtsy. "Thank you, kind sir. And might I say that your performance was wonderful, as well?"

With an *I-know* shrug, Trace gave her a mock bow. "You may, dear lady."

Her face still glowing with happiness, Cassie's tone grew more serious. "How much longer is this going to take?"

"I don't think it will take much longer. Did you see how Hopkins's face lit up when we walked in the door? Why, he practically knocked two men over in his hurry to get to us and let us know how glad he was to see us."

"And did you see how I couldn't lose at his tables tonight no matter what I did?"

Trace nodded his head. "He's hungry for something bigger than the little bit of gold you might lose at his tables. And as long as you're winning, he knows you'll keep coming to the Golden Goose. In fact, I wouldn't be surprised that by tomorrow night, our rat might be hungry enough to take a bit of the 'cheese' we're offering."

Turning down the alley beside the theater, Cassie and Trace dropped the subject of Cliff Hopkins and hurried to meet with Noah.

"Anything happen yet?" Trace asked as the large man materialized from the shadows.

Noah shook his head. "Either he's not coming, or Cassie's right and he sneaked in the front door in disguise. For all we know, he's come and gone by now. How'd it go at the Golden Goose?"

Trace looked up the alley toward the street and nodded his head. "Things went well. Hopkins ought to be ready to stick his head in our trap within the next day or so." He looked back at Noah, "I know you're right about Murieta. But I just can't get rid of this feeling that he's still here and we're practically on top of him."

"Well, maybe we'll spot him in the theater," Cassie suggested encouragingly. "Let's go inside so we can watch as people come in." She gave his arm an excited little tug.

Trace hesitated, then smiled his resignation. "All right." He clapped Noah on the back and said, "We'll let you know if anything happens."

Noah shook his head dejectedly. "I hope it's soon. I'm not sure I can take much more of this waiting around."

"Don't worry, it's all going to work out," Cassie told her friend. "Trace isn't going to let anything happen to Salina."

A few minutes later, as Trace and Cassie approached the theater door, Trace stopped and studied her. "Did you really believe what you said back there?"

"What did I say?"

"About me not letting anything happen to Salina. Do you really trust me that much?"

"I really do, you big galoot," she said, raising up on her toes to kiss his cheek. "Now, quit hemhawin' around and take me to see that theatrical!"

Despite its attractive false front, the theater inside was a long dirt-floored room with rows of backless benches facing a wooden platform at the far end of the room. The stage, such as it was, was arranged with a bench and two freestanding flats that displayed crudely painted trees. To each side of the stage, there were curtained doors. The outside edge of the acting platform was rimmed with a row of flickering oil lamps, their metal shades reflecting their lights toward the stage. On the two lengthwise walls, more lamps were hung, but their wicks were down low, giving the stark room a soft, magical glow that made it possible for the audience to forget how truly unlavish their surroundings were.

"It's really something, ain—I mean, isn't it?" Cassie asked, her momentary lapse doing nothing to dull her excitement.

It was impossible for Trace to resist her excitement. It was contagious. "Really something," he agreed with a smile. He bent his head and kissed her on the ear.

Cassie covered the side of her mouth with her cupped hand. "Don't look now, but isn't that Horace Gilbert?"

"The peddler? Where?"

388

She tilted her head and rolled her eyes toward the couple who had just come through the curtains that separated the narrow foyer and ticket desk from the actual theater. "There, with the lady in the yellow dress. Oh, no! They're coming this way."

"So, McAllister, we meet again," Horace called out, hurrying toward the place where Cassie and Trace stood trapped. "I understand congratulations are in order." He held out his hand to Trace. "You certainly had me fooled. Especially you, Miss Wyma—I mean, Mrs. McAllister. You were very convincing. Have you ever considered going onto the stage?"

"Me? Oh, heavens no. But thank you for the compliment, Mr. Gilbert," Cassie replied sweetly. "It is so kind of you to mention it."

The woman on Horace's arm cleared her throat. "Aren't you going to introduce me to your friends, darling?" Her voice was low and husky, and there was something vaguely familiar about it. Cassie's gaze, up till now barely tolerant, moved to study the woman's face, which was on the same level as her own.

"Oh, my pet! I'm so sorry!" Horace snatched up the woman's gloved hand and held it to his lips.

A flash of irritation darted across the woman's heavily made-up face, but was quickly disguised by a smile. She eased her hand out of Horace's grasp and held it out to Trace. Smiling, she looked at him, her dark eyes sparkling with challenge. "You must forgive Horace. I'm Angel Witherspoon, one of Mimi's girls."

The way she said "girls" made Cassie think she

meant something other than daughter. She shot a quick glance up at Trace to see how he was reacting to Angel.

Rather than taking Angel's hand, he furrowed his fingers into his hair at the back of his head. "Ah, yes, Angel. I believe I have you to thank for a bump I received on my head in Sacramento."

Angel threw back her head and laughed, a high, artificial sound. "I am so sorry. If I'd known you were one of Mimi's 'friends,' I never would have hit you."

A fuzzy memory flashed through Trace's thoughts, drawing his brows together in a puzzled frown. He studied her, trying to place when and where he'd seen that face. But it was no good. He couldn't get a grasp on it. "Have we met before, Miss Witherspoon?" He chuckled. "I mean, other than the time my head came into contact with your lamp."

"I'm sure we both would remember if we had, Mr. McAllister," Angel said, laying her hand on his arm and smiling up into his green eyes. "I know I would have," she added with a seductive lick of her bottom lip.

"I'm Cassandra McAllister," Cassie offered, a bit more loudly than necessary. "*Mrs.* McAllister," she said pointedly. "Don't you need to be getting backstage?"

Only taken slightly aback by Cassie's bluntness, Angel directed an amused glance at the younger woman. Her dark eyes roved disapprovingly from the flowers on the top of Cassie's hat to the tip of her high-heeled boots, then back up to look her directly in the eyes. "Tonight's my night to work backstage. We take turns being understudy, in case someone gets sick."

Cassie nodded her head, determined not to let the woman's superior attitude get to her. "What a shame we won't get to see you perform." She deliberately returned Angel's head-to-toe appraisal.

"Yes, a shame," Angel said, taking Horace's arm again. "Come, Horace, escort me backstage so I can help the others get ready."

"Yes, pet," he answered meekly, allowing himself to be led away.

"Poor Horace," Cassie said, watching as the unlikely couple disappeared through the door to the left of the stage.

"Why do you say that?" Trace asked offhandedly, his own attention also on the curtain, but for a different reason. He knew he'd met Angel before.

"He told me he's making a lot of money selling maps to newcomers to California, and Angel looks like the type of woman who would take a man for all he was worth, then toss him out with the trash."

"Mmm," Trace agreed, his eyes narrowing on the curtained door. "Indeed she does. Tell me, Cass. Was there something about Angel that didn't seem right to you?"

Chapter Twenty-three

Before Cassie could answer Trace's question, th
wicks on the oil lamps on the walls were turne
down, giving the warning that the show was abou
to begin; and there was a flurry of activity as th
audience hurried to gain the best seats. "Come on,
she said, grabbing his arm and dragging him to
bench.

"Didn't you notice anything odd about Angel?'
he repeated softly, once they were seated on
bench.

Sitting up straight and craning her neck to b
sure she would be able to see around the man i
front of her once the show started, Cassie shool
her head. "Not really. Except for being my height,
didn't notice anything unusual about her. I haven'
met too many gals as tall as I am. But other tha
that . . ."

"Mimi's tall, so it makes sense that her daughter

night be taller than average," he reasoned. "Wasn't here anything else?"

"Well, now that you mention it, I had the feeling recognized her when I first saw her. But that's illy. I know I've never se—"

"I had the same feeling! But where?"

"Maybe we saw her in a restaurant or on the street when we were all in Sacramento."

"Yeah, that could be it," he said thoughtfully. "But I don't think so. I feel like it was more than just passing her in the street or sitting across the room from her in an eating place. It's as if I've had a conversation with her before."

"Shh," Cassie ordered, tapping his shoulder and squirming animatedly on the bench as a man with a head of bushy white hair and side whiskers walked out onto the stage to announce the performers.

"Good evening, friends. Tonight the Witherspoon Acting Troupe will be performing the popular play, *Miss Esmerelda Tinky's Disgrace . . .*"

A cheer rose from the onlookers, and the announcer closed his mouth on his next words, a patient smile on his face as he waited for silence.

Cassie clapped excitedly with the rest of the crowd, unaware that Trace had leaned forward with interest the minute the master of ceremonies had begun speaking. The frown on his face deepened with each word the speaker uttered.

"I didn't know there were any men in Mimi's troupe," Cassie said to Trace as the applause died down.

"There aren't. Don't you know who that is?"

Her hands stopped in midclap, and Cassie stud-

393

ied the man on the stage. "Mimi?" she asked, her voice astounded. "That can't be Mimi!"

Trace nodded his head. "It took me a minute to recognize her, but that's who it is."

When the cheering ceased, the distinguished "man" on the stage proceeded. "—With the title role played by the lovely Jewel Witherspoon." He held out his hand, palm upward, indicating a curtained door to the side of the stage. A pretty girl in a frilly pink and white dress, her hair in gold ringlets, danced up onto the stage, smiling and curtsying to the boisterous applause and whistles.

Again the announcer waited. When some order was restored, he resumed his introductions. "And in the part of Reginald Goodman, our dauntless hero, we have another of your favorites, Miss Pearl Witherspoon—" Again the applause as Mimi held out her hand to introduce a handsome young man in prospector clothing, who swaggered onto the stage and struck a "hero" pose.

Cassie leaned over and whispered to Trace. "Are you sure? That sure looks like a man to me."

"I'm sure," Trace said, his tone serious as an idea began to form in his head.

"Tonight, Treasure Witherspoon will play Esmerelda's sweet grandmother, Mrs. Tinky," Mimi announced as a bent-over old woman hobbled slowly onto the stage. "And last, but, I hope, not least, I, Mrs. Witherspoon—" the applause grew louder than ever—"will portray the part of the eee-vil and siiin-sister—" As she spoke, Mimi's voice became nasal and her facial expression changed into a frightening sneer—"Barnabus Sneed!"

394

The other three actors on the stage grabbed at their chests and shrank back in horror. The cheers and clapping became boos and hisses.

Then, mesmerized by the transformation taking place on the stage, the crowd grew silent.

"The most daaas-tardly . . ." Mimi reached behind a tree flat and snatched up a black cape and hat. "Vile . . ." With theatrical flourish, she wrapped the cape around her shoulders and pulled the wide-brimmed hat low on her face. "Despicable . ." She curled into a furtive crouch. "Villain ever to test a good young woman's virtue!"

Releasing a cruel cackle that made the hair stand up on the back of Cassie's neck, Barnabus Sneed slinked off the stage.

"Sssss," Cassie hissed, her face vibrant with excitement. Bouncing up and down in her seat, she clapped her hands energetically and turned her smile toward Trace. "She really makes you believe she's him," she said, returning her gaze to the curtain Mimi had disappeared behind, as if she half expected the villain to reappear.

"Mmm," he answered, his thoughts elsewhere. "She's quite remarkable." Was that how Murieta had managed to come into the theater without being spotted by Noah? Had Mimi used her talent for creating disguises to change the Mexican's appearance?

Oblivious to the melodrama that was moving into full swing now, Trace turned his head and studied the enraptured faces of the people in the audience. *Murieta could be any one of them,* he thought, *searching for a familiar face. Or he could have al-*

ready been here and gone, he admitted in disgust a
he realized that the only face he recognized was tha
of Horace Gilbert, who stood at the back of th
theater, his arms crossed over his chest.

By the time the play had ended with the dramati
death of Barnabus Sneed, Trace had convinced him
self that Murieta was probably gone and that th
only way he was going to find the bandit now wa
through Mimi Witherspoon. "Why don't we g
backstage and reacquaint ourselves with Mimi?" h
said to Cassie, drawing her to her feet.

Cassie released a deep sigh and smiled up a
Trace. Her eyes, more gold than brown in the artifi
cial light, glistened with tears from the scene where
behind the dead body of Barnabus Sneed, the her
and heroine had proclaimed their love for one ar
other and vowed to never be parted again.

"Do you think we could?" she asked, her voic
rising with anticipation. She was still so caught u
in the play they'd just witnessed, she even forgo
that in Sacramento she had accused Trace of havin
Mimi Witherspoon as his "floozy." "You don
think she'd mind?"

"I'm sure she won't. Actors never mind being ad
mired." He put his hand on the small of he
back and prodded her toward the curtained doo

Before they could go through the curtains, Mim
still in costume, exploded through them, gingerl
pulling her side whiskers off as she came ou
"Trace McAllister! It is you! I thought I saw yo
out here." She directed her smile to Cassie, her ex
pression vague, obviously not recognizing the your
ger girl. "Did you enjoy our play, my dear?"

396

"It was *won*—" She felt Trace's hand tighten on her waist. She clamped her mouth shut on her exuberant praise. "—erful," she went on, forcing herself back into her role as the wife of the rich Easterner. "Truly delightful. You are quite talented, Mrs. Witherspoon."

"Why, thank you!" Mimi patted the back of her white wig in a decidedly feminine action, despite the incongruity of her costume. "I'm so glad you enjoyed it, Miss . . ." She looked at Trace questionly.

Trace wrapped his arm around Cassie's shoulders. "I'm sorry, Mimi. I just assumed you remembered my wife, Cassandra, from the night she met you by the stage door behind the Eagle Theater in Sacramento?"

"Your wife?" Mimi frowned and her gaze tripped over Cassie for some recognizable sign. The only person she ever talked to with Trace McAllister was that little . . . "You?"

Cassie nodded her head and grinned. "When I go out alone at night, I like to disguise myself in men's clothing. It's much safer. Rather like a wolf in sheep's clothing—in reverse," she added with a conspiratorial smile at Mimi. "And I wouldn't dream of traveling in any other garb. But I'm certain you understand how much more practical men's clothing is than all these layers of petticoats and skirts are."

"You didn't mention that you were married," Mimi said to Trace.

"We've only been married a short time, and I guess the subject just never came up," Trace quickly offered. Then, taking Cassie's arm, he tried to guide her toward the front door. They would just have to look around backstage some other time. Right now, it would be too obvious if he suggested they go backstage after Mimi had come out to see them. "Well, thanks for the entertaining evening, Mimi, but we'd better be going. Cassandra has her little heart set on opening her own casino, so we need to wake early in the morning to begin looking for the perfect spot for "The Pot O' Gold" Casino."

"And Theater!" Cassie inserted.

"Theater?" Mimi and Trace said together.

"I've decided — after seeing your lovely play to night, Mrs. Witherspoon — that I want a casino and a theater! You will let me have a theater, too, won' you?" She walked her fingers up Trace's lapel and raised her most beguiling gaze to meet his — which was at once confused and amused by her ad-lib performance for Mimi.

"If that's what you want, sweetheart, of course, you shall have it," he joined in, his eyes sparkling with mischief. He turned to Mimi, whose expression did not bother to hide the fact that the overt display of affection between the McAllisters was making her ill. "It might interest you to know that my wife is quite the little actress, herself," he explained proudly. "In fact, it wouldn't surprise me in the least to see her take to the boards one day."

Wrinkling her nose as if she'd received a whiff of a distasteful odor, Mimi forced a smile. "They do say there is a bit of the ham in everyone."

"I suppose you're right there," Trace agreed, then made their excuses. "Well, we really must be going. It's been good seeing you again, Mimi."

"You too," Mimi said. "I hope you—and your wife, of course—will come see me again." She poke directly to Trace, her voice husky with another unspoken invitation. "We're performing *The Drunkard* tomorrow night. Then next week, we're doing a dramatization of that new novel, *Uncle Tom's Cabin.*"

"*Uncle Tom's Cabin?*" Trace and Cassie asked in unison.

"Surely you've heard of it," Mimi said, her eyes narrowing suspiciously. "It has the South up in arms with indignation."

"Of course, we've heard about Mrs. Stowe's novel," Trace quickly improvised. "It's the talk of the country. I just didn't realize it had been dramatized. But we'll look forward to seeing it. Won't we, darling?"

Cassie looked at him questioningly. "What? Oh, yes, of course. We'll look forward to it." She tightened her grip on Trace's arm and tugged. "I've suddenly developed a bit of a headache. I'd like to go back to the hotel."

His tone doting, Trace said, "Of course," and hurriedly completed his farewells, then hustled Cassie out of the theater. Once outside, he dropped his concerned-husband pose and turned to face her. "What was that all about? Have you really got a headache?"

"Do you remember that clipping about *Uncle Tom's Cabin* we found outside of Drexell?"

Trace nodded, knowing what she was thinking because he was thinking the same thing. "It's probably just a coincidence." He was determined not to let his optimism run away with him this time. This could very well be just another in a long line of wild-goose chases. He began walking again.

"How can you say it's coincidence? Don't you think it's odd that we found a newspaper clipping about a play the Witherspoons are doing at the same place we found the silver concho we think belonged to Murieta?"

"Still, it doesn't mean they're connected. That paper was from Coloma and there were probably hundreds of them printed. Anyone could have dropped it."

Releasing an impatient sigh, Cassie said, "How much do you want to bet that if you checked the rest of that newspaper, you'd find out the Witherspoons were in town the same time that article was printed? *And* that a stage or two got robbed around the same time? I'll bet anything you were right about Murieta being a friend of Mimi's and that he dropped the clipping out of his pocket the same time he lost the concho!" Her face lit with a new idea. *"And!* That'd be why ever since we've been following his trail of robberies, we've kept running into the Witherspoon Acting Troupe. They've always been in a nearby town!"

"It makes sense, but we're still just assuming. We need some proof."

"You mark my words, the proof's in that gaudy wagon of theirs! All we've got to do is get in there when they're gone and find it!"

"That may not be so easy. Noah says a couple of the girls sleep in the wagon at night. It's never without an occupant."

Cassie's expression grew pensive. "Well, occupied or not, I'm getting into that wagon to look around! You just wait and see."

Trace's brow furrowed into a worried frown. "Now, Cassie," he started, his voice rising with warning. "I don't want you to go and do something crazy."

Cassie's eyes widened with pseudo-innocence. "Who me?"

"Yeah, you," he said with a grin. "We can't take a chance of exposing ourselves yet—not until we know Salina and her mother are safe."

"It's not going to expose us. I just want to get in there and look around."

"You won't expose us unless you get caught and hauled into jail. Then all the work we've done setting up Cliff Hopkins would be wasted."

"I'm not going to get caught."

"Are you willing to take that risk with Salina's life?"

"No, of course not." Her words were spoken in a perturbed grumble. "But it's going to kill me knowing my pa's gold might be inside that wagon and I can't go after it!"

"They're not going anywhere. You heard what Mimi said. They'll still be around next week. We should have Cliff Hopkins taken care of in the next few days; and then we'll give our full concentration to Mimi and Murieta."

Cassie screwed her mouth into a lopsided expression of distaste and said, "I guess that's the best thing to do. But it sure galls me thinking about them spending our gold right under our noses, and us not doing anything about it."

"What do you say we do something about something we can do something about right now?" he asked with a mischievous grin.

Her head tilted to the side and she smiled impishly at him. "Whatcha got in mind, McAllister?"

"Your headache. And Dr. McAllister's surefire remedy for headaches," he said, stopping and pulling her into his arms. He dipped his head and kissed the corner of her mouth. "Want to know what it is?" He moved his hips suggestively against hers.

Looking up into Trace's gleaming eyes, Cassie melted against him and answered huskily. "My head's getting better already. But I got another ache I need to talk to you about."

"Married!" Mimi said to the other occupant of her hotel room. "It would serve him right if I went to that simpering little female and told her how her big strong husband has been sniffing around my skirts."

"I told you to stay away from him — and the girl. They're nothing but trouble for us."

"For you, maybe, but not for me. He's got no reason to suspect me of anything." She sat down on the edge of the bed where her lover lay sprawled back against a stack of pillows, his nude body shimmering in the dim lamplight.

"You sound like your interest in McAllister is more than just casual." The man dragged a cheroot from the dresser and jabbed it into his mouth. "I'm warning you, *querida*," he said through his teeth as he struck a match with his thumbnail, "I don't hare what's mine."

Mimi's eyes brightened with passion. She liked it when her lover was angry with her. It gave their ovemaking an added intensity she craved. Her mouth spread in a taunting grin. "Are you jealous, angel?"

"You know what happened to the last bitch who betrayed me, don't you. You wouldn't want that to happen to you, would you?" He grabbed her by the hair and pressed her head down to his lap. "Now swear to me—on your life—that nothing's been going on between you and McAllister!"

Her fear intensifying her lust, Mimi shook her head. "Nothing happened. I swear it! You're the only one I've been with since we met! You're the only one I want."

"Then, show me."

"Are you sure Noah's all right?" Salina asked Sam Seifert when he "checked" on her the following morning.

"To tell the truth, he looks about ready to crack. I'm not sure how much longer he can hold out. I doubt he's had more than a couple hours of sleep since this whole thing began. But Trace and I are keeping a close eye on him. And as long as you're safe here and not working at the Golden Goose, we ought to be able to keep a rein on him." Sam lay the cover back over her freshly bandaged leg and stepped back, his manner suddenly shy. "He's a

403

lucky man, your Noah."

Salina studied the man who was her "doctor" and
smiled gratefully. About thirty, Sam Seifert was tall
though not as tall as Noah, and much more slim.
His hair was a rusty blond color and his face was
covered with freckles. Not really handsome, but still
there was an endearing quality to his features.
"Noah and I are *both* lucky to have found such
dear friends as Trace and Cassie and—you. We
never would have had a chance if you hadn't helped
us. I don't know how we'll ever be able to repay
you."

Sam slapped his hat on his head and reached for
the door. "Thanks aren't necessary, ma'am. Just
knowing you'll be safe and happy is all the thanks I
need. Now, I better get out of here and report your
progress to Hopkins. He's very anxious about you.
He's going to be real disappointed to hear the bad
news that you're not healing well at all!"

They exchanged understanding smiles and Sam
left, leaving Salina to while away the long hours
alone in her room. It was hell now knowing what
was happening, or if anything was even happening.
And she wasn't sure she could take much more of
it. If something didn't happen soon, she thought
she would lose her mind.

One way or another, it will all be over soon, she
tried to console herself, squeezing her eyes shut in
an effort to go back to sleep so the waiting would
be more bearable.

Cassie rolled over on her side and squirmed

404

closer to Trace, molding her own nude length to his. "Are you awake?" she asked, tickling her fingertips over his flat belly.

He clapped his hand over hers, stopping it before she could move it any lower. "No, I'm still asleep."

"I'm hungry." She took a playful nip of the muscle where his chest curved into his arm.

"Ouch!" He released her hand so he could protect his underarm.

Her fingertips immediately went back to work, raking through the dark hair on his chest, following the narrow line of fur that trailed down his body. "Don't you care if I'm hungry?"

"You're always hungry," he said, the sleep still evident in his voice, but he made no attempt to stop her now. His hips lifted upward. "I think those long legs of yours are hollow."

"But I've been hungrier lately. In fact . . ." She riffled her nails through the nest of hair at the root of his strength—which was already making Trace's "hunger" known. She ran a single finger along the column of his swelling passion, circled the throbbing tip, then trailed down the other side. "Right now, I'm so hungry I could . . ." She took a bite of the hard pectoral muscle nearest her mouth.

His body moving of its own accord, he rotated his hips against her hand to encourage her bold caresses. "You better stop that, or you're going to bite off more than you can chew."

"Promises, promises," she crooned, wrapping her fingers around his desire, now stretched tight, and bending her head so she could dip her tongue into his navel.

"I thought you were hungry for breakfast," he warned huskily as her hands moved up and down the length of him.

"Did I say anything about breakfast?" she asked, resting her chin on his middle and looking up at him. She smiled innocently as her hand continued its erotic manipulations and magic on him.

Trace dug his head back into the pillow, tossing it from side to side. "If you did," he panted, his words labored, "you missed your chance."

Without warning, he flipped her over onto her back and rammed into her with desperate force. "Fact is, you'll be lucky if you get lunch."

The thrill that sent her senses soaring every time Trace made love to her filled her with a completeness, as the two halves became one. One passion, one heartbeat, one soul.

Wrapping her arms and legs around his back and hips, she clung to him, determined this time not to let the ecstasy escape. "Yes, yes," she cried. "Don't ever stop!"

Cliff's agitated gaze skimmed over the figures on his ledger for the third time that evening. "There's got to be a mistake," he maintained determinedly. But no matter which direction he checked the figures from, the fact remained that after five days in business, the Golden Goose was losing money.

Oh, there had been customers. But most of them had been small-money gamblers, sometimes eating more of the free buffet than they lost at the tables. And with the high daily cost of operating the ca-

ino, coupled with bribes he had to pay for "protection," coming on top of the initial expenses he had
incurred to open in the first place, his financial
situation was at an all-time low. In fact, if he didn't
do something fast, he was going to lose everything.

"But that's not going to happen," he muttered,
closing the book with force and pitching it into the
safe in the floor of his office. "What I need is a
partner—a partner with lots of money and not a lot
of concern about where he spends it." He clicked
the lock on the safe shut and dropped the carpeted
trapdoor over it. Standing up, he crossed the room
and snatched up his hat and cane.

Fifteen minutes later, Cliff arrived in front of the
plush restaurant where the McAllisters were to meet
him. Taking off his hat, he ran his fingers through
his hair nervously. Just as he started to turn into
the doorway, a furtive movement and flash of color
across the street caught his attention. He paused
and directed a curious gaze toward the place he had
seen a woman he could have sworn was Mrs. McAllister disappear between two buildings.

Laughing at the ridiculous thought, he stepped
inside the restaurant. After all, what would a
woman like Cassandra McAllister be doing in a San
Francisco alley? He glanced around the large dining
room, searching for Trace and Cassie. They weren't
here yet.

Damn them! He had deliberately timed his arrival
so they would be waiting for him when he got
here. He didn't want to look too anxious. And
now they had ruined his entrance.

He bit the inside of his lip with frustrated indecision. What should he do? He supposed he could go on in and sit down at the table. Or . . . He looked over his shoulder at the doorway. Maybe all was not lost after all. If he went back out and found a spot to watch for them unobserved, when they arrived he could still make his planned appearance. Yes, that was what he would do, he decided. He wheeled around and scurried out the door, lest he run into the McAllisters coming in as he was leaving. Then he *would* have some explaining to do, wouldn't he?

Remembering the alley across the street, and thinking it a perfect observation point, he hurried toward it, furtively looking both ways as he did. When he was safely hidden in the shadows of the alley, he pulled a cheroot from his pocket and lit it, then leaned back against the plank building and waited.

The night sounds of the street mingled in a harsh chorus of shouts, clattering wagon wheels, squealing animals, and music. Somewhere at the other end of the alley, he heard a tomcat yowl and a dog bark. Growing more irritated by the instant, he shifted his weight and drew on the thin cigar.

At first he paid no attention to the hum of conversation inside the building he was leaning on. But when he heard the woman's voice rise with anger, his attention was drawn helplessly to the interchange. Though he couldn't quite make out what she was saying, something about the voice was familiar. He took off his hat and rolled his head to the side, pressing his ear against the wood.

"Can't you make that thing work any faster?" she asked, her voice rife with impatience. "We're already late for dinner!"

"I'm doing the best I can!" a man answered. A man whose voice was definitely familiar to Cliff!

Tossing his smoke to the ground, he turned to face the wall and pushed his ear harder against the plank. What were the McAllisters doing in there?

"Well, what's the problem? It usually isn't so slow!"

"I had to go out and get more . . ."

Cliff didn't get that word. Evidently McAllister had turned away or covered his mouth. "That's when I sent the message for you to meet me here. There! Almost done!"

What's almost done? Cliff asked, taking a step back to look for a way to see in. Spotting a small window above his head, he raised up on his toes. But it was no good. He couldn't quite stretch his squat body far enough to see in.

"Ahh," Cassie exclaimed, as a clacking and rumbling started up. "Here it comes. You know, after all this time, I still never quite get used to what a wonderful miracle this machine is!"

What machine? What kind of miracle? Frantic to know what was going on, Cliff dragged a small packing crate under the window. Checking its strength cautiously, and deciding it would hold his weight, he gripped the windowsill and eased one foot, then the other, onto the box. Gingerly, he moved his head so that he could peek in the dirty window with one eye.

There, just as he'd expected, were Cassandra and Trace McAllister. Trace was facing the window and his wife had her back to it, but Cliff was in no danger of being seen. They were both too engrossed with the noisy metal contraption between them.

The machine had a large funnel-shaped top to it that fed into what looked like a short water chute. The chute in turn disappeared into the upper side of a large metal box with a wheel on it.

As Cassie turned the wheel, Trace poured what looked like ordinary river pebbles into the funnel. Then, leaning behind him, he picked up an unmarked brown bottle and poured its contents into the funnel. Tossing the bottle aside, he moved to the other end of the machine and opened a hatch on top of the metal box, where he proceeded to pour in the white powdered contents of a cloth sack. "Do you want me to turn the wheel?" he asked.

"No, I like to do it," she answered, her head bent so she could watch the floor at the end of the machine. "Here they come!" she announced. "Oh, Trace, look how shiny. I think this is the best batch yet!"

I can't see, dammit! Cliff raged from his secret perch, moving to the end of the box and leaning to the side in an attempt to gain a better view. *What's so shiny? Batch of what?*

Trace stooped so that he was pretty much hidden behind Cassie's skirt. "I think you're right, sweetheart! I think this is going to be the best yet." He was obviously examining whatever it was that was coming out of the machine. "Yes," he said, standing up and patting the metal box affectionately. "This little wonder sure beats the hell out of clawing the ground for it, doesn't it?" He held up a

410

iny pebble to the light.

My God! They've got a machine that makes old! With that realization, Cliff lost his balance nd tumbled off the box to land in a stunned heap n the ground.

"Somebody's out there!" Trace exclaimed. Quick! Dismantle the machine while I check it ut!"

Chapter Twenty-four

Trace formed his thumb and forefinger into an ⊙ denoting success. With a quick wink at Cassie, h wrenched open the door and bolted outside, closin it securely behind him. "Hopkins!" he blurted ou as he practically tripped over the man who wa clumsily dragging himself to his feet. His expressio alarmed, Trace glanced uneasily over his shoulder a the door. "What're you doing here?"

"I might ask you the same question, McAllister, Cliff said, struggling to his feet, his smile that c the proverbial cat with a canary. He flicked th backs of this fingers down his trouser legs to re move the dirt, then brushed his coat front an sleeves as he waited for Trace's answer. "We wer supposed to meet at the restaurant forty-five mir utes ago."

Trace cleared his throat and wiped the back of h wrist across his upper lip. "Oh, yes . . . uh . . ." H tole another glance at the door he'd just exited. Well, you see it's this way. My wife had to come by ere to . . . uh . . . deliver some food to a sick riend. I'm sorry we kept you waiting."

"Sick friend, huh?"

Trace nodded profusely. "A woman we befriended n the ship when we came out from New York. She as very kind when Cassandra experienced seasick- ess."

"You can cut the act, McAllister. I'm on to you!" liff's round cheeks puffed into a sadistic sneer.

"What are you talking about?" Trace's innocent eatures didn't quite disguise his tenseness from liff. "What act?"

"I know you and your wife aren't what you ap- ear to be."

"Oh?"

"And just what are we, Mr. Hopkins?" a hard emale voice asked from the doorway as Cassie oined the conversation.

"You're gold counterfeiters! You've been flooding an Francisco with bogus gold."

"Bogus gold? Whatever gave you such a ridicu- ous idea?" Trace asked, his manner suddenly less ense.

"It's no good, McAllister. I saw the whole thing." lopkins's blue eyes sliced up toward the window, hen came back to the McAllisters. "Now, suppose ou give me a good reason not to expose your little peration."

"Because no one likes to be made a fool of, lopkins," Trace said, his smile slow and secretive. Which is exactly what will happen to you if you

413

try to tell the authorities such a preposterous story
Everyone knows you can't make counterfeit gold.

A shadow of uncertainty flashed across Cliff
face. He glimpsed up at the window again, the
back to Trace. "I saw you do it. I saw you tur
those river rocks into bogus gold."

"Do these look bogus to you?" Cassie aske
holding out a handful of nuggets. She popped on
between her teeth and bit down on it, then held th
misshapen metal out to Cliff. It had flatted out b
had not been bitten in half. "Fools gold would hav
broken my teeth because it's harder."

"Let me see that!" Cliff snarled, grabbing th
nugget out of her hand. He squatted down an
placed the nugget on the box he'd been standing o
Picking up a large stone from nearby, he slamme
it down on the nugget. He broke the box, but th
gold just contorted into a different shape. He sh
a questioning gaze at the smug couple watchin
him. Rising, he handed the nugget back to Cassi

"Keep it," she said generously. "We've got plenty.

Cliff closed his fingers around the bit of gol
"Where'd you get a machine that will make phon
gold that can pass a test for real gold?"

"Haven't you heard what we've said, M
Hopkins?" Cassie asked with an indignant huf
"We haven't made phony gold. The gold we ma—

"What my wife means to say," Trace interrupte
loudly, literally closing Cassie's mouth on the la
word with his stern glare, "is that the gold we *spen*
is perfectly genuine."

"Why'd you cut her off, McAllister? She wa
about to say the gold you *make* is genuine, wasn

414

e?"

"What if she was?"

"Then I want to know how you do it — *if* you do
"

Cassie and Trace exchanged desperate glances.
All right, Hopkins," Trace said finally. "I guess
is was too good to last. But I hope you'll keep it
 yourself, because once the word's out about what
 have, the bottom will drop out of the value of
ld. And if that happens, we'll all pay!"

Cliff's eyes were bright with eagerness. He licked
s lips hungrily "I won't say a word. I swear it on
y dear mother's grave. Just tell me. Have you
und a way to make real gold?"

Trace glimpsed from left to right, then took a
ep closer to Cliff. "Shh," he said, nodding his
ad affirmatively. He lowered his voice to a surrep-
ious whisper. "What would you say if I told you
 have a machine that, with only a few special
emicals, can separate the gold particles — which
e often too tiny to see with the naked eye — from
dinary river rocks and compress those same parti-
es into gold nuggets that can pass any test for real
ld? Because they *are* real gold."

"Do you expect me to believe you can turn ordi-
ry river rocks into genuine gold?" Cliff asked
eptically, doing his best to disguise an increasing
citement.

"Not just *any* river rocks," Cassie said with a roll
f her eyes. "Of course, some rocks are richer in
ld particles than others, and some don't contain
y. We've found that the best rocks come from
ver and creek bottoms where gold has already

415

been discovered."

"Usually from a dig that's *supposedly* alread[y] been panned out," Trace added with a cocky smir[k.]

"Just out of curiosity, how much would you say [a] machine like that would cost a man if he wante[d] one?" Cliff asked conversationally. "I mean, if [I] believed this whole preposterous story, that is?"

"Believe me, you couldn't afford it," Trace sai[d,] lounging back against the wall and crossing h[is] arms over his chest.

"Try me," Cliff insisted.

"Well, I never thought much about it — since [I] don't intend to sell it," Trace said, turning h[is] mouth down thoughtfully and looking up to th[e] sky. "I don't know. I guess we'd consider an offer o[f] a couple a million."

"A couple a million? For one machine? You'[re] crazy!"

Trace shrugged. "I told you you didn't want t[o] know."

"What's to stop me from buying one from som[e] one else?"

"Nothing. Except maybe the fact that we've g[ot] the only one in existence — and because there won['t] be another one any time soon. The inventor di[ed] right after he made this one."

"But you could build a duplicate, couldn't you? [I] heard you tell your wife to dismantle it, so you mu[st] know how to put it together!"

"Well, *maybe* I could build a duplicate, but [I] don't want to. With two or three of these litt[le] wonders in California, you could turn out so mu[ch] gold in a week that the value of gold would [be]

416

destroyed in a month."

"Just for a point of reference, how much gold do you suppose it can produce in a week?" Cliff's voice no longer harbored any disbelief. Now it fairly trembled with pure greed.

Trace waggled his head from side to side as he made a show of figuring out the answer. "Of course there are no guarantees when you're dealing with nature," he said slowly. "But . . . depending on the quality of the stones you use . . . and on how many hours you run it . . . I'd say you might be able to squeeze out a hundred thousand a day."

"A hundred thousand a day!" Cliff's eyes rounded and bulged.

Trace nodded.

"A day?" Cliff repeated.

"That's probably minimum if you ran it twenty-four hours. If you've got real quality stones—like we had tonight—you might be able to double that output."

"If you won't sell it and won't build another one, what would you say to renting it to me for a couple of days?"

"Rent it to you? For two days?"

"Two days," Cliff confirmed. "How much to use your gold machine for two days?"

"A hundred fifty thousand in gold—in advance," Trace said with a chuckle.

"A hundred fifty thousand?

"That doesn't seem too high a price for a machine that has the potential of producing twice that much in a couple of days, does it?"

"Not to me," Cassie said. "Not when you consider you could earn back the investment the first day and make pure profit the second day."

"I don't have a hundred fifty thousand dollars!" Cliff protested. "My cash is all tied up in the Golden Goose!"

"Then, what are we talking about?" Trace asked, shoving away from the wall. "I don't really want to rent it out anyway." He wrapped his arm around Cassie's shoulders and started toward the street. "Everything all locked up, sweetheart? I'm starved."

"Wait a minute!" Cliff called, running after them. "Aren't you going to leave a guard on—uh—it?"

"That's not necessary. No one but you knows what it is, and you wouldn't try to steal it from us, would you?" His pointed question was asked with a suspicious narrowing of his eyes. "Besides, it's in pieces and the special chemicals it needs are somewhere else. So you can see we've got nothing to worry about. You coming, Hopkins? I'm still buying dinner."

"What about my paying you at the end of the two days instead of in advance?" Cliff suggested eagerly.

"What guarantee would I have you wouldn't use it and just forget to pay us? No, I think we'd better drop the subject."

Directing a last baleful glance at the door to the room where the gold machine was now a useless pile of metal, Cliff followed Trace and Cassie out of the alley.

Once the threesome settled into their seats in the restaurant, and their orders had been given to the maître d', Trace introduced a new subject. "So,

418

Hopkins, how do you feel about the casino business, now that the Golden Goose has been open for nearly a week?"

Cliff made a face of disapproval and started to shake his head, then suddenly changed his action to a nod. His smile and enthusiasm obviously false, he said, "Couldn't be better. Tell me, are you still thinking of opening your own casino?"

Trace directed the question to Cassie. "You tell him, sweetheart. Since it's your idea."

Her eyes bright with excitement, Cassie scooted to the edge of her chair and leaned toward Cliff. "Most definitely. In fact, we found the perfect spot for it today. We just have to finalize the pap—"

"You know, hearing you talk of opening another casino has given me an idea," Cliff interrupted.

Cassie straightened indignantly at the interruption. "Oh?"

"What if I sold you the Golden Goose for the hundred fifty thousand, and you let me use your machine for the two days. Then at the end of the two days, you will sell me back the casino, at a profit, of course, and you will have your machine back as well."

"Why would we want to do that?" Cassie asked, her tone making no secret of the fact that she didn't appreciate having Cliff revert the conversation back to the gold machine.

"For one thing, you could keep the profits the casino brings in during your 'ownership.' And for another, it will give you a chance to see if you really like the business or not." Cliff's voice was silky.

"What kind of profit are we talking about here?"

Trace asked, a flicker of interest for Cliff's scheme skittering across his face.

"Well, let's see," Cliff mused. "You ought to make ten thousand a day at the casino. That'd be twenty thousand for the two days. Shall we say that twenty thousand and an additional twenty thousand in gold—for your troubles?"

"In advance," Trace said, his voice hard.

"In advance?" Cliff gulped.

"In advance?" Cassie said at the same time. "You're not thinking of going along with him, are you?" She threw herself back into her chair in a sulking snit.

Ignoring his pouting wife, Trace addressed Cliff. "Are you prepared to give me the twenty thousand dollars in advance, Hopkins?"

"Well, uh, I had really planned to—"

"That's what I thought. Either show me your good faith by putting your money where your mouth is, or let's drop the subject once and for all. On second thought, let's just drop it."

"Now, don't be that way," Cliff whined. "I didn' say I *wouldn't* give you the twenty thousand in advance. That'll be fine. But I'll need a day to work it out."

"Then, it's agreed. I'll have my lawyer draw up the papers first thing in the morning," Trace said with finality. "We'll bring them to you at the Golden Goose tomorrow afternoon at three. You have the deed and the twenty thousand dollars waiting for me, and you can use the machine for two days. Now, if you don't mind, I'd like to discuss something else. This subject seems to have

420

ired my beautiful wife!"

He turned to Cassie, apologizing for spending time on business and begging her to forgive him. Finally, Cassie relented and blessed him with a trembling half smile. "I suppose it might be fun to have a small taste of what it'll be like when I *really* own my own casino," she admitted.

"Of course it will," Trace promised, shooting Cliff Hopkins a glance that asked for understanding. "Now, no more business. We'll just relax and have a nice dinner. All right?"

"Actually, I have an engagement that I'll be late for if I stay any longer," Cliff said. "So, if you will excuse me . . ." His chair scraped back on the wooden floor.

"Of course," Trace said, smiling his gratitude. "I think we might make it an early evening ourselves. My wife hasn't been feeling her best lately. Headaches, you know."

"I'm sorry to hear that," Cliff said. "Well, I do hope you're feeling better, Mrs. McAllister." He picked up her hand and kissed it, not seeing the silly face Cassie made at Trace as Hopkins bent over her hand.

"You're too kind," she said, doing her best not to release the laugh building in her throat.

"Until tomorrow, McAllister," Cliff said, offering a limp-wristed handshake to Trace.

"Tomorrow at three," Trace reconfirmed, shaking Cliff's hand and dropping it as quickly as possible.

The minute Cliff disappeared through the door, Cassie released a very unladylike snort of laughter. "You would have to mention headaches!" she giggled. "You're shameless! I thought I was going to ruin the whole thing right then and there!"

"I couldn't help myself. I just couldn't stomach spending any more time with Cliff Hopkins. Besides I thought you might be feeling a 'headache coming on."

"Why would you think that?"

He licked his lips and skated his gaze over her to linger on the swell of her breasts exposed by her low neckline. "I know I feel a 'cure' coming on." He leaned toward her to trail his lips and tongue up the slender column of her neck to nuzzle her ear lobe.

"Then, let's get out of here, McAllister. I'd hate to let a perfectly good cure go to waste!"

Salina stood at the top of the stairs and peeked over the rail. Everything below was very quiet. It was only nine o'clock in the evening, but the servants had all evidently retired for the night. And Cliff would be gone for at least another four hours, so it should be safe for her to go downstairs for a few minutes. She just had to get out of her room for a while or she was going to go crazy.

Tiptoeing, though she was alone in the big house, Salina hurried down to the first floor and into the kitchen. Pausing at the pantry door, she listened for a sign she'd been detected. Not certain what to do now that she was out of her room, she looked around the kitchen, thinking it seemed as though she hadn't been in it in weeks, rather than days.

"Maybe a snack," she said to herself, lifting the lid on the pie safe and taking out an apple pie

Snatching up a saucer, she quickly slid a piece of the pie made from dried fruit on it and turned to leave the kitchen. She started to dash back upstairs, when she passed the library. *A glass of sherry might help me go to sleep,* she decided. "Though heaven knows I don't need any more sleep!" she reminded herself aloud, moving on silent feet to Cliff's bar. *I've slept enough this past few days to last a lifetime!*

Balancing her pie in one hand, she picked up a clean glass and hurriedly splashed a generous serving of the amber wine into it, then ran toward the stairs. She was suddenly very anxious to get back to the safety of her room.

"'Well, well, well," a man's voice sang out just as she reached the bottom step.

Cliff! Salina stopped short, the breath whooshing out of her as if she'd been kicked in the back by a horse. Desperation and panic deadened her every muscle so that she couldn't even turn around to see her adversary.

"I'm glad to see that you have made such a speedy recovery, after all, my dear," Cliff crooned unctuously.

She could tell by his voice that he must be sitting in the huge stuffed chair in the corner of the library by the fireplace. He must have been there the whole time, sitting there in the dimly lit room, waiting like a deadly spider for his victim to step into his web. How could she have missed him?

"Cliff," she finally managed to say, forcing herself to turn around. "I thought you were still at the casino." She took a limping step toward him.

423

Hopkins threw back his head and laughed "Spare me the theatrics, Salina! I know you're faking. In fact, it wouldn't surprise me if you'd been faking all along."

"I'm really injured," she insisted, stopping where she stood in the entry.

"Never mind. It doesn't matter now. It's probably worked out for the best this way. By saving you I've been able to build up the interest. When auction you off tomorrow evening, you ought to bring top dollar."

"Auction me off?" Salina gasped, memories of friends and family who'd been put on the auction block colliding grotesquely in her thoughts. "You can't do that. It's against the law in California. I'm free here. One person can't sell another one here!"

Cliff's mouth curved in a sly grin. "The auction I'm talking about is legal. The bidders will be vying for the honor of spending a night of reckless passion with you. I'm not selling *you* to the highest bidder, just your services. And this comes at a most opportune time, since I need to put all my other ready cash into a little business venture for a few days. Yes, your bruises have healed nicely and you ought to bring me a pretty penny."

"You can't mean it! For God's sake, Cliff! I'm your sister. What would our father say?"

"Making me angry won't work this time, Salina. I'm in too good a mood to let your little insults and jibes bother me. Now go on up to bed so you will look fresh and lovely tomorrow for your 'debut.'"

"I won't do it. I'll leave this house tonight."

Cliff shrugged his shoulders and rose from the

chair to fix himself another drink. "Have it your way. I never cared much for your mother anyway. It will give me great pleasure to think of her black hide being peeled from her, inch by torturous inch."

"You wouldn't."

He spun around and leaned back, resting his elbows on the bar behind him and holding his glass in both hands. "But of course I would. And you know that, don't you, Salina?"

Salina visibly shrank to a smaller height. "Yes, I know that," she answered, her head bent. "Good night, Cliff."

"Good night, Salina. See you in the morning. I'll tell the doctor about your miraculous recovery when he arrives. I'm sure he'll be glad to hear it."

By the time Salina got back to her room, she was shaking violently. She had managed delay after delay, but now the game was at an end and she had lost. It was all over, and there was nothing else she could do. Nowhere she could go. Cliff had beaten her totally this time.

"Oh, Noah!" she sobbed, gazing out the small window of her room. "We were so close." She bent her head and buried her face in her hands. "I was so sure we would make it this time," she wept hopelessly.

If only she could go to him, be with him one last time before . . .

Oh, God, how can this be happening? How can You have turned your back on us this way? How?

An idea suddenly occurred to her that might at least make what she had to do easier. If she could get a message to Noah to tell him good-bye, it might alleviate some of his pain.

But Salina shook her head the instant the thought occurred to her. Noah wouldn't be cast off that easily. He would know what was happening and would come crashing over here to take her away from Cliff—maybe even kill Cliff! And Noah would no doubt die for it.

No, she had already caused Noah enough hardship. She wouldn't be the cause of his death too. Either way, she was going to lose him. But the thought of him lost to her and *alive* was the only possibility she could bear to think of. And to ensure that happening, Noah couldn't know what she was going to do—until after the fact. The woman he had known and loved would simply have to disappear from his life. Forever.

By three o'clock the following afternoon, Cliff was sweating profusely, though the day was pleasantly cool; and he paced nervously back and forth inside the front door to his casino. Each time he made a sweep past the door, he peeked outside. Then, seeing no sign of the McAllisters, he would resume his agitated patrol.

When four o'clock rolled around, his face was a brilliant shade of red, and the veins in his temples were pounding visibly. Where were they? Had something gone wrong? Then, on perhaps his two hundredth turn past the door, he spotted them coming toward the Golden Goose.

Arm-in-arm, the laughing couple strolled leisurely across the street, as though they were on a Sunday outing rather than on their way to a business meeting. And Cliff fumed. Well, he wasn't going to let them see what a state he'd worked himself into.

"I'm expecting the McAllisters," he said to the burly bouncer who stood beside the door. "When they come in, tell them I'll be with them shortly!" He stomped into his office and closed the door behind him. *Let them see how it feels to wait on me for a change,* he raged, dropping into his desk chair and picking up a fan.

There was an immediate knock at the door. "Who is it?" he asked with feigned disinterest.

"It's Rogers, Mr. Hopkins," the bouncer answered.

"What is it, Rogers?" Cliff asked irritably, rising and walking to the door and flinging it open. "I told you I didn't want to be disturb— Oh! Mr. and Mrs. McAllister!" he exclaimed with forced friendliness. "Is it three o'clock already?"

"They said they had an appoi—"

"That'll be all, Rogers," he said with a dismissing wave. "Come in." He held out his hand in a welcoming gesture.

"Sorry we're late," Trace apologized.

"Late?" Cliff asked, pulling his watch out of his pocket and flipping it open. "You're not la— My goodness! So you are. I've been so busy I hadn't even noticed! But you're here now!" He shoved the watch back into his pocket and smiled. "So I suppose we might as well get down to business."

Trace gave Cassie an uncertain glance, then turned back to Cliff, his expression embarrassed. "Look, Hopkins, are you sure you want to do this?

427

If you want to back out, there will be no hard feelings."

"Back out! Why would I want to back out?"

"You know there are no guarantees that every river rock in California contains the gold particles. You could lose your casino if you don't get the right rocks. Do you really want to take that risk?"

"What are you trying to pull here, McAllister? Have you had a better offer? I'll match it! You've got to lend me that machine!"

"It's nothing like that!" Cassie protested. "It's just that my husband and I like you and would feel terrible if the machine didn't live up to your expectations and you were disappointed." Her face was genuinely concerned.

"You just let me worry about that," Cliff said. "Where are the papers?"

Trace inserted his hand in his breast pocket, but did not immediately withdraw it. "You're sure?"

"I'm sure." Cliff shoved his cash box toward Trace. "Here's my banknote for twenty thousand dollars and the deed to the Golden Goose, all signed and legal. Now let's see the contract."

Trace glanced at Cassie and shrugged his shoulders, then whipped out the neat papers he'd had drawn up that morning, the papers that would make the Golden Goose his.

He slapped the contract down on the desk for Cliff's perusal and shoved the cash box toward Cassie, who immediately checked its contents. She gave him a silent nod when she was through.

They waited silently for several minutes while Cliff glanced over the papers. "Looks good to me," he finally said, picking up the pen and scratching his signature hurriedly across the bottom of both copies. "When do I get the machine?"

"I'll have it delivered to you within the hour," Trace promised, snatching up the contract. He quickly scribbled his signature on both copies and handed one to Cliff, then folded one and returned it to his breast pocket. "Cassandra?" he said, with a nod of his head. "We'll see you in an hour, then. By the way, you'll need to have five thousand dollars to reimburse us for the necessary chemicals to operate the machine."

Cliff's face, already pale, drained of all color. "Five thousand for chemicals. You didn't tell me that! I thought—"

"Surely, you didn't expect *us* to provide your working materials, did you?" Cassie asked, her expression incredulous. "I suppose you expected us to find your river rocks for you too!"

When Cliff didn't answer, Trace and Cassie exchanged knowing expressions. "You *have* made arrangements for the rocks, haven't you?" Cassie asked skeptically.

Cliff shook his head.

"Look," Trace said with a friendly laugh. He stuck his hand in the pocket holding the contract. "Why don't we forget this whole thing?"

"No!" Cliff exploded. "We signed the papers and you promised to let me use your machine for forty-eight hours. You can't back out now."

"You don't have the chemicals or rocks," Cassie protested.

"I'll get them!"

"But you might waste half of your two days doing it!" she pointed out.

Trace flattened his hands together and tapped the tips of his fingers on his mouth thoughtfully. After thinking a few moments, he dropped his hands and slapped Cliff on the back. "What the hell!" he said. "What're a few hours between friends. Tell you what, Hopkins. We'll start your forty-eight hours this time tomorrow, instead of today. How's that sound to you?"

"That's a wonderful idea!" Cassie squealed. "That'll give you time to get your first load of stones *and* the money for the chemicals."

"I do appreciate this," Cliff said, his expression a mingle of relief and disappointment as he extended his hand to shake Trace's.

Trace took it and smiled. "Then, we'll see you tomorrow — with the machine and the chemicals."

"And I'll be here with the five thousand and the rocks."

Cassie tightened her grip on the cash box and turned to leave. "I wish you every success, Mr. Hopkins. I hope the machine lives up to its full potential for you. And you can be certain we will take good care of your establishment during your absence."

Chapter Twenty-five

"All right, Noah, you're on!" Trace bellowed as he and Cassie burst into Noah's room in back of the Chinese fan-tan parlor after converting Cliff's bank note into gold.

"Oh, Noah, I'd give anything if you coulda seen that scallywag beggin' us to take his money *and* the deed to his casino! I thought he was gonna bust out cryin' when he thought Trace was tryin' to back out o' the deal!" No one cared that in her excitement Cassie had slipped into her old speaking habits, least of all Cassie.

His expression tense, Noah reached for the suit coat they'd had specially made to accommodate his muscular proportions. "I sure do hope this works," he said, his tone not at all convinced. He shrugged into the jacket and adjusted his tie.

"It will!" Trace assured, reaching for Noah's lapels and adjusting the front of the coat the way a loving parent who was preparing his son for a special occasion would. "All you've got to do is go in there and flash that gold at him and he'll grab it. Every cent he's got is tied up in the Golden Goose."

"And our gold-making machine," Cassie added with a devilish grin.

A bitter smile on her lovely face, Salina stared with unseeing eyes at the closed door before her. Totally resigned to her fate now, she was numb to the lavish red velvet and gilt room on the second floor of the Golden Goose. Always overly modest, she didn't even seem aware of her nude body, which shimmered with a golden brown glow beneath the translucent red and black robe she'd been given to wear when her other clothing had been taken from her.

Her gaze swept the room with idle interest, staying for a moment on the large bed that dominated the room with its gold manacles and chains at each of the four posters. But she wasn't frightened. In fact, she had managed to detach herself from what was happening so completely that the bed and its chains made almost no impression on her at all — other than the fact that it was red and gold like the rest of the room.

She glanced down at the gold ropes that wrapped around her wrists, securing them to the carved arms of the wooden chair where she sat. A smile curved upward at the sight.

Wasn't that just like Cliff? He knew the ropes weren't necessary. Tied or not, she wasn't going anywhere. But he'd used them anyway, telling her the selling price would go higher if the bidders knew she was there against her will and had to be controlled.

Well, she would still have a victory over her half brother, small though it may be. For she would not fight. And she would not beg. So in the end, what Cliff wanted most—to destroy her spirit—would be denied him.

Noah stood outside the Golden Goose, took a deep breath, and stepped up on the boardwalk that ran across the front of the casino. He glanced from left to right to be certain Cassie and Trace, disguised in their sailors' garb, were in their strategic positions on the opposite side of the street. Assured that they were, he adjusted his vest over the derringer hidden there, then checked the guns in his holster.

Noah then nodded his readiness to "Doc" Seifert, who approached from the opposite direction. Sam returned the nod with a reassuring wink and hit the swinging doors to the casino with both hands.

Giving Sam a moment to get into the faro game closest to Cliff's office, Noah followed.

"Hold on there, boy!" a male voice chuckled as Noah stepped inside. "Where you think you're goin'? Mr. Hopkins don't 'low none o' your kind in here."

Noah drew himself up to his full height and narrowed his dark eyes at the speaker. The bouncer stood at least six inches shorter than Noah, though he did have the broad, rock-hard type of build that would force Noah to work for his victory should this confrontation come to blows. But hopefully, it wouldn't come to that.

"Get Hopkins. We have an appointment." Noah's tone was confident, authoritative. "Tell him it's Noah Simmons."

The bouncer squinted his eyes and angled his head to the side. Then he looked over his shoulder at the door to Cliff's office, his expression not so sure now. "You say he's expectin' you?"

Noah brushed past the hesitant hireling. "Never mind, I'll just go in," he said, striding with purpose toward the door he was now certain must be to Cliff's office.

"Wait a minute," the man yelled, running after Noah and catching his arm. "You can't go in there without me tellin' him you're here."

Noah glared down at the hand on his arm, obviously daring the man to leave it there. Under the heat of Noah's stare, the man's forehead broke out in a heavy sweat, and he shrank back a step—his hand falling away from Noah's arm as he did. "At least let me tell him you're . . ."

Noah showed his white teeth in a grin that said, *You're pushing your luck, mister.*

What the hell? He wasn't getting paid enough to take on a mountain that looked about as ready to explode as a stick of dynamite with the fuse burned down to half an inch. He took another step away from the black man. "On the other hand, you did say he was expectin' you, didn't you?"

Without knocking, Noah crashed through the

door to Cliff's private sanctuary, kicking it shut behind him.

Cliff, who'd had his back to the door, wheeled around to confront his intruder. "What do you mean coming in here unannounced?" As recognition dawned in his pale blue eyes, his expression changed from arrogance to fear. "What're you doing here?" he asked in a choking whisper. "I thought—"

"You thought you were rid of me, didn't you?" Noah asked, his smile cold and calculating as he sauntered across the office and sat down, unbuttoning his coat and opening it so the big revolvers he wore were in evidence.

"They told me you were on a ship bound for the East."

"Looks like they were wrong," Noah laughed, extending his hand, palm up, indicating the desk chair to the man who continued to stand there gawking at him. "Relax, Hopkins. I didn't come here to kill you. I wouldn't want to waste the bullets on the likes of you. I've just come to take care of our unfinished business."

Taking his seat, Cliff tried to affect a facade of confidence. However, this new Noah Simmons had thrown him for a loop. "By unfinished business, I assume you mean Salina."

"And her mother. We had a deal." He pitched a gold pouch onto the desk. "Here's one thousand dollars. You'll get the rest when you sign their emancipation papers."

"You have the whole ten thousand?" Cliff asked, his eyes on the heavy bag. "How soon could I get the rest?"

"How soon can you get the papers signed? I have friends outside just waiting for my signal to bring it in."

Cliff's gaze dropped to the floor where his safe was hidden beneath the carpet—and where all his important papers were stored. He could really use that money. He glanced up at the ceiling toward the room where Salina was waiting for her final degradation. But no matter how tempting Noah's gold was, he wouldn't cheat himself out of seeing her fall. Besides, the bidding could easily reach ten thousand dollars.

Cliff shook his head. "I don't think I want to . . ." On the other hand, why shouldn't he have the high bidder's gold *and* Noah's gold? It would serve the stupid buck right if he ended up paying for soiled goods—which was what Salina would be before this evening was over.

"Tell you what, boy. Since you and Salina are so determined to have each other, I'll sell the papers to you at our agreed-on price: ten thousand in gold. But it'll be a couple of hours before I can make the exchange."

He pulled out his watch and clicked it open. Six-thirty. Thirty minutes until the auction was to begin. Forty-five minutes for the auction, thirty more minutes for the winner to claim his prize and complete the fall of the saintly Salina.

"Meet me at my house at eight-thirty. I'll have the papers then—assuming of course, that you'll have the ten thousand in gold." Cliff stood up, his expression dismissing.

"I'll be there," Noah said, rising from the chair.

He leaned over the desk, bringing his face close to Cliff's, his lips stretched tight, baring gleaming teeth in a deadly snarl. "You just be sure you are. Because if you try to double-cross me, Hopkins, there won't be enough of you left after I get through for anyone to identify the remains."

The knowledge that Noah would do exactly as he promised ripped up Cliff's spine, and he was almost unable to hide the shudder that shook his shoulders. "I'll be there."

Noah straightened, keeping his threatening glare leveled on Cliff as he backed toward the door. "I'll see you at eight-thirty." He reached behind him and cracked the door. "By the way, my friends will be watching you until then. So don't think about having me jumped on my way to your place—unless you want to end up signing those papers using your own blood for ink!"

The coppery taste of blood filled Cliff's dry mouth as he realized he had bitten through the inside of his own cheek. "Just be there with the gold if you want Salina," he rasped, his voice shaking.

"Eight-thirty," Noah confirmed, his expression saying that he almost hoped Cliff did something to give him a reason to kill him. Noah pointed a finger at Cliff and ducked through the doorway. He was out of the casino before Cliff regained the courage to breathe.

"You'll never guess who's back in town," Cliff said to Salina twenty minutes later, when he had regathered his composure and was certain his plan could work. "Your old lover, Noah, is back in San Francisco."

Salina continued to stare straight ahead as Cliff draped a long black cape around her shoulders. Though her heart skipped frantically, she managed to keep her facial muscles and eyes from betraying her.

"He has the ten thousand dollars to pay me for your emancipation papers," he said in a singsong voice meant to dangle and taunt her freedom in front of her.

Why now, Noah?

"And I told him I'd meet him at eight-thirty to make the exchange."

Her eyes shifted in his direction, but she said nothing.

"There," he said with a sadistic smile, "I thought that might get your attention. Yes, I've decided that after tonight I'll have no more use for you. If a venture I'm working on proves to be as profitable as I think it will be, I'm seriously considering getting out of the casino business altogether. So, you can see you will be a liability to me—after tonight, of course."

He looped a gold cord in the rope that bound her wrists together and tugged on it. "Yes, after tonight, Noah Simmons is welcome to you. Unless you displease me," he taunted into her ear, reminding her that as close as freedom was, it still was not hers to have. "Then I will dispose of both of you *and* your mother."

He pressed a button and slid the wardrobe aside,

evealing another room, its far wall a ceiling-to-
loor curtain. He led her up onto a pedestal and
urned her so she was facing the curtain. "Now," he
aid softly, as he closed the wall behind them,
"knowing how close your freedom is, are you going
o behave yourself when I open the curtains? Or are
you going to let your mother die?"

Salina knew that once that curtain opened she
would never be able to go to Noah, but she still
nodded her agreement. She would do whatever it
ook to free her mother. And once her mother was
free, it wouldn't matter what happened to herself.

"I knew I could depend on you to make the wise
decision." Cliff clapped his hands and two scantily
clad women came forward, each carrying a golden
rod that they inserted into opposite sides of the
round pedestal where Salina stood. "Now turn
slowly," Cliff instructed. "We want to show her off
to her full advantage," he explained as the two
began to walk in the same direction around the
pedestal, pushing the sticks protruding from the
stand.

Unable to hold out her hands separately to steady
herself, Salina staggered slightly as the floor beneath her bare feet began to revolve.

Smiling his satisfaction, Cliff stood back and
watched his live statue. "Remember the consequences if you fail me, Salina," he hissed and disappeared through the slit in the curtains.

"Good evening, gentlemen," he said over the
sound of polite applause. "Tonight we have a treat
so rare for your pleasure that you will scarcely
believe your good fortune at having been invited to

439

simply view her. But the lucky one of you who will spend the night with this treasure is about to live out his most erotic fantasies. Gentlemen, I give you the African princess: Salina!" The curtain began to open, as two more girls, dressed as Roman slave girls pulled it apart.

There was a united intake of breath as the audience first saw the regal brown-skinned goddess revolving slowly on the stage.

Cliff stood to the side of the stage watching his audience's reaction to Salina, and he smiled. Every one of the fourteen men were enraptured by her loveliness—and they had only seen her face. Wait until they saw what the long flowing cape hid.

"Five hundred dollars," a gravelly voice announced from the back of the room.

Salina's head jerked up at the sound of the voice, but fear and humiliation and the stage lights blinded her to what the man looked like.

Cliff threw back his head and laughed. "Don't you want to see the rest of the package first?"

"Six hundred dollars," a youthful male voice called out.

"Seven hundred," the gravelly voice countered.

"A thousand," a third man offered, his baritone voice mellowed with a Southern drawl.

"I have a bid of a thousand," Cliff acknowledged. "What about you other gentlemen? Perhaps you would like to see what you will be getting for your money," he suggested, stepping over to the pedestal. The "slave" girls immediately stopped with Salina facing away from the audience. The girls dropped their poles, and each reached for a tie end that held Salina's cape at the throat. Cliff gave them a nod, and they walked in opposite directions, untying the cape and allowing it to shimmy over Salina's shoulders and down her petite body, to land in a black puddle of velvet at her feet.

"Twelve-fifty," the youth shouted, his words raking down Salina's back.

Grabbing a hook that descended on a rope from the ceiling, one of the slave girls caught it in the rope that bound Salina's wrists. When the girl signaled that the hook was secure, it began to rise again, stretching Salina's hands over her head, and the handmaiden resumed her position at the turning pole. Then the pedestal began to turn again.

As she was slowly turned to face the audience, Salina knew she might as well be naked, for the gauzy robe she wore hid nothing: not her rouged nipples, not the dark triangle of hair at the top of her thighs. Nothing. And she wished for death.

But it was in that moment, when she knew there would be no more delays, no more hope of help coming, that Salina vowed she would not die. She would live through this night for only one reason. She would live to kill Cliff Hopkins.

Raising her chin defiantly, Salina leveled her gaze on her smiling half brother.

Held captive by the intense glare, Cliff's smile faltered and disappeared until Salina was circled away from him. He released a relieved sigh and turned back to his audience. But each time she came round again, he was forced to endure another incapacitating assault from those staring, black-as-a-moonless-night eyes. And he felt a danger as real

441

as though she had a knife at his throat.

From their hiding place across the street from Cliff's house, Cassie and Trace watched as Noah knocked on the door at precisely eight-thirty. Cassie whipped out her revolver and spun the cartridge.

"That's about the fiftieth time you've checked that load," Trace said with an angry hiss, the tension in his face showing.

"I want to be sure—just in case. I don't trust Cliff Hopkins any further than I can throw him. And it'd be just like him to try to take Noah's gold without giving him the papers."

"He'll give him the papers, all right."

"Look! Here he comes."

Trace gave a bird whistle—which was answered from down the street—and he knew Sam was in his place too. "It shouldn't take him long," he muttered, as Noah and Cliff met at the front door, conversed a moment, then stepped inside. "We'll give them ten minutes and then we're going in."

Knowing Salina's room was on the third floor, once he was in the entry, Noah glanced up the stairs, looking for some sign that she knew he had come for her.

Cliff led him into the library. "Have you got the gold?" he asked, his attitude brusque as he crossed to his desk.

"I've got it," Noah bellowed, slapping the gold-filled saddlebags onto Cliff's desk. "Where's Salina?" He kept one hand on the leather strap between the bags, and rested the other on the handle of the .45 tied to his leg.

"Hold on there, boy. Don't be in such a hurry. You don't think I'm going to take your word for the fact that there's close to forty pounds of gold in those saddlebags, do you?" he retrieved a large scale from the credenza behind his desk. "I'll have to see for myself."

"Then, you'd better be quick about it. Because I've got three friends waiting outside who're liable to get trigger-happy if I don't show up out there in the next few minutes."

"Why, Noah! You mean you don't trust me?"

"Just weigh the gold," Noah said, shoving the saddlebags across the desk toward Cliff—and wrapping his fingers around the butt of the revolver.

Having no intention of shooting it out with Noah Simmons, Cliff shrugged his surrender and quickly weighed the gold.

"Forty pounds on the nose," he stated when he was through, leaning back in his chair and smiling.

"Get the papers," Noah ordered in a flat voice.

Cliff's mouth spread in an evil smile. "Why, of course." He reached into his pocket and extracted two documents. "There you go, emancipation papers for one Althea, and one Salina, two female slaves. All signed—and paid for!"

Keeping his right hand on his gun, Noah snatched up the papers and examined them quickly. They seemed to be in order. "Where's Salina?" he asked, shoving the papers into his breast pocket and slinging his empty saddlebags over his shoulder.

"Up in her room, I imagine. You know she's been bedridden for the past week. She took a nasty

443

fall." He clicked his tongue and shook his head. "You're welcome to go on up and get her. Her room's on the third floor."

"Salina!" Noah shouted, hurrying to the stairs. "I've got the papers. Come on down!"

Shouting her name as he went, Noah dashed up to Salina's room and burst the door open.

There, instead of the woman he'd expected, he only found an empty room. "She's not here!" Taking the stairs several at a time, he raced back to Cliff Hopkins.

Cliff sat behind the desk where he'd left him. But now, instead of wearing an uneasy expression on his face, Cliff smiled with confidence. Noah's gaze fell to the gun pointed at his belly. "What've you done with her, Hopkins?" he asked, raising his hands slowly.

"I gave her a job. That's all. After all, a California 'freedwoman' has to support herself, doesn't she? She can't depend on the master for everything like she can on the plantation." He moved his gun back and forth, pointing to the desk with the barrel. "Put those papers right here."

A chill of horror knifed in Noah's gut. He edged closer to the desk. "What kind of job?"

"Well, I already have a cook and a housekeeper, so there was only one other—"

"Where is she?" Noah's voice was rough with repressed violence. "What have you done with her?"

Cliff drug out his pocket watch and popped it open. "I'd say about now she's under that old man who paid me six thousand dollars for the pleasure of being the first to have her legs wrapped arou—"

The bellow that erupted from deep in Noah's belly bounced off the walls. Heedless of Cliff's firearm, he flew across the desk, catching Hopkins's fleshy neck in his hands and lifting the overweight man out of his chair as though he weighed nothing. "You slimy bastard!" he yelled, squeezing Cliff's neck and shaking him violently.

Cliff's eyes watered and protruded grotesquely. His mouth flapped open and shut in an effort to breathe.

"Let him go, Noah," a steady voice said from the doorway.

His expression pleading, Cliff's bulging eyes shifted to the man he'd come to know as Dr. Seifert.

Noah tightened his hold on Cliff. Just a couple more minutes and he would be able to squeeze the life out of the weasel once and for all.

"Noah, he won't do you any good dead. Let him go!"

This time when Sam spoke, Noah heard him. He didn't drop his grip on Cliff altogether, but he did release him enough to let him suck in a wheezing gasp of air. "I ought to kill him! Do you know what he did to Salina?"

"I heard. But what good will it do if you kill him? Is he worth a date with the noose?"

Noah relaxed his hold on Cliff and threw him back in his chair. "So help me, Hopkins, if she's been hurt, I'll be back. And next time the threat of the noose won't be enough to stop me from having the pleasure of seeing your eyes pop out of your head!"

445

He turned and ran from the room, leaving Cliff coughing and grasping his neck.

"I think he means it," Sam drawled, a lazy smile turning up on his mouth. "You'd better watch out, Cliff, old boy. Professionally speaking, I'd say San Francisco's about to become mighty unhealthy for you."

"I'll see you both hung for this," Cliff snarled, his voice raspy and wasted.

"Your word against mine, and I have several witnesses who say they saw you dealing in the slave trade in the State of California." Sam clicked his tongue. "Naughty, naughty, Cliff. You're liable to wind up in jail yet. If one of us decides to talk, that is."

His skin mottled with rage, Cliff gave in. "You win."

Naked, Salina lay staring up at the gold ceiling of the red room where she'd been kept until the auction began. Now she knew what the manacles and chains were for. Not that they were needed, because she had no intention of fighting the old man when he came to claim his reward for being the highest bidder. And nothing he could do could be as terrible as the thirty minutes she'd spent on that pedestal, finally stripped down to nothing when the last bid was made.

No, she would lie here, unmoving, and endure whatever repulsive advances the man cared to make, for nothing mattered to her now except surviving the night so that she could see Cliff dead. If it was true he was going to sell the papers to Noah to-night, then there was nothing to stop her. Perhaps she would cover his fat body with honey and stake him out for the ants to eat. That would be one way. Or she could hire Indians to torture him. She'd heard they had wonderful ways of making death come slowly. Or kerosene . . . Perhaps she could—

When the door to the room opened, Salina was so lost in her planning, she didn't even turn her head.

"Poor little princess," the gravelly voice cooed as the cover was ripped back, revealing her naked body to his rheumy gaze. "Do the manacles hurt?"

Maybe I'll do what he threatened to do to Mama. Inch by inch, I'll strip the flesh from his fat. Then I'll feed him to the fish in the bay.

"After a while, if you're a good girl, we'll take them off. Would you like that?" he asked, extending a gnarled hand toward her breast.

The door to the room burst open, ripping the hinges from the frame and sending the door crashing to the floor. "Get away from her!"

Chapter Twenty-six

"What's the meaning of this?" the old man shrieked, turning his heavily lined face toward the intruder.

Tramping over the door he had leveled, Noah gripped a skinny shoulder in his hand and drew back a fist.

"Don't hit me!" the man pleaded in a shaky squeal. Tears were streaming down his face.

Suddenly aware of the fragile bones he knew he could crush with one hand, Noah was able to check his rage. He'd come here to kill a man, not this shriveled old shell of a human being. "Get out, old man," he said, lifting the sniveling man out of his way and dropping him.

Without paying attention to where or how the man fell, Noah rushed to the bed. "Salina!" he keened, freezing at the sight of the woman he loved, naked and spread-eagled on the bed.

Salina turned her head slowly toward him, as though she had just realized someone was in the room with her. "Noah?"

Noah fell to his knees beside the bed and dragged the cover up over her naked body.

"Thank you." She managed a trembling smile.

"I should have killed him!" he roared, spying a large gold key on the table. He grabbed it, and with shaking hands freed a wrist from its shackle. "Once we get you out of this hellhole, I'm going back and beat the life out of that bastard." Scrambling on his knees to the end of the bed, he released an ankle from its manacle. "And I promise you, it's going to be a long, slow death." He freed her other ankle and scooted up to the head of the bed to work on the last cuff. "Nothing's too terrible for a man who'd do something like this to a woman. But to his own sister . . . !"

"Noah?" Salina asked softly, her eyes opening and closing as if she were just waking from a long, drugged sleep. "Is it over? Am I free?"

Tears blurring his vision, Noah stood and gathered her into his arms, blanket and all. "Yes, my sweet girl. It's all over. You and your mama are free. We're all free. You'll never have to bow down to another soul as long as you live."

"What about Cliff? You didn't kill him, did you?"

Taken off guard by the worry in her tone, Noah reared his head to examine her face. "No. But the night's not over yet."

"You can't kill him," she protested, squirming in his arms. "My mama will suffer if he dies."

"Didn't you hear what I said, Salina? I got him to sign the papers. Both you and your mama are free! Free, Salina! Nothing's going to happen to either one of you at Cliff Hopkins's hand ever again!"

"He really signed the papers?"

Noah nodded. "I've even got a witness."

"Are you sure it's not some trick? I don't think he ever intended to sign them."

"Well, thanks to Cassie and Trace, he got himself involved in a scheme that made it necessary for him to come up with some money real fast. It does look like he planned on signing the papers and taking my money, then stealing the papers back so he could keep his control over you. But he didn't plan on how mad I'd get — or on Sam Seifert backing me up. So we've got the papers, and Cliff Hopkins is living on borrowed time. I hope he's taking full advantage of this evening, because it's the last one he's going to be alive to enjoy!"

"I still don't want you to kill him," Salina said, her voice growing stronger with each word as the reality of her liberation sank deeper into her soul.

"Not kill him? After what he's done to you? After the way he's made you live? How can you say you don't want him dead?"

"I didn't say I don't wish him dead, Noah. I'd be lying if I said I could ever forgive him for what he's done. But I don't want you to kill him. Don't you see? He can't hurt us now! Not if we have my freedom papers. But if you kill him, he'll win after all — because if you're hung for his murder, we'll be separated forever."

An hour later, Noah and Salina were safely ensconced in Trace and Cassie's room at the hotel, and the initial occupants were on their way to the theater where the Witherspoons were appearing.

Still intoxicated by their success, Cassie felt invincible. "You should have seen that scrawny old man come bolting out of the room," she said with a laugh as she turned around backward and skipped ahead of Trace. "Not wearing a stitch and wetting all over himself in his hurry to get out of there. I don't think I ever saw anything so funny."

"I was too busy convincing the bouncer that I was his new boss, and that the black mountain who'd just thundered up the stairs of the casino was with me," Trace reminded her. *"And* that the redheaded whirlwind on his tail was the same proper lady I'd been in there with all week long."

Cassie slowed her buoyant pace and waited for Trace to catch up. "I guess I looked pretty unladylike with a holster strapped over my nice dress, and toting that .45, huh?"

"And taking the stairs two at a time," he added, catching her hand in his and tucking it securely in the crook of his arm. "Don't forget the stairs."

Hurt and chagrin knifed through her. She stopped and withdrew her hand from his arm. "I let you down, didn't I?"

"Let me down? What're you talking about? You haven't let me down."

"After all the work you did to turn me into a lady, I went and showed off my true colors, didn't

451

I? I'm hopeless. I'll never be a lady."

Trace grabbed her by the shoulders and pulled her to him, bending his knees to bring his face to the same level as hers. "Take my word for it, honey, you're a lady from the top of your head to the tip of your toes."

"Some lady." Her nose rimpled in disgust. "What kind of lady hikes up her skirts and races hell-bent-for-leather up the stairs of a saloon ready to shoot it out with someone?"

A smile twitched at the corner of Trace's mouth at the remembered sight. "The kind of a lady who's in a hurry to help a friend and doesn't intend to let anything or anyone get in her way. The kind of lady who cares more about other people than she does about the rules in the etiquette books. And the kind of lady who makes me proud to be her partner."

"You're proud to be my partner?" Her eyes widened with disbelieving surprise. "But I keep forgetting how I'm supposed to act, and I'm never going to quit making mistakes when I talk."

"To tell you the truth, kid, ladies who always know the right thing to do and say bore me to death. I'd much rather have you—'mistakes' and all—for my partner than all of those perfect ladies put together. Because one thing you're not, and that's boring!"

Her face felt hot with excitement. "Really?"

"Really! Believe me, out here, a woman who can handle a gun like you do, and who's not afraid of letting her hair down when there's trouble, is a lot handier than one that always knows the right fork to use at supper."

"As long as we're telling the truth, I've got an admission to make, too. I really do like having a partner who keeps me from jumping out of the frying pan into the fire every time I get a crazy notion in my head and don't think about the consequences before I do something dumb."

Trace wrapped his arm around her shoulders and squeezed her to him. "I guess when you think about it, we make a pretty good team, don't we?"

She wound her arm around his waist and returned his squeeze. "So, what fancy plan have you come up with for finding Murieta and flushing him out?"

"I think the first order of business is to figure out a way to get into that wagon and look around."

Cassie opened her mouth in an indignant gasp. "That's what I said we should do in the first place, and you said—"

"That we needed to take care of Salina first," he finished for her. "But I didn't say it wasn't a good idea, did I?"

"No," she admitted with a grin. "But you told me they always leave someone in there. So how're we going to do it without them catching us?"

"I don't know. You got any ideas?"

"How about we create a diversion? One of us could start a ruckus to get their attention, and the other one could slip into the wagon and look around!" She arched her eyebrows expectantly and nodded her head up and down. "What do you think?"

He wagged his head from side to side. "Yeah, that could work."

Cassie's eyes widened in surprise. Trace always thought her ideas were dumb. "You really think so?"

"I wouldn't say it if I didn't believe it. What kind of diversion are you thinking about using?"

Cassie's heart beat just a little faster. Not only had Trace liked one of her ideas, but he was actually asking for her opinion! "Well, uh, what if we started a fire outside the wagon near the front end?" Before he could respond, she answered her own question. "No, too dangerous. San Francisco's such a tinderbox, we're liable to burn the whole city down, including whatever's in that wagon."

"How about a fight?" he suggested.

"No guarantee whoever's in the wagon will come out to see it," she reasoned sensibly.

"Good thinking. We need something that will guarantee we can get into the wagon and have enough time to look around."

"I know!" Cassie squealed, hitting him on the arm excitedly. "What if we didn't try to sneak in there at all? What if we searched the wagon with them in it?

Trace shook his head, his face twisting in a doubtful wince. "You're not planning to go in there while they're asleep, are you? You'd bump into something and wake them up the minute you got inside."

"No. We'll just walk up to the door of that wagon and ask to come in," she said with a secretive smile.

"Oh, that's great! We just knock on the door and say, 'Excuse us, ladies, but would you mind if we

454

come in and search your wagon for evidence that you're connected with Joaquin Murieta?' "

Undaunted by his doubts, Cassie said, "You just watch, McAllister. You're not the only one who can make plans. How much you want to bet I can get inside that wagon to search it in the next five minutes?"

"Caaaaa-sie." There was an amused warning in his expression. "What are you planning?"

"Trust me," she said, lifting her chin naughtily as the alley that housed the acting troupe's wagon came into sight. "Just play along, and I'll be inside that wagon in the next five minutes."

"You're not still wearing your holster, are you?" he asked, following her into the alley. "You'd better not be thinking about pulling a gun on them." He was beginning to sound worried. "Before, in the Golden Goose, was one thing . . ."

"Relax, I'm not going to use my piece." About halfway down the alley, she held her forefinger up to her lips and lowered her voice. "Get ready."

He grabbed her arm and jerked her around. "All right, Cassie. That's enough. Whatever you've got planned is going to have to wait until you tell me what it is!"

"Get you vile hands off me, you monster!" Cassie shrilled at the top of her lungs, struggling against his grip on her and kicking out at his shins.

Trace's mouth fell open in shock as he sidestepped just in time to avoid her kick. "What the hell's gotten into you?"

"Unhand me, you beast!" This scream was even louder than the first. "I hate you," she wailed.

"Ohhhhhh." She wrenched herself out of his hold and made a frantic dash for the wagon. "Help me. Somebody help me!" She pounded hard on the wagon door. "Let me in before he kills me! Oh, my God, won't somebody help me!"

"Cassie, cut it out!" Trace said, catching her at the wagon. "Come on, let's go back to the hotel!"

"Never!" she yelled, banging on the door. "Please let me in!"

The door to the wagon opened slightly, then a little more. "Oh, thank God!" she cried, catching Trace off guard with a shove and scrambling through the door. She was inside the wagon before the woman in the doorway could stop her. "Quick, lock it!" she ordered, pressing her back against the door and holding it shut until the woman did as she was told.

Understanding dawning in his brain, Trace pounded on the door from the outside. "Cassandra McAllister, you get back out here right this minute."

"Go away," she responded. "I hate you and I never want to see you again!"

"You're my wife!" he protested. "A wife belongs with her husband."

"You should have thought of that before you . . . before you . . . Ohhhhhh!" She slid down to the floor and buried her face against her knees. "How could you do this to me?" she whined, peeking through her fingers at the room. "To think when Mother told me what a scoundrel you were, I refused to listen to her. I let my heart rule my actions, and now you've broken it into tiny little pieces."

The door shook behind her back as Trace's pounding became louder. "Cassandra, get out here right this minute, or I'm coming through the door after you!"

Her eyes full of tears, she lifted her desperate gaze to the woman who stood beside her, obviously not sure what she should do. "Please help me," Cassie begged, clutching the woman's skirt to her. "You can't let him in here! You've got to hide me."

The woman, who Cassie was certain she recognized as Treasure Witherspoon, the one who had played the grandmother in the play, looked from the violently shuddering door to her uninvited guest on the floor. A mingle of indecision and irritation crossed her face. "Look, why don't you go out there and make up with your old man?" she suggested in a voice so husky that it could have been a young man's. "You can see, there's no place for you to hide here." She reached for the lock.

"No!" Cassie pleaded, her face filled with terror as she flattened herself against the door to keep Treasure from opening it. "Don't let him in! You don't know what he's capable of when he's like this. He'll kill me. Please let me stay. Just until he's gone! I won't take up much room! And I promise, I'll be quiet as a mouse. You'll see. You won't even know I'm here." To prove her words, she scooted over into the corner against a trunk that had a red silk cloth draped over it. "See, I won't be in the way!"

Treasure looked at her unexpected company, then back to the door.

"All right, Cassandra! That's it. I'm going to kick

457

down the door!"

"Shit!" Treasure hit the lock on the door and ripped it open before the crazy man outside could tear it from its hinges. "Maybe I can talk him into leaving!" She stepped outside, slamming the door behind her.

No sooner had the door clicked shut than Cassie flew into action, lifting costumes, opening chests, drawers, and cabinets. Keeping her ears tuned to the hum of voices outside the wagon, she searched everywhere, growing more frantic by the minute because she found nothing that would help them. Able to tell, by the nearness of her voice, that Treasure had come back onto the wagon steps and was right outside the door, Cassie took a last defeated glance around the tiny room.

Then her eyes lighted on the trunk with the red cloth on it, and she realized she hadn't looked inside it. Watching the door, she hurried to the small trunk and sat down beside it. Praying there was something inside that would help them, she carefully lifted the silk fringed cloth.

Noah's trunk, she realized, her heart skipping a beat. Taking a cursory glimpse at the door, she reached for the brass latches on the trunk. Click. Good, they weren't locked. As though she expected something to pop out at her, she eased back the lid, all the time listening to the buzz of the conversation outside the door.

Immediately she saw that the trunk contained more costumes, fabrics of several rich colors, and braids and trims of gold and silver. Disappointment squeezed her shoulders into a slump.

Then, as she started to close the lid, something silver caught her eye.

Working with desperate haste, she shoved the costumes out of the way. And there it was, just as she had hoped it would be. The proof that Murieta was connected with the Witherspoons. There, before her eyes, were his black trousers and jacket, his red sash and sombrero, and his big silver-mounted revolvers and holster—even his mustache and wig!

Frantic to think of a way to get the suit out of the wagon to show Trace, she almost didn't hear the door click open until too late. But when Treasure spoke to Trace outside, her body hidden in the doorway, Cassie could hear that she was back inside.

Cassie's heart thrummed wildly in her ears, so loud she couldn't even hear what Treasure was saying. Sweat streamed down her forehead into her eyes, stinging them. Moving with painstaking caution, she eased the lid of the trunk back down and replaced the silk scarf.

Allowing herself a relieved sigh, she cowered into the corner again, her back to the trunk.

"All right, girlie, he's gone." Treasure stepped inside and closed the door behind her. "He said he'd leave you alone, so you can go on and leave too."

Cassie directed her most woeful look at the actress. "Where will I go? Can't I stay here with you for a while longer?" New tears filled her eyes.

Treasure tossed her a handkerchief. "Dry your tears and go get yourself a hotel room or something. But you can't stay here!" She jerked Cassie to her feet and shoved her toward the door.

"What if he's waiting out there for me?" Cassie asked.

"That's your problem. Not mine. I got him to leave you alone. The rest is up to you!" With that, Treasure flung open the door and pushed Cassie through it. "But don't come back here!" she said, banging the door shut.

Her face splitting into a grin, Cassie picked up her skirts and broke into a run toward the street.

"Not so fast, kid," a deep voice said as a man stepped out from behind a rain barrel, blocking her way.

For an instant, Cassie's heart stopped and the air in her lungs stayed trapped there. "Trace! You scared me!" she whispered, her breathing resuming its normal in-and-out action.

"You deserve to be scared!" He dug his fingers into her upper arm and started dragging her out of the alley. "In fact, you deserve a helluva lot more than that. You ought to have the daylights beat out of you for pulling such a stupid stunt!"

The intoxication with her success was too great to allow Trace's tirade to spoil it. "I guess this means you're not interested in knowing what I found in there?" Her words were delivered in a taunting tone.

"Just when I thought there was some hope for you to think things ou —" Trace stopped and stared down at her. "What did you say?"

Cassie turned her face away from him, thrusting her chin in a hurt pose. "I said, you probably wouldn't be interested in the evidence I found in the Witherspoons' wagon."

Trace caught her chin in his hand and turned her face to him. "All right, Cassie. No more games. What did you find?"

Enjoying the moment too much to let it be over yet, Cassie shrugged her shoulders and said, "Nothing . . ."

"Oh . . ." His chest deflated with disappointment.

"At first," she added with a mischievous grin.

"What do you mean, 'at first'? Did you find something or not?"

"Are you going to apologize for saying my idea was stupid?"

"Cassie . . ." he warned, dragging out her name in a significant drawl.

Realizing she was dangerously close to reaching the limits of Trace's tolerance, Cassie said, "All right, I'll tell you." Besides, she was too excited to keep it to herself any longer. "They've got Noah's trunk hidden under a red cloth in there. And you'll never guess in a million years what I found inside that trunk!"

"Your gold?" he asked hoarsely.

Cassie's smile fell slightly. "Well, it wasn't quite that good. But almost. Murieta's clothes are in the trunk! The black trousers with those little silver doodads down the sides, his jacket, his red sash, his sombrero—the whole outfit! So! McAllister, what have you got to say about my 'stupid' idea now?"

"You could have gotten in serious trouble if you'd been caught," he maintained, though the corner of his mouth twitched up crookedly.

"But it worked."

461

"You were lucky this time," he said, his grin straining to break into a full smile.

She punched him on the arm. "Admit it, Trace McAllister. It was a good idea."

"I guess it was a pretty good idea," he finally said, "But if you ever try anything like that again without telling me what you're up to, I'm going to tan your hide! You got that, kid?"

"Just you try it," she said cheekily, and spun away from him to scurry toward the hotel where they'd taken a second room for the night so Noah and Salina could have their privacy.

"Now that we know for sure the Witherspoons are helping Murieta, what are we going to do?" Cassie asked as they reached the door to their new hotel room. "I'm thinking that it might be time to face them head-on and call them down."

Trace assumed a thoughtful expression. She was right. It was time to lay all the cards on the table with Mimi. But this was something he had to do without Cassie. Murieta was a dangerous killer, and if there was going to be a showdown, he didn't want Cassie involved in it.

"Why don't we sleep on it tonight and decide what we need to do in the morning?" He inserted the key in the door and turned it. "Or better still," he said, his voice suddenly sultry as he prodded her into the room and closed the door behind him. He walked up behind her and wrapped his arms around her waist, dipping his head to kiss the side of her neck behind her ear. "Why don't I order us up a nice hot bath and a champagne dinner? We can discuss our dilemma over supper." He moved suggestively against her bottom and slid his hands up her rib cage to massage her breasts. "Unless we think of something more interesting to talk about, of course."

Fire spread from the heat of his hands on her breasts to settle in the depth of her belly. Her head lolled back on his shoulder. "Have you got anything special in mind?"

"Why don't you wait and see?" His voice was a soft caress against the shell of her ear. He put her from him and turned back to the door. "I'll send up the bath and be back in a little bit. I'm going to order you the best dinner I can find in San Francisco. This is going to be a real celebration."

She pivoted toward him, her mouth open to protest, to tell him she didn't care about dinner, that she was only hungry for him.

He grabbed her shoulders and covered her lips with his, kissing her soundly. "That ought to hold us." Opening the door, he stepped into the hall. "Don't bother with a gown," he said with a mischievous wink. "I won't be long." he closed the door behind him, calling back through the wood, "Lock it."

Smiling dreamily, Cassie did as he'd asked and turned up the lamps the innkeeper had lit for them. Maybe, just maybe, Trace had a celebration of a different sort planned for them. He was certainly acting suspiciously. Maybe he was going to ask her to— Cassie gave her head a firm shake. She wouldn't think about it. She wasn't going to let

463

herself get her hopes up. But no matter how she tried to erase the exciting dreams from her thoughts, they stayed there.

Trace stood in the shadows in the alley behind the theater. He could tell by the cheers of the audience inside that the show had just ended. He had to act now, or never.

Drawing his gun, he slipped out of his hiding place and hurried up the steps leading into the wagon. He took a quick glance around, then tapped lightly on the door.

Obviously thinking it was one of the other players, as he'd planned on her doing, Treasure swung the door open wide. "How'd it go . . ." Her mouth clamped shut as her gaze focused on the barrel of the pistol in his hand.

Knocking her aside, Trace barged past the surprised woman, slamming the door behind him. "So far, so good," he said through a tight grin as he signaled with the gun for her to back up.

"What do you want?" she said, raising her hands. "Your wife's not here any more. She left right after you did. Look around. You can see this wagon's too small for her to be hiding here."

Trace glanced around, quickly focusing on the red silk-covered chest in the corner. "What's in there?" he asked, indicating the trunk with his head.

"Just some costumes."

"Open it."

"You don't think I'd hide her in a trunk, do you?"

"Just do what I say." He pulled back on the hammer.

Treasure nodded her head nervously at the click of the hammer. "Sure. But you'll see, there's nothing in there." She squatted and threw the red scarf off the trunk.

"Go ahead," he said when she hesitated and looked back over her shoulder.

Working slowly, she clicked back the locks and flipped the lid up. "See?" she said, indicating the contents. "Like I said, it's just costumes."

"Let's see them." He waved the gun, indicating he wanted the trunk emptied.

Treasure looked at the door as if expecting help to be there. When there was none, she pulled a dress from the trunk.

"Move faster," Trace growled. "I'm in a real bad mood."

She reached in the trunk and pulled out a red sash and short black jacket, which she tossed casually on top of the other costumes.

Trace's eyes narrowed with satisfaction. Cassie was right. Not only was it Noah's trunk, but it was definitely the same suit Murieta had worn the day he robbed the stagecoach. "Where's the man who belongs to that jacket?" he said with a low, angry snarl.

"I don't know what you're talking about," she said. "It's just one of our costumes. No one's even worn it in a year or so."

"Cut the act, Treasure. I'm on to you. I know those clothes belong to Murieta, and that you've provided him with a disguise. Now, where is he?

465

He's got something that belongs to a couple of my friends."

"Are you looking for me, *señor?*" a familiar voice asked from behind Trace.

Taken off guard, Trace spun around to face the newcomer who'd just stepped through the curtains at the front of the wagon.

"You?" he rasped, his expression stunned. Then he saw the flash of silver, but it was too late. Pain was already ripping through his side as the knife tore through his clothes and flesh. Trace raised his gun to fire, but someone—Treasure, he decided in his pain-fogged brain—hit him from behind and sent the Colt .45 flying, as his knees folded beneath him.

"*Si, mi amigo.* You have found my little secret. But it will do a dead man no good."

Chapter Twenty-seven

Cassie ran her hand along the rim of the bathtub, then dipped her fingertips in the water. It was cold! She snatched her hand back and shook it off. "Damn! Where could he be?" She ambled over to the table set with the lovely dinner he'd had sent up. Lifting a cover from one of the plates, she made a face. The food was cold too. She clanged the cover back in place and bent to blow out the half-burned candles she had lit to make the meal even more romantic.

Frustrated, she got back into the bed. Falling heavily against the pillows, she drew the cover up over her bosom and held it there with her crossed arms.

For the hundredth time, she debated with herself as to what she should do. Her first inclination was to worry. What if something had happened to him? Maybe she should go look for him. But where would she go? And what if he came back and found her gone? He would be frantic!

On the other hand, if he wasn't hurt, it would serve him right! He should have been back by now. The bath had been delivered only a few minutes after he left, and the dinner and champagne had arrived over an hour ago. So where was he?

Then the entire answer exploded in her brain, and she bolted up straight in the bed, her expression panicked.

Trace had left her!

That was it! It was so clear now. Why hadn't she seen it right away? Now that they had taken care of Cliff Hopkins, he didn't need her any more. With Cliff out of the way, she had suddenly become excess baggage! A partner he'd have to split the Murieta reward with!

What a fool she'd been. She had fallen for his pretty words completely. She'd even convinced herself that tonight was going to be the prelude to a marriage proposal. And he had planned it to be a farewell dinner!

Tossing the sheet aside, she swung her feet to the floor. Marching across the room, she dug into the satchel she'd packed hurriedly when they had changed rooms. "He wanted to get me out of the way so he could go after Murieta — and my gold! — by himself." She stepped into her jeans with an angry kick and shrugged into a shirt. "Well, he's not going to get away with it."

Whipping up her holster, she strapped it on her hips and bent to tie it down to her thigh. She grabbed a leather vest and slipped it over her shirt to disguise her curves, then bent over, throwing all her hair to the crown of her head. Catching it with one hand, she slapped a hat on to keep it in place. "We'll just see who gets to Murieta first. You're going to be sorry for trying to cheat me, McAllister."

As Trace slowly regained his consciousness, he became aware of voices. Men's voices. Arguing.

"I hope you're satisfied with what you've done." The muscles of Trace's face gave an involuntary jerk as he wondered why the voice sounded familiar.

"And what would you have done, *madam?*" another slightly familiar voice returned.

Why would a man call another man "madam?" Trace pondered.

"I couldn't let him expose us! This is too sweet an operation."

"If you hadn't come in and made sure he knew the truth, I could have made up a convincing story about Murieta's clothes and gotten rid of him."

"But he knew they were there. His wife must have found them when she was here earlier." This voice Trace recognized as Treasure's, but with his eyes closed, she sounded more masculine than feminine.

"What are we going to do with him?"

"Since he knows about us, I don't see we have any choice but to finish him off and feed him to the fish." This voice wasn't particularly familiar.

"Too bad, Mimi, just when it looked like you might have a chance with him if his wife didn't come back to him."

That voice. It was so familiar. Where had he heard it? Trace rolled his head to the side and slitted his eyes, but his vision was blurred.

"That's the whole thing, isn't it, Angelo? The reason you stuck him had nothing to do with protecting our operation, did it? Admit it! You were afraid I'd throw you over for him."

Angelo? Angel? What the hell was going on here?

"I told you I don't share, *mi querida!*"

The Spanish endearment brought Trace's memory rushing back. Just before he'd felt the knife tear into his flesh, he had talked to Murieta. But it hadn't been Murieta. It had been Angel. She had only sounded like Murieta—and like Angelo, except for the accent.

Unable to lie still any longer, Trace opened his eyes all the way.

"He's awake!" another voice he didn't recognize exclaimed.

Certain he must be having an illusion, Trace blinked his eyes. The deep voices he'd been hearing belonged to the five Witherspoon women.

"You're Murieta?" he said to Angel, trying to sit up. White-hot pain radiated from his ribs, forcing him to fall back.

"At your service, *amigo,*" Angel said, affecting a courtly bow and a heavy Spanish accent. "And *mi compadres,*" she announced, indicating the others with a sweep of her hand.

"You mean to tell me Murieta's gang was five women all along?"

The five Witherspoons looked at each other and

470

grinned, as if sharing a private joke. "We might as well tell him, since he's going to be fish food before the night's over anyway," Angel said, her expression taunting as she reached up and pulled off her blond wig, exposing brown hair pomaded back from her forehead.

"You see, Mr. McAllister," she said, her voice particularly husky. She began unbuttoning her bodice. "Though we *are* the Murietas"—she slipped a button from its hole with each word—"we are not"—she inserted her fingers in the front edges of her blouse—"*señoritas!*" she said, completing her announcement by opening her top.

Trace stared in astonishment as the padded dress front fell away, leaving a bare male chest in its place. "All of you?" he finally said, understanding suddenly dawning in his eyes. "Even you?" he asked Mimi, remembering the feelings of revulsion he'd experienced every time Mimi had touched him. Now at least he knew why.

Mimi shrugged her shoulders and heaved a sigh full of regret. "It's too bad you had to go sticking your nose in where it didn't belong. You and I could have made beautiful music together."

Trace's stomach churned violently. "I'd rather be dead."

"Well," Treasure said with a laugh as she opened her dress and also became a "he." "Then, it looks as if you're going to like our plans." He tossed his wig aside and stripped off his dress.

"What plans?"

"As soon as we get that little troublemaker wife of yours, we're going to see you get your wish."

Angelo was speaking as he changed into attire more appropriate to his sex.

Panic beat frantically in Trace's veins. "What's Cassie got to do with this?"

"She knows too much. We have to dispose of her too," Pearl said.

"She doesn't! She doesn't know anything. I came here on my own."

"Can it, McAllister. We know you staged that little fight for our benefit, so you could get in here," Angelo said, now fully converted into a man, except for his makeup, which he was cold-creaming off.

"You had me going for a while," Treasure admitted, smearing some pomade in his hands and smoothing it over the sides of his hair. "But when you knew exactly where to look for Murieta's costume, I had no doubt about what she'd been doing while I was outside with you."

Desperate to think of a delaying tactic, Trace pressed his hand over the bloody pad at his waist and dragged himself to a sitting position. "As long as you're going to kill us, I wonder if you'd tell me what you did with the gold you took." Agony clouded his vision and slurred his speech, making each word an effort to produce and quickly draining the bit of strength he had mustered. He slumped back against a chest and winced.

"I don't suppose it would hurt anything to tell him," Jewel said to Mimi with a shrug.

"There's a false bottom under the wagon where we—"

Mimi was cut short by a sudden noise outside the

wagon. "What's that?"

"Probably some dog or pig rooting around," Pearl suggested.

"Better go check it out," Angelo ordered with a nod of his head.

"Goddammit!" Scrambling to her feet, Cassie glared at the wooden box she had just tripped over. *I gotta get help!*

Her balance still not fully regained from the fall, she began to run for the street.

"Just some drunk snooping around," she heard one of the Witherspoons announce to the others as she made her clumsy dash out of the alley.

She stumbled into the street, the words of the conversation she had overheard swimming and colliding in her head in a bizarre collage of horror and confusion.

"Cassie, is that you?" a man's voice asked as hands caught her by the shoulders. "What are you doing in those clothes?"

"Barton!" she said, a modicum of relief washing over her as she recognized the gambler. "You've got to help me! The Murietas have Trace, and they're going to kill him if I don't get hel—" Abruptly, the memory of how insistent Barton had been about sitting in that particular seat on the stagecoach flashed in her mind, cutting off her speech. *So he could signal the Murietas!* she realized in horror. She shot a desperate glimpse over her shoulder toward the alley.

"The Murietas? Are you sure?" Barton asked, his

473

eyes narrowing thoughtfully.

Anger and panic rioted in Cassie's brain and sh' grabbed for her gun. "You're one of them, aren' you?" she accused.

Barton's eyes bulged with disbelief as he stared a the gun barrel aimed at his chest. "What are you talking abou—"

The butt of a gun came down on the back o Barton's head with a loud crack. A look of confu sion flashed across his face as his knees buckled folding under him.

Cassie looked up to see the clothing-and-ma salesman, Horace Gilbert, standing over Barton' prone body. "Horace!" she exclaimed, shoving he revolver back into the holster. "Thank goodnes you're here! The Witherspoons and the Murietas ar the same people. And Barton is one of them! We'v got to get the police! They're going to kill Trace!"

When Horace said nothing, a sudden ripple o uncertainty tripped through her. "What are you doing here, anyway?" she asked, unable to keep from voicing her apprehension. "And why are you smiling?"

In that instant, full understanding erupted in he thoughts, and her frightened gaze jumped to hi weapon. It was pointed directly at her. "You?"

"You're such a clever girl, but you're wrong o two points," Horace said with a sneer as he wagge the gun, indicating she should take off her gunbelt "Talbot isn't one of us. He's just a poor fellow wh happened to come along at the wrong time. And n one's going for the law."

"What're you going to do?" Cassie asked, slowl

474

nfastening the buckle in an attempt to buy some
me. "You can't kill us all."

"Oh, we can. But it won't be necessary. Just you
nd McAllister need to be saying your prayers."

Cassie's gaze jumped to the unconscious man on
he ground, and a ray of hope filled her heart.

"Don't get too excited. Talbot doesn't know any-
hing that will help you." He stepped over Barton
nd took her holster from her, then prodded her
oward the alley.

Cassie threw a desperate glance at the empty
treet before she started forward. "Before you hit
im, I told him—"

"You told him the Murietas had McAllister,"
Horace finished for her. "That's all. But he doesn't
ave any idea who the Murietas really are—or that
'm involved." He nudged her with the point of his
un. "Walk faster," he growled. "So if he does go to
he police, his story will only help us. No one will
nake the connection between the Murietas and the
Witherspoons."

"Trace and I did. It's just a matter of time before
omeone else figures it out too and stops you."

"Well, you and McAllister aren't going to be
round to see it. Now, quit dragging your feet.
We've wasted enough time."

"Look what I found sneaking around outside," he
aid a minute later when Mimi, now dressed in
nasculine attire, answered his knock. "She says
ou've got a friend of hers in there and she's real
nxious to see him."

"Well, Mrs. McAllister," Mimi said, his manner
ust as feminine as it was when he wore a woman's

475

apparel, "you saved us a trip. I was just going t
send one of the 'girls' to find you." She turned back
to Pearl, who still wore a dress. "Get changed an
go tell C.H. what's happened while the others hitc
up a wagon."

Three men Cassie presumed to be the other thre
'daughters,' Treasure, Angel, and Jewel, filed out o
the wagon to hurry toward the stable at the othe
end of the alley.

"Trace!" Cassie cried, spying him propped agains
a chest on the far end of the wagon, his eye
closed. Heedless of the gun at her back, she shove
Mimi aside and ran to him. Dropping to her knees
her worried gaze zeroed in on the hand he hel
clamped over a bloody wad of cloth at his side
"What have they done to you?"

Trace opened his eyes slowly, as if it took a grea
effort to do so. When he saw Cassie, the confusio
in his expression cleared and became panic. "Wha
the hell are you doing here?" he asked. "I told yo
to say at the hotel!"

Ignoring his anger, Cassie removed his hand an
the stained pad. "Give me something to bandag
this wound with," she ordered, carefully tearing hi
shirt away from the wound so she could bette
judge the seriousness of it.

Horace laughed. "A lot of good that'll do wher
the two of you are going."

Cassie gingerly separated the edges of the cut i
Trace's side. She breathed a sign when she saw tha
it looked as though the knife had been deflected b
his ribs and hadn't gone in deep. Only slightl
relieved, she looked around for something to use t

476

andage it.

"I don't know why you're bothering with that," Horace said. "You're both going to be dead in a while anyway."

"Cassie, you've got to get out of here," Trace warned, his face sweating with pain.

"Shh," she comforted him. "Don't use your strength to talk." Working as if there were no gun pointed at her back, she snatched a petticoat from where it had been dropped on a chest and started ripping it into strips.

"Hey, what's the big idea?" Mimi gasped, grabbing at the slip.

"Let her bandage him. It'll keep her busy, and besides, there's no need to get more blood on the floor than he already has," Horace said in a tone that implied Cassie was wasting her time.

Mimi released his hold on the torn cloth, the frown on his face petulant.

Cassie went back to work. "Trace, honey," she said, folding a strip of the petticoat into a thick pad and placing it over the cut. She took his hand and positioned it on top of the pad. "Hold this here," she ordered.

Reaching around his back with both arms, she carried a strip of cloth across his back and brought it out the opposite side so she could wind it around his ribs to hold the bandage in place. "There," she said, removing his hand as she began the second turn around his back.

It was then her fingers brushed something hard, jutting out of the back waistband of Trace's trousers. *The spare pistol he always carries!* A twitch of a smile turned the corner of her mouth upward. But he captors didn't see because her back was still t them.

Holding her breath and catching her bottom li between her teeth, she eased the gun out of hi pants. She waited a brief instant, to be certain n one could see what she was doing, then brought th weapon out from behind him, hurriedly hiding i under her vest in the waistband of her own jeans She quickly tied off the bandage and turned bac to her captors. "So help me, if he dies, I'll mak every one of you pay," she swore, crossing her arm over her middle to be sure no bulges showed.

"From the bottom of the bay?" Horace asked mopping his brow with a white handkerchief.

It was at that moment everything fell in place Horace had had a white handkerchief in his han just before the stage had been stopped by the Mu rietas. *He tossed it out the window when he raise the shade to tell them the way was clear. The on we found with the clipping and concho at Mu rieta's campsite must have been from another on of their robberies.* It was all so clear now. Wh hadn't they seen it before?

"You won't get away with this, you know," sh said, "If we don't show up at the hotel, someon will come looking for us."

Before Mimi or Horace could respond, someon knocked on the door. Keeping his gun trained o the captives, Horace jerked his head at the doo Mimi cracked it open, then swung it wide. "Wagon here."

Horace crossed to Trace and nudged him with

ick, then grabbed his arm. "Let's go," he said.

Trace hunched his shoulders in pain.

"Get away from him!" Cassie hissed, fighting the rge to go for the hidden weapon right then, rather an wait until the time was right. But if Horace icked Trace again she wasn't sure she could stop erself from taking the cocky bully down first and inking about the consequences later. "Leave him lone. I'll get him up." She leaped to a crouch and rapped her arm around Trace's waist. "Come on, arlin', you've got to stand up."

"I'm sorry, Cassie" Trace apologized, doing his est to stand without putting too much weight on er. "I really got us into a mess, didn't I?"

"Serves you right for forgetting we're a team," she hided, bracing herself under his arm and starting im toward the door. "Haven't you figured it out yet at you need me to keep you out of trouble as uch as I need you?"

Trace managed a weak smile. "I think it's beginng to get through my thick skull."

"Pearl said you needed me. What's going on?" a igh-pitched male voice demanded from outside the agon.

Trace and Cassie both raised their heads attenvely. "What's Cliff Hopkins doing here?" she sked under her breath.

"I don't know what his connection is with these eople, but he may've just bought us some time," race said out of the corner of his mouth. Hopkins," he called out, "if you ever want to see at gold machine, you'd better tell your pals to ack off!"

479

"What gold machine?" Mimi asked, his tone ac cusing. "What's he talking about, Cliff?"

"McAllister?" Hopkins shrieked. "Is that wh you've got in there?"

"They figured out the truth about the Muriet and the Witherspoons," Horace explained, pushin Cassie and Trace out the doorway ahead of him "so we've got to get rid of them."

"Not until I get that machine and those chem cals, you're not!"

"Dammit! What machine?" Mimi asked again "What chemicals?"

Cliff shot Mimi a guilty look and opened h mouth to explain.

"Yeah, Hopkins, what machine?" Angelo pipe in. "You aren't holding something out on us, a you?" He turned to Mimi, a knowing leer on h face. "I told you we couldn't trust him."

"I don't owe you any explanation, Angelo!" Cli retorted indignantly, his dislike of the other ma obvious. "This whole Murieta setup was my ide and I'd say you've fared pretty well the last coup of months. In fact, you've been more than decentl compensated for the small service you did me which, I might add, did me no good in the lor run. That bastard got the money and tricked m into signing Salina over to him anyway. I should' had you kill the black son of a—"

"Well, you owe *me* an explanation!" Mimi inte rupted, coming down the stairs and poking h finger in the middle of Cliff's chest. "And I want know right now what machine you're talkin about."

480

"I was planning to surprise you, sweetness," Cliff xplained, his tone nauseatingly ingratiating.

Cassie turned to Trace and made a face. "Sweet-ess? I think I'm going to be sick. They sound like man and woman having a fight!"

Trace managed to smile at Cassie's innocence, in pite of the lightheadedness he was experiencing. You don't know the half of it."

"Don't you 'sweetness' me, Cliff Hopkins. You ell me right this minute what kind of deal you've ot going with these two, or we're through!"

"You mean you and he . . . ?" Angelo asked, his lark eyes narrowing angrily. He went for his gun. "I old you what I'd do if I found out you—"

"Will you bitches stop this quibbling, and decide vhat we're going to do about these two?" Horace sked angrily. "Do we kill them or not?"

"Yes," Angelo, Treasure, and Jewel said.

"Over my dead body," Cliff snapped.

"That suits me just fine." Angelo took a step oward Cliff, who took one back.

"Will you stop it?" Pearl interrupted. "Are you oing to tell us about this machine, or do we go on nd get rid of them now?"

Realizing his secret was no longer his, Cliff lanced at Angelo, then spoke to Mimi. "The McAllisters have a machine that separates gold par-icles from river rocks, and I gave them a hundred housand dollars to use it for a couple of days."

"You what?" Mimi asked, his mouth dropping pen in astonishment.

"Actually I only gave them twenty thousand in :ash along the deed to the Golden Goose, which

481

I'm going to buy back as soon as I've made th
gold. But they haven't delivered the machine yet — o
the chemicals it needs to work."

Angelo's mouth split in a triumphant grin. The
he threw back his head and broke into laughte
"Now I've heard it all. A machine that makes gold
Oh, Mimi, you really picked a prize this time!" h
chortled gleefully.

"Laugh all you want," Cliff whined, "but i
works. Doesn't it, McAllister?"

Trace stretched his lips in a secretive grin an
lifted his shoulders casually. "Oh, it works a
right — if you have the right rocks, and *if* Cassandr
and I are alive to tell you where it is and wha
chemicals to use in it."

"Of course, if we're dead, the machine dies wit
us." Cassie snapped her fingers in the air. "Gon
just like that!"

"Where is it?" Mimi asked, curiosity and gree
obvious on his expression.

"You don't really believe there's a machine tha
can make gold out of ordinary river rocks, d
you?" Angelo asked Mimi.

"I saw it do it!" Cliff vowed vehemently.

"No doubt you *think* you saw it!" Jewel said.

"Are you calling me crazy?" Cliff's voice ros
with each syllable.

"Stupid's more like it," Angelo snarled, "if yo
fell for such a dumb trick. Let's go. We're wastin
time here!"

"I'll show you," Cliff said. He grabbed Pearl in
headlock and held a derringer to his temple. "Dro
your gun, Horace, or Pearl gets it."

Horror flashed across Horace's features and he ossed down the gun without argument.

"McAllister," Cliff tightened his hold on Pearl, you and your wife come down here with me."

"Get ready," Trace warned Cassie as they came lown the stairs.

Hidden from view behind Cliff, Cassie brought •ut the pistol she'd tucked into her pants.

"Look out!" Mimi warned. "She's got a gun!"

Startled, Cliff spun toward Cassie, taking Pearl vith him.

That brief moment of inattention was all the •pportunity Angelo needed. With a skill born from rears of practice, he zipped a knife from his boot •nd flung it at Cliff's back in one efficient motion.

Chapter Twenty-eight

Cliff's pale eyes widened and his mouth dropped open as the meaning of the stabbing pain in his back penetrated his last thoughts. With a brief tortured sob, he relaxed his grip on Pearl's neck and his pudgy body dropped to the ground, his disbelieving gaze glassing over into an empty-eyed stare as death claimed him.

Her reflexes automatic, Cassie yelled, "Get out of here," at Trace and gave him a shove toward the street at the same time she squeezed the trigger of the gun, hitting her target exactly where she'd been aiming—square in the middle of the hand that had been the instrument of Cliff Hopkins's death.

"My God!" Angelo wailed, cradling his injured hand in the other. "You've destroyed my hand!" Like a wounded animal, he turned and ran screaming down the alley.

"Anybody else?" Cassie asked, her threatening tone belying the guilt she felt for harming another human being—even one as low as Angelo.

"Don't shoot!" Mimi and Horace said as one, raising their hands in surrender. Treasure, Jewel, and Pearl immediately did the same.

In the next instant, the alley was filled with San Francisco policemen, who Cassie assumed came in response to her shot. As soon as the lawmen took over, she hurried to Trace, who leaned against the wagon, his face ashen.

"Trace! Are you all right?"

He smiled, and nodded his head toward a man who stood apart from the others. "Look who brought the police."

Cassie turned around slowly. "Barton?"

"Sorry it took me so long," the gambler said as he approached them. He lifted his hat and rubbed the crown of his head. "It took me a while to get anyone to believe me. In fact, when you and Horace left me on the sidewalk, I wasn't sure I hadn't dreamed the whole conversation I'd heard."

"What changed your mind?" Cassie asked.

"I knew there was a reward for Murieta, so I owed it to myself to be sure. As soon as I could stand without falling down, I followed you. And what I heard told me it was no dream. That's when I went for the law."

"I guess we owe you our thanks," Trace said begrudgingly, holding out his hand to Barton.

Barton looked down at the extended hand and smiled. "I was thinking more along the lines of the reward money" he said.

"The reward money?" Trace said, his expressio angry. "We're the ones who exposed the Murie gang, not you."

A policeman joined them. "I couldn't help ove hearing your conversation, and I'm afraid I've g some bad news for you."

"Bad news?" Trace and Barton said together.

"Yeah, well, evidently these sissy boys aren't t real Murieta gang."

"Not the real gang? What're you talking abou They robbed the stagecoach we were all on ar took our gold."

"I know that, ma'am. But they were just one about four copycat gangs. The Rangers killed t real Joaquin Murieta in Tulare Valley just the oth day."

"How do you know the one they got is the 're Joaquin?" Cassie protested angrily.

"Because the governor of California says so. I already authorized paying them the reward."

"Does that mean there's no reward for this gang' Barton asked.

" 'Fraid not. There was only one reward, Harry Love 'n' his men got it for the Joaquin th brought in."

"That's just great," Barton complained indi nantly.

"Well," Trace said with an ironic chuckle, "w some, lose some."

"That's easy for you to say, since the reward's n even a drop in the bucket for you two. I mean, wi Cassie being a rich heiress and all. But I was coun ing on that money to give me a fresh stake!"

486

Cassie eyes bulged in surprise. "Who told you I was a rich heiress?"

Trace winced—and this time it wasn't from the knife wound.

"Why, your husband did, back in Auburn!"

"My husband?" Cassie asked, her eyes narrowing at Trace. But she didn't have to ask him if Barton was telling the truth. She could see in Trace's expression that he was. And that truth sliced into her heart with a cruel accuracy no knife could achieve more fully.

"Cassie," Trace said, reaching out to take her arm. "Let me explain."

"He was bragging all over town about how he'd met a rich heiress."

"Are you sure he told you I was an heiress in Auburn?" Her glare stayed leveled on Trace, though she directed her question to the gambler.

"Honey, it was just a coincid—"

"Of course, I'm sure. It was the night after the stagecoach was robbed. The night you and I went to the Imperial to see Lovey LaRue perform."

Cassie's vision blurred with tears as the full impact of Barton's revelation sank in.

"Yes, I remember the night," Cassie said, irritated with the way her voice cracked. Lifting her chin defiantly, she turned her back on Trace and directed a shaky smile at the gambler. "Thank you, Barton—for your help tonight. And for reminding me who and what I am. I won't forget again."

"Cassie," Trace said, her name a plea.

Gathering herself to her full height, she walked away from him without saying anything else.

Back in her room, an hour later, Cassie stare
into the darkness. She knew she should light a lam
and start packing her gear, but she just couldn
seem to gather the energy to move from the chai

When a knock at the door shattered the silence
she leaned forward and listened, only halfway curi
ous.

"Cassie, open the door. I know you're in there
We have to talk."

"Go away, Trace." she said woodenly, relaxing
back in the chair and returning her attention to the
way the fluttering curtains made the moonligh
dance on the floor.

"You've got to let me explain."

"I don't have to do anything."

"It's not like it seems."

She studied the door, able to tell by his muffled
words that his mouth was pressed against the wood.
A ripple of longing tightened in her womb as she
remembered the glorious feel of those lips pressed
on hers. She rolled her head against the back of the
chair and released a tortured whimper.

A spear of light from the hallway suddenly cut
into the darkness, jerking her attention back to the
present. She bolted up from the chair. "Get out of
here, McAllister!" she yelled. "I told you, I don't
want to talk to you."

Ignoring her, Trace walked to the lamp on the
bedside table and struck a match to light it. When
the wick was adjusted to his satisfaction, he moved
back to the door and closed it. Clutching his hand

his side, he turned to face her. His expression ntorted with pain, he sagged back against the or. "I thought you'd want to know that all of ah's and your gold was recovered. The Wither-oons had it hidden in a false floor of their gon. I brought you the receipt. All you've got to is go pick it up from the police station."

"Thanks," she said, determined not to give in to r desire to tell him to lie down before he fell wn. She pivoted away from him and pulled back e curtains to look outside. "I'll see to it in the orning."

"Cassie . . ."

Suddenly she could hold her anger back no nger. "You knew who I was all along, didn't you? at's why you kept popping up to help me out. u didn't care about me at all. Helping me was st a way to get to my grandparents' money, wasn't Tell me, is that why you were so quick to advise e to go back to Baltimore and see them?"

"No! You've got it all wrong!" He pushed away om the door and took a step toward her, his hand it to her. "You've got to be believe me. I didn't ow until —"

"Stop, it, McAllister!" She held her hands over r ears. "Leave. I don't want to hear any more of ur lies. And I don't ever want to see you again!"

"Cassie!" he said, covering her hands on her ears d bringing them down to wrap around her waist. didn't have any idea who you were. I only made that story because I thought Talbot was the one ho signaled the robbers to attack. I thought if I uld get him interested in you, I could trick him

489

into telling me something." He tightened his e[r]
brace around her waist and burrowed his face in h[er]
hair.

"Believe me, if I'd known how pretty you we[re]
under those gawdawful clothes and how sweet y[ou]
were behind that tough facade of yours, I ne[ver]
would have told Barton that story."

"You wouldn't?"

"From the minute I saw you step out of th[e]
bathtub, I knew I'd made a serious mistake."

"Because Barton wasn't the right man?"

Trace shook his head. "Because I wanted yo[u.]
More than I've ever wanted anything in my life, [I]
wanted you. And I couldn't bear the thought [of]
another man coming near you."

"You wanted me? You didn't tell me."

"You were so set on getting Talbot, and I to[ld]
myself it was for the best, since there wasn't roo[m]
in my life for a woman right then."

"And now?"

"Now" — he laughed — "there's one so embedded [in]
my heart, so much a part of me, that I can't ima[g]-
ine my life without her. And I'm scared sensel[ess]
that I'm going to lose her."

"Her?"

"You," he said, his voice breaking. "Don't lea[ve]
me, Cassie. Give me a chance to show you h[ow]
much I love you."

Cassie's heart soared at the words and her brea[th]
caught in her lungs. She had waited so long to he[ar]
him say that he loved her. But now, when he'd sa[id]
it at last, she knew she couldn't allow herself [to]
believe him. Not this time. She had let her fairy-ta[le]

490

ntasies lead her astray too many times. She had
nally learned her lesson. And she wasn't going to
ll into that trap again.

"It's too late, Trace," she said. "If you had told
e you loved me a week ago, even a day ago, I'd
ve been the happiest woman alive. But now, I
now what you're doing. Saying you love me is just
nother ploy to try and fool me into thinking a
an like you could really care for someone like me,
hen all you really want is my grandparents'
oney."

A low growl rumbled in Trace's chest, and he
opped his arms from around her waist. Moving
ith a halting gait, he staggered toward the door
d opened it.

A flood of guilt washed over Cassie, turning her
ce pale. She'd forgotten about his knife wound.
e ran into the hall after him. "Wait!" she called
his retreating back.

Trace stopped in his tracks, but he didn't turn
ound.

"Have you had a doctor look at that knife cut?"
e asked, her hands twisting together anxiously.

"Don't worry about it, kid. It's just a scratch."
e started walking again.

She ran down the hall after him and grabbed his
m. "Where will you go tonight?"

He stopped walking and turned to face her. Curl-
g his lip as though it disgusted him to even be
uched by her, he shook her hand off his arm and
aded for the stairs. "I'll send someone to pick up
y things."

Self-condemnation rose from deep in her belly,

491

culminating in a desperate wail. "Don't go."

At the top of the stairs, Trace paused and ble[?] out a sigh. "Why not?"

Cassie caught up to him at the stairs. "Becau[?] you're hurt. You need to have a doctor look at yo[?] side," she said to his back.

"Is that the only reason you want me to stay?" [?] asked, still not looking at her.

Cassie's face twisted into anger, anger at herse[?] for not being able to stop loving him in light [?] what she had learned. "No, it's not the only re[?] son," she admitted, her answer barely audible.

"Then why?" He turned slowly to look down in[?] her tearstained face. "Why do you want me [?] stay?"

Because I love you! she wanted to scream. *B[?] cause no matter what selfish reason brought y[?] into my life, I'll die if you walk out of it.*

When she didn't answer, he spoke, his voi[?] husky. "Why, Cassie?"

"Because I owe you for helping me get my go[?] back!" she spit out, wheeling away from him ar[?] proceeding back to the room.

Trace waited a minute, then followed her. "[?] long as you put it that way, I'll stay," he said, clo[?] ing the door behind himself.

Later, when the doctor had gone, and Trace w[?] resting comfortably, Cassie sat down on the edge [?] the bed. Her back to him, she studied her hands [?] her lap as they fidgeted with the folds of her ski[?]

Disappointment and hurt weighed heavily on h[?]

492

he heart she had so valiantly hardened against notions after her mother's death felt as if it were umbling, bit by bit, into a million tiny pieces in-de her chest. And the pain was so unbearable she ould give anything for the slightest letup.

Trace's explanation for the reason he had used r replayed in her mind over and over again; and ddenly she was struck with the realization that no atter how slim the chance was that he was telling e truth about his lack of knowledge of her past, e owed it to herself to find out. "Tell me again hy you told Barton I was an heiress," she said ftly.

His eyes filled with pain, Trace rolled his head ward her. "You said you didn't want to talk about "

"Maybe I shouldn't have said that. Maybe I ould've listened. I guess I was just too hurt at the ne."

He breathed in deeply, held his breath longer an necessary, then blew it out in a long, relieved ss. At least she was giving him another chance. "I ver meant to hurt you, Cassie."

" 'Cause you thought I was worth lots of money d you wanted to get your hands on it?" she asked tterly.

Trace shook his head. "I admit that at first I eant to use you."

Cassie choked back an anguished sob.

"But not for money!" he quickly explained. "I uly didn't know about your grandparents until you ld me about them."

"That's what you say."

493

"Like I told you, I thought Talbot was connected with Murieta, and that I could get him to give himself away if I got his guard down by distracting him with a pretty woman. It was a dumb idea. I admit it. But at the time it made sense."

"And that's why you showed up in my room wanting to make 'amends.'" She felt the bed move as he nodded his head—and another chunk of her heart chipped away.

"And why I told Talbot your father was a rich man and that you were just traveling in disguise to fool robbers. I knew it would make you more attractive to him."

"I guess it really gave you a big laugh when I believed a man like you—or even one like Barton—would really like me, just because I was me, didn't it?" She stood up and threw back her head to stare empty-eyed at the ceiling.

"No," he protested, reaching for her. "You've got it all wro—"

"I don't think I've got it wrong at all," she said, her tone hard. "On the contrary. I think I finally got it right. Good night, Trace. You'd better get some rest."

Trace awoke in the morning to a loud rapping on the hotel-room door. Groggy from the medicine the doctor had given him to drink, he blinked his eyes slowly. "Cassie? Get the door." He licked his lips in an effort to wet them.

"Open the door, McAllister."

"Cassie, see who's there, will you?" He lifted his

494

...ad off the pillow and stared at the door with one ...eary eye. "Cassie?" he called, a wave of apprehen-...n suddenly hitting him.

"McAllister. It's Noah and Salina. We've got to ...lk to you about Cassie. She's gone."

Trace propped himself up on his elbows and tried ... digest what Noah had just said. Cassie, gone? ...hat was crazy. He was just talking to her — wasn't ...?

He glanced around the room as if to prove his ...int. The empty silence told him he was totally ...one.

"Gone?" he bellowed, jackknifing up in the bed. ...argh!" he cried as agony speared through his ...dy from his wound. "She can't be gone," he pro-...sted, struggling to his feet in spite of the pain. ...rapping the sheet around himself, he stumbled to ...e door and hit the latch, then fell back into the ...d. "You must be mistaken. She's probably down ... the police station retrieving her gold. She was ...ing to do it first thing this morning. Did you go ...t yours yet? Was it all there?"

"The morning's almost gone, Trace," Salina ...inted out. "And when Noah says Cassie's gone, ... doesn't mean to the police station. He means ...ne — away!"

His head ached from the drug, and daggers of ...ain radiated from the knife wound in his side; but ...either pain compared to the toll the news took on ...m as it gripped his heart and squeezed all that ...as good out of his life. Cassie had left him. "She ...n't be gone," he insisted.

"She came to the room a little while ago and

495

packed up her things," Salina said. "She said sh
was leaving."

"She left you this," Noah said, dropping a saddl
bag Trace recognized as one of Cassie's on the be

"What is it?"

"She said since she might not have gotten h
gold back if you hadn't helped her, and since yo
missed out on the big money you were counting o
she wanted you to have it," Salina explaine
"There's five thousand dollars in gold in that bag

Trace stared at the bag on the bed and shook h
head. "Where is she?"

"She said she was going back to the gold cam
where she belongs."

Trace stood up and grabbed his shirt from th
back of a chair. "When did she leave?" Pressing h
hand to his side, he tramped behind the dressin
screen and tossed the sheet over it.

"She booked passage on a steamer that's sche
uled to leave for Sacramento at noon," Noah a
swered.

"What time is it now?"

"You've got thirty minutes to make it," Salin
answered, already gathering Trace's belongings an
shoving them into a satchel. She tilted her hea
toward the door, signaling Noah to bring in Trace
other suitcase, which they'd already packed. "You
better let me change your bandage before yo
leave."

"I'm fine," Trace answered, stepping out from b
hind the screen. Moving stiffly, he slipped on h
jacket as he walked.

"Then, let's go," Noah said, picking up the su

ase and saddlebag. "You've got a boat to catch."

"Ticket!" Trace said. "I need to get a ticket."

"Bought and paid for," Salina announced, producing the envelope containing his passage.

Trace looked around the room, then started for the door. Stopping short, he turned back to the smiling couple. He reached into his breast pocket and produced the deed to the Golden Goose. He dropped it into Noah's hand and patted him on the back. "In case I don't get back in time for the wedding, here's your wedding present from me and Cassie. It's already signed over to you."

"What are we going to do with a gambling casino?" Noah asked, stunned.

"That's your problem, my friend. Not mine. I've got a steamer to catch in thirty minutes."

"Make that fifteen," Salina said, pushing Trace and Noah out the door.

Cassie checked the time on her lapel watch. Five minutes after twelve. *Well, so much for Cinderella and Prince Charming,* she thought with a sad smile as the riverboat steamed out of San Francisco right on time. Of course she had known Trace wouldn't come for her—she had deliberately waited until the very last minute to tell Noah and Salina that she was leaving so he couldn't, out of some false sense of guilt, try to stop her. But that stubborn, optimistic romantic deep in her soul—the one that insisted on believing in happy endings—had still dared to hope he would come.

Maybe now you've learned your lesson, she told

herself. She glimpsed at the dress she wore, an
sniffed back the tears that refused to be quelled. A
least her father was going to be happy. She wa
coming back home a lady like her mother had beer
For all outward appearances, her trip to San Frar
cisco had been an enormous success, and one of hi
wishes had come true. On the inside? Well, that wa
another story, one her father would never know.

Tears now streaming profusely down her cheek:
she spun around and sagged against the rail of th
deck, no longer able to bear the sight of the cit
where she was leaving her heart.

A handkerchief was suddenly thrust in front o
her, and her bent head snapped up in surprise.

"Well?" Trace asked with a mischievous smile
"Are you going to use this, or would you prefer m
sleeve?" He bent his elbow and held it out to he.

Cassie gazed up into apprehensive green eyes, an
every nerve in her body cried out for her to thro
herself into his arms. But she reached for the hand
kerchief instead, ignoring the offer of his sleeve
"What are you doing here?" she asked, dabbing he
eyes as she turned back toward the rail so sh
wouldn't have to look at him.

"You left without telling me good-bye," he said
leaning over and resting his forearms on the ra
beside her, his hands clasped together. "Why, Cas
sie?"

"I didn't think it was necessary. We had alread
said all that needed to be said."

"That's not the reason, and you know it!"

"Well, whatever my reason is, it's none of you
business."

"Oh, I think it is. Especially if you ran away 'ithout saying good-bye because you knew you ouldn't look me in the eye and tell me you don't ver want to see me again."

She dared a furtive glance at him out of the cor-.er of her eye. "That's ridiculous."

"Is it? I don't think so."

"You don't know what you're talking about."

"Then, show me I'm wrong," he said, reaching up and catching her chin in his hand. He turned her ace toward his. "Look at me right now and tell me /ou don't ever want to see me again."

She met his gaze with hers and opened her mouth o speak. "I don't wan—" She looked away ner-/ously, needing to force herself to meet his eyes again. "I do—" Her lids dropped protectively over her eyes. "I—" A fresh onslaught of tears trailed down her cheeks.

Trace smiled, and straightened his posture, gath-ering her into his arms. "You can't do it, can you?"

Burying her face against his shirtfront, she rolled her head from side to side.

"Because you love me?" he asked, his tone prayer-ful.

She nodded her head. "But I don't want to love you."

Trace roved his hands over her back, snuggling her closer to him. "And Lord knows I tried not to love you. But what can I say? I fell in love with you anyway."

She drew back her head, her expression defensive. "I'd give anything if I could believe you."

"Then, just give me a chance to prove it to you."

She watched him skeptically. "It's only fair to te you that before I left San Francisco, I had a lawye draw up papers saying I'm giving up all claim t anything my grandparents might decide to leave t me."

"That's good," Trace said, his smile broad.

"Good? Didn't you hear what I said? I won inherit anything from my grandparents!"

"I heard you. And you just saved me from havin to convince you I want to marry you because I lov you and not because I have an ulterior motive."

"What did you say?" she asked, her expressio disbelieving.

"About ulterior motives?" he asked with a wicke grin.

"Trace McAllister, did you say you want to marr me?"

Trace zigzagged his eyes back and forth as if h was checking his memory. "Yep, I believe I did.

"But you said it was a crazy idea!"

"So how about it? Want to spend the rest of you life with a crazy man?"

Cassie threw her arms around his neck an squeezed him, covering his face with kisses. "Onl if it doesn't snow in the next two minutes."

"I love you, *kid.*"

"And I love you, *Prince Charming.*"

A spasm of pain made him grimace and h clutched at his side. "Now that's settled, do yo suppose we could find my white charger so I can s down before I fall down?"

Cassie draped his arm over her shoulders an grabbed him around the waist, encouraging him t

an on her. "I thought the fairy tale was supposed
end with the prince carrying Cinderella off. Not
the other way around."

"Honey, this is no fairy tale. This is the real
thing."

Epilogue

San Francisco—1857

"This is sure a far cry from the Golden Goos[e]
isn't it?" Cassie asked, taking in the unlikely-loo[k]
ing whitewashed building on Portsmouth Squar[e].

"It sure is," Trace agreed with a chuckle. "I b[et]
Cliff Hopkins rolled over in his grave when Sali[e]
and Noah sold off all his gaudy, imported furnis[h]
ings and turned this place into a homey hotel."

Cassie released a mischievous giggle. "If th[at]
made him roll over, the flowers in the window box[es]
and the white picket fence across the front por[ch]
probably had him doing somersaults!"

Trace grinned, and held open the gate in t[he]
fence for his wife and three-year-old son.

Cassie gave her neatly coiffed hairdo a quick p[at]
and guided the red-haired little boy up onto t[he]

502

orch. "Do I look all right?" she asked, her excitement impossible to disguise. It had been nearly three years since they'd last seen Noah and Salina. The happy couple had stopped over to visit the McAllisters at their ranch in Los Angeles when they were returning from Georgia, where they'd gone to retrieve Salina's mother.

Closing the gate behind him, Trace whisked his son up in his arms and wrapped his free arm around Cassie's shoulders. "You look better than 'all right,' sugar. You're positively 'blooming.' "

She glanced down at her protruding belly and winced with pretended embarrassment. "I was 'blooming' the last time we saw them, too," she reminded him.

"Daddy! Look!" The little boy pointed excitedly to the ornate double doors to the Simmons House, obviously fascinated by the way the sunlight caught and danced on the stained glass in the top half of the doors.

Before Trace could respond to the child with more than a nod of his head, the colorful doors were tugged open with an abrupt yank.

"Noah . . ." His name was an awed whisper on Cassie's lips as her eyes filled with tears, her gaze roving hungrily over the giant man who managed to fill the double doorway.

"Is that all you've got to say to me after three years?" Noah chuckled, opening his arms wide.

"Noah!" Cassie squealed as the fact that they were really together again sank into her mind. "Noah, Noah, Noah!" she exclaimed, eagerly throw-

ing herself into the waiting bear hug. "It's so won‐
derful to see you! Where's Salina? It's been so long
And the children! Where are your children?"

"Here we are," Salina called, rushing forward
from behind the registration desk, a four-year-old
and a two-year-old following closely on her heel

Cassie pushed out of Noah's hug, leaving th
men to greet each other as she ran to meet her
friend. "Look at you! You're more beautiful tha
ever! How do you do it? Run a hotel, take care o
three kids . . ." She stopped and glanced around
"Where's the baby?"

"She's in the kitchen with Mama," Salina said
her own excitement hard to contain. "We have
spare crib in there for naptime."

Cassie squatted down to smile at the two littl
boys who were peeking out from behind their moth‐
er's skirts. "Hello, there. I'm your Aunt Cassie. D
you want to come out here and meet my little boy
His name's Josh, and he's very excited about having
two new friends to play with." At that moment
Josh came up behind his mother and peered around
her, his expression very serious as he studied the
other children.

She drew her son around beside her and said
"Josh, this is your Aunt Salina, and these are the
new playmates I was telling you about, Benjamin
and Matthew. Why don't you give Benjamin and
Matthew the toy trains your grandpa carved for
them?"

His chin to his chest, his lips clamped tightly
together, Josh watched the brothers from under the

504

elf of his eyebrows as he produced two wooden
gines from his pocket and held them out in front
them. Benjamin took a hesitant step out from
hind Salina, and Matthew did the same.

"How *is* your father?" Noah asked. "Is he still
ospecting?"

"Still at it," Cassie said, watching as the three
tle boys inched cautiously toward each other.
hough we keep asking him to come live with us
the ranch, he won't do it. There's always one
ore lead to check out on finding the "mother
de." I guess once it's in your blood, it's always
ing to be there."

Satisfied that the three children were off to a
od start, Cassie started to stand up. However, her
gainly body protested, wobbling precariously as
e rocked back into her squat. "I guess I'm going
need some help," she admitted sheepishly.

Trace rushed forward and lifted her to her feet.
When are you ever going to get it into your head
at there are certain things "ladies"—especially
egnant ones—can't do?" he scolded good-na-
redly.

Smiling, Cassie gave Trace's cheek an affectionate
t. "When you're not there to pick me up and put
e back on my feet." She turned her mischievous
in toward Noah and Salina, cupping her hand
er the side of her mouth. "Or when hell freezes
er," she whispered. "Besides, how will you know
hat you 'can't' do if you don't try everything?"

Trace nodded his head in surrender. "What did I
er do to deserve a wife like you?"

Cassie gave his arm a punch. "I guess you ju
got lucky, McAllister!"

"I guess I did, Mrs. McAllister. I guess I did

Author's Note

Whether or not Joaquin Murieta actually existed as never been proven. Some say he is just a myth—the result of the anti-Mexican faction in California which was inclined to blame every crime committed in the gold country on the Spanish Americans. Others contend that there may have been several outlaw gangs who worked under the Murieta name—as many as five. And yet another group has elevated Joaquin to the position of a folk hero. They say he was not only a real man, but that he turned outlaw only after the rape of his wife, the stealing of his farm and gold claim, and a public beating with a cat-o'-nine-tails when he tried to stop a gang of Americans from hanging his brother for horse stealing.

However, in 1852, when Harry Love and his twenty volunteers were authorized by the State of

California to put an end to the reign of Joaqu[i]
Murieta, the reward they would receive when th[ey]
brought him in was probably a stronger incenti[ve]
than whether or not the bandit was genuine.

By July, with less than a month of their allott[ed]
three months remaining, the Rangers were no dou[bt]
getting anxious about losing out on the rewar[d]
they'd been working for. So, when they encountere[d]
a band of Mexicans camped out in the Panoch[e]
Pass in Tulare Valley, it must have been easy t[o]
convince themselves that they had at last cornere[d]
Joaquin Murieta and his gang, rather than seve[ral]
hapless cowboys who were rounding up wild mu[s]
tangs—as the *Alta California* newspaper later ac[?]
cused.

In the shootout that ensued, Love's men killed [a]
man they claimed to be Joaquin Murieta, as well a[s]
Three-Fingered Jack, Joaquin's main henchman[.]
Rather than chance having anyone argue with thei[r]
success, they put "Joaquin's" head in a jar of whis[-]
key to preserve it, then carried it to the governo[r]
along with the pickled hand of Three-Fingered Jac[k]
for additional proof.

Satisfied that Harry Love had indeed rid the Stat[e]
of California of Joaquin, the governor authorized [a]
$1,000 reward to be divided by all the Rangers, an[d]
an additional $5,000 bonus for Harry Love.

What of the gruesome souvenirs? They were cir[-]
culated and displayed at special exhibitions through[-]
out California for years to come. Even though n[o]
one ever really knew for sure if they were viewing
the head of the actual Joaquin Murieta or not (a
woman who identified herself as his sister insisted it

508

.sn't her brother), people came in droves to see
e head of the most famous bandit ever to ride in
lifornia, Joaquin Murieta.

ZEBRA ROMANCES FOR ALL SEASONS
From Bobbi Smith

IZONA TEMPTRESS   (1785, $3.95)

k Peralta found the freedom he craved only in his dis-
se as El Cazador. Then he saw the exquisitely alluring
nie among his compadres and the hotblooded male
ore she'd belong just to him.

PTIVE PRIDE   (2160, $3.95)

mmitted to the Colonial cause, the gorgeous and inde-
dent Cecelia Demorest swore she'd divert Captain
ah Kincade's weapons to help out the American rebels.
: the moment that the womanizing British privateer first
ched her, her scheming thoughts gave way to burning
d.

SERT HEART   (2010, $3.95)

cher Rand McAllister was furious when he became the
rdian of a scrawny girl from Arizona's mining country.
: when he finds that the pig-tailed brat is really a volup-
us beauty, his resentment turns to intense interest;
ıra Lee knew it would be the biggest mistake in her life
uccumb to the cowboy — but she can't fight against giv-
him her wild DESERT HEART.

*ilable wherever paperbacks are sold, or order direct from the
·lisher. Send cover price plus 50¢ per copy for mailing and
·dling to Zebra Books, Dept. 2374, 475 Park Avenue South,
· York, N.Y. 10016. Residents of New York, New Jersey and
·nsylvania must include sales tax. DO NOT SEND CASH.*

LOVE'S BRIGHTEST STARS SHINE
WITH ZEBRA BOOKS!

CATALINA'S CARESS   (2202, $3
by Sylvie F. Sommerfield

Catalina Carrington was determined to buy her riverb
back from the handsome gambler who'd beaten
brother at cards. But when dashing Marc Copeland nar
his price—three days as his mistress—Catalina swore sl
never meet his terms . . . even as she imagined the raptu
night in his arms would bring!

BELOVED EMBRACE   (2135, $3.
by Cassie Edwards

Leana Rutherford was terrified when the ship carrying
family from New York to Texas was attacked by savage
rates. But when she gazed upon the bold sea-bandit B
don Seton, Leana longed to share the ecstasy she was s
sure his passionate caress would ignite!

ELUSIVE SWAN   (2061, $3
by Sylvie F. Sommerfield

Just one glance from the handsome stranger in the d
side tavern in boisterous St. Augustine made Arianne tr
ble with excitement. But the innocent young woman
already running from one man . . . and no matter l
fiercely the flames of desire burned within her, Aria
dared not submit to another!

MOONLIT MAGIC   (1941, $3
by Sylvie F. Sommerfield

When she found the slick railroad negotiator Trace C
trespassing on her property and bathing in her river, in
cent Jenny Graham could barely contain her rage.
when she saw how the setting sun gilded Trace's mag
cent physique, Jenny's seething fury was transformed
burning desire!

*Available wherever paperbacks are sold, or order direct from
Publisher. Send cover price plus 50¢ per copy for mailing
handling to Zebra Books, Dept. 2374, 475 Park Avenue So
New York, N.Y. 10016. Residents of New York, New Jersey
Pennsylvania must include sales tax. DO NOT SEND CASH.*